THE LEGEND OF JIMMY DICK

`The Adventures of a Hillbilly Philosopher—

By Terry Howard

The Legend of Jimmy Dick Copyright © 2019 by Terry Howard. All Rights Reserved.

All rights reserved. No part of this book may be reproduced in any form or by any electronic or mechanical means including information storage and retrieval systems, without permission in writing from the author. The only exception is by a reviewer, who may quote short excerpts in a review.

Eric Flint's ring of Fire Press has a simple approach to digital rights management we trust the *honor* of our customers.

Cover designed by Laura Givens

This book is a work of fiction. Names, characters, places, and incidents either are products of the author's imagination or are used fictitiously. Any resemblance to actual persons, living or dead, events, or locales is entirely coincidental.

Printed in the United States of America

First Printing: June 2019
Eric Flint's ring of Fire Press

ebook ISBN-13 978-1-948818-42-1
Trade Paperback ISBN-13 978-1-948818-43-8

CONTENTS

Cast of Characters 1
Flash of Light 11
Grantville's Greatest Philosopher 19
Not a Princess Bride 39
Anna the Baptist 45
Inflation is a pain in the- 67
One last memory 71
Bremen or Bust 81
McDonald's Empire 89
A tale of Charles and Charles 97
Transference 115
Bowling Greens Aren't Just in Ohio any More 123
Dreams 127
A Prodigal's Son 137
A Piper on the Roof 145
Jimmy, have you got a kilt? 149
Foot in mouth disease 153
Death and Luggage 163
The Truth According to Buddha 167
E. Coli: A Tale of Redemption 173
The Baptist Basement Bar and Grill 185
Little Bird 211
One Night in the Flying Pig 215
Hair Club 250 221
Big Dog and a Bone of Contention 231
Dueling Philosophers 247
Overflow: A Salon 250 story 273
The McMansion 285

For old times' sake	287
Fire and Brimstone	291
Bound for Hamburg	311
Old Goats are hard of understanding	313
Sober in the Morning	317

CAST OF CHARACTERS

Aaron: Young Anabaptist from Magdeburg who rode with Old Joe on the caravan Trip from Grantville to Magdeburg

Abe Holt: Borrowed Pomal Conversion's truck when Wesley didn't know it.

Abbot: Up-time comedian mentioned in passing

Ad/Addison Miller: Office manager for Lamb's Commercial Properties which looked after Jimmy Dick's inherited real estate empire

Adam: Big Dog Carpenter's sidekick in betting with Jimmy Dick about the road worthiness of Old Joe's caravan

Albert: Teaching assistant at the University of Jena

Albert Green: Once the pastor of the Southern Baptist Church in Grantville and then Dean of the Mountain Top Bible Institute

Albert Underwood: Elder Deacon of the Southern Baptist Church in Grantville, a grouchy oldster who should have been a preacher but wouldn't not answer the call

Alberto Ugolini: Tombstone salesman in Grantville, amongst other things, since that alone was not enough to pay a living back up-time, or down-time either for that matter, since it was even more costly to live in Grantville after the Ring of Fire

Amanda Boyd: Friend of Marisa Beasley and organizer of the infamous Bachelorette party

Anabaptist: A religious movement that did not and does not recognize infant baptism

Anna: Any female employee of the Anabaptist Basement Bar and Grill answered to Anna while on the job

Anna: The mother of Mary, the mother of G-d (neither Mary nor Ann appear personally in these stories)

Anna: One of the two young blond secretary/receptionists for Marcantonio's machine shop

Anna Gisa: A barmaid at the Anabaptist bar and Grill

By Terry Howard

Anna McDonald: Wife of Charles and Mother of Jamey; matriarch of Jimmy Dick's household
Anna Baptist: Mistakenly thought to be the sister of John the Baptist by someone who did not know what an Anabaptist was
Ape: A denizen of Club 250
Arch Pennock: One of Club 250's lost souls
Arminians: The followers of Arminius, a Dutch theologian who conflicted with the teachings of Calvin
Armenians: The inhabitants of Armenia, not to be confused with Arminians
Artie Matewski: Interlocutor for the philosopher duel
Asa McDonald: Titled head of Clan McDonald in Grantville, husband of Dory McDonald
Audry Yost: Florist in Grantville who lunches at Tip's bar
Azrael: One of the names for the angel of death. He appears as a character in one of Jimmy Dick's stories and is very active but unnamed in the Ring of Fire universe
Beasley: Last name of Ken and Kim, owners of Club 250 and Hair Club 250
Becky: Rebecca Abrabanel, married to Mike Sterns, headed the Fourth of July party while Mike was off to the wars
Beire: Town in Germany between Grantville and Magdeburg
Bena Rae: Ex-wife of James Richard Shaver; mother of Merle Shaver
Benjamin Franklin Leek: Referee and ringside announcer for the philosopher's duel
Big Dog: See Bob/Bobby below
Birdie's farm: Located on the rim of the Ring wall. Birdie had a ramp cut into the cliff face to climb up instead of going around
Bob/Bobby/Big Dog Harlan Carpenter: Denizen of Club 250 and later the Flying Pig and Tips. A known welcher
Bobby Mcdougal: Of the Mcdougal family, who ran a restaurant in Grantville. A practical joker who contributed to the disastrous nude stripper incident at the infamous bachelorette party
Bollert: German Anabaptist
Boyd: Mistress Amanda Boyd (see Amanda above)
Bremen: German town with the statue of a donkey, a dog, a cat, and a rooster celebrating the famous or infamous story of the Musicians of Bremen
Brent: Sidekick accomplice of Bobby Mcdougal who helped lead Fred Astaire into the disastrous bachelorette party nude stripper incident
Brian Early: Got to ask a question at the philosopher's duel
Bubba: Mitchell Kovacs, a frequent foil for Jimmy Dick's barbed ~~tails~~ tales
Buddha: A character mentioned in a Jimmy Dick story who does not otherwise appear in these pages, at least not under his own name
Calvin: John Calvin, French theologian who is famous for holding beliefs which conflicted with those held by Arminius
Cameramen: A group of Scots bagpipers, mostly, who turned up seeking to join the McDonald Conquistadors in their quest to conquer Bremen

THE LEGEND OF JIMMY DICK

Carolyn: One of many gossipy old ladies of Grantville

Carolyn: The deceased wife of Zeppi. She lived in a physically abusive relationship and seemed content to do so

Casey's Take Out: A small eatery in Grantville

Charles: King of England who was known to enjoy bowling on the green

Charles McDonald: See Chucky, Charlie or London respectively

Charlie McDonald: The oldest of the three Charles McDonalds to take up residence with Jimmy Dick

Chief: Police Chief, see Chief Richards below, Richard Preston

Chucky McDonald: The second oldest of the three Charles McDonalds to take up residence with Jimmy Dick. Married to Anna and father of Jamey

Chief Richards: A police chief in Grantville (see Chief above)

Club 250: Disreputable bar owned by Ken Beasley

Costello: Side-kick of Abbot (see above); also mentioned in passing

Dave Marcantonio: Owner of a machine shop next door to Pomal Conversions. Employer of Asa McDonald

Dave Southerland: A lost soul of Club 250. His mother was an outstanding Bible scholar who prayed long and hard over her son's wayward ways

Dean Blackwood: One of Club 250's lost souls

Debbie Mora: Office worker at the newspaper who almost lost her job over the philosopher's debate

Dickhead/Dick Head: See James Richard Shaver

Diet of Speier: It has nothing to do with losing weight. A religious conclave in Speier where a letter of protest to the body established the uses of the word Protestant for non-Catholic/non-Orthodox Christians. The letter also confirmed that all Anabaptists should be executed whenever and wherever they were found since their crime of rebaptizing was self-evident. All Anabaptist are known anarchists, rabble rousers, and trouble makers, especially my father.

Dieter Schliemann: Night manager at the Thuringean Gardens

Don Quixote: Son of Ma Quixote (see reference below) or look for Don Quixote as the title of the most famous book to ever come out of Spain, on the list of Ten Books that Changed the World, AKA the Man of La Mancha

Donald Duck: Son of Ma Duck (see reference below) or look for him by name on the list of ten characters who made Walt Disney famous

Donny Murray: Husband of Melodie Murry, AKA Donny and Marie. Late of Club 250

Doris Debolt: Member of the Lions Club fundraising committee

Dory McDonald: Wife of Asa McDonald (see above)

Dupont: A character in a story told by Jimmy Dick, who had no interest in marrying the Jones family's daughter

Ed Ipus: See entry at Oedipus Rex (out of Greek legends)

Eisenhower: General in WWII and then President of the U.S. He does not appear personally in these stories.

By Terry Howard

Eli/Elizabeth: Hospital volunteer aide and then girlfriend and eventually the wife of Charles (London) McDonald. They will inherit the home of Asa and Dory McDonald after taking care of the old man when his wife dies.

Elijah: A character mentioned in a Jimmy Dick story, who does not otherwise appear in these pages.

Emmanuel Onofrio: Brother of Ralph Onofrio, uncle of Ralph Onofrio, Son of Ma Onofrio. Denied a vocation, he spent a lifetime teaching math in Catholic schools in New Jersey before retiring back home to Grantville to die. He came out of retirement to teach after the Ring of Fire.

Estil Congden: An outstanding ne'er-do-well of Grantville, who ended up making a fortune and a happy family in Venice, Italy, after fleeing Germany one step ahead of the angry husband of a young wife, who should have shot the lying, cheating, louse when he had the chance. Most famous in Grantville for having once put VW bug on the roof of the high school

Evan Jenkins: Son and partner of Walt the Barber

Fiedler: Pastor of German Anabaptist church not be confused with a Fiedler on the roof

Flying Pig: Bar opened in Grantville after the Ring of Fire

Fred Astaire: AKA Hans Gruber male stripper at the infamous bachelorette party

Freddy Genucci: An undertaker in Grantville who handled the arrangements for Jimmy Dick's daughter's funeral

Fritz Schuler: Owner of struggling new restaurant in Grantville. Only gambling at a casino is a faster way of going broke than opening an eatery in any universe.

Genucci: An undertaker in Grantville preferred by Bina when her daughter died

George Hess: Anabaptist Elder in Magdeburg

Gertrude: One of the two young blond secretary/receptionists for Marcantonio's machine shop

Gisa: Anna Gisa, barmaid at the Anabaptist bar and grill

Greiner: A pastor of the German Anabaptist church

Hair Club 250: Beauty Salon run by Kim Beasley, wife of Ken Beasley, mother of two daughters

Halle: Town in Germany between Grantville and Magdeburg

Hansel: Young Anabaptist from Magdeburg

Hans Gruber: AKA Fred Astaire, male stripper at the infamous bachelorette party

Hans Shruer: Down-time German policeman in Grantville. Not to be confused with Hans Shultz, a down-time policeman in Grantville. Hans is a Lutheran and cannot find it in his heart to forgive Catholics for slaughtering his family.

Hans Shultz: Down-time German policeman in Grantville. Not to be confused with Hans Shruer, a down-time policeman in Grantville. Hans is a Catholic and cannot find it in his heart to forgive Lutherans for slaughtering his family.

Hans Wyss: Medical student at the University of Jena

THE LEGEND OF JIMMY DICK

Nephew: Son of Doctor Wyss

Harlan Carpenter: AKA Big Dog, Bob, and then Bobby. Somehow he was once called a bobtailed dog. Bob and Bobby stuck while Bobtailed was soon forgotten.

Hazel: Breeder of Siamese cats

Head: See Dickhead above

Heloise: After hours cleaning lass at Hair Club 250 the night of the big fight

Heydenbluth: German Anabaptist

Hogan's Heroes: Up-time TV program shown in Grantville off of tapes

Hole in the Wall: Bar in Grantville

Holiday Lodge: An upscale hotel on the cliff face near Birdie's farm overlooking the Ring

Holocaust: See Strong's exhaustive concordance entry 5930. "To go up like smoke, i.e., a burnt offering to be fully consumed with nothing left but ash." Also a reference to Genocide in WWII

Holt: Pastor of a Lutheran Church in Rudoltstadt who was unhappy about the Anabaptist in the neighborhood

Ike: See Eisenhower above

James: A boy who met the philosopher James Shaver on a boat bound for Hamburg

James: See James Richard Shaver

James Richard Shaver: a drunken reprobate, of no account and of no interest to anyone, the titled war leader of the Grantville McDonalds and the titled Greatest Philosopher in Grantville. Neither title was worth a hill of beans.

Jamey Ann McDonald: Daughter of Charles and Anna McDonald, informally adopted granddaughter of James Richard Shaver, also the informally adopted granddaughter of Asa and Dory McDonald. The young lady is a prime candidate for being spoiled rotten.

Jason Shaver: A relative of Jimmy Dick. Briefly a suspect in the arson of the Anabaptist church

Jenny Ruffner: Wife of Tom/Tommy Ruffner, a convert to the Anabaptist church pursuant to a lost bar bet

Jim: Elderly next door neighbor of Jimmy Dick Shaver

Jimmy Dick: see James Richard Shaver

JFK: See John. F. Kennedy below

Joe, Joseph, Old Joe Jenkins: See below

Johan: Young Anabaptist from Magdeburg who rode on the caravan with Old Joe on the trip from Grantville to Magdeburg

Johann: Gas attendant when the cops were looking for the arsonist of the Anabaptist church

John III: Character in a story told by Jimmy Dick

John F. Kenny: Assassinated President of the U.S. who does not appear personally in these stories

John Ritter: Anabaptist Elder in Magdeburg

John's Son: Police officer Lyndon Johnson as pronounced by gas station attendant

John Samuels: Barbershop patron who wanted to build a bowling alley

By Terry Howard

Jones: a family with a daughter in a story told by Jimmy Dick
Joseph Dauod: Lions Club organizer for the philosopher's duel
Joseph Jenkins: Old Joe, once ordained up-time as a General Baptist preacher, as opposed to the more common Particular Baptists. He donated his farm to start a Bible college for Baptists.
Jenkins: Brother Who? See Joseph above
Julio: Ex-dish washer at Club 250, not to be confused with Julio the current dish washer at Club 250
Julio Mora: Current Dishwasher at Club 250, not to be confused with Julio the ex-dishwasher at Club 250
Ken Beasley: Owner of Club 250
Kim Beasley: Owner of Hair Club 250, mother of two daughters
Koehler: one of the families involved in the big fight at Hair Club 250
Korea: A hot spot in the cold war, attended by Asa McDonald and others
Krieger: See William Krieger, Bellow
Lamb Commercial Properties: The Real Estate agency in Grantville which managed Jimmy Dick's properties
LBJ: Lyndon B. Johnson, a President of the United States of America, sometimes mentioned in conspiracy theories concerning the death of John F. Kennedy. He is mentioned in passing and does not appear in person in these pages. Not to be confused with Lyndon Johnson, an up-time policeman in Grantville who does appear in these stories
Leo Nidus: A pen name used by Joseph Jenkins (above). Leonidas, King of the Spartans at Thermopylae
Leota: Customer at Hair club 250. A night manager at Willard Hotel
Lisa Alcom: Half owner of Pomal Conversions
London: The youngest of the three Charles McDonalds to take up residence with Jimmy Dick. Not to be confused with a small town in England
Lorena Maggard: One of the many gossipy old women of Grantville
Lowdown Jenkins: See Joseph Jinkins above
Luther: A theologian of note who was known to enjoy bowling on the green
Lyndon Johnson: Policeman in Grantville before and after the Ring of Fire, not to be confused with JFK's Vice-President Lyndon B. Johnson
Lyle Kindred: Owner of the newspaper that ran the ads for the philosopher's duel
Ma and Pa Kettle: Radio characters up-time. Notable as being cracker barrel philosophers
Ma Duck: Mother of Donald Duck referenced above
Ma Quixote: Mother of Don Quixote referenced above
Manny: SeeEmanuel Onofrio referenced above
Marisa Beasley: Daughter of Kim Beasley, party organizer for Hair Club 250s after-hours parties
Mark Castellani: One of Club 250's lost souls
Mary Jean Slater: Got to ask a question at the philosopher's duel

THE LEGEND OF JIMMY DICK

Mary Jo Kindred: Wife of Lyle Kindred, the owner of a newspaper in Grantville. She was the only reason Debbie Mora kept her job

Mary Katherine: Customer at Hair Club 250

Mary: Mary Kovacs, wife of Mitchell Kovacs (Bubba). Mary kept her husband on a tight budget to try to keep him out of the bars. It didn't work because Bubba was very good at getting other people to buy a beer or two for him

Maass: One of the families involved in the big fight at Hair Club 250

Mathew Bartholow: Grandson of Julio Mora referenced above, school student and messenger

McDee: McDonald, see Asa and Dory

Melle: Barmaid at the flying pig and friend of Anna McDonald

Menges: German Anabaptist

Merrie Davidson: Friend of Marisa Beasley; helped to organize the infamous bachelorette party

Miami: A small town in Florida where Mrs. Pomal thinks it would be a nice place to be a single lady

Mora: See Debbie above

Münster: A town in Germany once declared independent by a group of polygamist Anabaptists. It was fun while it lasted, which wasn't long.

Nam: Short for Vietnam, a country in Southeast Asia where James Richard Shaver and so many other young men and women fought in a hot episode of the cold war

Merle: Estranged daughter of James Richard Shaver and Bena Rae, James' ex-wife

Mitchell Kovacs: Bubba, a drinking buddy and a frequent foil for Jimmy Dick's barbed ~~tails~~ tales.

Monkey: Denizen of Club 250

Nazi: The spiritual inheritor of Kaiser Bismarck's (ruler of Prussia) dreams of world domination

Niles Hanover: The male stripper who replaced Fred Astaire (Hans), who was not about to come back after what happened

Nina Daoud: Wife of Joseph Daoud of the Lions Club

Oden: A character mentioned in a Jimmy Dick story who does not otherwise appear in these pages

Oedipus Rex: See entry at Ed Ipus

Old Joe: See Joe Jenkins above

Old Lady Lamb: Owner of Lamb's Commercial Properties, a real estate office in Grantville. No, she is not related to Brillo except by having personality traits in common.

Oman Frio: See Emmanuel Onofrio referenced above.

Onofrio: Onofrio was a large family in Grantville. But in these stories, the last name when used alone usually refers to Emmanuel

Peter: Young member of the Committee of Correspondence in Magdeburg

Phyllis Congden-Dobbs: A known gossip related to Estil Congden

Pomeroy: See Wesley below and Sheryl also below

By Terry Howard

Pomal Conversions: Partnership between Wesley Pomeroy and Lisa Alcom. Up-time they did van conversions, bodywork, and car interior repairs.

Renato Onofrio: Barbershop regular who came up with the idea of Dueling Philosophers

Prussian: Someone from Prussia, the future home of the Butterflied Kaiser Bismarck

Rebecca Abrabanel: Married to Mike Sterns; headed the Fourth of July party while Mike was off to the wars see above as Becky

Reyburn Berry: Member of the Lions Club fundraising committee

Richards: See entry at Chief Richards

Rick: A cop on the roof doing a stakeout of Pomel Conversions while investigating the fire at the Anabaptist church

Ritzman: German Anabaptist

Ronald McDonald: the clown and would be king of the Kingdom of The McDonalds after they conquer Bremen

Rudoltstadt: A German town near Grantville

Sarah: Young Anabaptist from Magdeburg who rode briefly on the caravan with Jimmy Dick

Schmitt: Frau in Halle who saw Old Joe's caravan passing through

Schroeder: Provost at the University of Jena

Schultz: The sergeant who knew nothing and saw nothing on Hogan's Heroes who is mentioned in passing but does not appear personally in these stories, see Hogan's Heroes above

Senewald: German Anabaptist

Sept Macbeth: Subset of Clan McDonald in Chucky's family tree

Sept Leitch: Subset of Clan McDonald in Chucky's family tree

Sheryl Pomeroy: Wife of Wesley Pomeroy (above)

Simone: The Bride jilted by her groom after the infamous Bachelorette party in Hair Club 250

Sondra Mae Prickett: Member of the Lions Club fundraising committee

St. Pepperoni: The patron saint of pizza makers. Not found in the catalog of saints, but like St. Rapido of New Orleans, still loved and prayed to by devout pizza makers and dock workers respectively. Neither saint appears personally in these stories

St. Carlos Borromeo: Patron saint of bakers and cooks including pizza makers

Stephen Wurmbrand: Co-owner and bartender at the Flying Pig. He doesn't like nobles, and that includes up-timers.

Terry Onofrio: Co-owner of the Flying Pig. Divorced mother of two children

Tip: owner of Tip's bar. Notable for being owned by a Siamese Cat

Tom Jordan: A lost soul of Club 250

Tom/Tommy Ruffner: Up-timer who joined the German Anabaptist church as a result of winning a bet with Jimmy Dick

Treiber: German Anabaptist

Thor: A Norse god and a character mentioned in a Jimmy Dick story who does not otherwise appear in these pages

THE LEGEND OF JIMMY DICK

Thuringian Gardens: The famous bar across the street (highway 250) from Club 250/Hair Club 250

Tyr: A Norse god and a character mentioned in a Jimmy Dick story who does not otherwise appear in these pages

Victoria: Queen of England. She does not personally appear in these stories but her age gets mentioned in passing

Walt/Walter Jenkins: The Barber; the third member of the four person Grand Triumvirate of philosophers in Grantville

Wesley Pomeroy: Half owner of Pomal conversions; husband of Sheryl, briefly one of the McDonald conquistadors

Watson: Sidekick of Sherlock Holmes mentioned in passing and does not appear in person in these stories

Wiley: A pastor in Grantville who had some bad luck in how his son William (see below) turned out as a grown-up

William Krieger: A famous German Philosopher, also a conceited stuffed shirt, who created the Berlin Philosophical Quarterly Review. Look for him in the index of Famous German Philosophers on the shelves of the library in Grantville. Don't bother looking elsewhere. No one maintains an index of fictional characters who never became famous.

William Wiley: Wayward son of Pastor Wiley

Wyss: Doctor from Schauhausen and the uncle/father of Hans Wyss

Zane: someone left up-time. A Four Point Calvinist believing Baptist, holding to the doctrine of once saved always saved, and therefore he believed he could drink to drunkenness without affecting his chances of going to heaven regardless of what the Baptist Church taught on total abstinence from alcohol. Sadly, he's right. The pastor who buried him was sure that the man was never saved in the first place, so his wayward ways had no effect on his salvation.

By Terry Howard

FLASH OF LIGHT

June 2000 / June 1631

Sighting the mailbox to the old Jenkin's place, and knowing what was coming next, James Richard, "Jimmy Dick" Shaver planted his scruffy docksiders against the firewall of Bubba's car and stiffened his skinny legs. Then he hung on tight to the bucket seat, for dear life. If he'd bother to wear the seatbelt, he wouldn't need to. But the day James found out that wearing seatbelts was legally mandatory was the last day he ever buckled up without the driver insisting "Hey Jimmy, watch this." Bubba pushed the gas pedal to the floor just before they reached the top of the hill. The faded black 1993 Pontiac came off the top of the hill airborne. The car was faded because Bubba didn't have a garage and he didn't keep the car waxed. But he did keep it in top mechanical condition. Bubba liked driving with the top down. He liked driving fast. He also enjoyed getting all four wheels off the ground. There was a firebird painted on the hood, as large as could be. James wondered, yet again, if the bird was part of the reason Bubba wanted the car to fly or if the desire to fly was the reason Bubba bought this particular used car.

Jimmy also wondered, yet again, why he kept asking Bubba to take him to the VA hospital in Huntington when every time he did he promised himself to never do it again. The man drove like a maniac. But a trip to the VA left James an emotional wreck from the dredged-up memories. Ergo they spent the nights after the appointments in a Huntington motel, and Bubba was good company. As long as you kept the beers coming, he'd keep his mouth shut once you told him to. So,

James put up with the hair-raising ride. Not to mention Bubba never hassled James about using the seatbelt.

"Eee-haa," Bubba screamed as they flew through the air. A flash of light hit like a lightning strike with the sound of thunder. Bubba was driving way too fast. And suddenly they were blind. The car bounced back to the blacktop. His foot came off the gas and slammed down on the brakes. There was a bend in the road on the way down the mountain, and even if the car cornered like it was on rails, taking the curve too fast would put them over the high side. At any speed even close to how fast they were going they needed to accelerate into the curve to have full control.

Fortunately, as James freely admitted, Bubba really was half as good of a driver as he thought he was, meaning Bubba was very good indeed. With the afterimage of the lightning flash filling the frame of reference, Bubba drove by feel and memory and kept the car on the pavement while he floored the brakes and put the car into a spin. They ended up with one front wheel in the driveway of the house the Rawls would end up living in since their old home place was on the other side of the ring wall. The owners of the new house were in Europe on vacation and had asked Mrs. Rawls to look after their cat. The other front wheel was off the driveway and had squashed the end of the culvert pipe.

"Did ya' see that, Jimmy? We made it all the way to the Rawls' mailbox! Eee-haa, am I good or am I good?"

"Ahh? Bubba, I didn't see much of anything but a flash of light."

"What the bleep was that?" Bubba asked.

Jimmy shrugged off the question. As for the bleep, Bubba's nagging wife was even plumper than Bubba and was forever trying to lose weight. She continually tried to persuade her husband to go on the various diets with her, to no avail. He would not join her, and she did not lose any weight. She also plagued him constantly to quit drinking. But that didn't work either. But when she griped about his foul language, he took to censoring himself by adding bleeps in the place of the words she objected to. He kept it up because it bugged her even worse than his using the words. Since it was clear he knew what he was doing and could control it, then why didn't he just stop? Jimmy knew all of this because, as much as she griped at her husband, her husband griped about her to his friends.

"It wasn't lightning," Bubba said, looking around. "There's not a cloud in the sky. So, what happened?"

"I don't know, Bubba," James replied.

Bubba smirked. "Well, if you don't know, nobody does." It was a fair dig. Jimmy was Bubba's go-to person on just about everything. Jimmy always had an opinion, and at least he *seemed* to be right almost all the time. Jimmy had a way of expressing his opinions as if they were unquestionable facts. Even when he wasn't right, he was still very good at arguing other opinions into the ground.

"Let's get out of here before somebody sees us," Bubba said, starting the car and throwing it into reverse. If no one saw them, then there would be no need to mention who squashed the tip of the culvert pipe the new owners put in last year when they built the new house after tearing the old one down and blacktopped the driveway. With a squeal of tires and the smell of burnt rubber the car dragged itself back onto the road. James let out a deep sigh as they went around the bend in the road. For once, Bubba was actually driving at a reasonable speed.

❋ ❋ ❋

When they got to the whitewashed cinderblock building which housed Club 250 on the outskirts of Grantville, the parking lot of the bar was in an uproar. Bubba and Jimmy stepped out of the car into the middle of shouting and what looked to be a showdown in the making.

"No way! That just ain't possible!" Dave Southerland yelled. At six feet six inches, he weighed in at nearly three hundred hard packed pounds. He was almost a head taller than Ken Beasley, who stood there in his ever-spotless white bartender's apron, with a fairly fresh, but used, small white bar towel over his left shoulder. Dave towered over Ken, shouting at the man almost face to face well inside, threateningly inside, Ken's comfort zone. It was plain to anybody who knew anything about belligerent blockheads that Dave was itching for any excuse to get into a fight. Everyone in the parking lot was waiting for Dave to start swinging. And for once Ken wasn't behind the bar where he could back up out of reach and then grab the sawed-off double barrel shotgun which hung under the cash register.

"You're right!" The club owner nodded but refused to give an inch of ground. "But, possible or not," Ken Beasley said quietly, "the sun is there." He pointed at the white-yellow orb hanging in the sky like a three hundred watt light bulb, "And, at this time of the day it should be there." The bartender pointed off into an empty stretch of blue sky. When he swung his arm from one point to the other, he used the movement as an excuse to put a little distance between himself and his antagonist.

"Ken, that just ain't possible!" Dave Southerland snarled.

"Look, before the lights went out, the sun coming through the window was shining on Tommy's table. That's where it should be at this time of the day. When the sun is shining, I don't need a clock. I can tell you the time give or take a quarter of an hour by where the sunny spot is on the floor. Before that flash of light, the sunny spot was where it was supposed to be. Then after the flash of light, it was almost all the way over to the pool table."

"The sun does not just up and jump around." Dave shook his head, "Ken, it's just not possible. You've got to be wrong. It can't happen."

Jimmy snickered loudly. Every set of eyes in the parking lot focused on the noise, except Dave's and Ken's. Theirs remained in a tight lock with each other. Some people noticed that James had a wicked gleam in his eyes. "Dave, why don't you go out to your parents' farm and tell your momma that the Bible ain't so." Dave's mother was a Bible-thumping Sunday school teacher, and everybody knew it. On more than one occasion, always when he got deep enough in his cups to get maudlin and feel guilty about what his momma called her son's wayward lifestyle, Dave loudly told everybody in the bar "

there ain't nothin' about the Bible my momma don't know." As far as Dave was concerned his momma was a living saint.

Dave turned and snarled, "What in hell are you talking about, Jimmy?"

Ken put some more distance between himself and the angry man.

"I mean, it's happened before. It's in the Bible."

"What?"

"Yeah. The sun turned back ten degrees."

"Jimmy, you are so full of shit! It ain't so. Ken's got to be wrong. Things like this just do not happen. He can't be right! It can't happen. So, it can't be in the Bible."

THE LEGEND OF JIMMY DICK

"Put your money where your mouth is Dave."

"I don't want to take your money, Jimmy."

"Oh, there's no chance of that, Dave." James' gaze followed Ken's slow progress back to the door of the bar where he stepped inside so fast it could have passed as magic. James' smile broadened just a hair. "You see, you don't know what you're talkin' about," James paused half a heartbeat for emphasis, "as usual. And I do," he paused yet again, "like always. And I don't mind takin' your money. So," James faced split, adding a shit eatin' grin of a smile, to the gleam of mischief in his eyes. Ken was back to the door, and his right hand was out of sight. James looked at him, and Ken nodded. "Dave," James paused, "it's time to put up or shut up."

"Jimmy, you are full of shit!"

"I got a hundred-dollar bill that says you're wrong and I'm right."

"I don't want to take your money, Jimmy."

"No chance of that. You don't know what you're talking about. And I do. Two to one odds."

Dave turned away.

"Four to one. Your twenty-five against my one-hundred."

Dave hesitated.

"You're so sure you know what can and can't be. You think your momma taught you the Bible!" James snorted in derision." Well, hell, I know you're wrong."

Dave continued to hesitate.

"And I know you're chicken!" Jimmy sneered.

"Ken, write it up," Dave said. "If that stupid idiot wants to throw his money away, I'll take it. If something like that was in the Bible, my momma would have taught me about it. She didn't, so it ain't there."

Because of the fights and feuds, the custom arose in Club 250 for Ken to write up the bets and hold the money. In the process, each party initialed the bet slip agreeing to what the bet was. It didn't stop the all the fights over bets, but it helped.

"How are you going to settle it?" Ken asked.

"If it's in there, Jimmy will have to show it to me," Dave said. Believe it or not, there was a Bible under the bar right on top a *Guinness Book of World Records*. Both were there for settling bets.

"Shit, I don't know where it is," Jimmy replied.

"That's 'cause it ain't there. Like I said, Jimmy, you are full of shit," Dave answered.

"Just because I don't know where it is, don't mean it's not in there. We'll get on the phone and call a preacher," Jimmy said.

"Can't," Ken said from the door. "The phone went out when the lights did."

All the customers who had been milling around in the parking lot, at first looking up at the sky, then waiting to see if Dave was going to swing at Ken, and then hoping Dave would flatten Jimmy Dick, lost interest when it became clear that the fight wasn't going to happen.

Tom Jordan muttered, "Too bad. I thought for a minute there Dave was going to give that little jerk Jimmy Dick what he's had coming."

Something caught someone's attention, and then several people gathered at the back of Bubba's Buick.

"Hey, Bubba? What happened to your bumper?" Tom Jordan asked.

"What's that, Tommy?" Bubba replied.

"Your back bumper? It's missing," Tom said.

"Shit, it was there when we put the bags in the trunk before we left Huntington."

Bubba walked around the car. Upon a glancing inspection, Bubba said, "Shit! It's sure is gone?" So were the facings of the rear taillights and the following edge of the spoiler. The ends of the bumper mounts were bright and shiny and smooth as glass as if a giant with a razor sliced them off at the same angle that matched the missing spoiler edge.

"Shit," Bubba said. "When did that happen?"

"Probably the same time G-d moved the sun around it the sky!" Dave mocked. "Is the missing bumper in the Bible too?" Dave got the laugh at Jimmy's expense that he was looking for.

"Go ahead and write it up, Ken," James said. The accompanying nod of his head said thank you, and it's all right. You can put the shotgun away. "I'll bring the chapter and verse in by one week from today if I've got to read the whole damned Bible to do it."

"Dave?" Ken asked. The question was, is that all right? The underlying question that Dave probably didn't even realize he was answering was, is the coming fight off for now or not?

"Yeah. I can wait a week for Jimmy to admit he's an idiot."

THE LEGEND OF JIMMY DICK

✳ ✳ ✳

It took three days.

"The thirty-eighth chapter of Isaiah," James called out as Dave came through the door of the bar. James was there because he habitually arrived shortly after the doors were open and usually stayed until the bar closed. Looking sheepish Dave just nodded. He'd already read it. His mother did indeed know her Bible. "Pay up Dave!" Jimmy snickered.

"Jimmy, you're right. It's there. But you are still a jackass."

A fortnight later Dave was hailed by Jimmy when he came through the door of the bar. "Hey Dave, it's been two weeks. You're past due."

"Hey, you had a week to settle the bet. And I've got a week after that to make good on the I.O.U."

"Yeah. But that was two weeks ago. You're late."

"Check the date on the bet slip, Jimmy. I've got over three hundred years before that note is due." The date was on the slip both men signed when Ken agreed to hold it. "I don't have to pay it until it's due."

The bar roared with laughter.

"I'll hold you to it," Jimmy replied, trying to salvage a scrap of dignity. But Dave had a loophole big enough to drive a truck through.

By Terry Howard

GRANTVILLE'S GREATEST PHILOSOPHER

Ken looked up when the door opened. When he saw the men who were entering, he moved down to the cash register. Once there, he put his hand on the sawed-off shotgun that hung in a rack on the underside of the bar. "Julio," he called.

"Yeah?" Julio Mora replied.

"Nine one one, *now!*"

"On it." Julio left the sink of dirty dishes and headed for the phone in the back room.

Three men walked through the door. Each was well dressed, one more so than the others. They were armed, but that was common enough. Two of them had that air of 'trouble on a short leash.' Muscle, Ken thought. Bodyguards, competent, deadly, dangerous. They were also down-timers. Under the big "Club 250" sign on the door, a little sign read "No Dogs and No Germans Allowed." All down-timers were "Krauts" as far as the denizens of Ken's bar were concerned.

If it had been a bit later in the day, Ken would have told them to get out, knowing there was enough firepower at hand to make it stick. It was, after all, that kind of bar. At this hour, though, the "I want a drink for lunch crowd" was mostly gone. There were only three patrons left. Ken knew they were nothing but three more targets. It was time to stall and pray that the police came quickly, so Ken waited nervously for the down-timers to speak first.

After standing inside the door for half a minute, the trio consulted briefly, and one of the guards spoke in fairly understandable English. "We have read the sign."

Uh oh, Ken thought.

"We are not staying," the guard said.

Relief swept through the owner of the bar. Ken had never killed anyone in the bar and didn't want to start now. For that matter, he had never been killed and sure didn't want to start that now, either.

"We were told that the great philosopher, Herr Head, always had lunch here."

James Richard Shaver, Jimmy Dick, often referred to behind his back as Dick Head, a name he richly deserved for being a jerk of the first water, actually managed to blush. Ken, from long practice, managed to swallow his laughter completely. Some of his patrons were a mite touchy, especially when they were drunk.

"Herr Krieger wishes to converse with him," the guard continued. "It need not be here, where we are not allowed. Over dinner tonight, at the newly opened salon, perhaps?"

Ken let out the breath he was holding and took his moist hand off the shotgun. The tension flowed out of his muscles and evaporated without leaving any residue on the floor. Politely, he answered the trio with complete honesty. "There is no one here right now who answers to the name Herr Head. Can I ask who sent you?"

"We sought the gathering place of the local philosophical society at the . . ." The guard did not quite pause, "'front counter,' where we took lodgings. We were directed to the . . ." This time he did pause while he wrapped his tongue around a more difficult, recently learned, word phrase, "'Police Station.' They directed us to the . . ." Again a new word. "'Post office.' There we were told that the only full-time, practicing philosopher in town was Herr, excuse me, Mister Head, and he could be found here having lunch since there was no longer a Cracker-barrel in town."

"Did the post office say Mister Head or dickhead?" Ken inquired.

"Yes, Dick Head is the name we were given."

The other two patrons snickered, and James blushed again.

"Where are you staying?" Ken asked. "If Herr Head comes in today, I'll give him the message. And then, if the greatest of Grantville's philosophers wishes to talk to you, he can send a disciple to make arrangements."

All the while Ken spoke, Jimmy Dick was thinking hard. He was never going to live this down. He knew it. People who hadn't spoken to him in years, if ever, would hail him on the streets of Grantville at the slightest of excuse, just to have the opportunity of addressing him as "Herr Head." The more polite of them would seek the opinion of Grantville's greatest philosopher. Small towns can be quite cruel that way.

It was almost a relief when the door opened, and two cops walked in.

"Is there a problem, Mister Beasley?" one of them asked.

"No. No problem at all. These gentlemen were just leaving."

One cop looked at the other and tilted his head slightly towards the door. The second nodded ever more slightly. Then Hans, the down-time cop, went out with the three strangers to make sure they didn't have any complaints that should be addressed.

Lyndon approached the bar. When he reached the cash register, he asked, "What happened, Ken?" Officer Johnson was probably the only cop who ever addressed Ken Beasley by his first name. He once briefly dated Ken's step-daughter, and Ken still thought well of him.

"Sorry about that, Lyndon," Ken said. "When three armed Krauts came through the door looking dangerous, I thought I had a problem. Turns out someone down at the post office sent them here on a wild goose chase; just to get rid of them, I suspect."

Lyndon worked so hard to swallow his laughter that he almost choked on it. "Sorry about that, Ken," Lyndon apologized. "I guess that's our fault. When the three wise men came wandering into the station looking for our philosophers so they could commune with them, the person behind the desk tried to explain that we didn't have any. She finally got rid of them by sending them to the Post Office. After all, they have everybody's address. Well, someone thought it was funny, I guess, to let them chase their tails all over town and called the post office and suggested Jimmy Dick."

"Thanks a hell of a lot!" James added from the sidelines.

Lyndon continued. "If the post office had given them his home address they never would have come here."

"Hey?" Jimmy Dick called out. "Hello." He waved his hand in a big "bring on the train" wave. "I'm down here. If you can't talk to me, you could at least not talk about me as if I ain't here, damn it."

"Oh, I'm sorry, Jimmy," Lyndon said. "When I didn't see you talking to them I figured you weren't here."

"Why the hell should I talk to them? And why was it funny to give them my name?" James demanded. Then before that could be answered, if indeed it could be, he also asked, "And just who do I thank for that anyway? And why would I want them poking around my house?"

Lyndon started to answer the first or second question and then bit his tongue. He didn't answer the third question either, but he did reply to it. "Jeez, Jimmy, I'm not sure who made that call."

✷ ✷ ✷

In truth, Lyndon knew exactly who made the call. He knew it had been discussed for almost three minutes and everybody in the office, including the chief, knew about it and thought it was funny.

The conversation started out with someone suggesting that they call the post office and have them send the three wise men down to the stables to look for Don.

"Don who?" someone asked.

"Donald Duck," someone else suggested.

"That would do, but I was thinking of Ma Quixote's oldest boy."

The people in the room had chuckled. Then someone showed his age by saying, "If they want philosophy, we should send them to Ma and Pa Kettle."

"Who's that?" At least two people asked.

As he tried to explain who Ma and Pa Kettle were and then what a cracker-barrel philosopher was, the name Dick Head came up.

The truth was that they were, perhaps, just a little embarrassed that they did not have a Philosophical Society in town nor did they have anybody they considered a philosopher. So they sought to hide the embarrassment in humor. Pain turned inward is depression. Pain turned outward is anger. Pain turned sideways is humor. All three can be destructive.

THE LEGEND OF JIMMY DICK

✱ ✱ ✱

"If there's no problem, I'd better get back to work," Lyndon said. Ken noticed he hadn't answered the fourth question, either.

The other two patrons were out the door behind him before it shut all the way. The closing of the door seemed to trigger a wave of laughter.

"Ken, bring me a bottle of whatever you're calling whiskey these days," Jimmy Dick said. "That story is all over town by now. Looks like I'll be doing my drinking at home for a good long while."

"Shoot, Jimmy. That won't help, and you know it. The only thing you can do is make it your joke on the Krauts and ride it out."

James picked up his beer and took a long slow sip and thought for a minute. You can't talk while you're drinking and you can't talk while you're thinking. Or is it you can't think while you're talking? James mind went back to junior high school. If someone insulted you it was best to turn it back on them; it was almost as good if you could turn it on someone else, then you were doing the laughing instead of being laughed at.

"Oh, come on, Jimmy," Ken said, "why do you think I told them you'd have a disciple come to their hotel? You can have the whole town laughin' at you, or you can have the town laughin' at them."

"I don't know, Ken."

"Go have a free dinner. Order two of the most expensive meals on the menu. Hand them some bullshit. Then tell everybody in town what saps the puffed up highbrow Krauts are."

"I don't know, Ken," James said, again. The answer came a bit slower this time.

Ken knew he was coming around. "Well, why not?" Ken pushed.

"That interpreter he had was hard on the ears," James said. It was lame, and he knew it. He also knew that he would be taking Ken's advice. He just couldn't give in without arguing. It wasn't in his nature.

"So when you send the messenger, tell 'em you're bringing your own. Better still, tell them you're bringing two, so it'll be three on three."

Julio brought half a tray of glasses to add to the stack under the bar. The only time he ever brought less than a full tray was when he wanted an excuse to come out front. "I'll get my grandson to deliver the message," he said.

"He's in school, ain't he? I want to get this over with." James said.

"I'll call over there and get him out," Julio said.

"Why don't we just call the hotel?" James asked.

"Naw! It ain't dignified enough. Grantville's greatest philosopher would send a formal note. While we're waiting for the boy, I'll call home and get a blank card. Don't just stand there, Julio," Ken said. "Call the school and get the kid over here."

❋ ❋ ❋

When Matthew got back to school, he had missed one class and was late for the next. When he entered Mister Onofrio's math class, he handed the teacher a note from the office. The note said simply "Matthew Bartholow was excused and may be admitted to class at this time."

After forty years of teaching, Emmanuel Onofrio knew a rat when he smelled one. "You will speak to me after class, young man. Do you have today's assignment?" It was the last class of the day, and Emmanuel knew Matthew's shift as a busboy didn't start until dinner time. The lad had tried, once, to use it as an excuse for not having his homework done.

When the room was empty except for the two of them, Mister Onofrio asked, "Just where were you, young man?" in his well-practiced "I can see your soul so don't mess with me" voice.

"My grandfather sent for me to run an errand," Matthew replied.

"And what was this errand that was so important that it couldn't wait?"

"They needed a message delivered." The boy's answer sounded rather lame to the old man.

"And what was this important message, that had to be delivered, by you, before school was out?" The mathematician wanted to know. The boy blushed but did not say a word.

"Come, come," the graybeard said. He knew he was near a confession when the lad blushed. "Speak up."

"Well, they didn't tell me not to read it," Matthew said.

"So you read it. What did it say?"

"Dick Head, along with an interpreter and an associate, will be pleased to accept Herr Krieger's dinner invitation tonight at seven. Please make reservations for six at Grantville Fine Foods."

At the name Dick Head, Emmanuel Onofrio started to dismiss the whole thing as a bad joke. But the name Krieger caught his full attention. "Krieger?" He almost gasped. "Not Wilhelm Krieger?"

"That's the one. I got his first name at the counter when I delivered the note," Matthew said.

"Why would he want to see that idiot Jimmy Dick?" Emmanuel asked the universe, all but forgetting that there was another person in the room.

"All I know is that the post office sent 'em lookin' for Dick Head and they found him where Grandpa works afternoons," Matthew said.

"The post office?!" The puzzled teacher nearly yelped. "Why would they send him there?"

"I don't know."

"That will be all."

* * *

Shortly after Matthew left, Emmanuel was on his bicycle. He was heading for the post office and determined to get to the bottom of it all.

* * *

The gray-haired man stepped up to the window to be promptly told, "Sorry, Emmanuel, there isn't any mail for you. I'd send it on to the school anyway."

"No, I'm not expecting anything. I was wondering, though . . . Well, I heard something improbable from a student and thought I ought to check before I called him on it. You didn't see Wilhelm Krieger today, did you?" Emmanuel asked.

"Not that I know of," she answered.

"Thank goodness. That's a relief. I was told you sent him looking for Jimmy Dick," he said.

"Oh! The three wise men. Yeah, I sent them to Club 250 to see the Dick, ah, Jimmy Dick." Even grown-ups can be intimidated by an old teacher.

"Why?" Emmanuel practically shouted.

The postmistress must have "got her back up" at his tone of voice, at the implied criticism, and at being made to feel like a naughty little girl. "Cause the cops called over here and told me to. If you got a problem with that, go and talk to them." With those words, she turned away from the window.

※ ※ ※

Shortly thereafter, Emmanuel found himself at the police station. Shortly after that, he found himself in Chief Richards' office. Oddly, it was the chief who was uncomfortable.

"Chief Richards, do you know why one of your people sent Wilhelm Krieger to speak to Jimmy Dick?"

"Well, Mister Onofrio, what can I say? It seemed like a good idea at the time."

"Chief, you just sent the biggest jerk in the whole town to represent us to the greatest intellectual mind that Germany is likely to produce this century."

"Never heard of him," Chief Richards replied.

"He probably didn't live long enough to make it into our history books. Beyond doubt, he will be in the ones we're writing now. His published work on philosophy guarantees that even if he never writes another word. We can't have him thinking that jackass, Jimmy Dick, represents Grantville. You've got to stop it." Chief Richards knew Emmanuel must be a very flustered academic. He wasn't just speaking forcefully; he was nearly shouting.

"I don't see what I can do about it. Having dinner isn't a crime. If you feel that strongly about it, go talk to Jimmy Dick. Now, is there anything else I can help you with before I get back to work?" Chief

Richards was getting a bit annoyed. He wasn't used to being yelled at in his own office.

* * *

Emmanuel put his kickstand down outside of Club 250 within a few minutes of leaving the police station. As he read the sign, 'No Dogs And No germans Allowed,' his mind corrected the missed capital letter. Then he realized it had been done that way on purpose. He took a deep breath, squared his shoulders and entered the den to bait the lions.

* * *

Ken looked up as Emmanuel walked in. Emmanuel could see that Ken didn't immediately recognize him. Then he apparently decided that Emmanuel was obviously an up-timer, probably okay. The old man approached the bar, and Ken asked, "What can I get ya'?"

"I'm looking for Jimmy Dick," Emmanuel said.

"He ain't here," Ken answered.

"You're Ken Beasley, right?" Emmanuel asked.

"Yeah," Ken answered.

"I'm Emmanuel Onofrio," Emmanuel said.

"Ralph's uncle?" Ken asked.

"Or his brother, depending on which Ralph you're referring to. Perhaps you can help me. I need to convince Jimmy Dick to not keep that dinner date tonight."

"Why?"

"Mister Beasley," Emmanuel started to explain but was interrupted.

"Call me Ken," Ken said. "The only people who call me Mister Beasley in here are cops here on official business."

"Ken, Jimmy Dick is the butt of a horrible joke. A joke that's in very bad taste, I might add, perpetrated by the police department."

"Manny, we knew that when we sent the note accepting the invitation," Ken said.

Emmanuel ignored being called Manny. The old man detested that nickname but was dealing with a shock of his own at the moment. "You knew?"

"Sure," Ken said.

"Then why did he accept?"

"Well, Grantville is going to be laughing about this for years to come. We decided we'd rather have them laughing at some damned Kraut stuffed shirt than at one of our own," Ken explained.

"But, Mister Beasley, Ken, that Kraut stuffed shirt is Wilhelm Krieger. He's here to research our philosophy before he writes about it for all of Europe to read." When it came to Herr Krieger's purpose, Emmanuel was guessing. Correctly, as it turned out, but still just guessing.

"Really?"

"Do you really want all of Europe to judge us by Herr Krieger's impression of Jimmy Dick?" Emmanuel asked.

Ken looked taken aback for a moment. The stakes were a lot higher than he had realized, apparently. Still, he asked, "Do you really want Jimmy to spend the rest of his life being laughed at over this?"

Emmanuel started to speak and paused with his mouth open. He hadn't thought of that. He was angry with himself. In an argument, you take the time that your opponent is speaking to plan your next point. In a discussion, you listen to the other party and think about what was said before responding. He hated arguing and was annoyed with himself for having slipped into one. Still, he had to try. "Mister Beasley, this is important. Way too important to leave in the hands of Jimmy Dick Shaver."

"Well, the cops should've thought of that before they set him up to take a pratfall. Shouldn't they have?"

"I can't agree with you more. Their behavior is reprehensible. But what can you do, report them to the police?" Emmanuel asked.

Ken actually laughed. The hostility that had been building was, provisionally, set aside, though it was ready to hand and could be easily put back in play.

"Where is Jimmy Dick? Perhaps I can reason with him," Emmanuel said.

"I doubt it." Ken smiled. "His mind is pretty well made up. Have a seat and a beer on the house. Jimmy will be back shortly. He's gone out to nail down his interpreter for tonight."

That caught Emmanuel's curiosity. "Who is he getting?"

"He wants Old Joe Jenkins."

"That old hillbilly?"

"Yep." Ken nodded. "Jimmy said he heard him translatin' sermons, German to English and English to German right down to the emotional slant of the preacher and was never more than one word behind. He also said that Old Joe Jenkins was the smartest man he had ever met."

Emmanuel was shocked to find that he was angry or jealous and chided himself for it. Why should he care about the opinion of the biggest jackass in a town half full of petty, close-minded people? Besides he had never really met Jimmy Dick, so the poor man didn't really know what a smart man was. Then he chided himself for being overly proud and again for being uncharitable to the village he grew up in and had chosen to retire to.

"Who's his other second?" Emmanuel asked.

"Huh?" Ken looked confused.

"Jimmy has been challenged to a duel of wits. He's taking two seconds. One is Joe Jenkins. Who is the other one?"

"I don't think that's been settled yet," Ken said. He knew for a fact that Jimmy was assuming he would be the third member of the party. He wasn't thrilled with the idea. Fresh organic fertilizer had a way of splattering anyone close by when it hit the fan, and he didn't want to deal with it. A thought grew in his mind, and a smile grew on his face. "But I think it should be you."

✢ ✢ ✢

Fritz Shuler was ecstatic. On a weeknight his struggling restaurant, Grantville Fine Foods was booked to capacity. He hadn't had a night like this since the opening rush. The crowd was almost all up-timers, for a change. There was one reservation from a down-timer. Then the calls started trickling in. The trickle steadily increased until he was turning people away.

By Terry Howard

Fritz was frantically putting the final touches on the new policy that he hoped would be the salvation of his investment. He had researched up-time dining before he opened. He found a paper maker who would make paper plates and napkins. His niece bought plastic flatware and cups at school from anyone who would sell them.

He had set out to provide an authentic West Virginia dining experience. He featured catfish, Kentucky style chicken cooked in a very expensive "pressure cooker," and beef grilled to order, on top of a full menu. The down-timers found it charming, but up-timers didn't come back.

Someone finally explained the difference between fast food and fine food. After tonight when diners arrived, they would be asked, "Paper or cloth napkins?" But tonight, except for the one table, everyone would have real linen, silver flatware, fine china, and glass. He hadn't planned to start that until next week but when the river floods, it's time to float the logs.

After a hard day of frantic preparations, the night was not going well. People who arrived at six were lingering over coffee and wine as if waiting for something. People who had a seven o'clock reservation were arriving early as if they were afraid they would miss something. Customers were piling up in the waiting area. There were no open tables except for the one set for six with paper and plastic. Fritz was not going to put an up-time patron there. He gritted his teeth and started passing out free wine.

The down-timers arrived a bit early. Oddly, no one in the waiting area objected to being passed over. Fritz showed them to the table where they immediately examined the place settings in detail as was typical of a first time down-timer diner. Fritz was shocked when the rest of the party arrived and were up-timers. Well, it was too late to change things now.

Fritz showed the new arrivals to the table. Before they could seat themselves one of the down-timers stood up. Fritz was startled and just a bit worried.

In passable English, the standing man said, "Herr Krieger suspects that he is being played for a fool." From the look on his face, the interpreter was completely convinced of it and was more than a little pleased about it for some reason.

Emmanuel's heart dropped. He had hoped he could take the conversation into Latin, the language of scholarship, and control the night. Now the game was lost before it started. All he could think to do was apologize profusely. Before he could start Joe Jenkins spoke up.

"Why does he suspect that?" Joe asked.

It was a fair question, Emmanuel thought, but something about the way Joe said it was . . . Latin! It was Latin; accented but understandable Latin. Where did a dumb hillbilly learn Latin?

The interpreter looked perplexed. Emmanuel guessed that he didn't know Latin, just his native dialect of German and the passable English he had picked up somewhere. Herr Krieger, on the other hand, was suddenly focused completely on Joseph. He motioned for the interpreter to sit down.

"My man here claimed to have overheard a conversation leading him to believe Dick Head is not a name but an insult," he said in crisp Latin. His voice was quite tainted with suspicion and hostility.

"Well, he is right about it being no one's proper name." Joseph continued speaking in Latin, to Emmanuel's ongoing amazement. "I am Joseph Loudoun Jenkins, now commonly known as Old Joe. When I was young, I was known as Low Down Jenkins. Over there is Emmanuel Onofrio, known to his students as Oman Frio, meaning Old man 'Frio. Don't look sour, Emmanuel. You know it's so. Emmanuel is otherwise known as Ralph's brother or Ralph's uncle, depending upon the age of the speaker. Your third guest is James Richard Shaver, commonly known as Jimmy Dick, sometimes called Dick Head."

"Why?" Wilhelm asked.

Joe began to answer. "Well, sir." Hearing the West Virginia accent and word choice coming out of Joseph's mouth while speaking Latin was amazing to Emmanuel. Still, somehow, it felt like Joseph was yet going to pull it out of the soup. "We came from a very busy time. Anything we could do to get things done faster we did it. Even our language was rushed. We didn't have time to say 'The United States of America,' so we said 'the U.S.A.' When I was a young man we had a 'President,' a leader named Eisenhower. He was very highly esteemed. Everyone referred to him as Ike. Later two Presidents in a row were known by initials, J.F.K. and then L.B.J." Joseph answered the question while completely ignoring what was asked.

"Are we just goin' t' stand here or what?" Jimmy Dick spoke up.

Herr Krieger's interpreter translated the question into German. Wilhelm nodded slightly and motioned to the chairs with a slight hand movement. Emmanuel realized that James was a loose cannon who was getting irate about not knowing what was going on. He started translating the Latin into English for him.

"So you shorten names for convenience. That is nothing that we do not do. But he is Dick Head. Is that not an insult?" Wilhelm asked.

"Have you studied Hebrew, Herr Krieger?" Joseph asked.

"Briefly," Wilhelm said. "There were works I wanted to read, but in the end, it proved more workable to have them translated."

"I know what you mean. I tried to learn Hebrew and Greek, but it was more time than I could spare back then. Knowing French helped when I decided to learn Latin six months ago," Joseph said.

"You have only been working on Latin for six months? Incredible," Wilhelm said. Emmanuel agreed.

"We Americans do things in a hurry. I thought I might need it for dealing with the Catholics, so I was motivated. As I was saying about Hebrew, you know that the word 'Rosh' can translate as 'first' or 'top' or 'head.' Dick can be used in English to mean 'penis.' But it also can mean 'any man' for obvious reasons. Like the words," he shifted to English for two words "lumberjack and steeplejack. So, yes, it can be an insult. But then, to misquote scripture, 'a philosopher is not without honor except in his own home.'"

Wilhelm smiled and started to call for wine by picking up his glass and holding it in the air. But he stopped with the red plastic cup only inches off the table. "Why are we the only ones who have these?" he asked.

"Shit," Jimmy Dick said. "They came from up-time with us, and when they're gone, they're gone. You're being honored." He swallowed the words, 'ya dumb Kraut,' because Emmanuel had impressed on him how important the dinner was. "Honored with a piece of the future. Everybody else here tonight has to make do with the here and now."

Emmanuel started translating what was said into Latin before Herr Krieger's man could give an uncensored version. People at the nearby tables seemed to be taken with sudden fits of coughing.

"Waiter, wine for my guests," Wilhelm Krieger called out. When he did, it seemed as if there was a pause in conversation while he spoke. The noise level in the room unquestionably went back up when he set his glass down. "This," he waved his hand to include everything on the table, "is truly amazing, so light, yet strong." He picked up a fork and looked at it skeptically. "Can you truly eat with this? It seems like it would break."

Emmanuel was busy translating German to English for Jimmy Dick, who was amongst the minority in Grantville who refused to learn German. So the conversation fell to Joseph, who responded in German. "They can break if you try cutting meat with them, so you use the knife. They were made to be thrown away after one use."

"Truly?" Wilhelm asked with raised eyebrows. "What of the expense?"

"You could buy a box of one hundred for less than you earned in an hour," Joseph replied. "They were not highly esteemed, but it saved the time of washing up. Our thought was 'anything to save time.' We were a very busy people."

Herr Krieger's eyebrows went up again. Emmanuel could almost see him thinking that there was a fortune to be made here.

"Unfortunately, we can't make anymore. Even if we had the equipment, the materials are not available. These are the last for at least ten years," Joseph said.

"Unfortunate, indeed. Do you teach at the local academy also?" Krieger asked.

"No. I don't have the credentials it takes to do that," Joseph said.

"But with your Latin . . . and you are a philosopher, surely?"

"Neither Latin nor philosophy are much regarded." Turning to Emmanuel, Joseph said, "Why don't you tell Herr Krieger about the school system."

Emmanuel set about giving a detailed account of Grantville's schools. As far as he was concerned, he was justifiably proud of them, even if they were on the low side of average up-time. Joseph translated for Jimmy this time. Ordering food interrupted the flow of Emmanuel's lecture, but he eventually concluded with, "I would put our high school graduates up against Jena's University students when it comes to general knowledge. When it comes to specialized knowledge, I would match Jena graduates with ours in the same field. Of course, we have areas of study that they do not." He was thinking drivers' ed, and then others.

The food arrived. Diners began to leave while others arrived and took seats. It didn't look like the hoped-for fireworks were going to happen. No one had the Latin to follow the conversation, so why stay?

"Your colleague says Latin and philosophy are not esteemed?" Wilhelm asked.

"We offer Latin as an elective. Philosophy is covered as part of English literature," Emmanuel answered.

Herr Krieger cautiously cut at his steak with the plastic knife and was visibly surprised that it worked. The silent bodyguard tried cutting his with the fork. It broke in his hand. A staff member immediately turned up with a set of silver utensils for him and took the knife and spoon away. Emmanuel had the chicken. It was quite good. It had been so long since he last had Kentucky chicken that he couldn't tell the difference. The slaw, mashed potatoes, and gravy were superlative.

After his first bite, Wilhelm Krieger reverted to Latin. "Herr Head, is war mankind's greatest glory or its greatest shame?"

Emmanuel translated the question.

"Hell, it's neither," Jimmy Dick Shaver answered. Joseph translated the answer.

"Neither?" Herr Krieger prompted.

"War is a great adventure," Jimmy Dick quoted. "But, an adventure is someone else havin' a hard time of it somewhere else. War is glorious when you win with an acceptable casualty rate. But no casualty rate is acceptable to the casualty. And since someone always loses, war is glorious less than half the time.

"To the men in the middle of it," James continued, "war is at best boring drudgery spiked with moments of terror. For some, it is a walking nightmare that never leaves them this side of the grave."

"Then it is our greatest shame?" Krieger asked.

"There are greater shames," James said after Emmanuel translated the question. "The holocaust comes to mind."

"Do you want me to explain that?" Joe asked.

"Might as well," James said.

"In our history, Herr Krieger," Joseph said, "in the years of the nineteen thirties and forties, a Prussian government rounded up twelve million people they did not approve of. Jews, gypsies, Poles, Slavs, and others. Then they exterminated them."

"Like Vlad the Impaler killing every beggar in the kingdom," Herr Krieger said. "But, that many?"

"It was a very full world," Joseph said. "Look it up at the library. The key words are Nazi and Holocaust. It will surely confirm the six million Jews. You may have to dig to find the others. They are often forgotten."

Wilhelm Krieger looked at James. "But, this Holocaust is surely a fluke?"

"No!" James replied. "Pol Pot, five million, Saddam, three million, Stalin . . . who knows how many millions."

"So these holocausts are man's greatest shame?" Krieger asked. The undertone of skeptical unbelief was less than perfectly hidden.

"Hell no!" James answered.

A frustrated Wilhelm finally demanded, "If it is not war and it is not slaughter, then what is it?"

Emanuel translated the question. Joseph waited for the answer. James paused. His last "hell no" was a reaction without conscious thought. Now he needed a response. "Tell him that mankind's greatest shame is running out of good whiskey. No, wait." A memory of personal pain gushed into his mind like a torrent of water from a long-forgotten dam that crumbled. "Tell him our greatest shame is an uncherished child. A man's greatest glory is to love his wife and raise his children well."

Joseph translated it. Wilhelm started at him like a pole-axed steer for at least five seconds. Then he turned to Emmanuel. "Did he translate that correctly?"

"Yes," was all Emmanuel said.

Wilhelm looked back at Joseph. "Do you agree with him?"

"Well, it was my greatest joy. And yes, it is my greatest glory. So I agree with him." Joseph said.

"And you?" Herr Krieger asked, looking at Emmanuel.

Onofrio's memories flashed back through a list of unloved, bright children who faded into dull commonness or blossomed into brilliant horrors. "Yes. An uncherished child is our greatest shame."

"You people are hopeless romantics." Krieger's tone made it clear he thought the idea contemptible.

Both up-timer translators laughed. When Emmanuel explained why, James smirked.

"What is so funny?" an obviously angry Wilhelm demanded.

Joseph dried his eyes. "My wife has often told me that I was a typical male with no idea of what romance is."

Wilhelm humphed before asking, "Herr Head, how many children did you and your wife raise?"

"I ain't mankind. I'm one man. Nam was my greatest glory and my greatest shame. When I returned no women worth puttin' up with would have me and any women who would put up with me weren't worth havin'."

※ ※ ※

He saw no reason to tell this damned Kraut about his personal life. When Bina Rae found out their baby had "bad bones," probably from something he brought back from Nam—something he hadn't told her about—she moved out on him. She acted like Agent Orange was some sort of venereal disease he could have avoided. When she left, he took to hitting the bottle hard and lost his job. Bina Rae wouldn't talk to him, wouldn't go to counseling, and wouldn't let him see Little Merle without a big fight each and every time.

Now Merle was living in the nursing home, and as long as the bills were paid, he never heard from or of her. Merle would not speak to him for abandoning her. She never even heard his side of the story.

The only happy year of his miserable life crashed in 1973. Bina Rae came home from the doctor and was packed up and gone when he got home from work. He got drunk and stayed drunk. Along the way, he got divorced and listed as sixty percent disabled instead of the usual thirty percent for a head case. Up to the Ring of Fire, the Veterans Administration paid for Merle out of his disability check. Now he was making do with family money off of rental properties that an agent managed.

None of that was anybody's damned business, especially some damned Kraut.

THE LEGEND OF JIMMY DICK

* * *

"So you admit that your greatest glory and your greatest shame is war. But you would have me believe it is raising children." Herr Krieger turned to his interpreter and spoke in loud, angry, German while rising to his feet and pocketing the plastic spoon. "You are right! I am being played for a fool. Settle up with the proprietor and return to the lodgings." Then without a fare-thee-well, he and the silent bodyguard stalked out of the totally silent room.

Jimmy Dick was the first to speak. "Ya know, this catfish is really quite good."

The dining room burst into roaring laughter.

When it had mostly died down, Emmanuel Onofrio stood and extended his hand to Jimmy "Dickhead" Shaver. "Mister Shaver," he said in a voice pitched to carry, "it was truly a pleasure translating for Grantville's only fulltime practicing philosopher."

By Terry Howard

NOT A PRINCESS BRIDE

James Richard, or Jimmy Dick, Shaver (known to his close associates, and almost everyone else, as Dickhead) was in the grocery store. The old drunk was not there buying food. Most of his calories came from beer, followed by pretzels. Yes, believe it or not, despite the Ring of Fire, the Club 250 still sold pretzels. They were much better or a whole lot worse than the old ones, depending on who you asked. Hamburgers and fries rounded out his usual diet. You weren't always sure that the ground meat was pure beef, the bun was hand sliced, and the pickle wasn't Vlassic. But someone had managed to get the mustard right.

Jimmy Dick was in the store buying tobacco. As far as he was concerned what you could get was shit. Most folk—everyone who smoked, really—agreed with that opinion. They also agreed that it was way over-priced, but then they had complained about that back in the real world. Still, when the local crop failed because the growing season was too short, you bought what was available or quit. As he left the checkout lane a man was waiting for him at the baggers' station. There was no bagger, of course. That was because there were no bags, paper or plastic. You brought a canvas bag, a basket, a tote sack or something from home. Cardboard boxes were popular at first, but they wore out. The ones that were still in good shape were bringing a good price on the curiosity market all over Europe, so the price went up as the supply went down. One little old lady thought of her hoard as her retirement fund.

As Jimmy Dick passed him, the man spoke. His English was good. It was understandable, with a heavy German accent of some sort that Jimmy did not place. "Herr Sha—Mister Shaver?" Jimmy stopped. "Forgive me for stopping you; I heard the girl call you Mister Shaver. Are you the Mister Shaver who is the famous philosopher?"

Jimmy had given up fighting it. Only the Dutch can stop the tide. "That's me." Jimmy waited. Next would come a joke or an insult or—rarely—a compliment. Jimmy had learned that to wait, laugh and leave was the best way of taking the steam out of the sails of whoever was trying to be funny at his expense.

"I would be honored if you would let me buy you a beer and ask you a question," the stranger said.

Club 250, Jimmy's usual watering hole, would not admit a Kraut. The Gardens, though, were just across the street and they would let anyone in. Jimmy was well known for buying beer for anyone who would listen to him. He was also known to never turn down a free beer. "Throw in a ham sandwich and you're on."

The stranger looked puzzled. "That was a yes?"

"Hell, yes, that was a yes," Jimmy said.

The stranger beamed.

❋ ❋ ❋

It was a quiet walk to the Gardens. They ordered the potables and, oddly enough, ate in silence. When the sandwiches and beer were done, the down-timer ordered two more beers.

"Herr Shaver, I have a question of practical philosophy," the Kraut said.

Jimmy grunted over the rim of his beer.

"My daughter . . ." The man paused to swallow a lump in his throat. "She wishes to marry. We, her mother and I, have said no. We feel that the boy is beneath her. We think she should wait until she is older and that she should wait for someone better. We would prefer to arrange for her to marry a man from back home. We have forbidden her to see this boy. But she comes home from school with that gleam in her eye. We have spoken to her about it. She smiles now and says nothing. Once she told us that when they have graduated and he will find a job and they will marry and that there is nothing we can do about it.

"We threatened to return home. She knows it is only a threat. We want only the best for her. We don't understand a culture that encourages the children to disobey the parents. It is not ri . . . it does not seem right. What are we to do?"

"You want your daughter to wait for someone better?" Jimmy set down his empty beer.

The odd man nodded.

Jimmy waited. The Kraut waved for another round.

"When I was a kid growing up in the hills," Jimmy began, "there was a family in the neighborhood by the name of Jones. They owned half a mountain with a good farm on it that the old man bought with the money he brought back from being in the army in World War One, along with an uppity French bride.

"He was in the quartermaster's outfit and made the money by selling things off before they could get to the front, then marking them down as being destroyed in route.

"Anyway, the Joneses had themselves a daughter. She was a looker like her Ma. As she grew up, her Ma filled her head with the idea that none of the local boys were good enough for her. Most folks thought that Mrs. Jones wasn't quite right in the head. They seemed to think she was living in a dream world. She thought that the family ought to go to France and let their daughter find someone suitable. But the old man hadn't managed to steal that much money, or he hadn't managed to hang onto enough for that, so it just wasn't going to happen.

"Well now, the odd part of the story was that most of the women in town seemed to agree that she shouldn't settle for a local boy. My Pa told me once he thought it was because they didn't want their daughters to have to compete with her.

"At any rate, a fellow by the name of Dupont showed up in town along with a Frenchman who couldn't speak a word of English. Now, I don't know whether this Dupont was related to the Duponts that had all the money or not, but folks assumed that he was. They had come to go bear hunting. Most of the bears were shot out by that time. But, there was a she-bear with cubs in a cave down in a holler on the Jones place. The only reason they were still around was because old man Jones was a really bad shot, and he sure wouldn't let anyone else go hunting on his place.

"Well, they went up to Jones' place to see if they could get permission to bag that bear. Mrs. Jones had heard all about them, of course. A rich industrialist and a world-touring French noble showing up at the same time was just too much. She suddenly had to decide which man they were going to let marry their daughter.

"Of course, the two of them had heard all about the beautiful daughter of the Joneses, and when they arrived, they were met in the front yard by Papa Jones, Mama Jones, and Pretty Little Miss Jones. Mama Jones was a bit put out when all they wanted to know was about the bear. But then she got a gleam in her eyes and insisted that her husband take them all up there right that instant.

"Well, when they got to the top of the bluff looking down into the rift where the cave was, Mrs. Jones took her daughter's hat and sailed it off over the edge into the mouth of the cave. Then she announced that whichever one of them brought her daughter's hat back to her would have her hand in marriage. The Dupont fellow looked at the daughter, looked at the hat in the cave, looked at the climb in between and the noises coming out of the cave, and shook his head no. The Frenchman, without a word, climbed down, retrieved the hat, climbed back up, used the hat to dust himself off and then sailed it off back into the gulch. "It's your hat," he said, "if you want it, get it yourself.

"Thanks for the beer." Jimmy Dick rose to leave.

"But Herr Shaver, what does it mean? Are you saying I should let my daughter marry this no-account that she is taken with?"

"I ain't got no idea. But let me tell you something about American kids, which includes your daughter if she's been in the public school for more than a year. You tell them they can't have something and you make them want it all the more. Shoot, we took over an entire continent just because one party or another kept telling us we couldn't have it. If you're convinced that this kid she wants to take up with is no good, then why don't you help her to see it?"

"We have told her. She will not listen."

Jimmy Dick shook his head. "I can see why. She came by it honest like. You don't listen either. I didn't say tell her. I said help her see it."

"How do we do that?" the Kraut asked.

Jimmy sighed and sat back down. Then he waved for a round of beers that he paid for. "Okay, if this kid is beneath you, then his table manners ain't up to your standards. Have him over to dinner with the family. Pull out the stops. Put out the best china, the real silver, have soup and salad, lay out three or four forks, and let her see what an embarrassment he is. Does she really want to set across the table and watch him slurp his soup for the rest her life?

"If you ain't got the wherewithal to spread the table, take the kids out to Grantville's Fine Dining and tell the fancy pants with the menus that you want a cloth napkins table, not paper.

"Put them together often." Jimmy held up a hand to forestall an objection. "Have him over to your house or let them go where you or someone can keep an eye on things. If he ain't no good, give her plenty of time up close and personal to figure it out. I guarantee he'll look different up close."

Having said that he tipped his beer and walked out.

It was a month or more later that Jimmy saw the troubled father in the store.

"Hey there, guy. How did you come out on that trouble with your daughter?" Jimmy asked.

The man looked sad. "What you said, about things looking different up close and personal? You were right. He is a nice boy, a good boy; he is working hard and doing well in school. He has a promising future. I would be proud to have my daughter marry him. But, it is so sad! She will not, how was it said? She will not give him the time of day."

By Terry Howard

ANNA THE BAPTIST

December 1634

Julio stacked clean glasses under the bar. "Damn it, Ken! I don't know what's got you riled, but I'm sick of it! Back off or I'm goin' home. I don't have t' have this job. I only took it to help you out."

Julio didn't mention his fear of losing his regular job to what he thought of as cheap foreign labor. The fear drove him to drink, something he'd done little of before the Ring of Fire. He did his drinking in the one place a man didn't have to put up with "krauts." This led to a part-time job.

✳ ✳ ✳

Julio had been sitting at the bar, contemplating the world at the bottom of his beer, when Ken yelled, "Julio!"

He looked up and said, "Yes?"

Ken Beasley calmed down immediately. "I'm sorry, Mister Mora. I'm almost out of glasses, and I was yelling at my dish washer. I forgot he quit."

"You need a dish washer?" Julio tipped his beer, set the empty down on the bar and headed for the swinging door to the kitchen.

"Hey, the bathroom's that way." Ken pointed.

"I know," Julio answered.

"Where're you goin'?"

"To wash dishes."

Someone called out, "Hey, Ken, where's my beer?" First things first, Ken took care of the customer, then another one, then he cleaned up a spill. By this time there was a tray of glasses under the bar. Glasses and customers kept coming. The stack stayed topped off, and all the glasses were clean. Ken quit checking.

At closing, Ken remembered someone was working for him that he hadn't hired. He found Julio mopping the kitchen floor. To Ken's disappointment, Julio would only take the job part-time. Short of hiring a kraut, what was he going to do?

❋ ❋ ❋

"Sorry, Julio," Ken said. "It's the damned krauts."

Julio relaxed. Ken had his full sympathy. The Ring of Fire changed everything, mostly. He still spent third shift mopping, vacuuming, cleaning bathrooms, and washing windows at the bank and elsewhere. Food had changed. Bread didn't come pre-sliced in plastic bags. Canning jars came up out of the basement. Pepper had to be ground. Salt didn't come in round boxes anymore. Ken had him take an ice pick and make the holes in all of the salt shakers bigger, but getting it out was still a problem. The big difference, though, was "the krauts."

"I'm sorry," Ken continued. "I'd hardly gotten to sleep last night when, at the crack of dawn, a bunch of damned krauts woke me up singing hymns off key, right outside my window!"

"What're you talkin' about?"

"My neighbor, damned hypocrite, is letting a bunch of damn Bible-thumping krauts use his storage shed for a church," Ken said.

"They can't do that! It's not been consecrated. You can't have a church without an altar, or an altar without a relic. The saint has to be installed by a bishop. They sure wouldn't put one in a garage." Julio didn't get to Mass as often as he should but knew his catechism from when he was an altar boy. "When the cops stop in, you tell 'em about it. If people can complain about us making noise late at night, then they ought'a do something about the krauts waking you up."

"The cops?" Ken growled. "Just great! What in hell are they doin' here?"

THE LEGEND OF JIMMY DICK

"They're here every Sunday," Julio said. The police investigated every complaint. As sure as God made little green hypocrites, one of the old ladies in town called the station after Sunday dinner and complained.

* * *

As Julio predicted the cops showed up on a noise complaint.

The cops were Hans and Hans. One was Hans Shruer; the other was Hans Shultz. Ken Beasley couldn't remember which was which. It didn't matter. They came in a matched set, Catholic, and Lutheran. It was too bad the sign on the door, "No Dogs And No germans Allowed," didn't apply to cops.

As cops went, Hans and Hans were all business. If they talked to each other about anything else, it ended in an argument about religion. They sure couldn't talk of families. Hans Shruer had watched from the hill while a Catholic troop burned his home, raped his mother and sister and tortured his father. Hans hated Catholics, collectively and individually. The only redeeming fact in a Catholic's favor was he would be spending eternity in Hell. The sooner he got there, the better.

Hans Shultz's family had been well off before the Lutherans came. They lost over half of the family and everything but the clothes on their backs. Compared to Hans Shultz's attitude towards Lutherans, Hans Shruer was a soft-spoken, forgiving moderate.

"You want to talk about noise?" Ken blew up. "What are you going to do about those damned Baptists waking me up at the crack of dawn with their singing?"

"Mister Beasley, you live over a mile from the Baptist church, and they start at ten," Hans Shultz said.

"Well, maybe it wasn't dawn but I'd just gotten to sleep. And I'm talkin' about the ones who've moved into the garage behind my house!"

A blond haired, heavy set man in a plaid shirt sitting at the bar spoke up. "They ain't Baptist. That's why they got thrown out of the church. They're Anna Baptist. But I got no idea who Anna is."

Jimmy Dick called out, "Read your Bible, Bubba. Anna Baptist is John Baptist's sister."

Julio spoke up to straighten Dick out. "Anna is the mother of the Blessed Virgin Mary, the mother of God." He had stacked a half full tray of glasses on the pile under the bar as an excuse to leave the sink when the cops showed up.

"Well, if that don't beat all," Bubba said. "No wonder they got tossed. It's bad enough, the Catholics worshipin' Mary. Now you got people worshipin' her mother! Humf." He snorted. "Sssshit! Does that make her the grandmother of God?"

* * *

At the accusation that Catholics worshiped Mary, Hans Shultz started to object. Veneration is not worship. It might be a small hair to split, but the difference is very important to knowledgeable Catholics. At the words "Anna Baptist" Hans lost all interest in straightening out one ignorant, obnoxious up-timer.

"Anabaptist?" Hans Shruer asked in a shocked voice.

"Yeah." Bubba agreed. "That's what I said. Anna Baptist."

Hans and Hans looked at each other in apprehension bordering on fear.

Hans Shultz spoke slowly in a soft voice as if it were bad luck to speak the name aloud. "Anabaptist."

* * *

Ken was very good at reading people, especially people who were scared or angry or just plain crazy enough to start a fight. Fights were bad for business. Hans and Hans suddenly needed watching. "What's wrong with Anna Baptist?"

"Mister Beasley, they're trouble! Everyone knows that! Even the English heretics have outlawed them! They are . . . what is the word . . . people without respect for authority, who do whatever they please, without concern for decency or order."

"Rednecks?" Bubba volunteered.

Hans ignored him.

"Antichrist?" Hans Shruer supplied cautiously.

"That will do. I was looking for anarchist. Anabaptists are anarchist, rebels, nihilists, fanatics, troublemakers! Luther, Calvin, the king of England and the pope all outlawed them!"

"Sounds like rednecks to me," Bubba said.

"Shut up, Bubba," Ken said. "So what's so wrong with Anna Baptist?"

"They do not give proper respect to the civil authorities. Their practice of re-baptizing strikes at the very root of Christianity. They want to tear the church down and start over, their way. Have you heard of Munster?" Hans Shruer asked.

Ken shook his head.

"A thousand Anabaptists took six wives each, declared the city of Munster an independent republic. It took a war to stop them!" You don't need all the facts completely right when you are spreading slander.

Bubba was on a roll. "Sounds like my kind of rednecks. Six wives? Where do I join up?"

Ken tried to shut him down. "Shush up! You can't handle the wife you've got, or you wouldn't be in here every other night, drinking."

"Do you know of the peasant's revolt?" Hans Shultz asked.

Ken shook his head.

"They nailed priests to the doors and burned the churches. They raped the nuns. They burned manor houses, convents, castles, entire villages. They drank the cellars dry, looted. . ."

"Sounds like rednecks to me," Bubba said.

"I said shut up, Bubba!"

Hans ignored the interruption. ". . . everything they could carry and burned everything they couldn't. Even Luther condemned them.

"It took the armies from four countries to put the revolt down and the nobles back in charge. Anabaptists are evil incarnate." The last four words were rote dogma.

"We need to tell the chief! He needs to do something before it gets bad."

"Like what?" Ken asked. "Run them out of town?" Hans and Hans didn't catch the note of sarcasm.

"That would work," Hans Shultz said.

"Like hell, it will!" Bubba didn't catch the note of sarcasm either.

"Shut up, Bubba," Ken said.

"Hey, Ken. What cha' got against religious freedom?" Bubba asked.

"I ain't got nothin' against it, Bubba. I just don't want it in my backyard."

* * *

Later in the night, Lyndon Johnson stopped in. Departmental policy required a follow-up call to anyone making a complaint after an investigation.

"Mister Beasley," Lyndon said with the serious demeanor he used for official police business, "Hans and Hans said you want some people run out of town and they agree with you.

"The two of them were adamant. Hans said 'the disease-carrying vermin should be exterminated for the good health of the community and the general improvement of mankind.' They were distraught and sure there would be trouble. Chief Richards told me to check it out and file a report."

Ken shook his head. "Officer, they said something had to be done, not me. Usually, when I hear talk like that, it's from some old lady talking about the bar. The next words would be 'run it out of town.'

"So I asked, 'You mean something like, run out of town' and they agreed. I don't want them run out of town. I just don't want them over my back fence." Ken glanced both ways and leaned forward before asking, in a voice too soft to carry, "Lyndon, what's goin' on? Who are these people?"

Officer Johnson leaned forward over the bar. "Ken, that's what is really strange about this whole thing!

"Hans and Hans came into the station all hot and bothered. I mean to tell you they were really wound tight. They're pretty good cops for a couple of krauts. So Chief Richards told me to look into it, quick! I went over and had a chat with Shultz's pastor, then with Shruer's pastor, then with Reverend Green down at the Southern Baptist church. Green said Joe Jenkins was the pastor of the Anabaptist church and I should go talk to him if there was a problem."

"Old Joe?" Ken asked. "A pastor? Can he do that?"

THE LEGEND OF JIMMY DICK

"I asked Green about it," Lyndon answered. "Green said he could. Seems he was ordained in some off-brand Baptist denomination years ago. Green says it's still valid.

"As I was saying, Hans and Hans were making some mighty wild claims! Shultz's pastor said they were true. Shruer's pastor agreed."

* * *

The down-timer Shultz called Father, and Lyndon addressed as Reverend, assured Lyndon the Anabaptists were trouble just waiting to happen.

The Lutheran pastor's first words were "Spawn of Satan! The Augsburg confession clearly condemned them." He was sure they were Arminians. It was the only one of Pastor Holt's six syllable words Lyndon remembered, only because he knew where Armenia was. Holt made it sound contagious, vile, and shameful. Any Anabaptists discovered in a Lutheran country would be lucky to escape with their lives. He was sure they were nothing but lawless, reckless, rioters without morals, decency or self-control.

By the end of the second conversation, Officer Johnson was convinced Grantville had a real problem on its hands. He was wondering how they had managed to miss it so far.

* * *

"I caught Reverend Green right before his evening service," Lyn told Ken. "He didn't have time to talk right then, but he had someone go to the office and get me a list of the Anabaptists who'd left and those who agreed with Southern Baptist doctrine and stayed, which was over half of them.

"I asked about them being thrown out. He said they left by mutual agreement, which means 'left quietly.' I took the lists down to the office to have names cross-referenced to complaints for the report.

"Then I drove out to the Jenkin's place to let Joe know what he'd gotten into so he could get out before he got hurt. And let me tell you did I get an ear full!"

* * *

"Joe, what's this I hear about you starting a church for a mess of bad news Germans the Baptists threw out because they're Armenian Anabaptist?"

"Lyndon, first off, *all* Baptists are Anabaptist. They only baptize adults. It is true most Baptists are Calvinist, but a few of us are Arminians."

Lyndon was shocked and puzzled. Joe sounded proud of it. So he asked, "What is an Armenian?"

"An Armenian is someone from Armenia. An Arminian holds a doctrine the Calvinists dislike."

* * *

Lyndon leaned a bit farther over the bar. "You know what 'once saved, always saved' means?"

"I think it means if you're born Baptist you can do whatever you want and still think you're not goin' to hell," Ken answered. It was an impression he got from listening to drunks.

"Well," Lyndon said, "according to Old Joe, an Arminian is the other side of it."

* * *

Officer Johnson looked at Old Joe Jenkins, who was on his back porch in an old rocking chair. The last light faded from the sky along the ridgeline. Joe nursed a shot of corn squeezin's his father had put in the cellar. He smoked a hand-rolled cigarette made from tobacco raised in a cobbled-up greenhouse behind the barn. There was a crate of papers, bought wholesale, in the house. He had offered Lyndon some of each, but Lyndon didn't drink or smoke.

"That's it?" Lyndon asked. "That is what all the fuss is about?"

Joe looked at Lyndon and smiled. "If it's already decided, why bother tryin' to change things? If it's a matter of choice, then if things are bad you're obliged to try an' change 'em."

Lyndon didn't think through the implications of Joe's statement. "You know there are a lot of people mighty riled up over this. They're sayin' these people are trouble."

Joe smiled again. "Check the records."

"They're being checked now," Lyndon replied.

"You won't find nothin'."

"If that's the case, why is everybody so upset with them?"

"It's not their theology," Joe replied. "It's their politics."

Lyndon thought *what does theology have to do with politics?* Then in short order, his mind clicked through the Moral Majority, the Christian Coalition, and Right to Life. *Maybe theology does affect politics.*

Joe explained. "They want the government to stay out of religion and religion to stay out of government."

"Separation of church and state?"

Joe snorted. "Where did you think the idea came from?"

"The Constitution," Lyndon said. "People went to America for religious freedom."

"Yeah," Joe said. "Freedom to have their own church. But when Roger Williams started preaching free will, he got chased out of Massachusetts for heresy and went down to nowhere and started the Rhode Island colony where you could believe anything you wanted and worship God any way you pleased. And from there it got into the Constitution."

"You mean we got these Arminians to thank for freedom of religion?"

"Pretty much," Joe said.

Lyndon didn't know whether to believe him or not but decided he'd ask a history teacher first chance he got.

❈ ❈ ❈

Ken Beasley looked at the young, clean-cut police officer in puzzlement for a few seconds. Ken knew the kid and liked him. Lyndon had briefly dated his stepdaughter, Morgan. The boy had been polite. He got her home before the deadline with time to spare. He had treated Morgan well and her mother with respect. Ken and Lyndon had formed an odd friendship in spite of the difference in age and attitude. Morgan broke the relationship off when Lyndon wanted her to start going to church with him. Finally, Ken asked, "That's all this is about?"

"Looks like it, Ken." Lyndon stepped back from the bar and back into the voice and demeanor he used when he first entered. "Mister Beasley, they ain't doin' nothin' I can do anything about. Shoot, if everybody was as good at staying out of trouble as these folks, I'd be out of a job.

"I mentioned the noise to Joe. He said he was sorry but didn't think it was overly loud. I'll stop by Sunday and see for myself, but I'm afraid I won't be able to do much about it."

"Why am I not surprised?" Ken let sarcasm drip off the end of every word.

* * *

Lyndon started his written report with a one-paragraph summation concluding with his recommendation.

"This alleged noise violation is nearly the only complaint to be lodged against anyone on either list of Anabaptists Rev. Green gave me. All other accusations are lodged against the group in general and arise from blatant prejudice. I recommend no action be taken at this time."

February 1635

"Hey, Tom. Let me buy ya' a beer," Dick said when Tom stepped up to the bar.

Tom was chronically short on money. His wife counted his pocket change to keep track of how much he was spending on beer and bad company. Dick was chronically short on someone to drink with. He rubbed everybody the wrong way.

"Ain't seen much of ya' lately. What's the matter? Won't the little lady let ya' stop for a drink on your way home from work?"

Tom didn't say anything.

Dick saw a sore spot and pushed. "Hey, buddy! What's the matter? Cat got your tongue?" The attitude, a malicious condescension, was raw. "The old henpecked problem, huh?" Dick was not going to drop it.

Tom needed a reason why he hadn't been in lately. "I don't like drinkin' in a place that lets in krauts."

Dick smirked and looked around. "No krauts here."

"Yeah? What about Sunday morning?"

"Shoot, they don't count. They're gone before the bar opens," Dick said. "Besides, there's krauts and there's krauts. These are our kind of krauts."

* * *

Ken heard it and shook his head. Just yesterday, Dick was complaining about the krauts using the place to hold church on Sunday morning. Jimmy Dick would argue either side of anything.

* * *

"Don't see it," Tom said.

"Then ya' haven't looked. Open your eyes man! These krauts are rednecks."

"How do ya' figure?"

"Well first, how many churches ya' know who'd ever hold services in a bar?" Dick asked.

"None," Tom said.

"Wrong! Wrong! Wrong! Ya' know one. This one, so they ain't your average, run of the mill, goody two-shoes. Second, Zane was a good old boy, right?" Dick asked. Zane was a drunken reprobate who wasn't home for the Ring of Fire.

"What's your point?" Tom answered.

"Well, the Baptist church threw him out. They threw these krauts out too. Makes 'em our kind of people."

Tom shook his head. "Don't see it."

"Three," Dick said. "Half the people in here can't stand somebody else in here. Right?"

"So?"

"So these here krauts can't get along with each other either. Ken didn't offer to let them use the place until they started havin' two services back to back 'cause they couldn't get along. So ya' see, they're our kind of people."

※ ※ ※

This time Jimmy was half right. Some of the Anabaptists were non-violent, amongst other things. They wanted to hear their own speaker. The other group liked Brother Fiedler's preaching. The building was getting too small for all of them at once, so they went to two services. If Ken had known they'd take him up on the offer, he wouldn't have made it. Still, the rent helped.

※ ※ ※

"Don't see it," Tom said.

"Well, we don't like krauts, and the krauts don't like us. Right?"

"And?" Tom asked.

"So the other krauts can't stand these people. I mean Catholics pick on Lutherans and Lutherans don't like Calvinists. But all three of them got it in for Anna Baptists."

Tom became half interested in spite of himself. "Yeah? Why's that?"

"'Cause they won't buckle down and go along. They insist on doin' things their own way. Like only baptizin' adults and to hell with the consequences. Sounds like rednecks to me." Dick grinned.

"Don't see it." Tom shook his head.

"And I hear tell, back in the world, it was these people who got freedom of religion put in the constitution."

THE LEGEND OF JIMMY DICK

"They didn't do it from Germany," Tom answered.
"Well, how about the place bein' cleaner since they started usin' it?" Dick asked.

* * *

They came in the first Sunday and moved the tables and set up the chairs. Before they put the place back together, they mopped the floors and wiped down the chairs and the tables.

* * *

"So? Ken could hire an American to do it," Tom said.
"Yeah? With what? So many of us are in the army or off somewhere else; business is way off. Shoot, with the rate we're droppin', all of his regulars will be dead shortly anyway. He can't afford to hire more help. Besides they were keeping Ken awake, singing and preaching just over his back fence."
"He could sleep here Sunday nights," Tom suggested.
Dick grunted. "And not go home to the missus? Not Ken. But then he's not henpecked."
"I ain't henpecked," Tom muttered.
Dick took out his wallet and put five twenty dollar bills on the bar. "Hundred dollars right here says ya' are."
"Well, I ain't. Who we goin' get to settle it?" Tom asked.
"Uh uh. If you ain't henpecked, then she'll do what you tell her." Jimmy Dick pointed at the door. "The day she walks through that door and stays for one hour you win the bet."
"I ain't got a hundred dollars on me."
Dick sneered. "And you won't have it come payday. Shoot, you won't have it at twenty a week. Hell, you won't have it at five a week, 'cause you're a loser. I tell ya' what, I'll put up the hundred against you admitting you're henpecked. Hey, Ken."

"Just a minute, Jimmy Dick," Ken called back. Ken finished the order he was working on. Since the bartender quit, he'd gone back to doing it all himself. "What do ya' need?"

"Tommy and me got a bet goin'. Can you put this in the box until we settle it?"

Ken went down to the cash register and grabbed a lockbox out of the cabinet. When he got back, he opened it and took out a pad of paper. "Okay, what's the bet?"

"I bet Tommy one hundred dollars he's henpecked."

"How ya' gonna settle it?"

"If his wife comes in and stays for an hour any time in the next month, the hundred is his. If she don't, then he answers to henpecked."

"You agree, Tom?" Ken asked.

* * *

Tom was caught in a web. "Sure. Why not?" What in hell did I just get myself into, he thought. Maybe if I agree to go to church with her? Naw, won't work she won't agree to come in here anyway. Then it clicked.

Tom smiled. "Sure! If she comes through that door and stays for an hour anytime in the next month the money is mine. Give me the pen."

Tom snickered as he signed his initials to the bet slip. "You just lost your hundred dollars, Dickhead." Then he tipped back his beer and drained it.

All the way home he tried to figure out the best way to get his wife to agree to the plan. He settled on goading her into bugging him to go to church. She did it often enough without his trying. Then he would agree to go if he got to pick the church. When she balked, he'd offer to go with her to her church after she went with him to the church of his choice.

The bet was any time in the next month. Sunday morning would do just fine.

April 1635

"What can I do for you fellows?" Ken asked as Hans and Hans approached the bar. He had talked to them on Sunday when they routinely "investigated" the noise complaints called in on Sunday afternoon. Now it was Monday, and the cops were back.

"Mister Beasley, do you know where your congregation was on Sunday?" Hans Shruer asked.

Ken Beasley broke into a deep belly laugh. Somehow, they were his congregation and he was supposed to know what they were up to. The cops seemed to think he knew what his regular patrons were doing twenty-four seven. Now he was supposed to keep track of the Anabaptists, too.

The fact was he knew exactly where they were on Sunday morning. Tom Ruffner and his wife Jenny were part of the congregation now. Tom had stopped in for a beer last night. Oddly, his wife didn't mind his having a beer now and again anymore. She even came with him for an hour one evening. She found out about the bet with Jimmy Dick and said it wasn't right. He said he wasn't giving it back. So she traipsed in one evening, hopped up on a bar stool and ordered a cup of coffee. Then she announced it was six minutes after six. At seven minutes after seven, she walked out the door.

When Tom stopped in for a beer, Ken complained about the mess.

"Ain't our fault," Tom said. "Weren't none of us here. We all went over to Rudoltstadt for the first service of a church Joe is starting over there. They're gonna have some trouble on account of Rudolstadt being nothin' but Lutheran. We went over to show support. If there was a mess, it was your mess."

Ken had to concede the point. Still, just because he knew where they were didn't mean he was going to tell the cops anything, especially not in front of Jimmy Dick. James Richard Schaver was the only patron in the place at the moment. The lunch drinkers were gone, the "beer or two on the way home" crowd wouldn't trickle in for a while, and it was way too early for the every-night late-night regulars. If he told the cops anything, sure as Saint Patrick wasn't Jewish, Jimmy Dick would see to it everybody knew it. His patrons expected privacy with their beer.

When his laughter ran down, Ken responded to the question without answering it. "Joe Jenkins hasn't been in yet to pay this week's rent. When he does, I'm going to complain about the mess they left me. It almost looked as if there hadn't been anyone here at all."

Hans and Hans exchanged knowing glances.

"What's up?" Ken asked.

"We got a query from over in Rudoltstadt. It seems someone with a truck was at an unauthorized church service," Hans said.

The description of the truck matched Joe's ancient (early fifties vintage) coal hauler to a "T." Joe ended up with the old thing when the company he was working for went bankrupt. It was so old the army didn't want it. Even the tires weren't worth taking. Now, it had a propane tank for natural gas over the cab. The bed was boxed in against the weather with benches down each side, with a door and steps to the rear for people. Joe was using it for a church bus.

"Unauthorized?" Jimmy Dick piped in. "It was Sunday. How much more authorized do you need to be?"

"Mister Schaver," Hans said. "The ruler in Rudoltstadt is Lutheran. So the church in Rudoltstadt is Lutheran."

"And if you ain't Lutheran?"

"Then you convert, or you move," Hans said.

"That ain't right! Whatever happened to freedom of religion?!"

"Rudoltstadt is not America. Not being Lutheran in Rudoltstadt is a punishable offense!"

The law in the USE called for religious tolerance, but the gap between custom and law is often quite large.

"That just ain't right," Jimmy said.

"Punishable, how?" Ken asked.

"Fines, confiscation, exile, imprisonment, beheading." Hans knew full well capital punishment was rare even before the USE. Still, getting sick or starving to death in prison or on the road was not in the least uncommon.

Jimmy practically squealed. "That's medieval!"

"And just when do you think you are, Mister Schaver? This is the year of our Lord sixteen hundred and thirty-five. You are in Germany, and this is the way things are done," Hans said.

THE LEGEND OF JIMMY DICK

"Mister Beasley, when . . ." It was clearly when, not if. ". . . you see Joe Jenkins, please let him know we would like him to stop in at the station. We need to assure the people over in Rudoltstadt that it won't happen again."

Having made that pronouncement Hans and Hans stalked out. Ken watched them leave with a feeling of anxiety.

"That's bull shit!" Jimmy Dick said. "They can't tell our krauts what to do."

Ken's head snapped around. "Our krauts? Since when did any of those shit-heads become our krauts?"

"Ken, there ain't a conversation in this bar you don't know about." It was a slight exaggeration, but only a slight one. "You know we've been sayin' the krauts holdin' church here are rednecks and our kind of krauts."

When Jimmy said "we" he was talking about himself. But no one was shutting him down, which he took as agreement. "We ain't gonna let them push our krauts around. Not when it comes to religious freedom."

"Jimmy Dick, you're full of shit!"

"Well, sell me another beer."

* * *

Later, Jimmy Dick was riding a high horse hell bent for leather. What surprised Ken was that people were listening. Normally, Jimmy had to buy to get anyone to drink with him and listen to his ranting insults. But he started talking about religious freedom.

"We shouldn't let them outside krauts over the border push our good old boy, red neck krauts around. Our krauts ain't too stuck up to hold church in a bar. Are we goin'a let some asshole over the border tell them what they can and can't do? We ought to take our shotguns and go over there to church next Sunday and however many Sundays it takes until they figure it out and leave our krauts alone." Jimmy actually had people buying him drinks.

Ken heard it, and the sinking feeling in his stomach started turning into a large knot.

By Terry Howard

* * *

Joe Jenkins turned up the next day after the lunch crowd was gone. Ken let him know right away the cops had been in looking for him.

"I've already talked to them."

"Then you're shutting down the church over there?" Jimmy Dick asked. He was there for lunch, as usual, and would likely stay to closing. Between his disability from the army and family money, he hadn't held a job since coming back from Nam.

"No," Joe answered.

"Good. Me and a few of the boys are talkin' about comin'."

"Be glad to have you."

"You got this week's rent?" Ken planned to tell Joe it would be going up.

"We didn't use the place this week."

"Why, you cheap S.O.B. Get your worthless, sorry ass out of my place and don't let me ever catch you in here again." In truth, Ken was relieved. He knew in his bones something bad was going to happen and he didn't need to be part of it.

"Sorry ya' feel that way about it." Joe sighed.

* * *

Hans Shruer requested permission to handle the follow up on the complaint that Grantville was exporting heresy. Hans wanted it handled by someone sympathetic. He was not sure an up-timer would show proper respect for a pastor.

Despite everything he loved in Grantville, there were things which troubled him. Their willingness to treat all men as equals was refreshing. It was amusing when the emperor became Captain-General Gars upon entering Grantville. It would not be amusing if someone were less than deferential to a pastor.

Hans rose early, mounted a borrowed horse, and made his way across the border. Pastor Holt received him in the study. The room's fireplace was welcome on a chilly April day. A writing desk, a magnificent library of seven books and two comfortable chairs in front of the fire furnished the room.

"Pastor, I am here in response to the complaint you lodged with the Grantville Police."

"Good." Pastor Holt said. "We need this nipped in the bud with as little fuss as possible."

"I couldn't agree with you more, Pastor. But I am afraid I must inform you the chief of police feels there is nothing he can do."

"What?"

"He says it is outside his jurisdiction."

"He intends to let these, these blasphemers, carry on their criminal activities because they cross the border to do it?"

"Pastor, first, he does not see it as criminal."

"Nonsense! It is against the laws of God and man!"

"Pastor, the laws of God are not the laws of the USE. Or of Grantville."

"They should be!"

"I agree. But unfortunately, they are not. The different churches cannot agree as to what those laws are and . . ."

"On this point, we are in agreement! The re-baptizers strike at the very root of Christianity. How can anyone have confidence in their salvation when someone claims baptism does not save?" Pastor Holt shuddered. "Where does this leave those children who die an early death?"

"I understand completely. You are absolutely right. Except all of the churches do not agree on . . ."

"Nonsense. It was settled at the second Diet of Speier. The Catholics, the Lutherans, and now the Calvinists, all agreed the Anabaptists are not to be tolerated."

"Pastor, there are three established churches in Grantville who practice only adult baptism. They have, or will have, existed for hundreds of years in America. Their existence is not a threat to the Lutheran church or Christianity. The chief feels you will just have to make an accommodation in your thinking. You know they have a radical concept of religious freedom."

"I can do nothing about what 'they' do in Grantville." It is amazing how much can be said with how a word is pronounced. "But, I will not allow this travesty to be inflicted on the people of my parish."

"Pastor, Joseph Jenkins claims to have the count's permission."

"Nonsense! The count is a loyal member of the Lutheran faith. He would never condone this."

"The chief has known Mr. Jenkins for years. He accepted his statement without bothering to verify it. I overheard the conversation. Mr. Jenkins claimed to have talked with the count. He claimed the count does not want to lose a large party of gunsmiths who were about to move so they could attend church without walking miles and miles. The count, according to Jenkins, feels this acceptance of any faith as long as it does not create social disorder is one of the secrets of Grantville's prosperity."

"Social disorder? What does he think rebaptism is? Doesn't he know about Munster?"

"Pastor, you will have to ask the count. I fully sympathize with your problem. Believe me; I will do anything I can to help. But the response I was sent to deliver is: the officials in Grantville are not prepared to do anything."

"Surely you jest?"

"I wish I did."

* * *

The count did not relieve Pastor Holt's frustration. "Pastor Holt, I know you are aware the Emperor has declared religious freedom."

"Religious freedom? Yes. But surely it does not include these people."

"Yes. It does."

Next Sunday's sermon was a railing accusation against Godless polygamists and anarchists. On Monday, word came from the count to drop it. Pastor Holt had no choice but to obey. After all, the count was the one who appointed him to the pulpit and paid his salary.

* * *

THE LEGEND OF JIMMY DICK

About three months later, the English version of the Magdeburg Freedom Arches propaganda broadside started turning up in Grantville. When Jimmy Dick saw the lead article, he wondered just how long he would have to do his drinking at home.

Rednecks to the Rescue by Leo Nidus

If you have not been to Grantville, then you may not know of a private drinking establishment called "Club 250." There is a sign on the door "No Dogs and No Germans Allowed."

The people who drink there are referred to by the general population of Grantville as "rednecks." This is a derogatory term designating a lower class of people. They are presumed to be louts, willfully ignorant, belligerently pugnacious, and ethnocentric in the extreme, as noted by the sign on the door. They are not well considered and clearly stand in opposition to the general policy of acceptance which is a hallmark of Grantville. But since tolerance is so highly esteemed by Grantville's ethos, even rednecks are secure by law from any disapproval beyond verbal condemnation.

Why should I write of these dregs of their culture, the lowest order of society? That is simple. I write of them because of the nobility of their actions and the generosity of their spirit.

When no place to worship could be found amongst the established churches—yes, churches: Grantville's tolerance fosters over half a dozen different faiths existing side by side without even covert violence—for a small Anabaptist sect, the rednecks of Club 250 opened the doors of the club to them in off hours, asking only that they be gone well before the club opened for business. When the sect opened a church across the border and encountered active opposition, including the threat and actualization of violence, these same "degenerate louts" undertook to guarantee the safety of the congregation by standing armed vigil over the services until the violence subsided.

Why would the dregs of society, the despised lowest order, the willfully ignorant do such a thing? Because they know in their hearts, they hold the conviction deep in their souls, that freedom is not free. They understand that when one man is not free, then none are truly free.

If today we allow the Anabaptists to be denied the right to freely assemble, then tomorrow that freedom could be denied to others and then to us.

By Terry Howard

The price of freedom is the defense of the rights of others, even if it is the right to be wrong. As one red neck put it, "The price of freedom is the defense of idiots."

INFLATION IS A PAIN IN THE –

November of 1634

Adam looked at the price list painted in tempera on the mirrors behind the bar. "Shit, Ken. You want me to do my drinking elsewhere?"

"Go check, Adam." Ken's voice was resigned, and he looked tired. "They just raised their prices too."

"Yeah, but other places have a full menu and live entertainment."

"And Krauts. Don't forget the Krauts. This is the only Kraut free zone in town." Ken answered tartly.

"Ken, that beer price is over twice what it was last year."

"And my percentage is down by half." Ken was clearly defensive and perhaps a touch angry. "I am making the same profit per bottle, not the same percentage, mind you, the same profit per bottle as I was last year. My take home is the same, but my buying power is half of what it was. And my property taxes went up the same as yours did. If the wife's hair salon wasn't hoppin', I'd have to shut done and go get a job. That's the best I can do for you. Shit, I can't even afford to hire a full-time bartender anymore, I have to cover it myself from open to close. Do you want a cold one or not?"

Adam nodded; everything was more expensive these days. There was no reason why beer and pretzels shouldn't be also. But if you can't gripe in a bar why bother going? Adam took the first sip of his beer and turned to his good buddy Harlan. "Shit. It ain't right, Big Dog!"

There was a reason why Harlan was known as a big dog. He had Abbot's height and Costello's girth. His partner, Adam, was thin and short. Neither one of them had Costello's magic or Abbot's intelligence. No one ever called the duo funny. "My wages sure haven't doubled in the last year. If I wasn't workin' a lot of overtime, I don't know how we'd get by. I'd have to find a part-time job."

"Where would you look?" Harlan wanted to know. "The Krauts have them all sewn up. Those damned creeps will work twenty-four seven for room and board. I tell you, Adam: someone is making a fortune out of low wages and high prices."

"Yeah, you never get ahead workin' for the other guy. We ought to go into business for ourselves."

"Doin' what? Anything we could come up with is already taken."

"Damn it, that's because the library is givin' away ideas that are worth millions to anyone who walks in off of the street. That library ought to be lock up tighter than a virgin's chastity belt in a whore house. That information belongs to us. It ought to be reserved for our use. Do you realize that some Kraut outfit in Magdeburg is building river boats with steam engines? Shit, they even named the first one the African Queen. That oughta be some up-timer makin' the money offa them boats," Adam Rice said.

Harlan/Big Dog/Carpenter sipped his beer before saying, "I hear ya. But no one cares. Shit, even that asshole Simpson's sold out since they made him an admiral. Sterns could care less if we all end up workin' for Krauts or losin' our jobs and starvin' to death 'cause some Kraut will work cheaper. Now if they'd hung onto all of that stuff in the library, by and by we'd all be sitting on the top of the world."

Jimmy Dick butted in, "You ever hear the saying 'tis safer a pretender in public than a true prince in hiding?"

"What the hell are you talkin' about Jimmy," Adam asked.

Big Dog looked at the old drunk. He still looked strange without the skinny little ponytail he wore for years before he gave it up when he became Grantville's resident philosopher. Big Dog whispered loud enough to he heard all over the bar. "Now you done it, Adam. You went and gave him an opening. He's gonna up and tell us one of his dumb stories."

Jimmy ignored it and said, "It's like the fella who collected rare things. I don't mean just rare stamps or rare baseball cards or rare books: if it was rare he wanted one. The rarer it was, the more he wanted it.

"One day someone showed up with a hairy tennis ball with feet. 'What is it?' the collector asked. 'Don't know. It's so rare no one knows what it is or where it came from. I mean have you ever seen one? Ever heard of one? I sure ain't. This is the only one alive. I just call it a rary. It's yours for only ten dollars.'

"Well for ten dollars he bought it? Then he asked, 'What does it eat?'

'Set it down in the back yard and let it eat bugs. That's what it was doing when I found it.'

"Well, that worked fine until it got to be the size of a beach ball. Then it started eating the cat's food. Later it started eating the dog's food. Then the cat disappeared. When it got to be the size of a weather balloon, they caught it eating the dog. That's when his wife told him he had to get rid of it.

"So, he loaded it into the back of his dump truck and drove three miles to the Grand Canyon. He had it backed up to dump it over the edge when he heard a voice. 'Hey, what are you doing?'

"He looked around thinking he was busted for dumping in the Grand Canyon but he didn't see anyone. That's when the voice said, 'Up here, dummy.'

"Well, the man was shocked. 'I didn't know you could talk.'

'I didn't need to, until now. Just what do you think you're doing? If you tip this thing any further, I'll go over the edge.'

'That's the point. My wife said I've got to get rid of you, so I'm dumping you into the canyon.'

'You don't want to do that. I know the secret cure for cancer, I know the secret of cold fusion. I can tell you how to make anti-gravity devices.'

'Yeah, but it's too late. The wife said I have to get rid of you. Why didn't you say something sooner?'

'Well, I didn't want to just give it away.'

"The collector hit the lever and started dumping the critter. 'I can tell you how to turn lead into gold. But you've got to stop tipping this thing right now. That's a long way to tip a rary'."

Big Dog groaned. "Why do you have to be that way, Jimmy?"

Jimmy shrugged and continued the tale. "But with that, it was too late. The critter was over the tailgate and on its way down. The collector stepped to the end of the truck and watched it fall. 'Too bad, he said to himself. I could have used a pile of gold'."

"So, other than that atrocious pun, what's the point, Jimmy?"

"The point is; if we don't want the world to decide to get rid of a rare and strange thing that turned up out of nowhere, we need to let the world know that we're worth keeping around. All of that knowledge in the library won't do us one bit of good if someone doesn't think we're worthwhile."

"Just let them try and get rid of us. We'll blow 'em away." Harlan replied.

"How many time, Harlan? How many times do you think we can stop them if they decide to get rid of us and we don't have any local help?"

"Shit, Jimmy, what are you a Kraut lover now?"

"No, but, I am kind of in love with breathing. If you know what I mean? Ken, give us another round."

ONE LAST MEMORY

Friday evening December twenty-third, 1634

On Christmas Eve, white-haired, skinny as a rail Asa, and gray-haired, frail and nearly emaciated Dory, dressed in their pajamas, were ready for bed. Wrapped in bathrobes, they sat on the French Provincial couch in front of the fireplace with its glazed Italian tiles and a roaring fire. The imported tiles of the small, eighteen-nineties vintage, one bedroom house complemented the ornate oak woodwork. The two of them sipped a fine old Amontillado out of her Grandmother's crystal stemware as they had almost every Christmas Eve for nearly fifty years. They had just exchanged gifts. Having never had children, they slept in on Christmas day. He had given her a new set of boots and several pairs of warm socks. Her feet were getting wet walking to the tram getting to and from school now that she had temporarily come out of retirement. She gave him a fired clay building.

She thought she had the perfect Christmas present. A perfect present needed to be three things. First, it must be something the person wants. They may not have known it exists, but when they find out it does, they want it. Secondly, it should be something they would not buy for themselves. Thirdly, it must be a surprise. Years ago he had started collecting a Christmas village, and they had added to it year by year. Now, of course, there was no catalog to supply them. She showed a potter a picture of what she wanted, and she showed him one of the buildings they already had, then she rejected several firings until he made something close to what she wanted. Unfortunately, the fat fingered Hungarian put the rejects on display. Asa saw them in the shop's window.

"I'm sorry Asa. I really thought I had you surprised this year."

"It was sweet of you dear. It really does look like it is part of the set. I'm sorry I got you something practical. But it is all I could think of." He had taken an old pair of shoes down to the shoemaker. The cobbler made the lasts to fit the shoes, and then he made the boots to fit the lasts. They were the best fitting, and perhaps the best made, shoes she had ever had. Still, it was not a particularly romantic present.

"Asa, there is only one thing in the whole wide world you could give me which I actually want." They gave up on having a family, years ago. They thought about adopting when they were younger but really didn't think they could afford it. They thought about it again when the Ring of Fire moved them to Germany, but they decided it would not be fair to take on children they would not live to see grown. It was a loss they had buried so deeply they didn't even think about it. He knew exactly what she was talking about. They had traveled some when he was in Germany in the army. One of the places they went was Bremen. The story of the musicians of Bremen was a favorite of Dory's. The statue in the town of the animals standing on each other's back caught her imagination at the time. And it had been a life-long dream to go back. It was an unfulfilled dream.

They had planned to go several times. But each time but something always came up. In 1970 they hadn't saved up the money. In 1980 the roof blew off the house and the furnace went out. When that happened, Dory sighed and said, "It looks like our trip to Europe is gone with the wind." A decade later Asa was in the hospital.

"We had the reservations made, Dory. The money is still in the bank. We would have gone. I know how much it meant to you."

"We could still go."

"Dory! Remember?" Asa sighed. He hated starting any conversation with the word, 'remember.' And it was happening more and more often. "It's 1634. In a few days, it will be 1635. There's no airlines to take us there."

"Asa, we're already in Germany. We don't need an airline."

"Dory," Asa sighed again, "I'll be seventy-five next month. You just turned seventy-two. Neither one of us are in what you would call good health. There is no way we can go traipsing off half way around the world at our age."

"It's not half way around the world." Dory put her glass down and folded her knurled, arthritic hands in her lap. When she did, Asa knew he was in for an argument. "It's less than a hundred and fifty miles as the crow flies. I've checked. We walked farther than that when we hiked the Appalachian Trail."

"We weren't seventy-two and seventy-five at the time, and it was in America where it was safe."

"It was safe?" Dory's hands did not move from her lap. But she raised a single eyebrow in a studied gesture. "Is that why you insisted on carrying a pistol?"

"Dory, it's out of the question. There's a war on. And even if there weren't you have to think about the bandits. On top of everything else, it's not like we can hop in the car and be there in two or three hours, no matter how fast I drive. A trip like that could kill us."

"Asa, you know I'm losing my mind."

"You're getting Alzheimer's; it's not the same thing as losing your mind."

"Asa, you can call it whatever you want. My memory is slipping. In another year or two, I may not know what day it is. I might not even know who you are. Just like my mother and my grandmother at the end. If the trip kills me, what will I lose? A handful of years of being tied to a bed down at the nursing home so I don't wonder out into the snow and forget how to get back in. Back in 1970, Asa McDonald, you promised you would take me. I don't care that there isn't a highway. I want to see Bremen again before I die. It is less than two hundred miles away by road. Are you going to take me or am I going by myself?"

"You can't do that!" Asa raised his voice sharply.

"You just watch me."

"You'll get yourself killed."

"Then I'll die trying!"

"For crying out loud, woman, be reasonable!"

"Mr. McDonald. I have been reasonable my whole life. What has it gotten me? In another year or two, I won't be able to remember. It's all falling in on itself even as we speak. Husband, give me something to remember. My mother and her mother both ended up talking about the same thing over and over again each and every day. Give me something interesting to talk about. Take me to Bremen. You promised!"

When she picked up her glass, Asa knew the argument was over.

Noon, Monday, January third, 1635

"Herr McDonald!" Anna, the young blond secretary/receptionist, sat behind the old, gray steel desk in the front office of the machine shop. David Marcantonio paid ten dollars for the desk in a Salvation Army thrift store years ago when he started the business. A customer offered him a small fortune for it early in 1632. He decided to sell it when he found out he could buy a newly made hardwood desk of the same size or larger and still have money left over. When he mentioned this, the furniture maker offered a swap of two for one. Well if they could give him two desks and still make money on it, that put a stop to the first deal. Every year since, he'd had two or three offers for the up-time desk, and the price kept going up. So, a beautiful young blond sat behind the ugly piece of junk that continued in use. David didn't need the money. The shop was more than busy.

Anna was dressed in a thick sweater to ward off the chill, which radiated through the single pane glass of the office's picture window. "It is freezing out there." She scolded the white-haired man with a cane as he limped from the shop door towards the front door and the street. "You must not go out without your coat and hat. You will catch pneumonia and die. If you are not here, what will Herr Marcantonio do the next time he cannot figure out how to do something and needs to know how the old-timers used to do it?"

Her last phrase was what Asa McDonald was noted for, remembering obsolete processes from the old days.

"Dave will figure it out without me if he has to. I'm just running next door, Anna. I don't need my coat."

"And you are not wearing your boots! There is ice on the road. What will happen if you fall and break your hip? Who will look after your wife? She is getting forgetful and needs you even more than Herr Marcantonio does."

"That's rather personal. Just who have you been talking to, girl?" The smile in his voice softened the harsh words.

Anna ignored the question. The lives of the up-timers were grist for the rumor mill in Grantville. Dory McDonald's pending Alzheimer's and the school's decision not to renew her contract for next year were common knowledge. "You wait there, and I will fetch your hat and coat from the time clock."

"That's okay. I'm just running next door." And with those words, he left through the steel front door which also had a standing offer if David ever wanted to sell it.

The wind-chill made its affect known and Asa's shoes slipped on the ice, as he trod the asphalt between the two standard, one story, flat-topped cinderblock industrial buildings. "You old fool. You should have let her go get your coat. She's right: Dory needs you."

*** * ***

"Wesley, how's business?" Asa asked as he approached the counter. The sign on the picture window at his back read 'Pomal Conversions' in a recently touched up crisp Gothic script in royal blue with gold highlights. The walls inside and out had been painted late in the summer and were still neat and pristine. Next door the sign painted on the window in the dirty whitewashed cinderblock building announced that it was Marcantonio's machine shop. The script was plain, and the paint was faded. But, with more work than he could handle, Dave Marcantonio wasn't overly worried about making a good first impression.

"Staying busy." The much younger but balding, dark-haired Wesley Pomeroy replied proudly. More than once since the Ring of Fire he had feared that he would not be able to keep the door of his shop open, van conversion being, at least at first glance, a distinctly up-time business.

He did not have to look up more than an inch to make eye contact with the six foot two still shivering machinist, "What can I do for you, Mister McDonald?"

Asa opened a vanilla folder and put a pile of drawings as thick as a nickel on the counter, leaving slightly oily finger prints on the top and bottom sheets. "It's pretty straightforward."

By Terry Howard

Wesley thumbed through them. His hands left no visible smudge even though there was a black line ingrained around his fingernails and in the creases of his knuckles from working on dirty engines.

"Asa, if this is straightforward, I would hate to see what you call complicated. But then if you admit that it's complicated, you can't argue it should be done cheaply." The top one showed a V.W. mini-bus exterior, converted to a coach and six. It was a different sort of van conversion than Wesley did up-time, but it was still a conversion. Wesley nodded. It was what he was doing for a living these days, converting up-time automobiles to horse drawn carriages, mostly for rich down-time nobles who wanted to show off just how much money they had to throw away. It was profitable work, and it kept him in business, since the conversion of cars and tractors from unleaded to natural gas, which kept him busy right after the flash of light, was pretty much over.

"You've got a driver's seat on the roof and a slot under the window for the reins."

"I like options." Asa pointed to the next picture, "I want the two front bucket seats on turntables so they can face forward to drive or backwards to ride and chat with other passengers."

Wesley nodded again.

"Now this's interesting," Wesley said, pointing to a drawing of a generator and a hydraulic pump being turned by the drive axle to feed a series of batteries and a power fluid system where the engine used to sit.

"Just because the engine went to the Air Force I don't see why I should give up on the lights or the electric heater. I paid extra for the heater. I want to use it. I want the brakes working too, at least while the bus is moving. The handbrake can hold it when it's standing still. I'll supply the parts. All you have to do is install the system." He flipped to the next page. "You can see we will want a second set of brake controls for the seat up top."

"Have you thought of how much drag that is going to add?" Wesley asked.

"No."

"I think you will find it's not a good idea."

"Well, I want to try it, at least."

Wesley nodded. "You're paying for it. Now this here," Wesley said, pointing at the front axle. "Mostly we've been pulling the front suspension and putting in a hay trailer axle. You've got us tying into the existing system."

"It will work."

"Cost a lot to get it made, though."

"I'll make up the parts. All you have to do is install it when you pull the steering wheel. I've seen what you usually do. It works fine, but you have to cut the old wheel wells away for the thing to turn. This," Wesley wrapped his knuckles, on the next picture, "will look better, it keeps the springs intact, and I get to keep those fancy air-filled shock absorbers I had put on."

"Well, if we cut it away we can move the lights up to the top to shine over the horses," Wesley said.

Asa rubbed his jaw, "I hadn't thought– No, leave them, I've got the front lights off of a 1932 Ford 'B' Model in the rafters over the garage. They were there when we bought the place, and I never bothered taking them down. Let's leave the lights where they are for aesthetics and mount those up top."

"Do they still work?" Wesley asked.

"If they don't we can use the housings and have them rewired."

"I suppose you want this tomorrow." Wesley unconsciously rubbed his temple to massage a headache that was not there, as he started to marshal the reasons why it couldn't be done quickly.

"No." Asa forestalled Wesley's thoughts with a dismissive wave of his hand. "No hurry. Middle of next month will be fine."

"I see. You've got rigging for a six horse team and a full luggage rack over the whole roof behind the driver's seat. You don't need six horses here in town. Are you going into passenger service or something?"

"We're going to be doing some traveling come late spring after the weather clears."

"Oh, where are you going?"

"My wife wants to go to Bremen."

"Bremen? I guess that makes sense the way she has always loved it. She told us all about it when I had her for a teacher. She told us the story of the Musicians of Bremen and showed us the picture of the statue. And then she told us all about how she went to Germany when you were in the army after your tour in Korea."

By Terry Howard

"Yeah," Asa said, "that was a long time ago. We got married just before I shipped out for Korea. To get me to sign up for a second tour, they offered me a tour in Germany. But I said I wanted to go home to my wife, so they said I could bring a dependent over to Germany. Dory agreed, so I signed on for a second tour. There was just something about that statue in Bremen that she fell in love with. All these years she's wanted to go back. And now that we're here she says she's going."

Wesley asked, "Doesn't she know there's a war on?"

Asa winced. "There's a war on?" Asa asked, inflecting his voice to make the statement a question while bumping his forehead with the heel of his hand in mock surprise. "Really?"

Then in a calm voice, he said, "Trust me, Wesley. I tried that argument."

Wesley started to say something.

"I tried that one, too," Asa said before he even heard what the man was going to say. "She's got her mind made up. I can take her or she's going without me."

"Well, Mr. McDonald, if you've got to go, you've got to go. I've got to admit if I were going, especially at your age, I'd want the best ride I could get, and it looks like we will be getting that for you." Wesley said, tapping the pile of drawings.

Lisa Alcom, Wesley's partner and co-owner in the conversion business, came into the office from her section of the shop. The short, blond-haired woman was as plump as her partner. They looked like a married couple even though they weren't. She handled the upholstering end of the business and the bookkeeping. He did everything else. Lisa looked at the top picture on the pile while the men were talking.

"I remember when I had your wife as a teacher, Lisa said. "She took one whole afternoon and told us all about her trip and the history of Bremen and the statue of the musicians." She didn't mention the student's bright idea of distracting their teacher with a question about it whenever someone didn't have their homework done. If you could get her started, she could and sometimes would talk all afternoon on the subject. It was nearly thirty years ago, but Lisa still felt a little guilty about it.

"Yeah. I remember it too." Wesley added. "Shoot, it was nearly fifty years ago. I was in the first class she ever taught. I still remember how excited she was and how exciting she made it sound. Shoot, I've dreamed of going myself."

"You and everybody else who ever had her for a teacher," Lisa said.

That evening Lisa told a girlfriend about Old Lady McDonald's planned trip. It would be an exaggeration to say everybody in town knew all about by the next morning, but not by much.

* * *

Wesley helped his wife Sheryl, still in her white cooking apron with its red-tipped ruffled edges, put the pot roast dinner on the table. Sheryl was a good match for her husband's personality, but she was not at all a match for Wesley's build, being as she was on the skinny side. Since the Ring of Fire, in the absence of home hair dyes, Sheryl's hair had grown out gray, and she had it cut short, so it was all gray just as soon as the gray was long enough to let her do so without looking butch. She had taken to keeping it covered when it started growing out, and she still kept it covered even after she had it cut short. As he set the table, he told her, about Asa putting in the order.

"Asa sold the motor out of his old VW bus to Jesse to make an airplane. So now he wants it rigged to be pulled by horses." Then he told her why. Over dinner, he told her about Mrs. McDonald reading her class the story of the Musicians of Bremen and then showing her third-grade class a picture of the statue in Bremen, with the rooster standing on the cat, standing on the dog, standing on the donkey. "Then she told us about her trip and seeing the statue in person."

When he ran down, his wife looked at him and said, "You want to go, don't you!"

"Don't be ridiculous."

Sheryl put her fork down and focused her cornflower blue eyes on her husband's chubby face. "I'm not being ridiculous. You would like to go."

"I'd like to go to China too!" he said with a laugh.

"Yes. But you can't go to China. You could go to Bremen. You've been dreaming of it your whole life ever since you were in the third grade. Admit it."

By Terry Howard

Wesley looked down at his plate, so Sheryl saw his horseshoe haircut instead of his blushing cheeks. "Honey, I've had a lot of dreams. I even wanted to be an astronaut once."

"So, you can't go to the moon. You could go to Bremen." She picked her fork back up and took a bite of the apple pie she had made for dessert.

"It's too dangerous."

"Wesley Pomeroy," Sheryl said with a touch of impishness in her voice—Wesley fell in love with it all those years ago when they were dating—"are you going to sit there and tell me you are ready to stand by and watch as those two old people do something you want to do but don't have the balls to even try?"

Well, when a fellow's wife puts it to him that way, what can a man say? He looked up, placed both palms on the table, made hard eye contact, and in a firm and no-nonsense voice asked, "Do you want your own coach or are we going to share theirs?"

"What?" She snorted. "What makes you think I'm going?"

"Sheryl Pomeroy, are you going to admit he loves his wife enough to go with her on the trip of a lifetime but you don't love your husband enough to do the same? Or are you hoping I'll get myself killed so you can sell the business and run off to Miami?"

She broke out in laughter. Her husband smiled in return. Every time they ever got into a fight about anything it always ended with her threatening to run off to Florida, especially since the Ring of Fire.

The next day Wesley stopped into the machine shop next door to his business and wandered out onto the shop floor. He found Asa sitting on a stool watching a turret lathe do what a turret lathe does. Asa's walking stick, which he had cut from a young oak on the hillside, leaned against the stool. "Asa, the wife and I were wondering if we can ride with you to Bremen. If not, then I need to get two of these things built in time for the trip."

"Wesley," Asa said, looking so solemn that he would have looked sour if he had been anyone else. But being sour just was not in him. "I should tell you: I'm building this mostly to keep Dory happy. When it comes right down to the wire, I plan to ask for official permission, and I expect to get turned down. But yes, if we go you are more than welcome to ride with us."

BREMEN OR BUST

January 5, 1635, Grantville

Around lunch time, Wesley came through the green front door of the single-story, whitewashed cinderblock building, housing Club 250, the almost forgotten smell of tobacco smoke hit him like a brick wall. Ken was selling the tobacco to fill pipes, a dollar a fill. If you didn't bring your own pipe or paper to roll your own cigarette, you could borrow a long-stemmed clay pipe kept in a jar on the back-bar. Ken broke about an inch off of the stem after each use. So you got a clean mouthpiece each time. It was something he'd seen done at a black-powder rendezvous once.

Tobacco had come close to disappearing after the Ring of Fire, and now it was shipped in at very high prices. It wasn't the mild tobacco of up-time cigarettes. There was a lot of research and development in the tobacco industry that got passed over when Grantville came back in time. But it was what there was. Wesley hadn't smoked before the Ring of Fire. He sang solos in the high school choir and now in the Methodist choir. Smoking cut into your wind, so he never took it up. He had never thought about how much he didn't miss it until Ken started selling it. Now his reaction was a wrinkled nose. "Why does anyone put up with it?"

He started to leave, but a voice called out, "Hey, Wes. Let me buy you a beer." The voice was James Richard Shaver's. And since Jimmy Dick owned the building Wesley ran his business out of, Wesley thought better of leaving.

By Terry Howard

Jimmy Dick looked odd to Wesley with a short haircut after decades of wearing it pulled back in a ponytail. The Vietnam Vet perched on a bar stool in jeans, a button-down white shirt, and an old tan, Mr. Roger's style cardigan sweater, with pockets, that the drunken reprobate wore from fall to spring. There was an empty stool on each side of the man while the rest were full. Jimmy Dick's notoriety for being a loud-mouthed, obnoxious, annoying, drunk was hard-earned, well-deserved and not soon forgotten.

Wesley found himself wondering just how it was that Jimmy Dick could spend all day, every day, drinking beer and still stay as skinny as he did. There didn't seem to be an ounce of fat on the man anywhere. Up-time, Wesley had to watch what he ate. It was a never-ending struggle to keep from bloating up like a blowfish. The first winter after the Ring of Fire there wasn't much extra, and he managed to lose weight. Now there was enough of a surplus to make plenty of beer, and Wesley had to watch it. Every time he had a beer it seemed to go right to his waist.

Wesley exposed his horseshoe haircut when he took off his stocking cap and stuffed it in his pocket. As he hung the coat he wore over his coveralls on a wall peg by the door he said, "Sure, Jimmy. A beer is what I came in for."

Ken set two newly made dark glass bottles on the counter. Beer bottles were amongst the first thing the local glass industry turned out. As soon as someone imported cork, a tinker started making caps, and newly bottled beer was back with the return of the church key. Bottles from up-time were collectible and pretty much worth their weight in gold by this time.

Bottled beer was nearly synonymous with cold beer in Grantville; a glass or mug usually meant room temperature beer out of a keg. Drinking out of the bottle was a practically a fashion statement or a declaration of culture. If you didn't want to drink out of the bottle, you had to ask for a glass in club 250 these days. If you did, you ran the risk of being teased for being a sissy, or worse, a kraut lover.

"Burger, Wes?" Ken asked, as Wesley approached the bar.

Wes nodded.

"Fries?" Ken asked.

Wes shook his head no. Potatoes were expensive, and Ken's prices reflected that fact; an order of fries cost more than a hamburger did. On top of that, they were fried in lard and even worse about putting weight under his belt than beer.

When Wesley's bottom interfaced with the vinyl covered foam padded seat of the bar stool, Jimmy said, "I hear you're taking Old Lady McDonald to Bremen."

Jimmy turned the bottom of the bottle he was working on to the tin tray ceiling to get the last few drops. The genuine antique ceiling came from the same closed tavern as the dark wood bar, mirrored-back bar, and brass cash register. The cinderblock building holding the hundred-year-old ceiling was less than fifty years old, and the bar had been in the building for the last twenty years.

"Well, I'm converting Asa's mini-bus to horse power for the trip, but I don't think they'll actually go," Wesley answered before he took a small sip. He limited himself to one or two beers a week in his battle of the bulge. So when he drank beer, he drank them slowly to savor every drop.

"Ain't how I heard it!" Jimmy Dick snorted, reinforcing his words by plunking his empty bottle down hard on the bar and grabbing the new one, in a continuous motion which left his hand empty for only a fraction of a second. "What I heard was you were going with him."

Wesley's mind went back to the conversation with his wife. When it found its way back to where his bottom was squishing the foam of a vinyl covered bar stool, Wesley noticed Jimmy Dick staring at him.

"Earth to Wesley, over?" Jimmy Dick smirked.

"Well," Wesley told Jimmy Dick, "if Asa and Mrs. McDee do go, the wife an' I are going with them. But Asa said he doesn't think they will get too. He'll wait until the last minute and then ask for clearance. There's a war on you know. So it probably ain't safe."

"Shit, these days there's always a war on. If that were a consideration, nobody would ever go anywhere. So that's pure bull shit! I mean it, Wes. If Old Lady McDonald wants to go to Bremen, then damnit she should go! You tell Asa to forget about askin' for permission from the government. When she's ready to leave, there's enough of her students around willing to swat any bugs that get in the way to see to it the old lady gets there and back."

"You think there might be that kind of interest?"

"Shit yeah, Of course, there is." Jimmy Dick continued, "I remember her telling us about it back in the third grade. She made it sound exciting.

I've always thought I'd like to see it. If she wants to go, we'll get her there. You tell that to Mister McDee. But Wesley, there's something I'm puzzled about." Jimmy took a swig of beer.

"Is the statue there yet? I mean, what's the point of going if it ain't?"

"I don't know," Wesley answered.

"Well," Jimmy Dick said when he when he set the beer down and wiped his mouth with the back of his sleeve, "it really doesn't matter. You tell Asa that if she wants to go to Bremen, we'll get her there."

Ken was back with the burger. It was lunchtime, and the patties were on the cast iron grill. It was winter, so there was no lettuce or tomato, but there were pickles and ketchup and mustard. Some people even made their own back before the Ring of Fire. Wes filled his mouth, taking note of the better quality of the bun than what would have been commonly available before the flash of light. The wheat was a coarser grind than up-time, and it had more milk and eggs, so it was a heavier, darker bread. Light white bread was something else he didn't miss from up-time.

The door opened. Addison Miller came in. He was not a regular, but he had business with Jimmy Dick, and since Jimmy didn't keep a working phone and his mail was delivered to the office Addison worked in, catching Jimmy at the bar was just about the only sure way of getting a message to him. Jimmy called out, "Hey Ad, you had Mrs. McDonald for the third grade. We're putting an escort to see her to Bremen in the spring. You in?"

"Don't know if the wife would let me do that."

"Wes here is taking his wife with him," Jimmy said.

"Jimmy," Wes said, "Don't you think we ought to ask Asa before you go making plans?"

"Shoot, Wes, what will it hurt to see who's interested?"

"I think you should wait and ask."

"Well, you check with Asa and get back to me."

Addison hopped up on the last empty barstool and Jimmy waved three fingers at the bartender.

"Jimmy, we've got a stack of papers for you to sign. And we got some mail you need to look at."

"I'll stop by when I get the time," Jimmy replied.

Wesley made an exception and had a second beer. When the burger was only a memory, he pushed the plate away and reached for his wallet.

"I've got it," Jimmy said. "You're a tenant. I can take it off my income taxes as a business lunch."

"Thanks, Jimmy. I'll check with Asa."

* * *

Of course, Jimmy Dick did not wait for a reply from Asa McDonald. By the time the bar closed for the night, anyone who came through who might be interested in helping 'old lady McDee', and everybody who wasn't at all interested, for that matter, were all very aware that Jimmy Dick was organizing an armed escort for the McDonald's spring trip to Bremen. The number of people who were, metaphorically, looking at their early summer schedules said a great deal for the quality of Mrs. McDonald as a person and as a teacher. The number of men who were reviewing their traveling gear and wardrobe said even more.

Grantville was never a very big place. The news that the McDonalds were going to Bremen had already penetrated to the saturation point before Wes and Jimmy had a beer over lunch. Jimmy's raising of an armed escort found its way to the last nook and cranny within forty-eight hours. By then, of course, the tale had only a passing acquaintance with facts. Up-time such would have been good for a chuckle and a comment on the credulity of gossips. But in the early winter of 1635, in Grantville, in the Germanies, gossip didn't stop over the back fence or at the city limits.

* * *

"Hey?" Jimmy Dick said to Addison Miller, the office manager of Lamb Commercial Properties, as he walked into the office. "What ya' got for me?" They ran the business out of what had once been a first-class dwelling house on the edge of downtown when Victoria was Queen of England. Addison Miller now ran the business for Old Lady Lamb. He and Jimmy had been in Mrs. McDee's third-grade class, and they had graduated together. The draft sent Jimmy to Nam and tagged Addison as 4F. A relative of Jimmy Dick's started buying up downtown properties as business closed down. He left them all to Jimmy Dick while the boy was still in Vietnam, to the annoyance of the rest of the family. Owning the properties didn't mean squat before the Ring of Fire. After paying the taxes and upkeep and the fees to the management company, very little remained out of the rents. And nobody wanted to buy the buildings.

Everything changed with the Ring of Fire. Every roof had a family or three under it. One family to a bedroom with a shared bathroom and kitchen was a very common arrangement in Grantville now. Ground floor business space was suddenly once again premium real estate. The rents were paying Jimmy's living, which was a good thing since his VA disability check stopped coming.

"Jimmy, we've got a stack of papers for you to sign. And we got some mail you need to look at."

"Shoot, Ad. If I owe it, pay it. If I don't owe it tell them no."

"We told them no, but they keep saying they need to talk to you. There's three different private security groups who want to bid on providing security for your trip to Bremen."

"I bet that's the same people who keep sending notes to me at Club 250. Ad, tell them we ain't interested."

"One of them stopped in, and I told him. He just smiled and winked and said, of course, you need to hire a professional outfit. A ragtag group of amateurs isn't up to taking on a job of that size.

"Well, I told him it was just a tourist trip for a little old lady. He gave me a nod and left a business card. And he said, Tell Mister Shaver that we will be speaking to him. Jimmy, are you sure you haven't gotten in over your head?"

"Yeah. Don't worry about it."

"Look, Jimmy, I know you haven't had a phone in years. But when we agreed to take care of your mail we thought that might mean dealing with an occasional bill collector."

Addison held up a hand to forestall Jimmy's reply. "It hasn't ever happened. We pay your property taxes, and now we pay your gas bill when it comes in, and you don't hardly get any mail, so that's fine. After we pay the bills, we make a deposit at the bank, and everything is fine. But we never thought it would mean we'd have mercenaries showing up looking for you. We're not set up to handle that. The girls are all nervous and upset over it. I need you to take care of this, Jimmy."

"Okay, Ad. Send them a letter telling them to meet me at the Thuringian Gardens on the first of the month at noon. I'll get a private dining room and tell them to quit bothering you."

By Terry Howard

MCDONALD'S EMPIRE

January 15, 1635

It was nine o'clock in the morning. Jimmy was half awake in bed, just beginning to think of a hot shower before heading to 'Club 250' for his first beer of the day around ten o'clock when Ken unlocked the doors to be officially open at eleven for lunch. The insistent pounding on his kitchen door was getting louder. Jimmy finally had to admit it probably wasn't a door to door vacuum sweeper salesman who would go away if ignored. So, he stumbled his blurry- "All right, I'm coming. Knock it off."

Officer Lyndon Johnson was standing in the still falling snow at the door. The kid Jimmy hired to clear his back walk to the kitchen door and his sidewalk along the street had been there already and would have to come back later, the way the snow was coming down.

"What's with the pounding on my door at the crack of dawn?" Jimmy snarled as he opened the door.

"Shoot, Jimmy, I pushed the button to the front doorbell, but I didn't get an answer." Jimmy knew Lyndon was fully aware of the doorbell's disabled state. Lyndon, a rookie at the time, was there the day Jimmy Dick ripped the annoying noise maker off the wall rather than answer the door.

"Look, Lyndon, whatever it was, I didn't do it. Okay?" Jimmy said with a halfhearted attempt to close the door. He could not do it because there was a combat boot-covered foot in the way.

"What you mean is you haven't done it yet!" The policeman responded.

"What are you talking about? I ain't done anything illegal and I ain't planning to."

"Well, if there isn't a law against opening up a private front in an ongoing war there ought to be."

"Unhhh?" Was Jimmy's first response. "What are you talking about?"

"Jimmy, you know we've got spies crawling out of the woodworks around here. Did you give any thought to just what the rumor mill would do with your Bremen plans or how those rumors would get reported back to every capital in Europe?" Lyndon watched as comprehension crept over Jimmy's face.

"Shit!"

"Yeah." The officer said. "The chief has a letter from Magdeburg. They've got one report back that the up-time branch of Clan McDonald is seceding from Grantville to pursue plans of conquering an independent kingdom. They told him to take care of it, and he told me to come see you and get it cleared up."

"So that's why the mercenary outfits want to talk to me?" Jimmy cracked up.

"Probably."

"King Ronald the first?" Jimmy started laughing.

Lyndon kept the smile off of his face, but couldn't keep it out of his eyes. "It ain't funny, Jimmy."

"Yes, it is," Jimmy said, still laughing.

"Okay, it's funny. I admit it. But, damn it, Jimmy, it's serious too."

"Lyndon, are you sure the spy they've got spying on the other spies ain't talking about what's goin' on down at the good old golden arches?" Jimmy laughed again.

Lyndon's face paled. "Holy shit! I wonder if they even thought of that. I know I didn't. I sure hoped no one else had either. If they do, - shit!"

"Yeah," Jimmy said without a trace of humor in his voice. The committee of correspondence who met in the old McDonald restaurant really was a revolutionary cartel. If their name got tangled up in this, there could be hell to pay. "Things sure ain't what they used to be."

THE LEGEND OF JIMMY DICK

"Jimmy, do me a favor, please, and start a rumor that there ain't but two or three of you who're going to Bremen."

"I don't know if I should do that," Jimmy said, shivering in the cold breeze that came through the shoe-wide crack in the door. He liked the young cop but, he wasn't about to open it any wider. It was an old habit; he wasn't about to invite a police officer inside, not since the day, years ago, when he ripped the doorbell off the wall and told the cops to come back with a warrant if they wanted to talk to him. "Last count I had is somewhere around thirty people have asked about it. If we start claiming it's only two or three, it might look like we're trying to hide something. If you've got spies taking this seriously, then looking like we're hiding something might not be such a good idea. But I've got a meeting set up with the security contractors for the first of the month at the Gardens. I'll tell them this ain't nothing but a tourist trip. The meeting is for noon. Maybe you and some of the boys should stop by for lunch that day just in case."

"That should help," Lyndon admitted. "And I've got to eat lunch somewhere. So, the Gardens on the first might be a good idea. Just see if you can ratchet this down a little between then and now."

"I'll see what I can do," Jimmy said.

Then Lyndon tugged at his foot, and Jimmy opened the door just a crack more so he could pull his foot out. Jimmy watched through the glass as the snowfall collected on the man's hat and the shoulders of his military-style overcoat as he walked down the walk, back to his car in the alley. When he was gone, out of curiosity, Jimmy looked out the front window of the house. The gate in the picket fence stood closed; the snow on the unshovelled walk remained pristine.

❋ ❋ ❋

As Asa made his way to the tram which was waiting in front of the machine shop for the shift change, someone in a police cruiser flashed the lights on the car. Lyndon Johnson rolled the driver's window down and called out, "Asa."

Asa stopped. The car crept forward. "Hop in," the clean-cut young police officer said. "I'll give you a ride home."

Asa hobbled around the car and slid in. "Thanks. What's up?"

"That's what I was told to ask you."

The blank look on Asa's face prompted Lyndon to continue. "Magdeburg wants to know what's going on with this army that Jimmy Dick is raising."

"Magdeburg? And Jimmy Dick is raising an army?" Asa asked.

"You've got no idea what I'm talking about, do you?"

"Well, Wesley said something about Jimmy Dick maybe arranging for an escort for Dory's trip to Bremen."

"The chief got a letter asking about the army Jimmy Dick is raising, and they want to know why."

Asa chuckled. "Dory wants to go to Bremen. It seems that Wesley told Jimmy that I thought we call it off at the last minute because it was too dangerous. So, Jimmy volunteered to put together an armed escort of some of Dory's old students to see us there and back."

"So, you don't have any plans of conquering a kingdom for the local branch of the Clan McDonald?"

At this Asa laughed so hard tears ran down his face. "King Ronald McDonald the first? I wouldn't look good in a clown suit."

Lyndon smiled and prompted, "So you don't know anything about it?"

"Lyndon," Asa said soberly, "this is the first I've heard about plans to conquer a kingdom. I'm too old to work that hard."

"Okay," Lyndon said. "I've already talked to Jimmy."

That night, Asa asked Dory if she wanted to be a queen. When he finally managed to explain what he was talking about she was not amused. "Jimmy was a scamp when I had him in class. And it looks like the boy never did grow up."

When Asa didn't hear anything else about it, he figured it had all blown over.

※ ※ ※

At ten minutes to noon on February first, Jimmy was leaving Club 250 to head across the street to the Thuringian Gardens, which was a larger, more popular bar than the Club. Built after the Ring of Fire, it was across the street from Club 250, mostly to rub certain noses in the fact that an open-door policy (Club 250 had a sign on the front door reading 'no dogs and no Krauts allowed') was much more profitable. And the owner of the land was willing to go into partnership, so land didn't have to be bought or leased. It was a traditional post and beam, wattle and daub, two-story construction with a fireplace at each end of the great room and exposed beams on the ceiling. What it didn't have was parking. Indeed, the empty lot had at times been used for overflow parking by patrons of Club 250 in years past and gone. But with the trolleys running and most cars not running, parking didn't matter like it once did.

Jimmy encountered Officer Lyndon Johnson at the green door. Each man had a hand on a doorknob at the same time.

"I was afraid you'd forgotten," Lyndon said. "I knew you wouldn't just blow it." The latter was a social lie, and both men knew it. Lyndon indeed worried that the old drunk might do exactly that. And the Chief of Police would not be at all happy about it if he did.

"I didn't see no need to be early," Jimmy answered.

"Well, you've got quite a crowd waiting for you."

"Lyndon, there were only three invitations sent out."

"Then you've got some uninvited guests, 'cause there is a bigger bunch than that waiting and more still just watching. Just about all the openly reporting agents in town are just accidentally having lunch there today. And half of the suspects who don't admit who they are spying for are there too. I've got to make notes on who else is there. They might bear watching."

As they entered the front door of the gardens, Jimmy noted that there was a gas fire in both of the big fireplaces. They held a large heat exchange unit in the flue with forced air, so the whole room was warm. Without taking off his coat or his hat, Jimmy went to the small the stage on the wall, half way between the fires and across the room from the kitchen. The stage was just big enough to hold an average sized band.

"Your attention, please. I've called this meeting to clear up some rumors that have gotten out of hand. The McDonalds have no plans of setting up an independent kingdom. I am putting together an escort to accompany Mrs. McDonald and her husband to Bremen on a tourist trip. And Mr. McDonald says that if there is official opposition to the trip, then it will not be happening. So, if you are here because you thought I was recruiting an army, then you are out of luck and have wasted your time. Thank you for coming. Now leave me alone and quit bothering my real estate broker."

Jimmy stalked out of the building to a background of grumbling.

"Shoot, Jimmy, don't you think you could have ticked them off just a bit more than that? You know, called stupid Krauts or something?"

"Nope. Now that I'm Grantville's resident philosopher, I need to watch what I say." Jimmy said with a straight face.

Lyndon snorted. "Someone will be by to give you a ride home for the next few nights. Some of those fellows might be a bit upset that you wasted their time. Don't you up and leave early, you hear me, Jimmy?"

"You think there might be trouble?"

"Jimmy, you just killed a dream. The word in the walls is that each man would get five acres of land and each officer would get an additional acre for each man he brought to the expedition."

"The word in the walls, Lyndon?" Jimmy asked.

"Yes. When they come crawling out of the woodwork, that's the tale they are bringing with them. And you know how these people feel about land ownership. So, watch your back and wait for your ride."

The cop started to turn away.

"Let me buy you a beer," Jimmy said.

"Jimmy, if you'd offered when we were in the gardens I'd have let you. But I'm a paid public official, and I can't be seen hanging out with you lowlifes in Ken's bar."

"Shoot, Lyndon. Don't you think you could have ticked me off a bit more than that? You know, you could have called me a dumb hillbilly or a red neck or somethin' besides just a lowlife."

The cop snickered and made an invisible mark on a scoreboard in the air. "Your point Jimmy. Just watch out for a bit."

※ ※ ※

Not quite two weeks later, Jimmy Dick turned the large collar of his nearly new sheepskin coat up against the howling wind as he stepped out of his back door. It was a bit before ten A.M. Jimmy was surprised to find Lyndon sitting in a patrol car in the alley, waiting for him. When

Jimmy came through the back gate, Lyndon rolled his window down—in the bitter cold—and told Jimmy, "Get in."

As they pulled away, Jimmy asked, "Where we goin'?"

"To see Asa." Lyndon didn't even glance at Jimmy when he answered. He was busy watching the road. The wind was blowing small crystals of snow and visibility was poor. People were hunkering down, and with greatly reduced traffic and so many emigrants, some people were not as cautious about watching for cars as they would have been up-time. "I've got a letter from Magdeburg, and I don't want to go through it two or three times, so I need all of you together."

They parked in front of the machine shop where Asa worked. The single-story cinderblock building was next door to a similar one housing Pomal Conversions. In the front office of the machine shop, Lyndon nodded to the receptionist. The young German lass was wearing a thick sweater, and there was an electric heater at her feet. The single paned glass of the picture window radiated cold, and the block walls weren't insulated.

"Officer Johnson? What can we do for you?" She asked with more than the prerecorded smile that she gave to most people who came through the door. She was not married, and in her opinion, Lyndon was a hunk.

"Gertrude, would you call next door and ask Wesley to come here and then get Asa from out on the floor, please."

"Of course. Officer Johnson." She picked up the phone with one hand while flipping the rolodex with the other.

Gertrude came out onto the shop floor to tell him Lyndon wanted him in the office. Asa slapped a hand to his forehead and followed her.

A few minutes later Wesley came in with a blast of cold air and a nod of recognition from Lyndon. "Wesley."

"Man, it's cold out there. What's up, Lyndon?" Wes asked at about the same time Gertrude came in the other door with a blast of noise. A walking stick followed her in Asa's hand.

"Fellas, I won't keep you long," the cop told Wesley and Asa. "The Chief got another letter from Magdeburg. This trip to Bremen is stirred up a hornet's nest, and it isn't calming down. I know all you wanted to do was make a trip, to see someplace you have fond memories of, and that shouldn't be a problem. But the news of Clan McDonald's plans for conquering a kingdom just is getting all kinds of attention from all over."

"Word has arrived from the government in Magdeburg. You wouldn't believe the flack this is stirring up. Jimmy, I know you told the mercenary recruiters that they were not wanted. I was there when you made it plain to then that there were no plans to conquer a kingdom. But that didn't calm thing down any."

"So, here's the bottom line." Lyndon caught Asa's gaze and made hard eye contact. "Tell your wife that they've decided to accredit her as a goodwill ambassador, and they will be escorted on the trip by a squad of marines. The only people on the trip who will be armed will be the marines. Period! You will not be mounting machine guns and cannons on armored busses. And the party of non-combatants will be limited to a total of four people. And one of them is not you, Jimmy!"

"Sheeit!" Jimmy said. "They can't tell us that."

"Jimmy, if you give us any trouble over this, you will find your reserve status invoked, and you'll end up somewhere far away. And it will be somewhere where you are being shot at if that can be managed."

"Shit!" Jimmy said. "I was looking forward to seeing that statue after all these years."

"Too bad, Jimmy. Suck it up and get over it."

"Will Asa need the bus, then? I mean if they're going to be official and all and with the Marines going." Wes asked. "I've got a tentative offer for it when it gets back, but they'd like it now."

"You can put it on a barge down the river," Lyndon said. "I can't think of anything that will draw more attention than it will and drawing attention is what this is all going to be about. Tell your customer he'll just have to wait."

"Sheeit!" Jimmy said.

"Yeah, Jimmy," Lyndon smirked. "It sucks to be you, don't it?"

A TALE OF CHARLES AND CHARLES

March 35

Lyndon Johnson entered Club 250, the most infamous bar in Grantville, across the street from the Thuringian Gardens, the most famous bar in Grantville. Though Lyndon still thought of 'The Gardens' as the new bar. It was late in the afternoon on a dreary and windy day.

Ken Beasley, owner and bartender of the club, called to him in a friendly way as he came through the door, "What's up?" Ken knew that the police officer was not there as a patron. But Lyndon had briefly dated one of his daughters, and Ken liked the young man.

"They need Jimmy Dick at the hospital," Lyndon answered.

Jimmy turned away from the bar and asked, "What for?"

"I got a call over the radio telling me they need you at the hospital. Let's go?"

"What for?"

"If you want to know, you're going to have to go find out. Let's go."

Jimmy turned the current bottle to the antique tray ceiling and slid off the stool.

In the car, when Lyndon had not said a word Jimmy finally asked, "What's going on Lyndon?"

"Best you wait until we get there." The rest of the drive was strangely quiet for two men who were both usually very talkative. When they got to the hospital, Lyndon took Jimmy to the delousing station, which confirmed to Jimmy that Lyndon knew more than he was sharing.

The white-haired matron who ran the station looked up when Jimmy and Lyndon came through the door. "Your people are still showering, Herr Shaver?" An interior door opened and a stout, broad-shouldered, redhead man in his late thirties or early forties came into the room in a bathrobe. "Herr McDonald," she said, pointing at Jimmy Dick. "Here is the man you are looking for."

In a heavy Scotts accent, the man asked, "Are you Lord Jimmy Dick, war leader for the local clan McDonald?"

Jimmy's mouth fell open, and a snickering Lyndon said, "He's your man."

"Lord Jimmy, I am Charles McDonald of the McDonalds from the Isles. When I left home, we had one hundred and six good men ready to join your conquest. I suspect that number has doubled since I left. They are waiting to hear from me that the offer is for real."

A younger less stout man and pregnant young women also in bathrobes came through the same interior door.

"This is Charles McDonald and his wife Anna from the Clan in Ireland. They barely have a word of English between them. I met them on the boat upriver from Hamburg. They're here for the five acres. I gather they were in some bit of trouble, so they came early. They tell me there is more coming later in a group."

Jimmy's eyes got big, and he finally closed his mouth. Lyndon tried hard to swallow his laughter and almost succeeded.

Jimmy turned to the cop and asked, "What the hell am I supposed to do?"

"Shoot, Jimmy, as far as they're concerned, they're here at your invitation."

"But I never—"

"I know that, and you know that, but they don't. Someone has to put them up until they go home or get a job and get settled. You've got two empty bedrooms, and you're just about the only person in Grantville who didn't take in boarders."

"I like my privacy," Jimmy said defensively.

THE LEGEND OF JIMMY DICK

"Asa and Dory have that dinky little one bedroom house. They can't put them up. Chief Richards says this is your fault and for you to fix it. I think you're stuck, Jimmy."

Jimmy looked the Clansmen over. "Lyndon, let's talk outside."

✻ ✻ ✻

"Dammit, Lyndon, you can't do this to me!" An artificial calm masked a tightly controlled anger as Jimmy Dick addressed the younger police officer while standing in the cold.

Lyndon Johnson looked at the reprobate old drunk, okay, to be fair, the semi-reformed old drunk, without even a hint of sympathy. "This is what you wanted to talk about outside? Forget it, Jimmy. The chief said you made this mess so you can clean it up."

"But I didn't invite them. All I wanted was to go with Old Lady McDee to Bremen, and then 'those people in Magdeburg' squashed that."

"Of course, the government in Magdeburg squashed it." Lyndon shivered in the cold. "Just looks like these people haven't heard that yet. So, they're here to answer your call for conquistadors."

"I never said that and I didn't invite these people!"

"Well, this is what happened when word got to Scotland that you were offering five acres per man and an acre per head to each officer for each man he brought to help you conquer a new country for Clan McDonald. These three showed up, and they say there are more coming in the spring. You need to get some letters in the mail and head them off."

"I never said that. I did not invite them. This is not my fault!" Jimmy said putting both hands to his head, rubbing his temples, trying to deal with a sudden headache. "Damn it, Lyndon!" Jimmy repeated himself, "You know good and well, all I wanted to do was go to Bremen. The old lady deserved that much after teaching third grade for thirty years. These people are not my responsibility."

"The Chief doesn't see it that way. These people wouldn't be here if it weren't for you. You made this problem. Take care of it."

"But— Damn it. This is not my fault!"

"Jimmy, you play the part of a dumb, red neck, hillbilly better than anybody I know." Lyndon turned the collar of his coat up and turned his back the wind which left him at right angles to Jimmy. "But I know there is a first-class brain behind your brown eyes when you bother to use it."

"My eyes are blue." Jimmy objected.

"Not when you're full of shit," Lyndon answered. "What did you think was going to happen when word got out?"

"I didn't think-"

"You got that right,-" Lyndon said overriding Jimmy's last two words.

"-of this," Jimmy concluded.

"- you didn't think." Lyndon continued, "Well, this time it came back to bite you. The chief is adamant. As long as they are in Grantville, they are your problem. You've never taken in boarders, so you've got an empty house."

"Dammit, Lyndon, I like my privacy."

Lyndon ignored him. "And these are Scotts, so you can't complain about not wanting to deal with Krauts. It's a good thing that one of them speaks English and understands whatever it is that the other two speak or I don't know what you would do. And one of them is a young lady so she can handle the cooking. I can hang around until their clothes are done and give you a ride home. And we can stop at the grocery store on the way. If I know you there isn't anything in your kitchen that isn't ten years old."

"I cleaned out the cupboards back when the church ladies were feeding the refugees. There ain't nothin' left."

Lyndon nodded. "So you need to buy everything."

"But, Lyndon—"

The cop interrupted him. "Forget it, Jimmy. I don't want to hear it. You're not getting out of it. You've got to explain to them that there is no invasion, so there is no free land. And if they can't pay their way back home, which I sure at least two of them can't, then you need to help them find jobs and put them up until they can afford to rent a room.

"Now, I'm going back inside where it's warm."

Jimmy's hands moved from rubbing his temples to rubbing his eyes and then back to his temples. "Sheeit!" he said to the closing door. "Damn it's cold out here." And with these words, he followed Lyndon back inside to face the white painted empty room with the white-haired German matron behind the counter.

"Your guests are getting dressed, Herr Shaver." The matron said.

Jimmy growled some inarticulate response and Lyndon stifled a chuckle before telling the woman, "That means thank you, in Scotts Gaelic. But his pronunciation is awful."

The matron looked at Lyndon skeptically but didn't say anything. The three of them waited in a mood of tense silence until the inside door opened. The young Charles McDonald and his wife Anna, both a bit shorter than average with red hair and freckles, came out first. Jimmy glanced and then stopped and stared at the girl. She looked familiar. She looked like his ex-wife. She looked like what his daughter might have looked like if she had ever been healthy.

They were wearing everything they had with them, and the lass was wrinkling up her nose at the smell of the light petroleum distillates used for dry cleaning solution that lingered on her wool clothes. The older Charles McDonald from the Isles took longer, having to repack his bag. When he came through the door, he looked a lot like the two younger folks but was a generation older.

"Let's go," Lyndon said.

Old Charles translated for the young McDonalds, and they followed him as he followed Lyndon out into the cold, leaving Jimmy to bring up the rear.

"Good luck." The bathhouse matron said to his back. Jimmy's only response was an unhappy snort.

Lyndon opened the back door of the squad car. The three McDonalds got into the back seat with the lass in the middle after a few sharp words, from first one Charles and then the other. Lyndon leaned down and asked, "Is there a problem?"

Old Charles looked at Lyndon and shrugged. Then he explained. "Anna was not happy on the riverboat that moved without sail or oars." He glanced at Anna. "We showed her the engine, and when we stopped, we showed her the propeller. But it still seemed like magic, and she was scared. But no one else seemed to care, so she calmed down. She was even more unhappy on the train going so fast. The coach that brought us here from the train dock scared her even more. It moved on its own without horse or oxen. There was nothing pulling it. At least with the train, there was an engine pulling the coaches." His focus returned to Lyndon. "So she didn't want to get in this one. She will be all right. I have assured them that these things are no more magical than a watermill. But it seems like magic. Where there is magic, there are elves, and elves leave changelings in a newborn's crib. She is scared, and she worries. I have told her on the train: the elves will not come for her baby. But still, there were lights in a closed room without flames, and she is wondering again, and the clothes smell odd, and she wonders about that. When she wonders, she worries. It will be all right."

"Yes, Grantville does take some getting used to," Lyndon said closing one door and opening another to get in behind the steering wheel. Anna's trembling hands were clasped tightly in her lap. Her lips moved in a silent prayer. Her husband placed his right hand over hers. Jimmy opened the passenger's side front door.

"Hurry up, Jimmy. It's cold out there." Lyndon told him, and then got underway.

In short order, Jimmy asked, "Why?"

When Lyndon glanced at Jimmy, Lyndon saw he was looking at the speedometer which was reading less than twenty miles an hour. Lyndon tilted his head at the back seat. Jimmy glanced back and noticed that the girl was white as the March Hare's waistcoat. "Oh." Was all Jimmy said!

"Lyndon, can you have the station call McDougal's Restaurant and order a carryout dinner for four?"

"Jimmy, that little lady is scared to death already. If I turn the radio on and a voice starts talking out of thin air, what do you think she will do?"

"Yeah, good point. We can walk down to the Flying Pig for supper, I guess. It ain't but a block and a half."

There were almost no cars in the grocery store parking lot. Even with gas once again at the pumps, it was still expensive. And after sitting unused for years, some tires had gone flat and wouldn't hold air, and there were other problems. So most people took the trolley, and the stores made deliveries if you wanted to call in an order. The store was fairly busy with people stopping on their way home from work. Lyndon ushered them all inside. Anna freaked out at the plate glass windows until she figured out they were just big pieces of glass when Lyndon pushed open the door. But, at least with the windows for natural light, she didn't get upset with the electric lights.

Three of the four checkout lanes were manned. On the wall, off to the left, as they came through the door, someone was behind the bakery and ice cream counter. What produce there was, was on the wall off to the right. Johnson's Grocery had some greenhouse tomatoes and such, but mostly there were root crops. Traditional shelves were on the other side of the cashiers. When you walked past the produce, you came to the butcher's counter, and then the back wall held the bulk food counter.

"Lord," the elder Charles asked Lyndon, "Anna wants to know how you have summer garden harvest for sale if it is not magic."

"Greenhouses," Lyndon replied. And with a look of incomprehension by Charles, Lyndon explained, "Like the front windows, the greenhouses are made of glass so the plants will grow. And they keep them warm through the winter."

Charles nodded and translated. After a brief discussion, he told Lyndon, "Anna says you must be very rich."

Lyndon nodded, "We hear that a lot. Tell Anna she needs to buy everything she needs to fix meals. She will have a complete kitchen but no food."

"We cannot pay for it. When I left the Scotland, I assumed the army would feed me when I got here. And they," he tilted his head at the young couple, "did not think that far ahead. I still don't know what kind of trouble they were in. They were just in a hurry to be someplace else, anyplace else when they fled Ireland."

"Jimmy will cover that until you're on your feet," Lyndon said, looking at the old reprobate and smiling when all Jimmy did was glare and scowl.

"How often is the market day? Anna will need to know how much to get."

"The grocery store is open at least dawn to dark, seven days a week."

"Even Sunday? Doesn't the Church object?" The older Charles asked in surprise.

"Which one?" Lyndon asked. "And even if they all got together and demanded it, they'd have to get the government to agree, and that would take a vote, and they'd most likely lose. The stores can close if they want, and they would if no one came on Sunday, but they have enough customers, so they don't. Which means if the churches did get a proposal on the ballot they'd lose, and they know it."

Anna didn't even look at what was on the shelves, which were dominated by just about anything you could put up in glass jars. Most of them had the dome and wire tops sealed with cork. But there were a few with metal lids. None were from up-time. Up-time jars—up-time almost anything—was worth its weight in gold. She talked with the older Charles, and he asked Jimmy, "Don't you need to go home and get your beer buckets and sacks?"

Lyndon intervened, "He doesn't have any. Just buy what you need to carry home what you're getting."

Jimmy was scowling again. "Jimmy!" Lyndon stared him down.

"They will buy the cans back if they're clean. Same for the glass jars. You wanted a carryout dinner from McDougal's. You'd have paid a deposit on the beer buckets. So what's the difference? Nobody had Styrofoam boxes anymore."

Anna chatted with Old Charles again, and Charles asked, "She wants to know if she can get yeast from a neighbor?"

"Don't count on it," Jimmy said.

"You can buy yeast here." Lyndon volunteered. "It's good now. They've finally worked out the bugs, so you get good yeast every time."

At the checkout, Jimmy said to Lyndon, "It looks like we're buying paint and plaster." The beer cans that the tinkers were turning out looked a lot like paint cans at a glance. There were three five-pound cloth bags: oats, wheat, and rye, along with a pint can of salt, two gallons of beer, one of milk, one of lard, and one can with a one pound block of yeast and another with a pound block of butter. There was a covered wooden box divided into six chambers for an egg each. A paper-wrapped pound of pork, that could have been bacon if it had been smoked, filled out the purchase.

"Yeah," Lyndon agreed. "It does look like paint and plaster doesn't it."

✽ ✽ ✽

THE LEGEND OF JIMMY DICK

Lyndon drove down the alley behind Jimmy's house because he knew the front door was never used. As Jimmy got out of the car, Lyndon asked, "You're going to take care of this? Right?"

Jimmy snarled but nodded.

"Good luck," Lyndon replied. He popped the trunk, Jimmy grabbed two cans and headed for the door. As soon as the groceries were out of the trunk, Lyndon got in and drove off. The McDonalds followed Jimmy up the cleared path. Jimmy glanced back and saw them ogling the house. Jimmy looked at it and at first wondered why, until he remembered where they were from. The house was quite ordinary for the neighborhood. But it was a far cry from what they were used to. It needed to be painted come spring and really should have been painted last spring. The white house with green shutters, built in the late 1800s or early 1900s like the rest of the neighborhood, stood two stories plus the attic over a basement.

Jimmy went through the kitchen door. One of his cans was milk. It went into the frig which was empty except for the bottles of beer in the door. He realized they had been there for years. He never drank at home anymore and hadn't in years.

Anna said something. Her tone of was off. Jimmy turned to the older Charles and demanded. "What did she say?"

At his tone of voice, all three of the McDonalds turned white and became quiet.

"I want to know what she said!"

The older Charles bit his lip. His eyes reminded Jimmy of a treed raccoon.

"Well?"

"My Lord, -hmm- she said, -uhh-"

"Yes?!" the rising note of inflection promised trouble.

It came out in a rush. "She said, your lady wife obviously never comes into the kitchen, or she would beat your servants half to death for letting it get this way."

Jimmy broke out into a laugh that started just north of his belly button and didn't end until he was gasping for breath. The McDonalds did not move so much as to blink. Jimmy caught his breath. He looked at them and started laughing again. "You look like three deer on the road caught in the headlights. Tell Anna that as of now she is the lady of the house for as long as she is here. I have no lady wife. And I have no servants."

"But, sir? She won't believe me. A grand house like this should have at least four or five servants to look after the house and the family."

"No servants, no family. Yes, it's a mess with everything covered in dust. But at least it's neat. I don't do much here but sleep." He opened a closet door. "Broom, dustpan, mop, and bucket." He pointed to the shelf in the broom closet. "Soap." He turned and opened cabinet drawer. "Towels and washcloths." He opened the door under the sink, "Dish soap, dish rack, and drainboard." He pointed to the cabinets either side of the sink. "Glasses, plates." Then he opened a top drawer, "silverware, and utensils. Make yourselves at home."

Older Charles translated as Jimmy went.

Anna spoke again. "She wants to know where your oven is and where do you keep your peat or firewood."

Jimmy went to the stove and turned on a burner. He opened the oven door and pointed at a knob. "Oven."

When Jimmy turned on the burner, Anna gasped and crossed herself.

"Tell her it is not witchcraft," Jimmy told Charles while turning the burner off. "See, turn the knob to the right, and it comes on." He did so. "Turn it to the left, and it goes off."

"Where are your millstones?"

"What?" Jimmy asked

"For grinding the grain she bought to make porridge, and flour for bread."

Jimmy took one of the cloth sacks from the younger Charles. He untied it and dropped a handful in the blender. It made a horrible noise and all three of his guests back away from it. Jimmy turned it off and poured some of it out in his hand. He stepped toward Anna so she could see it. "If you want it finer then leave it in longer."

Anna gasped. Charles translated. Anna spoke, and Charles translated again. "That is perfect for porridge. And you did it so fast."

"Look. Put the meat in the refrigerator and take off your coats if you're staying." With these words, he shrugged out of his sheepskin coat and hung it on one of a half-dozen empty pegs near the door and added his matching hat.

"The house is so warm," Charles said. "Surely you jest about no family and no servants. Surely you do not leave a fire burning when no one is here to tend it."

"The furnace is in the basement. It tends itself."

"Does it work like the stove without peat or wood?"

"Yeah." Jimmy nodded. "It's gas. Now let me show you to your rooms." In the front entryway, he stopped at the thermostat and told Charles, "If you want more or less heat you turn this." Jimmy turned it, and the furnace kicked in. Charles looked impressed. But when the floor grate started blowing hot air, Anna grew wide-eyed and babbled away. Jimmy looked at Charles and raised an eyebrow.

"She wants to know if you keep *sidhe* ah elves under the house, and is the heat vented from hell?"

"I think I'd better show y'all the furnace before we go upstairs." He opened a door, where a second stairway descended under the one going up. At the flick of the light switch Anna jumped and backed up. But her husband held her hand tightly and spoke to her firmly and then almost dragged her down the stairs. An old octopus furnace with a gas conversion add-on dominated the basement. "That's it," Jimmy said. "Open the door," Jimmy pointed, "and you will see the fire."

The older Charles did. And the younger man looked over his shoulder. The older Charles stepped aside so Anna could see. They chatted for a bit. Then Charles told Jimmy, "It's all right. It is not a gate to hell, and there are no elves. She is afraid of changelings."

"That white thing is the hot water heater. And those two are the washer and dryer. But let's not show Anna that yet."

Charles looked at the dust-covered packed back half of the basement. Jimmy answered the unasked question, "All of that junk came with the house. We were going to clean it out but never got around to it."

They went up the grand open stairs. The dark oak banister was a bit battered, having lived through the raising of four children by a previous owner. It matched the rest of the woodwork in the Victorian house. There was a carpet strip up the middle of the stairs with hardwood on each side. It was a green leaf patterned wool carpet that was showing a lot of wear in the middle. It may have been as old as the house.

Upstairs, Jimmy said to the older Charles, "You can throw your bag in here," pointing at the first door on the left. He threw a thumb over his shoulder. That's the door to the attic." As he walked down the hall, he said, "That's my room there." Jimmy pointed at the middle room on the left. They followed him down the hall, and he opened the last door on the left side. The bathroom is there." You could see one end of the claw foot tub and the porcelain pedestal sink that was once white but now had a patina of age. "You've been shown modern plumbing. Right?"

"Yes. The bathhouse. They showed us." Old Charles nodded.

"Good." Jimmy opened a closet door at the end of the hall. It was the only door that did not match the rest. "Towels, sheets, extra blankets, soap is in the tub." From the discoloration of the floor, there used to be a carpet runner down the middle of the hall. He pointed at the single door on the right side of the hall. "They can have the big room."

When he opened the door, and the young couple walked in, she started babbling again and seemed on the edge of hysterics.

"Charley?" Jimmy yelled. "I need some help in here."

The room was as long as the house. At one end there was a modern king sized bed, which was out of keeping with the rest of the furniture. A cedar chest set at the footboard. There were two nightstands at the pillow end. There was a chest of drawers and an old fashion standing wardrobe. There was no built-in closet. Across from the door stood an old-fashioned vanity with a mirror and next to it was an antique wash stand with a full-length mirror. The indoor flush plumbing was a late addition in what was once a fourth bedroom over the kitchen. But the washstand belonged to the last owner's mother and grandmother, who had built the house. And it was still in place. At the other end of the room was a baby's bed, a rocking chair, and a dresser, padded and dressed to use as a changing table. When Jimmy's wife had lived there, they had planned on adding a master bathroom on that end once the baby was in her own room.

Lastly, two overstuffed wing chairs sat at a small fireplace near the door where the chimney rose up from the basement.

Old Charles came in. He listened for a bit and then said, "She wants to know if you mean for them to sleep in this room. She says it's fit for a queen and it's as big as the cottage on the croft she grew up in."

"My room and your room have twin beds," Jimmy said. "So this is it."

He translated and then translated back. "She says such a fine room is for the lord of the manor. They can sleep in the kitchen. They don't need a bed."

"No! This room has the baby's bed, and they will need that by and by. A pregnant woman doesn't need to be sleeping on a cold floor. I'll not have it. Tell them this is their room. Period. They are welcome to anything in the drawers or hanging in the wardrobe. What my ex-wife left when she moved out is still there, which is mostly her maternity clothes. And the two of them are about the same size."

Again they talked. Then Old Charles laughed. Anna looked fierce. Old Charles held up his hand as if in mock fear. "She wants to know if the bedclothes are as stale and musty as the rest of the house and–" Charles laughed again. "And she wants to know if you have a door into summer so the sheets and blankets can be hung on a clothesline so they can be aired out?"

"The sheets on the bed were washed last spring when I had the house cleaned." Someone needed some money, so Jimmy hired the fellow and his wife to clean the house. And it was over two years ago, not last spring. The truth was something that Jimmy considered mutable. "But if she wants a door into summer to air out the sheets, then strip the bed and let's get that done."

Old Charles mouth fell open.

Down in the basement, Jimmy stood in front of the washer and dryer. "A door into summer?" He opened the dryer and threw the sheets in then he hit the start button. "Now let's go find supper at the flying pig. These will be fresh when we return, and we can fluff the blankets when we take out the sheet."

✳ ✳ ✳

The pig' was one of Grantville's several new bars that came into existence after the Ring of Fire. The name was Mrs. Onofrio's idea. When her ex-father-in-law heard she was opening a bar, he was rumored to have said, "That will work–when pigs fly." So that was the name painted on the front window, just to rub the pious fellow's nose in it. There was no love lost between Terry and her children's grandparents on their father's side. With Grantville's boom growth, more people needed more services, and enterprising people provided them. Besides, the up-time bars just did not feel comfortable to most down-timers.

Stephan Wurmbrand, with his wife and two boys, had rented a room from Terry Onofrio early on in that first year, when everyone was scrambling to help house and feed the refugees. When she started talking about finishing off the garage as an apartment, he talked her into letting him open a tavern instead. In short order, she was looking for a better location for her partner's business. She wanted her privacy back. She was tired of people traipsing into the house to use the bathroom. Some of them left a mess. Just closing the business down was out of the question. Stephan's tavern was making way too much money even to think of quitting. They settled on a cinderblock building which had once been a small neighborhood grocery store at the corner of Monroe and Washington. Terry took out a mortgage on her house and then told the people living in the old store to vacate. In the end, they moved into her house and garage because they couldn't find anything else short of splitting the families up and going to the dormitories. But two more families using the bathroom was better than a string of strangers. Wurmbrand ripped the interior walls out, leaving the kitchen and the bathroom at the back of the building. Terry added a bar down one side, and two staggered rows of tables because that's what she thought a bar should look like. And then they took out half of the light bulbs because a bar should be dark.

Stephan ran the bar; his wife ran the kitchen. His boys, ten and twelve-year-olds, bussed table and delivered food, and they hired several barmaids on different shifts to take orders at the tables and deliver drinks. And while they weren't famous like the Thuringian Gardens or infamous like Club 250, the Flying Pig did a steady business between neighborhood customers and a band of ex-mercenaries who use it almost as a clubhouse.

After the first winter, Stephan added a second story over the flat roof of the old block building and moved his family upstairs instead of living in the kitchen and sleeping on the tavern floor after hours.

The three McDonalds and Jimmy took up a table. Melle, the barmaid, approached. "Three beers and a tea," Jimmy said. "Two mugs and one bottle. What's for dinner?" The unspoken understanding was that the bottle would be cold and the mugs room temperature.

"Sauerkraut and sausage," Melle said.

"Four plates," Jimmy said.

When the drinks arrived, Anna demanded to know why she didn't get a beer. Before Charles could translate Melle answered.

"You understand Gaelic," Charles said in English.

"I speak Bretton. My boyfriend speaks Welch. We can understand each other mostly. I don't think I could discuss philosophy even if I were a philosopher like your host. But I understood her. If she didn't understand me, tell her that the up-timers don't think a pregnant woman should drink alcohol. Their physicians claim that too much of it can hurt the baby in her womb."

Charles translated. Anna objected. Melle responded. Jimmy looked puzzled.

"The maid told Anna to forget it. She said there was no way you were going to buy beer for a woman with a baby in her belly." Charles told Jimmy. Melle walked off.

"Damn straight," Jimmy said. "If she doesn't promise to lay off the beer until after the baby comes, I'll see to it that there isn't any in the house. It can really mess a kid up."

Charles translated. The other Charles responded.

"He said to tell you that women drink beer all the time in Ireland, and the babies are fine." The older Charles added, "They do in Scotland too."

"Charley, you tell Chucky that we know better. Enough alcohol can pickle the brain. Surely you've seen enough old drunks to know that. And when the brain is just forming even a little alcohol can shave points off of the baby's IQ."

"What is IQ?"

"Intelligence quotient. It measures how smart a person is."

The McDonalds chatted. Then Charles translated. "She doesn't agree. And drinking water isn't safe."

"Charley, you tell her, that the water here in Grantville is safe, especially the tap water. And you tell her that as long as she's living under my roof, she will live by my rules." Jimmy stopped and smiled a big shit-eating grin of a smile. "G-d, I've dreamed of saying that for years. If she don't like it, that's too bad. But those are the house rules, and she will abide by them. You got that Charley?"

"Yes, Lord Jimmy."

While the McDonalds were chatting, Melle came back with the dinner plates. She said to Jimmy, "Your young friend is not happy about it. Her father told her 'too bad.' He's telling her that it looks like the people here have some strange superstitions, which is true. You do. But, he told her she is just going to have to put up with it."

Melle said something. Anna looked at her, and Melle nodded and said something else. "I told her you were right. The water is safe to drink, and you really do believe alcohol is bad for the baby."

When Jimmy headed downstairs the next morning, a bit before ten o'clock, he could tell while he was still on the stairs that it was a dreary day outside. The stained glass window over the front door in the formal entryway was dull. On a sunny day, the round window with the white dove splashed colored light all over the stairs in the morning. The light came nearly to the top of the stairs at sunrise. It illuminated ever fewer steps as the morning grew older. Then it disappeared around noon when the sun was overhead. The wind chime on the front porch was banging like it was a full orchestra, so he knew it was not just gloomy, but blowing to beat the band.

In the kitchen, Anna had a counter full of dishes out of the cabinet. She was washing them and putting them back. But at the moment she was up standing on a chair washing out the plate shelves. The kitchen smell like baking bread. When she saw Jimmy, she got down and asked, "Break-fast?"

Jimmy smiled at her charming accent. "I never eat in the morning."

"Break-fast." She pointed to a saucepan on the stove and grabbed a bowl and spoon.

Jimmy walked over and lifted the lid while she snatched up a ladle, and waited patiently for him to step aside. It looked like cream of wheat or grits. He put the lid back down. "No thanks. I never eat before lunch."

"Break-fast?" were the only words he understood, and she had a mouthful.

"No."

"Break-fast?"

"No!" Jimmy shook his head.

THE LEGEND OF JIMMY DICK

Anna, having exhausted her ready English vocabulary on the topic again said something Jimmy did not understand.

"Where's Charlie?"

"Charles lookingwork."

"Charles is looking for work?" The tone and inflection made it a question.

Anna screwed up her face in concentration and carefully repeated herself and then pronounced it as close to Jimmy's way as she could manage.

"Good," Jimmy said.

She repeated, "Charles is looking for work."

"You don't understand a word I am saying do you?"

"Break-fast?"

Jimmy shook his head as put on his coat. Outside, he went out to the garage and got a kitchen step ladder made for reaching the high cabinets safely. He brought it back, set it up, and put the chair back at the table. "See ya later."

Anna stared at him. So he waved bye-bye. She waved back.

By Terry Howard

THE LEGEND OF JIMMY DICK

TRANSFERENCE

Jimmy pushed open the green door to Club 250 without really noting the sign that read no Germans and no Dogs. Little had changed inside since before the Ring of Fire. True, the beer was different for a while, but Ken, the owner, and the chief bartender had finally found someone who could and would brew and bottle something close to what they were used to. The buns on the hamburgers were better as long as they were fresh. And they went stale fast. The bar offered pipes and some rather harsh tobacco if you wanted to smoke. But the oaken tables and chairs were still there, in two staggered rows of five and four.

The bar and back-bar were genuine mahogany, as were the barstools, and came out of a tavern in the next county over, back up-time, that closed after being in business for the better part of a hundred years. The back bar had three rows of mirrors framed by wood with newer glass shelves holding a dwindling number of bottles of the ever-more-expensive odd stuff that people bought from time to time. The house whiskey was moonshine, now. It was raw and unaged. What little up-time whiskey was still on the shelf went for a hefty premium. The metal tray ceiling, like the brass cash register, came out of the same tavern as the bar.

Off to the right of the bar as you came through the front door was the door to the kitchen, and then next to it, the door to the bathrooms. That end of the tavern held the pool table and the jukebox. The only thing that had changed was the addition of a new line of pegs to hold coats, to the left of the front door. With the colder weather, people were wearing heavier coats, and everybody was walking more. The old pegs to the right of the door were no longer sufficient to the task.

By Terry Howard

Jimmy hung up his coat and hat on what he considered to be his peg on the end, near one of the beer posters of scantily-clad, well-endowed models. As always, he looked at the picture.

"How did you come out with the cops?" Someone asked from farther down the bar, as Ken, the barkeeper, popped the cap off of a beer for the man who used to be his first customer of the day almost every day of the week.

"It seems some McDonalds showed up looking to join the conquest of a McDonald kingdom. The cops asked me to put them up until they can save up enough money to go back where they came from."

"You told them where they could stick it didn't you?"

"It's kind of hard to tell the chief of police where to shove it, especially after they point out that these people were practically here by my invitation. The two guys are out looking for work. And the woman is home cleaning my house."

Ken snickered, "What's it been? Ten years?"

Jimmy scowled. "I had it cleaned just last fall."

"That Kraut and his wife?" The scorn was plain in Ken's voice.

"They couldn't pay their rent, so I let them work it off," Jimmy said a bit guiltily.

Ken raised an eyebrow. "Last fall?"

"Well, the fall before that anyway."

"If she's cleaning your house, she'll probably wear out your vacuum sweeper."

"I didn't show her the vacuum. She's afraid of the light switches. She thinks they're magic. I had to show her the fire in the furnace before she decided the heat wasn't coming from hell."

"So you need to get those Scottish monks to go talk with her, especially if you're keeping them for any length of time."

"Ken, that's a first-rate idea," Jimmy said, taking the first sip out of the bottle. "Or I need to get that barmaid from the Flying Pig, since they seem to understand each other."

✽ ✽ ✽

THE LEGEND OF JIMMY DICK

For the first time in his life, Jimmy came home at the end of the night and tried to be quiet as he went to bed. Before his wife left him, he never stayed out until closing time. After that, there was no one in the house to be quiet for.

In the morning, Charles and Charles were eating bread and porridge at the kitchen table while Anna sat and watched with a glass of milk in front of her. When Jimmy walked in, she hopped up and filled a bowl from the pot on the stove. Then she put it in front of the last chair.

"Lord Jimmy, good morning," the older Charles said. "Anna said you left yesterday without eating."

"I haven't eaten breakfast in years," Jimmy replied. "How is the job hunt going?"

"We went to work yesterday; we are working third shift making what goes in the hats for guns. We just got back a bit ago."

Jimmy turned pale. "You mean caps?"

"Yes."

"You are making mercury fulminate? That is dangerous work."

Charles shrugged. "But it pays well. The coal mine pays better. But, we need to save up the money to buy boots with steel toes and helmets with lights."

"You go back to the hiring agency and get signed up for the mine. I'll cover the steel-toed boots, and I think I saw some old carbide lamps in the basement. If there aren't, I'll cover those too. The mine is dangerous, but they do their best to keep it safe. You can't say that about the fellows running the business you worked for last night." Jimmy glanced at Anna. "I don't want to see her a widow before she's twenty."

"But we owe you too much already." He waved a hand at the food on the table and glanced at the ceiling to where the bedrooms were. "We were told what it cost to rent a room in Grantville."

"You can't pay me back if you end up in an explosion. Did they tell you how often that happened?"

Charles looked pained and nodded. The young couple, who did not have any English that they had not just learned, did not follow the conversation.

"At least they told you," Jimmy said. "Look, Charley, you just called me lord. Well, my understanding is that part of that job is taking care of your people and keeping the land in production. I don't want to see you fellows working for those idiots making caps or reloading shells. And working third shift is the most dangerous shift of the day. We're not meant to work all night. The mine is only running one shift now.

"You two finish up while I go rummage around in the basement. Then we'll go get you signed up for the mine and get what you need to start." He never even sat down.

When Jimmy came up and into the kitchen, he had a dusty mining helmet. "The fellow who left me this house never threw anything away." He turned it over in his hands and looked inside. "The leather head band's brittle. But we can get that reworked. But I think we'll go sell this to a curios shop and buy new ones from the tinker and probably pay for the steel toes out of the same money. That way you'll know it didn't cost me anything. I always planned on just throwing everything out down there but just never got around to it."

Anna was washing dishes in the sink. One bowl of porridge was still on the table with the bread and butter and a glass of warm, flat, beer. "It's a nice day out. The sun has to be shining because the sunshine has the stairs all lit up, and the wind chime is quiet."

Charles interrupted. "The stained glass over the front door is like a church. You are very rich."

Jimmy snorted. "I guess I am by most standards these days. But I never thought I was, at least not before we came here. As I was saying, it's nice out today. Ask Anna if she wants to come. We'll stop at the grocery store on the way back. You need a better diet than bread and cream-of-wheat."

"Anna said she's happy you have a cathedral window in the house. There is no way the *sidhe* can possibly trouble a baby in a house protected by a church window no matter how much magic there is in town. She said it is like the story of John the Baptist baptizing Jesus when the dove came down. Every time the sun comes up the Holy Spirit blesses the house."

"Well, whatever you do, don't tell her differently."

* * *

THE LEGEND OF JIMMY DICK

When the younger Charles took off his shoes, the young clerk in the shoe store crinkled up his face. The man's socks were worn out and dirty.

"Let's start with clean socks, then get his size, okay?" Jimmy said.

The red-headed boy, well, strawberry blond might come closer, smiled. "Certainly, Herr Shaver." When he nodded, his payois bounced.

Jimmy looked at the older Charles. "Do you need socks too?"

Charles answered, "If you need clean socks to measure for making new boots, then yes. I have two more pairs at your house. But they're dirty."

"When we get home remind me to tell you about the washing machine." Jimmy called after the clerk, "Bring a half dozen pair of socks."

The shop's last business up-time had been a shoe store. The last owner's heirs had sold it stock and all, cheap, not wanting to fuss with the out-of-date inventory. Everything got moved to the attic, but the ground floor set empty until the Ring of Fire. The shop held refugees briefly but without a kitchen, that didn't work out too well, and it was amongst the first sites to be emptied out. Jimmy donated the shoes on hand to the relief effort right after the Ring of Fire. A tailor shop opened up for a while. But the rents got too high, and he moved in with someone else.

Now that there were shoe mills in Magdeburg, someone decided to open a retail shop in competition with the cobblers. They moved the furniture back down. And, except for the lack of cardboard shoe boxes; the store looked very much like it had in the 1960s when the last owner had remodeled for the last time. The one really odd item in the attic was an x-ray machine from the 1950s. You stuck your toes in the machine and looked at the screen to see whether your bones were squashed up or not. They quit using them when people started getting radiation burns. The machine had been up there, completely forgotten, for decades. When the hospital found out about it, they went apeshit.

"We need steel-toed boots for Charley and Chucky." Jimmy glanced at Anna's feet and told the clerk, "Then, show us what you've got in her size."

Both fellows were in a common size range, so work boots were not a problem. When the clerk put the Brannock device for measuring shoe size on the floor in front of Anna, she shook her head and said something.

The older Charles translated. "She says she doesn't need new shoes."

"Tell her that her shoes are worn out and that I insist. She's the lady of the house for as long as you stay, and I will not have her getting wet feet when she goes out."

"She says her shoes can be repaired."

"Yes, but she needs something to wear while her old shoes are at the cobblers." Jimmy looked at the clerk, "Bring three pairs of socks in her size."

Old Charles and Anna talked for a bit. Young Charles chipped in. Then old Charles said, "She says she can go barefooted while her husband fixes her shoes. And he says they should wait to buy her new shoes until she needs them."

"Tell him that as lord of the house I won't have it. And we're getting her a new coat while we're out, too." Jimmy smiled. "My house, my rules."

After a confab, old Charles said, "They'll give in on the shoes. But there is a good winter coat In the wardrobe."

"Well, why ain't she wearing it? I told her to use anything she found."

"She thought it was too good for her."

"Nonsense. You tell her that everything up there is second hand and I should have already thrown it out. I don't want to see her in rags ever again. You got that?"

"Yes, my lord."

When the clerk had her shoe size, he asked, "What shoes would she like to try on?"

Charles translated, and Anna pointed at the steel toed work boots.

The clerk smiled. "We do have a pair in her size. My uncle is going to be tickled pink to have them sold. He was sure no one would ever want them."

"That's okay," Jimmy said. "But bring a pair of penny loafers in her size, too. Those boots are too heavy to wear around the house."

When she figured out that Jimmy was buying her two pairs of shoes she started babbling away, shaking her head firmly.

Charley translated, and Jimmy smirked. "Tell her it's just too bad. My house, my rules. She can leave anytime she wants."

At the grocery store, Jimmy bought a roast for dinner along with potatoes, carrots, onions and a half pint of pepper. Anna bought some collard greens. At the bulk food section, he bought three kinds of herbal teas and a pound of sugar, along with another gallon of milk and a gallon of fresh apple juice. Then, on the way to the checkout, he grabbed a wooden six-pack of bottled root beer. He didn't want Anna to have any excuse for drinking beer.

On the trolley, Jimmy told Charles, "When we get home, we'll go up to the attic and see what we can find in the way of men's clothing. If you guys are going to work in the mine, you are going to need a change of clothes or two."

* * *

"Hey, Jimmy? Where ya going?" Bubba asked as Jimmy put his coat on around five o'clock, well before closing time.

Jimmy turned red as a beet. "Home to dinner."

When he was gone, Bubba turned to Ken. "What's that about? It's as bad as the time he took to staying in the library all day studying philosophy. I just got here, he bought me one beer, and now he's gone. Who's gonna buy the beers?"

"Sucks to be broke, Bubba," Ken replied.

"I'm serious Ken. What's goin' on with Jimmy?"

"Jimmy's in love, Bubba."

"Hun?" The pudgy fellow said.

"Yep." The bartender answered. "I got it from my wife. Someone down at Johnson's Grocery was getting her hair done and told Kim, the Scottish girl. Anna is a skinny little-redheaded thing that looks a lot like Jimmy's wife Bina looked when they got married. Kim says it's transference."

"Huh? What's that?" Bubba asked.

"One of those fancy words Kim got when she went to reading psychology books when our teenagers started acting out so bad. In the back of Jimmy's mind, he's getting mixed up on who Bina was and who

Anna is. She looks about Bina's age when they got married. She's wearing Bina's clothes. She's sleeping in Bina's bed. She's keeping Bina's house and cooking in Bina's kitchen. And she's got a bun in the oven just like Bina did for most of the year she lived with Jimmy after he came back from Nam and they got married. When she took their daughter and left him, he went to pieces. Now in the back of his mind, she's back. Or maybe she's his daughter that he never got to raise."

"That sounds messed up."

"Yeah," was all Ken had to say about it. "Another beer, Bubba?"

"No. You're right. I'm broke. I was counting on hanging out with Jimmy."

BOWLING GREENS AREN'T JUST IN OHIO ANY MORE

On a Saturday, Jimmy took his new roommates, Charles and Charles McDonald, to the barbershop. With Charlie and Chucky working in the coal mine they didn't need the bother of unruly hair under a miner's helmet. Anna, Chucky's wife, said she could cut their hair.

"Lord Jimmy, you do not need to be spending money going to a barber. They do not need to be bled. I can cut hair."

"Anna, going to the barbershop is a social thing like going to a bar. You hang out with the guys and chew the fat. You'll have to get Melle to take you to the beauty parlor. Tell her to make the appointment, and I'll pay for you both. Ken Beasley's wife, Kim, runs it out of the front room of their house. You need to start getting acquainted here in town."

The padded waiting chairs were all full. The folding chairs set up in front of the large picture window had room for two of them.

"Sit," Jimmy told Charles and Charles.

"But Lord Jimmy, it should be the one of us who stands." The older Charles said.

At the words 'Lord Jimmy' the shop kerfuffled with chuckles and snickers. Jimmy blushed. He was trying to get them not to do it. But it was not working.

"Charlie, I said, sit!"

By Terry Howard

"But, Lord Jimmy,–" At the look on Jimmy's face Charles sat down, and a with few words of Gaelic and a glance at Jimmy's continence, the younger Charles did too. But someone got up from the barber's chair, and the next fellow stood up from one of the regular chairs, so Jimmy had a place to sit down.

"I don't know, John." Walt was saying to the man in his son's barber chair. "You're talking about tying up a lot of money. You need pin setting machines for a bowling alley."

"Nope, before there were machines there was a pit behind the pins. After the ball stopped, someone hopped down in the pit and returned the ball and set the pins. There's plenty of school kids looking for part-time work."

"Okay, I hadn't thought of that. That will work. But you still need a big building. You need enough lanes to make it worthwhile. Where are you going to put a building that size?" Walt asked.

John Samuels, who was sitting in the second barber's chair having his hair cut by Walt's son, said, "Up on the ridge, just past Birdie's farm, near the Holiday Lodge. The trolley goes all the way to the village. Besides, if you build an upscale bowling alley, it wouldn't have to be that big. Then when the Lodge's bowling green is closed, you can pick up the business from the tourists."

"Going for the high-end trade with a bowling alley won't work." Jimmy offer his unsolicited opinion.

"Why not?" John demanded. "King Charles is an avid bowler. Luther bowled."

Jimmy spoke up. "Two different games, John. If you're counting on high-end trade to make a go of it, you'll go bust. Bowling on the green is all balls. Not a man alive who don't like to play with balls. But a bowling alley is all about knocking down pins. So back up-time, bowling was the sport of the masses. You didn't see any management types, and you sure didn't see any upper management types hanging out in bowling alleys."

"Yeah," John said. "But that was then. This is now. If it's from up-time, they'll come, and they'll pay if it's nice with good service. And you make your real money off of drinks and food."

"Nope. Didn't work that way up-time. And won't now. If you want upscale business open a billiards parlor, not a pool hall, but a billiards parlor. Pool and billiards are two very different games, like lawn bowling and bowling alleys."

"Well, mister philosopher?" John asked with a slight touch of ridicule to his voice, "Why wouldn't bowling catch on with the upper-class tourist? They don't know the difference."

"John, you'd have to change the game. The upscale tourists who stay at the lodge are mostly nobles or rich merchants. Either way, they're management types. And they just aren't going to get into bowling."

"Why not?"

"Can you see them, in their fancy clothes, hanging out in alleys and trying to stay out of the gutter?" There were snickers from the peanut gallery. "But mostly the game is about knocking down as many pins as possible. And there is no way a management type, here and now or anywhere else, will ever see a strike as a good thing."

The shop roared with laughter.

When the laughter dwindled, John said, "Seriously, Jimmy, do you think it's a bad idea or not?"

"John, if you do it, design the building to cover your ass. Either build it with a second story or to hold a second story, and lay your drain pipes under the slab you pour to put your lanes on so you can repurpose the building without tearing the floor up. You do that, and I'll go in for ten percent or more if I like the building plans. Or better still, figure out how big you want it and let me build the building and lease you the floor space."

"Then if you're my landlord can I call you Lord Jimmy?"

"Sure." Jimmy paused for a beat and a half. After all, timing is everything, "And if you do, I'll raise the rent."

Once again, the philosopher got the laugh he was looking for. You see, Jimmy had figured out that a philosopher and a comedian had a lot in common.

By Terry Howard

DREAMS

May 1635

Jimmy woke up in a cold sweat. The dream was back. Not the one where the North Vietnamese Regulars were charging the perimeter out of the jungle and the fallback position around the command post had already been overrun. And not the one where they were patrolling through a village and the sergeant shot the five-year-old little girl holding a bunch of flowers ten feet short of her handing them to him, just seconds before she blew up. And not the one where he came home to look in every room of the house over and over again only to find that his wife and daughter were not there. This was the July nightmare.

Jimmy's daughter Merle was born in July . . It was a hot and muggy night. The windows were open, hoping for a breeze. The curtains were tied back and still as a painting of a fruit bowl. Bina was a month short of her due date, and in the middle of the night she woke him with a blood curdling, half-strangled scream that had him running for the bunker. At the bedroom door, he came to himself and stopped. Then Bina screamed again, "Damn it, Jimmy, call an ambulance." The bed was soaked in blood. The dream came at least three times every July since.

Jimmy lay there wondering why the July dream was coming in May when he heard the same scream again. Out in the hall, the concerned looking elder Charles was standing talking quietly with the younger Charles outside of the couple's bedroom. He told Jimmy, "She's been having mild contractions at least every hour or so all night. They've been getting worse and more frequent. Her water just broke. It's time. We need the midwife."

A blurry-eyed Jimmy Dick nodded to acknowledge his understanding. The older Charles followed Jimmy as he made his way down to the kitchen to the phone which he had recently had turned back on after two decades of being out of service. Jimmy called the police station. "This is Jimmy Dick Shaver on Franklin Street. We need a ride to the hospital." Jimmy looked at Charley who was putting the tea kettle on the stove to boil, and smiled. "No. We don't need an ambulance. A squad car will do. Anna's having her baby."

Anna waddled into the kitchen followed by the younger Charles, who had her hospital bag in hand. The elder Charles was pouring raspberry-mint tea into cups. It was Anna's favorite. Jimmy preferred coffee and the two clansmen preferred chamomile. But today it was all about Anna.

Jimmy hopped up and pulled a chair out for her. The elder Charles put the teacup in front of her and put the sugar bowl on the table. Anna liked it best with sugar but usually drank it unsweetened. Anna frowned. "Charley, you know how much sugar costs."

"Anna, today is special. You will need your strength. Besides, Jimmy can afford it." Charles chuckled. It was almost a running joke. Jimmy spent money way too freely in Anna's opinion. Whenever he went to the grocery store, he brought home generous portions instead of the frugal amounts she would have bought. And he usually had something in the way of a treat. She would always chide him for being wasteful, and he would always answer, "I can afford it."

When the squad car stopped in the alley behind the house, Hans flicked its roof lights on and off, but not the siren. The very first faint line of false dawn was showing on the horizon, and most people were still asleep.

Anna gulped down the last of her tea. Her husband held her coat for her and then donned his own. The elder Charles was already heading for the back gate with Anna's suitcase. Anna held tightly to the handrail and her husband as she negotiated the back steps.

Jimmy brought up the rear. As the younger Charles opened the back door of the squad car, Jimmy called out, "Chucky, put her in the front seat for crying out loud. It's easier to get in and out of."

"But, Lord Jimmy, that's your place."

"Not today it ain't."

The older Charles put the suitcase in the trunk, and Hans closed it.

At the hospital, the wheelchairs had caned seats and backs. The hubs, axles, and front casters were iron, but the rest of the chair was wood with leather over the iron tire that held the wooden spokes and fellies in place. They checked Anna in, and the younger Charles wheeled her to the midwife's room. Jimmy and the older Charles ended up in the waiting area.

At first glance, it looked like an up-time waiting room. When you sat down, you might notice that the cushions were real leather stuffed with horsehair. The chair legs were wooden as was the coffee table. The reading materials were all newly printed. Luther's Bible and a Catholic approved German translation along with an up-time printing of the King James and a Latin Bible were setting on the coffee table. Bilingual newspapers and German magazine or quarterlies, along with a wide variety of pamphlets, were in a wall rack. A samovar of herbal tea and a stack of clean cups on a table along a wall rounded out the white painted room's furniture.

"Now we wait," Jimmy said.

"I should go to work," Charles said.

"Naw. But call in and tell them you and Chucky won't be in today. They will understand. You're family, and you might need to translate."

"No, they're picking it up fast. His English is good. And with Melle coaching her and teaching her to read, hers is better than his."

Jimmy chuckled.

✻ ✻ ✻

Anna had shown Melle their room and the clothes in the wardrobe that Jimmy told her to use. Then Melle told Anna just how much Jimmy could get for the rent on a room like that. And it was more than her husband made in a month. It would take a visiting noble or a very rich merchant to afford the rent. Melle looked at the baby supplies Jimmy had bought or scrounged. "And it looks like he's planning on you staying right here even after the baby comes."

"But why?" Anna asked. "We aren't even his clan, much less his family?"

"Anna," Melle answered, "you are just going to have to accept that these up-timers are strange and have a lot of strange ideas. My boyfriend is a painter. His boss treats him almost like family. He has practically adopted him. It looks like Jimmy Dick has done the same thing in your case."

"But what does he want?"

The red-headed waitress shrugged. "I told you, they are strange."

"Melle, that's a lot of money."

"Anna, he owns half of downtown. I don't think you realize how rich he is. I don't think he realizes just how rich he is. He sure does not live like it. He could sell the clothes he told you to wear and pay the rent you are not paying for a year. Just accept it." She pointed at the bilingual Doctor Suisse books with the dialog page divided into quarters. Half the page was English over a word for word translation to German, and the other half of the page reversed the order. The second page in every fold held the very familiar pictures. Every one that was available in town was on the bookshelf. "Those aren't cheap. And if he wasn't planning on you staying why would he buy them? He is going to expect you to read them to the baby."

"Melle. I can't read. I don't know German or English."

"Well, then, it is high time you learned all three. You don't want to disappoint your landlord that's for sure."

✻ ✻ ✻

"Yeah, with Melle's help she's memorized Doctor Seuss. And it's affecting her English. She's rhyming everything. It's kind of cute. But don't worry about going to work. Just go find a phone and call in. Now that I think about it, let's go find the cafeteria. You need breakfast, and I need a cup of coffee. Then we will find a phone."

✻ ✻ ✻

THE LEGEND OF JIMMY DICK

The cafeteria had between thirty and forty chairs. It had a separate outside entrance. It was open twenty-four hours a day. The help-yourself soups and day-old bread were free. Starvation breeds illness as does uncleanliness. So the hospital had a delousing station which doubled as a public bathhouse. And the cafeteria doubled as a warming center/soup kitchen. The hospital saw it as their job to keep the community healthy while hopefully making enough money to break even.

Charles started to get a bowl of free soup. "Charley, let's go through the line and get breakfast," Jimmy said.

"But, Lord Jimmy, the soup is free."

"But the beer isn't. And I want a cold one. But I don't like to drink alone."

"Get me a beer to go with the soup. They do have good beer here, don't they?" By that, Jimmy knew the man meant room temperature draft beer. Charles thought chilling it ruined the taste.

As Jimmy left the cash register, two men in knee-length white coats came in through the inside entrance from the hospital chatting away in Alemannic, an obscure dialect of German.

"That is the man you said you wanted to meet," the young man who looked to be early- to mid-twenties said to his gray-haired companion.

The old man, with half raised eyebrows, raised both hand palms up in front of his breasts with a slight shrug to his shoulders. By which he asked, who, or what, or why?

"You said you were interested in meeting the philosopher Herr Shaver."

"Yes. I very much wish to talk to him."

The younger man nodded and then approached Jimmy, "Herr Shaver?" His English was good, but the accent was a bit thick.

"Yes?"

"Herr Shaver, I am Hans Wyss. I am a student at the University of Jena. My uncle, Doctor Wyss from Schaufhausen, is here observing up-time medical practices. He has read of you in the Berlin Philosophical Journal and would very much like to make your acquaintance. Would you join us." No one in Grantville ever knew that the elder doctor Wyss had no brothers or sister with children.

Jimmy took a long sip of beer from his bottle and then gestured with the full mug at the table where Charles was sitting. "I already have a table."

"Well, then may we join you?"

"We're waiting for our roommate to pop a bun out of the oven. So, we will be here awhile." He took another swig. "So, if you want to buy the beers, well, I make it practice to never turn down free beer."

Hans glanced at the kitchen, and Jimmy chuckled. "It means she's in labor."

Hans translated for his uncle and then asked, "Uncle wishes to know if, in your up-time English, you often refer to children as buns?"

"Only when they're in the oven. Normally we call them kids. *We call them young goats,*" Jimmy added in Latin.

Doctor Wyss smiled and answered in Latin, "I am glad that you have Latin. I was under the impression that you disdained it."

Jimmy looked puzzled, and Hans translated his uncle's words.

"I am afraid my Latin is not good enough to handle your uncle's accent." By this time, they were at the table. Charles stood at their approach.

"Charley, shake hands with Doctor Wyss and his uncle, Doctor Wyss. They want to talk about philosophy." Jimmy sat down. "Doctors Wyss, this is my other roommate, Charles McDonald. He's from the old McDonalds from the Iles."

Hans asked second hand, "And you are waiting for another roommate to deliver a child?"

"Yeah."

Hans listened to his uncle and then said, "Is it true as reported that you once said war is neither mankind's greatest glory nor our greatest disgrace."

"Well, that Kraut from Berlin got that much right at least. Most of what he has said since is hogwash."

"And did you also say that a man's greatest glory was to love his wife and raise his children well?"

"Yeah. He got that right, too."

"So, this roommate?" Hans asked. "Roommate is room and mate. Mate can be wife?"

Charles worked very hard to swallow his laughter. Jimmy turned as red as an Indian.

"The young woman is upstairs with her husband," Jimmy said quietly.

Hans listened and then said, "As a roommate, then do you take responsibility for raising the child well?"

Jimmy renewed his blush. "Raising the child is the responsibility of the mother and the father. The two of them are young enough to be my kids. But as long as they live in my house I will have some say in the matter. Until they move out, I will do my best to see to it."

Hans listened and said, "My uncle says he will have to return in a decade or two to see how things work out. And he is interested in what the journals had to say about the mass slaughter of Jews that happened in your up-time history."

The beers kept coming, and Jimmy answered questions for the next three hours. A young nurse's aide approached the table to say, "Excuse me, but you are wanted upstairs. We are having some trouble. Your people don't have a lot of English. There is some disagreement about what they can name the baby girl."

"Shit? It's over?" Jimmy said while standing. He left without a word, polite or otherwise, to his guest. Old Charles was already halfway to the door.

It would later be reported that he left a full bottle of beer on the table. This report is malicious slander and not at all accurate. Jimmy's bottle was only half full. It was Charles who left a full beer behind. Doctor and Doctor Wyss followed at a slightly more sedate pace. When they got to the midwife's room, the elder Charles had all the details and was turning to explain the problem to Jimmy Dick.

"Lord Jimmy, the problem is simple. Apparently, there is some legal or customary reason why the name they wish to give the child is meeting with some resistance from," he tilted his head at the midwife in the starched white nurses uniform, "her."

"Herr Shaver, I tried to explain why it is not right, but they do not understand." She put her hands on her hips and huffed. "Or they simply are refusing to understand."

"If it was a boy they had decided to name it Jimmy Dick Shaver. So, they want to name the girl Jamey Charlotte Shaver." The older Charles informed Jimmy.

Jimmy was quiet for almost thirty seconds. Which is an eternity in the middle of a conversation. At last, he spoke in a hushed voice. "Anna, Chuck, I'm flattered. I really am. But the midwife is right. It is contrary to how things are done here. The child should be named McDonald."

The younger Charles said something that hardly anyone understood. The elder Charles nodded and answered in kind. Then he said to Jimmy, "McDonald is the name of the clan. It is not the name of everyone in the clan. You are war leader of the Clan McDonald here in Grantville."

Jimmy started to interrupt but held his peace while Charles continued to talk. "You are a member of Clan McDonald even though your name is Shaver. They should have talked to you first and asked if they could be part of your sept. But, they didn't think they had to. The way you treat us, not charging rent, buying extravagant foods for our meals, buying us boots and giving us clothes, and buying expensive books and things for the child: to their mind they are part of your household. You let us call you Lord Jimmy–"

Jimmy muttered loudly, "I knew I should have put a stop to that."

"–so the child is born in your household, and they thought it proper to give it the name of the local sept of Clan McDonald for which it is now part. They meant no disrespect." Charles had been to the library and spent some time reading things of interest to him. He had picked up some odd ideas that he shared with his compatriots.

"The child should be named after a saint." The Midwife insisted in very good West Virginian English.

Anna understood the woman and said something. Old Charles nodded and translated. "Anna said that Lord Jimmy is a living saint."

Jimmy blushed. The midwife snorted. The elder Doctor Wyss drew his eyebrows down and together while puckering his lips. The three McDonalds stood there straight-faced.

"Charles, very few people know what a sept is. Shoot, if they ever saw it they probably thought it was an abbreviation for September. The custom is to give the child the father's family name."

"But Lord Jimmy, that has changed throughout history. Young Charles is a McDonald of Sept Macbeth that became Sept Leitch, that changed again in Ireland though they have not used that name or told me what it is. They see no reason not to change names again since they have moved to a new country. I read that in your history, it happened sometimes."

"Usually when the people changing their names were running away from something," Jimmy said.

The three McDonalds became very still and very quiet.

"Look, how about we give the kid the last name of McDonald since that is the name Chucky has been using here. I'll give you the name Jamey, and I'll acknowledge that she is part of my household she can stay in my house as long as she wants, as long as I have a house. Shoot, I'll go down and get the lawyer to make me a will, and she can have the house when I'm gone if she wants it. Everybody else in the family has been ticked off at me for years anyway, since I got all the downtown property, and they thought they were going to get part of it. But let's keep," Jimmy glanced at the midwife, "the old biddy happy and give her a saint's name after her mother and put the name Jamey Ann McDonald on the birth certificate."

The three McDonalds babbled away amongst themselves. The midwife did not wait for an answer. She wrote down the name as announced by Jimmy. The elder Doctor Wyss spoke in their weird German to his bastard son and said that he would be interested in keeping track of what becomes of little Miss McDonald. And wasn't Macbeth the name of a Scottish King in a Shakespeare play?

※ ※ ※

The next quarterly issue of the Berlin Philosophical Journal included a letter from Doctor Wyss in its section set aside for correspondence. The letter informed the world that James Richard Shaver, and Grantville for that matter, did not disdain Latin as previously reported. "Latin is commonly used amongst the medical practitioners in Town. But, that while Herr Shaver can surely read it and write it, like so many others his accent is atrocious and he has trouble understanding other accents when it is spoken." The letter went on to say: "If you converse with Herr Shaver in his own English, you will find that the man has a firm grasp of traditional philosophical ideas. He seems particularly fond of the classical Greeks and early church fathers -

- while he does have some wild-eyed radical ideas about social order —

- preponderance for quoting men who have yet to be born-

- it is surprising to note that he is the war leader for the local Clan McDonald –

- what is most notable is that he takes his personal philosophy on the importance of cherishing children very seriously –"

A PRODIGAL'S SON.

Officer Lyndon Johnson walked through the green front door of Club 250 in the middle of the lunch rush. The bar was not half as full as it used to be. More and more people were leaving town, joining the military, or drinking elsewhere with coworkers who weren't welcome in the club, especially younger men or boys who were coming of age. It was late May in 1635. Lyndon was still wearing his military-style greatcoat, but it was not buttoned up, and his head and hands were bare.

"Lyndon," Ken called out cheerfully from behind the bar when one of his favorite young men came in, "What's up?"

"We need Jimmy Dick down at the hospital," the young police officer answered the older bartender and owner of the bar.

Jimmy looked up and into the mahogany framed mirror behind the bar. He turned to face Lyndon. His face was full of concern. "What's wrong? Who's hurt? Was there a problem at the mine?" Two of his roommates worked the coal.

"No. Everything is fine. Well, here at least." Lyndon replied. "But, they've got that kid that Hans pick up on the road into town the other day while he was coming back from checking out a complaint. And I mean literally on the road. Hans first radioed that he had a dead man in the road. Then he said the man was still breathing and he was taking him to the hospital. Let's go," Lyndon said to Jimmy.

"Why me?" Jimmy asked.

"Because," Lyndon replied, "he's one of yours."

"Shit!" Jimmy said. He turned his beer bottle to the antique metal tray ceiling and chugged until it was empty, before sliding off the bar stool and heading for his coat hanging on a wall peg.

"What makes him mine?" Jimmy asked.

By Terry Howard

Lyndon sighed as he held the door for the semi-reformed reprobate. "When Hans got him to the hospital he was out of it. Hans says he didn't weigh more than a hundred pounds, that he looked about twelve years old, and that he was barefoot and dressed in rags that barely covered his body. And other than a wheel lock pistol and a big knife, he didn't have a thing with him. He was suffering from exposure, starvation, dehydration, and a high fever. And if they'd been busy enough to triage, they would have let him die. But things were slow, so they got a feeding tube down him and gave him something for the fever, got him cleaned up, and into a warm bed. That was three days ago. He's finally started coming to. He hasn't said much, but he says he's a McDonald, and he wanted to know if he was in time for the invasion."

"Shit," Jimmy said getting into the panda bear. The Grantville police still had two black and white cruisers left from before the Ring of Fire. "We sent out letters to everywhere we could think of telling everyone not to come."

"Well, it seems this kid didn't read his mail," Lyndon said, turning the key in the ignition. "How's things working out with the new baby in the house?" he asked, changing the topic.

"Jamey Ann is a little princess." Jimmy's toothy smile lit up his face like a proud grandpa. "She hardly ever cries. And she's tracking sounds and movement with her eyes. If I didn't know better, I'd think that she recognizes me. But the truth is she smiles and gurgles to anyone who picks her up and talks sweet to her. Old lady McDee didn't want to let go of her and only gave her up when she got wet and had to be changed. We've had Asa and Dory over to dinner every Sunday since Ann and Jamey got home from the hospital. When Dory got to hold Jamey, she finally stopped talking about going to Bremen next month. Now the way she carries on you'd think she was the baby's grandmother."

Lyndon smirked but kept his mouth shut, mostly anyway, "Yeah, well, there's a lot of that going around."

Jimmy got a twinkle in his eye and laughed. "Yes. I Guess there is at that."

Lyndon took a route to the hospital that avoided the downtown part of Grantville. Just because the public safety vehicles were exempt from the dawn to the midnight ban on vehicular traffic downtown was no reason to drive down a pedestrian dominated main street when there wasn't any need.

The hospital parking lot, paved to hold a whole congregation's worth of cars back when the hospital was still a church, was mostly empty. Even with gas for sale at the gas stations, a lot of cars were still sitting idle. Tires were an issue, a lot of them went bad while sitting that long. Batteries were expensive and so was fuel. The trolley system was cheap and easy to use, so why fuss with a car? The expanded building now took up most of the unpaved land that the church once owned. Lyndon got out and went in with Jimmy. He had been instructed by his boss, Chief Richards, to see to it that Jimmy took responsibility for the young Scotsman.

The floor nurse spotted them and met them in the hall. "Thank goodness you're here," the white-haired matron, with the stiffly starched cap perched on top of her head, said in relief. "Hopefully you can calm the lad down and convince him to stay put. He's worried about running up a bill he can't pay. We told him the local McDonalds would cover his hospital bill. But he's still worried about it."

Jimmy mumbled, "Shit, people sure are free with spending my hard-earned money."

Lyndon laughed softly. "Hard earned money? When was the last time you did a day's work, Jimmy? Not since right after the flash of light when you chipped in to help get the new railroad track laid from the mine to the power plant. Now all you do is collect the rent off of half the buildings downtown, and Lamb Properties does the actual collecting for you."

"Well, it's still my money everyone else is spending."

The nurse paid the two of them no heed at all but talked over and through the conversation as if it never happened. "And he's afraid the McDonald army will leave town without him, so he's insisting we release him. He isn't ready to leave, and we'll tie him down if we have to."

"How is he doing?" Lyndon asked.

"He's alive," she answered, with a residue of surprise in her voice. "And that is saying something. You can count every rib he has, clear as day. He hasn't been eating well for the last year if ever. I don't see how he didn't have frostbite on his feet, being bare in this weather, but his callouses are so thick he might as well have been wearing shoes, I guess. I

By Terry Howard

don't think his feet know what shoes are. He's weak as a kitten and as stubborn as a mule. He doesn't want to answer questions. We barely have a name; we don't know where he's from other than he speaks English with what I'm told is a London dockside gutter accent. He wants out of here, and he wants to join the McDonald army. We finally had to fetch his pistol and that sword he had out of storage before he'd calm down and quit worrying that they were stolen. Once he saw them, he was okay with us putting them back in lockup with the promise he could have them when he left."

"But you did get a name out of him?"

"Yes, he said he was Charles McDonald," the nurse replied.

"Great. Another Charles." Jimmy said with an air of disgust. "It seems like every other McDonald is named Charles. Now I've got three of them. I take it it's the equivalent of Hans for the Krauts."

"If you two will come this way, I'll take you to him." They followed the woman in her bright white uniform down the hall of white painted walls and shiny waxed oaken floors. "We've got him in a private room because we didn't expect him to make it. Having a roommate die can upset a whole ward full of patients."

In the room, a petite blond high school volunteer was sitting in the wooden armchair keeping an eye on the sullen young man, making sure he stayed in bed. Apparently wearing nothing but a hospital gown that tied in the back wasn't enough to keep the boy under the sheet and woolen blanket. He'd kicked the sheet and blanket off as if they were too hot to put up with. It was Saturday, so the volunteer wasn't skipping school. The young lady was dressed in the same starched white uniform as the nurse, except she didn't have a hat and there was blue trim on the skirt. She'd given up trying to engage him in conversation and was reading a book aloud. "– but viewing that the wench strove to depart, and Don Quixote labored to withhold her, the jesting seemed–"

"Thank you, Elizabeth." The floor nurse said to the volunteer. "These gentlemen need to talk with our patient." She turned to the boy in the bed, "Charles, this is Officer Lyndon Johnson." She waved at the policeman." And this is the man you came looking for." She pointed at Jimmy Dick. "Lord James Shaver, the war leader for the local Clan McDonald. Please do not make us roust out The McDonald himself. The old man in is frail health and refuses to quit working. He needs his evening to relax. But if you can't work out your problems with Lord James, we *will* bring in Laird Asa to set you straight." She glanced at Lyndon. "We will leave you gentlemen to your business. Come, Elizabeth."

Jimmy looked the boy over. He wasn't as bad as a picture of a holocaust victim. But he would do until a real one turned up. His reddish hair was cropped close to help deal with lice, since they couldn't run him through the decontamination station downstairs and had to settle for a bed bath. There was a faint trace of freckles promising a full crop come summer. Jimmy guessed the lad to be maybe five feet, and if he weighed a pound over ninety, it sure didn't show. He looked to be all of twelve years old. "Charles," Jimmy said to the boy who was busy looking back at him in apprehension, "for my sins, it seems that I am now *Lord* James Richard Shaver, the war leader for the local Clan McDonald, such as it is. How old are you, boy?"

"Sixteen, sir."

Jimmy silently stared at the lad and waited.

"Well, fifteen." The boy conceded.

Jimmy continued to stare.

The lad grimaced and finally added, "Almost, anyway."

At last, Jimmy nodded. "So, you claim to the fourteen, and you look like you might be eleven or twelve?"

"Lord, I might be small for my age. But I swear on my mother's grave that I am just shy of fifteen."

"So your mother is dead. What of your father?"

"Where are you from, boy?" Jimmy asked.

"I'm a McDonald, sir."

"I'll give you that much. No one would admit it if they didn't have to. But that does not answer my question. You are not from the northern isles. I know that accent. And you aren't from the clan in Ireland. I know that accent too. So where are you from?"

"London, my lord."

"Whether or not I am *your* lord is yet to be settled, boy. So far you are a stray stick figure of a lad who claims to be a McDonald. But you aren't from any of the clans. If you were, they never would have let you get into the shape you're in or let you go traipsing off at the end of the winter to come to Grantville. What were you doing in London?"

"Surviving, your grace."

"I'll answer to Lord James, boy, and if you're lucky maybe someday I'll let you think of me as 'my lord.' But call me 'your grace' again, and I'm out of here, and you are on your own. Is that clear?"

"Yes, you-, m-, yes Lord James."

"Now what were you doing in London? And don't say surviving, because it's clear to me that you weren't or just barely."

"Momma worked as a weaver until the fever took her. I worked her loom for a bit until the owner came back after the fever was over, and he found a country lass to work the loom. After that, I scrounged the docks and water side when the tide was out."

"And what changed?" Jimmy asked.

"I took up with a girl who worked for an old man who ran a gang, mostly pickpockets, mostly kids. He was going to sell the girl to a brothel, so she ran away. I helped her learn the ins and outs of picking the tidal mudflats, and she shared my nest. Then her gang caught up with her and beat her to death. They were looking for me for stealing her, so I needed to run. I heard that the McDonalds of Grantville were raising an army and any McDonald was welcome. I knew where I could pinch a pistol, and I stowed away on a boat bound for Hamburg. Then I headed this way."

"And your only claim to being a McDonald is your claim that your mother told you so?" Jimmy asked.

"Yes, Lord James. But you need fighting men, and I want the five acres you're promising to everyone who signs up."

"I see." James stared at the boy for a while, and the lad squirmed like a live bug pinned to a collection card. In the end, James sigh and nodded. "Okay. I will acknowledge that you can think of me as 'my lord.' But I never want to hear it. And I sure don't want to hear 'your grace.' That will be enough to get you disowned. I'll answer to Lord James but I'd rather you called me Jimmy Dick or Mr. Shaver if you can't handle Jimmy Dick. But Lord James or Lord Jimmy will do. Is that clear?"

"Yes, sir."

"Now, first of all, you will quit giving the hospital staff problems. You will be a perfect patient. Don't worry about the bill. It is covered, and yes, you will work it off or pay it back. Can you read and write?"

"No, Lord James."

"We will see to that."

"Why?" The boy asked genuinely puzzled. "What would I ever do with that? I'm no priest or gentleman."

"Because I said so. Because this is Grantville and here you will go to school until you are at least sixteen. Because we have an odd definition of gentleman here. A gentleman means you have manners and act politely. It has nothing to do with noble birth, and since you just became part of my household, part of my family, I will insist that you learn to be a gentleman by local standards. And because when you have learned to read you will be surprised at the world that will suddenly open up to you."

"But a fighting man doesn't need to read and write. And a farmer with five acres doesn't need it either."

"Lad, there is no army. We are not planning on conquering a homeland for the clan. So you are going to have to learn a trade, and in Grantville, I am not going to be able to get you an apprenticeship if you can't read."

"Sir, if you don't need fighting men, then why are you taking me in?"

Jimmy looked at Lyndon. "I find myself asking the same question. But I have a feeling that this man and his boss would have a few choice words with me if I didn't. I think the bottom line is that you need help and I have been elected as the man best able to provide that help."

"You can afford it, Jimmy," Lyndon said.

Jimmy never took his eyes off of Lyndon. "From each according to his ability, to each according to his needs. Is that the case, Lyndon?"

"I don't think that is exactly how Chief Richards would put it, Jimmy."

"No. I don't suppose he would. But that pretty much sums it up, doesn't it?"

Lyndon stood mute and, if the truth be told, a little red in the face.

"As a personal philosophy, it isn't that bad of one," Jimmy said barely audibly. "It just doesn't work well for a large group or multiple generations. Someone needs to take care of those who can't take care of themselves. I guess that's part and parcel of what it means to be part of a clan. And whether I want it or not, I guess Grantville's greatest philosopher is now famous for being part of the Grantville sept of Clan McDonald."

Jimmy looked back to the boy in the bed. "I've already got two guys answering to Charles at home; don't need a third one."

Lyndon looked concerned, and panic flashed across the boy's face.

"So, until further notice, you will answer to London. Is that clear?"

The relieved lad nodded.

"Okay. For now, your job is to get stronger. And I suggest you get that pretty little girl to teach you the alphabet, so you've got a jump on learning to read." He looked at a likewise relieved police officer. "Lyndon, lets get out of here and let London get some rest."

When they left the room, the floor nurse was back at the counter and her workstation. Elizabeth headed back to the room to keep watch. When she sat down and started reading aloud London startled her. "Lass, Lord James tells me that I must learn to read. Can you teach me?"

She looked at the suddenly changed demeanor of the patient. "Well, we can get started on it, I guess. Let me get a clipboard and some paper. I'll be right back."

At the counter, Elizabeth said, "Nurse Marta,– "

"Is he up again?" the nurse said with clear frustration. "You should have just called out."

"No, ma'am. He's in bed and calm as can be. But his Lord told him he must learn to read, and he asked me to teach him, so I need a clipboard and paper to get started."

"Well, that is almost a miracle."

When the hospital released London, the boy settled in on the couch in the living room, where Anna could keep an eye on him while he finished recovering. Elizabeth stopped by after school each day to continue with his education. Anna brought down the bilingual Doctor Seuss books Jimmy had bought for the nursery. Shortly, London had them memorized in English and German and read through them daily before tackling something harder. It wasn't long before Elizabeth became Eli. She was sixteen, but London seemed older than he was so she didn't seem to mind the age difference.

A PIPER ON THE ROOF.

While London was still in the hospital, Lyndon stepped through the door of Club 250 around four o'clock. Ken wasn't behind the bar. But Jimmy Dick, in his usual blue jeans, white shirt, and tan cardigan sweater, was enthroned on his usual bar stool, slowly working on his usual endless bottle of beer.

"Jimmy?" Lyndon called out.

"Is the kid okay, Lyndon?" Jimmy turned around and slipped off the bar stool.

"Yeah, last I knew."

Jimmy drained the last swallow out of the bottom of his bottle and set the empty on the bar behind him without looking. "What's up?"

"I'm here to give you a ride to the train station." Lyndon mostly succeeded in suppressing a smile.

"Let me guess? You've found another McDonald!" Jimmy sneered.

"Something like that." Lyndon smiled.

"It ain't fair, Lyndon."

"If anyone told you life was fair, they were lying, Jimmy."

Jimmy growled but grabbed his coat. The two men were silent for the whole trip to the train station; Lyndon wore a smirk and Jimmy effected a scowl.

At the station, they heard the train long before they saw it. But it wasn't the usual train noises. It was a calm day, but the train sounded like the worst howling windstorm one could imagine. The train came into clear view, and the reason for the noise was clear. Two kilted pipers were standing on top of a rail carriage bending the air with a squeeze of a bag and fingers dancing on a chanter while another three reeds drearily droned away. As the train drew closer, the people at the station could hear the beat of a bodhran underneath the screaming pipes. The drummer was standing in the steps of the car. The pipers on the roof stopped with a flourish as the train came to a halt. The drummer continued, and a much gentler rendition of the song came through the open windows of the railcar. The drummer stopped when the music of the small pipes ended.

"Could someone be telling me where we could be finding Lord James of Clan McDonald?" one of the pipers on the roof called out.

"Here he is," Lyndon said loudly, with a wave of his arm that ended up pointing at Jimmy.

"Lord James, could you be using two more pipers for the coming campaign?" the piper on the roof asked.

The drummer stepped down, followed by a man carrying the small pipes under his arm, and a claymore, the two-handed kind that stretched from chin to floor, over his shoulder. The drummer had a basket-hilted sword and targe hanging over the hilt. Both were wearing kilts, and not the up-time skirt but a great kilt that is just a large piece of fabric folded into pleats and wrapped around under a belt.

"Didn't you get the letter? There isn't going to be a campaign," Jimmy shouted.

"What letter?" came the reply from the roof.

"The letter we sent to any McDonald sept or clan holding we could think of that might be heading this way. There is no invasion planned. So, no one is getting five acres."

"Oh, that's the problem. No, we never got your letter because we're Clan Cameron."

"Shit! First I have to deal with every stray McDonald who comes along, and now I've got Cameramen playing bag pipes."

The pipers on the roof climbed down, and two more kilted fellows appeared from the car, schlepping baggage, including two more claymores.

Someone in the livery of the Holladay Lodge, wearing white pants and dark blue jacket with the logo on the breast, was chatting with the small piper and the drummer. The pair started up a song. It was soft mellow and pleasant. The second piper, who was just reaching the ground, began to sing in a fine tenor voice in something other than English. The steward from the lodge who was there to meet the train glanced at the singer and then started nodding in time to the music. As he listened, he took a business card out of a pocket, wrote a note on the back, and handed it to the tenor with a few words of explanation.

Jimmy turned to Lyndon, "They ain't McDonalds. So, they aren't mine. Right?"

"I don't think the chief will see it that way, Jimmy. They're here to join up. He'll figure they're yours. Look, I can't fit all of you in the car. You'll have to walk them out to the hospital to run them through delousing and quarantine check."

"Quarantine check? When did that start?"

"Since London showed up with a fever. Anybody from England should be checked until further notice."

"Mr. Shaver?" The steward from the Holladay Lodge seemed to appear out of nowhere at Jimmy's elbow.

"What do you want?" Jimmy snarled.

"The musicians said I would need to talk to you. They will have to audition, of course, but that won't be a problem; I'm sure the director will want them when he's heard them."

"What?" Confusion overshadowed the snarl.

"The lodge needs a new dinner act, and they'll be perfect." He handed Jimmy a business card that he seemed to have in endless numbers. "So if they're available, call this number and ask for the program director. And there's my client. I've got to go." Which he did.

Jimmy sighed. "Well, let's get you guys cleaned up to start with, and then we'll have to figure out what to do with you. At least some of you have a job waiting."

They insisted on making music while they walked, and of course that got them noticed.

By Terry Howard

JIMMY, HAVE YOU GOT A KILT?

One week later, when Lyndon answered a summons to the chief's office, the chief was sitting behind his clutter-free desk perusing a letter. The chief looked up and very solemnly asked, "How would you feel about going to Bremen?"

"Not interested," Lyndon replied.

"Too bad. I was hoping you would see it as a vacation. It seems that Jimmy Dick is now identified as the war chief for the local Clan McDonald. If Laird Asa and Dory aren't going, someone in Magdeburg is of the opinion that it has to be Jimmy or the people kicking up a fuss will think we're trying to pull a fast one. You've got a better chance of keeping the old sot in line than anybody else in town since he seems to like you."

"Chief, no one can keep that man in line."

Richards let out a deep sigh. "You'd better. It's your job." The chief dropped the letter, wrapped one hand around a fist, planted his elbows on the desk and put his hands to his mouth. He wanted to nibble on a knuckle, but he refrained. "Go collect him and bring him in, and we'll see if the two of us can't get him to see reason."

"Chief, is it all right if I wait until after the lunch crowd has cleared out of Club 250? Getting him to come in to see you will be a whole lot easier if he doesn't have a full house to play to."

"Good point," the chief agreed.

✻ ✻ ✻

When Lyndon opened the door for Jimmy to enter the chief's office, the old sot belligerently demanded, "What do you want this time?"

"We need to talk about Bremen," the chief said.

"That's settled," Jimmy grumped. "I've already told the boys that the trip is off."

"Dory's in the hospital," the chief said. "She won't be able to travel for two or three months."

"So?" Jimmy asked.

"The trip is scheduled for right after the Fourth of July. Magdeburg is insisting that we stick to the plan. With Asa and Dory out of the picture, Magdeburg wants you to make the trip as the representative of Clan McDonald."

"Hello? The name is James Richard Shaver. Not McDonald."

"Yes. But since you're listed in that Berlin Philosophical Quarterly as the war chief for the local clan McDonald, and with Laird Asa not going, Magdeburg says you need to."

"What? First, you tell me I can't go. And now you're telling me I have to go?"

"That's about it, Jimmy. Someone from Clan McDonald of Grantville has to be in Bremen in July or there will be diplomatic hell to pay."

"Chief, the point was to take Dory."

The chief nodded. "She can go anytime she wants too. We just need someone to go in July to put an end to the idea that Clan McDonald is planning on conquering a kingdom. That's your fault. So you get to go."

"Without Dory, I ain't interested."

"That doesn't matter." The chief put both palms flat on the desktop and stared back at Jimmy, who was standing in front of the desk with Lyndon standing behind him. "Magdeburg wants an end to all of the wild stories that are causing no end of problems."

"You need some McDonalds. Shoot, chief, even with a bagpipe and a kilt, no one is going to believe that I'm a McDonald."

The chief raised his eyebrows. "Jimmy, weren't you listening? The Berlin philosophical quarterly has published a letter telling all of Europe that you are the war leader for the local McDonalds. But a bagpiper is a good idea. And I know where we can get one. Come to think of it, I think you've got two or three of them to make the trip with you. And I'm sending Lyndon along to keep you out of trouble."

"You're putting me on, right?"

The chief solemnly shook his head.

"You want me to lead a team of bagpipers to Bremen to look at a statue of a chicken, on a cat, on a dog, on a donkey?"

"Yes."

"Chief, I'll admit it. You can make me go. But if you think for one minute that you are going to get me to wear a kilt, you had better think again."

"Then, you'll do it?" The chief asked.

"Have I got a choice?" Jimmy replied.

"No. Not really."

By Terry Howard

FOOT IN MOUTH DISEASE

It was Wednesday night. Bubba was broke early this week. Before he got drunk enough not to care what happened when he got home, he started whining about his wife. This cut into the audience Jimmy was paying for. Jimmy would buy a drink for anyone who would drink with him, and he would keep buying as long as they would put up with his caustic wit. Jimmy broke with his policy of staying out of other people's lives. It was a good policy. The shame was he almost never followed it.

"Bubba, for crying out loud, be a man. If you're unhappy with your wife, make her change," Jimmy said.

"Make her change? Jimmy, God himself couldn't get that jackass wife of mine to change," Bubba replied.

"First off Bubba, the word is jenny. A female ass is a jenny not a jack. Second, you can get a whole lot of work out of a good ass if you can get it harnessed and keep it motivated. Grandpa had a jenny as stubborn as rock. You put a rope on it and it would not move to save your life. There was no way you were going to get it into a collar and make it plow the field. But grandpa would give it a treat, an apple core, the paring off a carrot, a taste of salt or sugar. Then he'd whisper something into that old jenny's ear and he didn't have a bit of trouble with her the rest of the day." Jimmy took a pull off of his beer.

"I asked one time just what it was he whispered into that jenny's ear. Grandpa just smiled at me. Jimmy, he said, a good ass is like a good woman. Give them a little sugar and a few soft words and they'll bust their butt for you.

By Terry Howard

"Now Bubba, when you finish that beer, head on home. Stop down at the new pottery shop." The fellow had just turned up from somewhere unpronounceable. He was short, broad and ugly. He wore a full beard, and his long hair was not pulled back nor controlled in any fashion. But anything to help hide his face was welcome. His hands looked like undersized catcher's mitts with four and a half sausages attached. You know, the fat ones you put on the grill in the summer, not the little ones that came with eggs in a café. Folks didn't mind what he looked like. He was turning out beautiful, thin delicate pieces of almost art. "He's got a pearly white bud vase down there," Jimmy said, "that almost made me wish I was still married just so I could give it to my wife. You stop in and buy it then pick up a rose to give to your wife. When she gets suspicious tell it was beautiful and it made you think of her."

"Damn it Jimmy, I'm broke," Bubba said. "I wouldn't be drinkin' with you if I wasn't."

Jimmy Dick pulled out his wallet and handed Bubba two twenty dollar bills, "Go buy your wife a rose."

"I don't need a loan," Bubba said.

"It's not a loan."

"I don't want charity, Dickhead," Bubba said.

"No. You just want me to buy when you're broke. Well, you're broke and I'm buying," Jimmy said. Something about the way Jimmy said it, the tone of his voice, his body language or telepathy told Bubba to shut up and do as he was told.

On Thursday Bubba came into Club 250 and headed to the middle of the bar instead of the left end where he usually hung out. By Thursdays Bubba was usually out of pocket money. His wife cashed his check and paid the bills before the Ring of Fire. Now, since he was paid in cash, she took his pay envelope and doled back a sum calculated to keep him away from beer. Bubba leaned up against the bar next to Jimmy Dick, smiled and said, "Hey Jimmy, let me buy you a drink."

This was notable. Bubba never smiled. Okay he did smile once at a Christmas party when someone called his boss a horse's ass and got away with it because she was the boss's wife. Otherwise Bubba was a bitter, beaten man, who saw little or nothing in his life to smile about.

Secondly, it was Thursday. Bubba should have been broke, and would have been if he hadn't had some of Jimmy's money left over from buying the bud vase. If he wasn't broke he should have been hanging out at the far left end of the bar in the shadows next to the wall where he could feel like he was hidden from sight in case any other Baptist came in. If Baptists ever started drinking together they might have something to smile about.

Thirdly, he offered to buy Jimmy Dick a drink. Bubba never offered to buy. He rarely had the money, and he was too stingy even when he did.

Jimmy Dick looked at Bubba while blindly waving two fingers at the bartender. There was no need to make eye contact with Ken. The owner of the bar knew everything that was going on, in sight and out of sight. When Bubba leaned up against the bar next to Jimmy Dick, Ken had snaked two cold ones out of the ice. Bubba would be thirsty, Jimmy would buy, and Jimmy would want a new one to keep Bubba's beer company.

When Ken set the beers down and a smiling Bubba paid, Ken's radar went off. Bubba was not broke, Bubba was smiling, and Bubba was paying. This was completely out of character. Bubba would be watched, closely, until he was out the door.

"Mmhm," Jimmy Dick hummed. "It worked, didn't it."

"Like a charm," the smiling Bubba said. "Damn it Jimmy, your grandpa knew what he was talkin' about and so did you. She liked the rose but she got all goggle eyed over that bud vase."

A very smug Jimmy Dick smiled, "Knew she would."

"How come you were so sure? You were right, but how did you know?" Bubba asked.

"Flowers, Bubba, are an aphrodisiac," Jimmy said. Bubba frowned. "Fancy word for sex magic, Bubba."

"Yeah, but she was really taken by the vase," Bubba said.

"Of course," Jimmy replied.

"Yeah, but, how did ya' know?" Bubba asked.

"Open your eyes and observe, my dear Watson. Of course, it worked magic. You got it from the hairy potter. He can't keep his shelves stocked and there is always someone looking in his front window.

"Now that you got her attention with a treat, it's time for you to whisper a few soft words in her ear. Hmm, let's see what you think she'd most like to hear?"

"Honey, I got a raise."

"Well we can't do anything about that one," Jimmy said.

"I wish *was* getting' a raise." Grantville's booming economy was reflected in the price of everything. "Shit, Jimmy, I wish I'd been born rich instead of good lookin'?" The second half of the sentence was stretching things, but oddly, Jimmy chose to respond to the first half.

Jimmy Dick just looked at Bubba for four whole seconds and finally said, "Wouldn't help."

Bubba's face got scrunched up around the eyes. "Why do ya' say that?"

"Because, Bubba, you *were* born rich."

Bubba responded in a stilted voice, with drawn out vowels and complete words, "Jimmy, you are so full of shit your eyes are brown."

"Na, they're blue and I'm serious. You were born rich."

"Like I said, Jimmy, you're full of shit. I'm a working stiff and always have been."

"True enough. But you were still born rich. You just wish you'd been born richer and it wouldn't have been enough. Never is."

Bubba savored the cold beer. "Okay, Jimmy how do ya' figure I was born rich?"

"Look Bubba, let's start with the difference between being broke and being poor."

"Same thing."

Jimmy's dinner arrived. He didn't offer to buy a burger for Bubba. "Far from it. Being broke means you are out of money, right?"

"Yeah."

"Being poor is a frame of mind."

Bubba's eyes got crinkled up again. It was strange thought, and Bubba was not used to thinking. "What?"

"Think about it, Bubba. You remember the Lee sisters over in Fairmont?"

Bubba nodded. The old gals were life-long spinsters. They were fixtures around town next to forever until they died a few years before we got dumped here. They were always seen together, walking to the store where they bought one pound of the cheapest meat once or twice a week, walking to the bus stop to go out of town, walking to church, or just walking the streets for something to do to get out of the house. They wore clothes they bought at second-hand thrift shops. They wore shoes until the soles would no longer hold in a piece of cardboard put inside to cover the holes. They cooked and heated with wood a neighbor cut to help the old women out in exchange for fresh produce from their garden.

Jimmy tilted his beer bottle up while Bubba answered. When he took the bottle down he said, "That's them. They caught the flu one winter and died rather than go to the doctor. When the house was cleared it was packed full of antiques and collectables. The biggest shock was the one hundred and ninety-three thousand dollars that they had in the bank. The banking staff counted on them making a deposit on the last business day of every month. No one could remember them ever making a withdrawal. The stock portfolio that their father left them was still worth over half a million dollars."

Bubba shook his head, "Crazy old fools, livin' like that when they had all that money."

"They lived that way because they were poor. Not broke, Bubba, poor. When they were young they were taught to pinch pennies. The louder the change in their pockets cried, the happier they were. They were always afraid that there'd be another stock market crash, and then they'd need that money to live on. And, if the bank failed, they'd have the collectables they kept in the house. Shoot, there was a gun collector from England at the auction, for crying out loud."

Jimmy wetted his whistle. "If they lost all their money they would have been broke. Someone who's rich can be broke, too. I knew a realtor back in the world. He spent part of every winter in the Virgin Islands. He drove a Beemer, always flew first class, wouldn't put on a pair of scuffed shoes even to go fishing, he and his third wife lived in a six-bedroom house until she got it in the divorce. He golfed at least three times a week when the courses were open. Sound rich?"

"I'd love to live like that," Bubba said.

"He was always broke, always playing catch up with his creditors and Uncle Sam. Being rich or being poor has nothing to do with how much money you got. It has everything to do with how you see the world. Someone once asked J.P. Morgan how much money was enough. He told them, 'You always need just a little bit more.' "

"Don't matter. There ain't no gas."

"Just answer the question, Bubba."

"Two."

Jimmy raised an eyebrow.

Bubba said, "There's mine and my wife's."

Jimmy continued to look at him.

"What?" Bubba finally asked, in frustration.

"What's those black things back behind your house?"

"Shoot, Jimmy. They're up on blocks. They don't count."

"You know how you can tell a rich boy in Georgia? He's got two cars up on blocks in his yard. That's you Bubba; you're rich. So you got four cars. Back up-time, in over sixty percent of the world, a family with a car, whether it ran or not, qualified as rich. Here and now, you can get a coach and six for each and every one of them. As soon as they get the petroleum industry up and running you'll have enough to retire on."

"What'a'ya do that for, Jimmy?"

"Do what?"

"Make that awful pun?"

The perplexed town drunk replied, "What in hell are you going on about? You know good and well that by the time they get gas back at the pump every tire in town is going to be ruined from sittin' that long. Everybody is going to have to re-tire and there ain't no tire factory for three hundred years."

"Oh. I missed that one. Where was I? You got a four-bedroom house."

"Three," Bubba corrected.

"Four," Jimmy argued. "Your wife uses one for a sewing room even if she doesn't sew. Most everybody else in this world would be happy to have only four people per bed. Shoot, most of them would count themselves well off to have a bed. It's all relative, Bubba. You were rich by world standards back in the world, and you are rich by world standards here and now."

"But I got to work for a livin'." It was a not so subtle dig at Jimmy Dick. His monthly check from the military stayed up-time, but the real estate holdings in town would see him out with some to spare. Right after the translation he took a job when everybody was scrambling and he stuck with it until they were over the hump. The V.A. wasn't watching any more. Still, when the crisis was over Jimmy went back to doing nothing.

THE LEGEND OF JIMMY DICK

"If you were willing to live like everybody else, you could manage very well on what you could get from renting out the house. Move into the garage. You could make a comfortable one room apartment out of it."

"Man alive, Jimmy. Here I am, complaining that I wish I was better off and you go and tell me I need to live like I was dirt poor."

"That's my point exactly. You are *not* living like you're poor. You *are* living like you're rich. You're just not as rich as you want to be.

"You wish you'd been born richer, but it wouldn't have been enough. Never is. Look at the king of Trashkanistan. He owns the whole country. You'd think anybody would be content owning a whole country. But, no. He wants more, so he starts a war and the people pay for his new territory with their lives. I'm telling you Bubba, wealth is relative. It's all in how you look at the world."

"Well," an unconvinced Bubba responded. "I hear what you're sayin' and it makes sense, but that just ain't my way of lookin' at it. I'm broke, and I'm poor, and I wish I'd been born rich."

"That's your problem. You *are* rich. You're just bound and determined not to see it. Wealth is relative, and if you wanted to be wealthy, you should have picked your relatives more carefully."

Bubba's eyes got crinkled up, *again*. Something about what Jimmy said didn't sound just right. Finally it sunk in. The only time you get to pick your relatives is when you're married. So if he wanted to be rich he should have married a rich wife. "Jimmy? Why do you have to be like that?"

Jimmy Dick smirked into his beer. "Like what, Bubba?"

"This whole thing started when I complained about my wife. You were telling me how to get her to change and then you go and make that gaud awful pun about how I should have married someone with money if I wanted to be rich."

"So we were talking about getting your wife to change. Now let's see, what could you whisper in her ear that she would really like to hear?"

"Only other thing I can think of besides, Honey I got a raise is, Honey, I'd really like to go to church with you." She woke him up every Sunday and bugged him about going to mass, but he didn't want to. She made him go occasionally and she really did wish he was going because he wanted.

"Okay, let's see if we can work with that."

"Huh, no way, Jimmy. No way in hell. I can't stand going down to church. Those people treat me like I'm a leper or something."

"What is a leper, Bubba?"

"I don't know. It's in the Bible; some kind of disease or something."

"It's deadly and you got it. You *are* a leper, Bubba. Do you really think they don't know where you spend most of your spare time? Then they got to pretend they don't know and that makes them feel like the hypocrites they know they are. So every time you go to church you make them feel guilty. I ought to leave you right there, just for that, but we were talking about getting your wife to change.

"Now, the truth is, you could get her to change all along. You just don't want to."

"How's that, Jimmy?"

"If you'd become the kind of man she wants you to be . . ."

"I can't get rich."

"That's something else. I mean, she would like you to be a good churchman."

"I ain't cut out for it. Lying don't come natural to me and I ain't goin' to change."

"We aren't talking about you changing, Bubba. We're talking about you changing your wife. Now, you don't want to go to church with her. So turn the tables on her. Tell her you want her to go to church with you."

"Shit Bubba, you know what con fuse ius said, 'Man who pass gas in church sets in own pew.' Bubba, use your ears. I didn't say go to church. I said tell her you wanted her to go to church with *you*. Old Joe's people are meeting in tent down at the fair-grounds since they got tossed out of here. Tell her you want her to go to church with you *there*. She will say, 'No way in hell am I going to some church meeting in a bar.' And you can start the negotiations. If she won't go to church with you, why should you have to go to church with her?"

The light dawned and Bubba smiled, again.

"And if you aren't going to church then there's no point of you acting like you're a goody-two-shoes. So she should shut up about you spending a little time down here."

THE LEGEND OF JIMMY DICK

On Saturday Bubba stopped for a cold one on his way home from working overtime. From the look on his face and the posture of his walk as he came through the door Ken made a note to keep an eye on him. He looked like he was ready to blow. It was Saturday. He got paid on Friday so he should have had money, which meant he should have slid off to the left end of the bar to drink alone. Instead he stalked stiff legged to the middle of the bar, where he said, "Damn it, Dickhead. Do you have any idea what kind of mess you got me into?"

"What are you talking about Bubba?"

"Your damned idea of changin' my wife? I told her I wanted her to go to church with me and she said, 'Honey that's a great idea.' Turns out she just had a fight with Miz Fussbritches over the flower arrangements. Now we're stuck going to church at the fairgrounds tomorrow, with the krauts."

"Well, it shouldn't be all that bad, Bubba. I'll buy you a beer Monday night and you can tell me about it."

"You weren't listenin', Dickhead! I said, we're stuck going to church tomorrow. It was your idea. You're goin' with me."

"Ah, bubba, that's not something I'm likely to do very much of. I usually sleep in on Sundays."

"Just like every other day of the week, Jimmy. Not this time, Jimmy. It was your idea, it's time to put up or shut up. Or I'll tell everyone you welshed."

"That would be a lie, Bubba."

Bubba did not need to say he didn't care. He didn't need to say anything, his shit-eating grin said it all.

After going to the fairgrounds early on Sunday morning, Mary let her husband sleep on Sundays after that and slipped off to church without waking him.

By Terry Howard

DEATH AND LUGGAGE

"Hey, Jimmy. Why don't I ever see you down at the rail yard anymore?" It was a cold winter night, and Club 250 had its every-night regulars and as many more folks who weren't. The young man talking to Jimmy Dick was one of the latter.

Jimmy Dick gazed down the length of his beer bottle at the fellow he thought of as "the kid." Right after the Ring of Fire, when everyone was scrambling to pitch in and make things work, he'd taken a job with the railroad and joined the army. The rails kept the power plant in coal, and the army kept the town from being overrun. Now he was in the reserves and the scramble to stay alive was over.

"They don't need me," Jimmy replied.

"Bull shit. You were a lot of help."

"Yeah. They could use me . . . but they don't need me. There's enough people to get the job done."

"Yeah, okay. But the money's good, and you were good at it."

"Don't need the money. Why work?"

"Ah, come on. You can always use a little more."

Jimmy had gotten by up-time without working because of the disability payments he picked up in Nam (Agent Orange was a bit more effective than it needed to be), and what little profit there was from the real estate holdings he had inherited. There were a lot of vacancies in town at the time. Now the pension was gone but the real estate more than covered things. He didn't need to work to get by, and he saw no reason to get ahead.

"Hey, Ken, give me a glass and another beer." Jimmy had to ask for a glass. Bottled beer was becoming synonymous with cold beer. Down-timers wanted it at room temperature in a mug, and it was tapped out of a keg. Up-timers wanted it cold. It's easier to chill bottles in ice than it is to cool a keg. Mugs were a down-time thing, so most members of the 250 clan had taken to drinking out of the bottle as a social statement. When it arrived, Jimmy poured the rest of his current beer into the glass and then started pouring the new bottle in after it.

"Damn it, Jimmy, stop pouring. It's overflowing already," the kid said.

"Oh? So, there is such a thing as not needing a little more."

"I was talking about money."

"Same thing. When you got enough, why get more?"

"Save it for retirement."

"You ever saved half a beer overnight?"

"'Course not. It goes flat."

"That's my point."

"I wasn't talking about beer. Money's different."

Jimmy sighed. How do you convince a young man that he needs to enjoy the journey because the destination might be disappointing? "Kid, let me tell ya a story.

"Seems a rich man died. When the angel of death came to collect him the fellow was setting there on a pile of baggage. Well, Azrael looked at him and . . ."

Jimmy's drinking partner interrupted. "Who's Azrael? I thought he was a character on the *Smurfs*?"

"Kid, Azrael is the name of the angel of death. I don't know nothin' about what's written on no sponge football.

"Anyway, Azrael says to the rich man, 'Time to go.'

" 'Well give me a hand with this,' the rich man said, meaning his luggage.

" 'Leave it. You don't need it where you're goin'.'

" 'No way,' says the rich man. 'I worked all my life for this and I ain't leaving it.'

" 'Well, you can't take it with you.'

" 'Then I ain't goin',' says the rich man.

"They argued about it for a while, and Azrael finally said, 'Look, I don't have all eternity. I'll let you bring whatever you can carry. Grab what you can and leave the rest and let's get goin'.' The rich fellow, he agonizes over what to leave and what to take and finally grabs a suitcase in each hand. By the time they got to the pearly gates, he was down to one and covered in sweat.

"Peter looked down at it and said, 'What's that?'

" 'It's all the luggage the angel would let me bring.' "

" 'Well, I can tell you right now it ain't goin' in with you. What did you bring, anyway?' The rich man huffed the tote up on the counter and opened it up. It was full of gold bars. A puzzled Peter looked at it and said, 'Paving stones? Why did you bring paving stones?' "

The kid laughed. "That's funny. What's the point?"

Jimmy sighed again and gave up. Sometimes it was just plain too much work to get an idea across. "The point is, I think we need a couple of cold ones down here. Hey, Ken, two more." Jimmy knew there weren't very many problems in this world you couldn't get to go away, at least for a while, if you just kept the beers coming. Maybe someday the kid would figure it out, but probably not.

By Terry Howard

THE TRUTH ACCORDING TO BUDDHA

"Hey, Jimmy Dick." Bubba sidled up to the bar and waited for Jimmy to order him a beer. It was Thursday and Bubba was broke. "You hear about the horrible way the school treated preacher Wiley's kid?"

"No. What happened?"

"He was up there giving his Indian arrow presentation, and they flat kicked him out in the street 'cause he said he believed in science."

"Bubba?" Jimmy said, waving two fingers at the bartender, "You'll believe anything, won't you?"

"Whata' ya mean, Jimmy?"

"You heard Will's side of the tale and swallowed it whole. You didn't bother to find out the other side or to even think that there might be one. I bet ya' this is just another who-ha Wiley's brat is stirring up."

"Well hell, Jimmy. How am I supposed to know what the truth is?"

"Bubba, let me tell you a story. I had a dream last night. In my dream, I heard a voice—

" 'Docket number 659,656, being an alleged violation of the protocol compact limiting direct intervention in the affairs of the worlds of men by gods.'

" 'Now comes Tyr, speaking for the complainant Odin and all others, before the supreme council of all the gods.' "

"Hey, Jimmy? I know who Odin is. He's Thor's sidekick in Super Heroes, but who's Tire?"

"Other way around, Bubba. Thor is Odin's sidekick. Tyr is a god just like Thor, another sidekick of Odin's. Thor was famous for his hammer, Tyr was famous for always telling the truth. He got his hand bitten off by a wolf while he was saving the world."

"You sure about that, Jimmy?"

"Yeah, I'm sure about that. Now can I tell the story?"

"Sure, Jimmy."

" 'Well,' Tyr said, 'Most gracious judge, for nearly two thousand years, ever since the Roman Christians brought the Semitic god, Jehovah—' "

"Roman Christians? You mean Catholics, Jimmy?"

Jimmy sighed. "Yeah, Bubba. I mean Catholics. Now can I tell the story?"

"Oh, sure, Jimmy. Sorry."

" 'Ever since the Roman Christians brought the Semitic god Jehovah into the lands of the Germans—' "

"Semitic? You mean like in anti-Jewish?"

"Bubba, have I ever told you you're dumber than a box of rocks?" a frustrated Jimmy Dick asked.

"Yeah. But does that mean Semitic means anti-Jewish or not?"

"*Huuuuuh*. Semitic mostly means Jewish. It doesn't mean anti-Jewish unless you say anti-Semitic. You got that?"

"Sure, Jimmy. I was just wondering."

"Now, can I tell you this story or not?"

"I'm listening."

"'Ever since the Roman Christians brought the Semitic god, Jehovah, into the lands of the Germans, we have bided our time without having farther disturbed this council once you ruled that the saints were not gods nor were they avatars, and therefore what they did in the world could not be considered a violation of the compact of non-interference. We have watched their direct intervention in the world of men, an absolute violation of the compact if a god did it, and—save for the complaint that the saints were being prayed to as gods and not just petitioned as venerable ancestors, a claim supported by the accusation of the reformed Christian priests against the Roman Christians—we have said nothing.' "

THE LEGEND OF JIMMY DICK

Ken put two cold bottles down in front of them. Jimmy grabbed them both.

"Hey, I thought you were gonna buy me a beer," Bubba said.

"I thought you were going to listen to a story?"

Bubba started to say something and stopped. He got the message. Jimmy slid the bottle over to his captive audience and continued the tale.

" 'We have wept at the abuses fostered on our peoples at the hands of their priests. And though we have often contemplated doing so, we have not bothered this council with that complaint. Nay, we have said nothing.'

"'We have watched in silence while they have destroyed our holy places on every high hill, their believers being stronger than ours, because they had the aid and succor of the saints. And we have said nothing.'

"'We have said nothing while the mother of their god has appeared to every shepherd girl in Europe, making and fulfilling promises that are a direct violation of the compact. But we have said nothing, for even the mother of their god is protected as a saint.' "

Bubba started to ask a question. Jimmy looked at the beer, and Bubba shut up.

"'We have watched their priests steal our customs and our holidays. We have watched as they changed the names of the high holy days, perverted the meanings of the observances and the symbols, and not given credit where it was due for their origin, even though they have nothing to do with the history or customs of the Semitic faith. And we have said nothing.'

"'We have waited in peace for their influence to fade so we could reclaim our territorial rights.'

"'But this is too much. The Semite has moved a village from half the world away and four hundred years out of time into the middle of Germany. Even if it were the work of a saint, which it is not, any saint that can do that surely must be considered a god and must be under the ban of non-interference.'

"'We submit that this council is obliged to require the Semite to return the town to its proper place and time. We further feel that it is only fitting, in light of this clear and flagrant violation of the compact, that the Semite's saints be barred from the farther usurpation of the duties of gods, and that for a period of at least three hundred years we, the true gods of the Germanies, be allowed to commune directly with our few remaining believers and aid them directly in overcoming this gross invasion. I thank the most gracious judge for hearing our petition.'

"'Now comes the saint Elijah speaking for the defendant Jehovah in each of his three forms.' "

Finally, it was more than Bubba could take. He had a question he just could not hold in. "You mean Elijah, like in the Bible? I thought you were talking about a made-up Jewish god. I didn't know you meant *God*. This ain't funny, Jimmy."

"Bubba, do you want to drink my beer or not?"

Bubba shut up by sticking the rim of the bottle to his lips and lifting the bottom high.

" 'Well,' Elijah said, 'Most gracious judge, once again we are forced to answer the whining snivels of Oden from his grave in Valhalla. My god has abided by the compact that he asked for in the days of the Babylonian exile when his, his and her chosen people asked that he end the oracles of other gods. To do so, he has given up the giving of prophecies and direct appearances and assistance, even to the bother of his becoming a man to teach as a man and to die as a man. It was a wise choice that has stopped much destructive warfare between the gods.'

" 'I have checked with my god, and neither he, nor he, nor she had anything in the least to do with the anachronistic appearance of Grantville in the 1600s. It is a clear violation of the compact. We agree. Something should be done. But it was not done by my god.' "

"Tyr, waving the empty stump where his hand was bitten off, called out from the bar, 'Your high priest in Rome and your high priest in Moscow say your god has done this thing!'

" 'My good god Tyr,' Elijah responded, 'surely you of all beings know, priests, lie!'

" 'If your god did not do this then who did?' Tyr demanded.

" 'Our best guess is that it was an act of Science.'

" 'Shit!' screamed Tyr, 'Science again? Gracious judge, something must be done!'

"Buddha, whose turn it was this eon to sit in the seat of the judge and be chair-deity of the council, spoke. 'I AM AFRAID, TYR, THAT science IS NOT SIGNATORY TO THE COMPACT AND DOES NOT RECOGNIZE THE AUTHORITY OF THIS COUNCIL.' "

Bubba had the bottom of his beer bottle between his face and the ceiling until it was dry. He set the empty down on the bar. "What's all that supposed to mean, Jimmy?"

Jimmy sighed. "I think it means we need another couple of beers down here."

By Terry Howard

E. COLI: A TALE OF REDEMPTION

Ken paused in front of Jimmy Dick barely long enough to say, "Incoming," before moving down the bar and taking shelter in the back room. Jimmy glanced in the mirror to see his ex-wife, Bina Rae, framed by the early afternoon sun, walking toward him from the slowly closing door of the otherwise empty bar.

"James, I sent you a letter. You didn't answer it."

Jimmy didn't say anything.

"I went down to Genucci's and made the arrangements. Everything will be out of the way when the time comes. You need to stop in and pay for it."

Their only child, Merle, had brittle bones. Jimmy had been exposed to Agent Orange in Vietnam. When the baby was diagnosed, the pediatrician told her Jimmy's exposure might be the reason why. He came home from working overtime to find his wife had taken his daughter and moved out. She blamed him for the baby's condition.

The court gave him visitation rights along with the child support payments but it never worked out. There was always some conflicting schedule, or a big fight, or both. Merle eventually ended up in assisted living, and Veteran's Affairs paid the bills. Jimmy had tried to visit her in the home after she moved in, but Merle made it clear she didn't want to see him. This was, pretty much, his entire contact with his ex-wife and child.

Now, the home was telling Bina that Merle wouldn't last much longer. So Bina made arrangements with the funeral home.

"Aren't you going to say anything, James?"

"Have a beer."

Her voice was scornful, "You drink too much. It's bad for you. You never did take care of yourself."

"Back up-time, before we left, in a number of carefully controlled studies, it was determined that if a person drank a half gallon of water each day, at the end of the year they would have absorbed more than half a pound of E. coli. In other words, when you drink water you're drinking shit.

"However, if you drink whiskey or beer or any other liquor, you're safe because alcohol has to go through a purification process of fermentation.

"So, you've got a choice. You can drink beer and talk stupid, or you can drink water and be full of shit."

Her voice dripped with disgust. "What did I ever see in you?"

"A good living?"

"Stop down to the funeral home and pay the bill, Jimmy." With that, she walked out of his life, again.

"Ken," Jimmy Dick said softly, "whiskey, and leave the bottle."

✳ ✳ ✳

A few weeks, later Genucci's Funeral Home opened up the overflow area and then put out extra chairs for Merle's funeral. They had been told to expect a small turnout. After all, Merle had spent half of her life in assisted living, her father's family never visited, she had no friends outside of the home, and her friends from the home would not be attending. Her mother's family, her mother and three adopted children were all the guests they were told to expect.

"Merle's father will pay for things. He will not be attending," Bina Rae told Freddy when she made the arrangements.

When Jimmy stopped in, Freddy asked, "Bina Rae says you won't be attending?"

"Bina . . ." Jimmy was trying to be polite so did not pronounce it Bi'tch'na as he normally did. "Does not know what she is talking about. Again, as usual."

THE LEGEND OF JIMMY DICK

Freddy concluded that separate seating would be in order. The family area in many funeral homes is often at right angles to the general seating. This provides privacy to the bereaved. Providentially, the converted dwelling he ran the funeral business out of just worked out that way. When the time came, he would seat Jimmy in the general seating area, out of sight of the family.

While not many people were familiar with Merle, a lot of people knew Jimmy Dick. Many of them knew him as 'Dick Head,' a name even Jimmy would admit to being fully deserved on the rare occasions he was fully sober. Yet somehow they managed to respect him. And while he never talked about it, Grantville was a small town where your business was everybody's. They knew the story. They felt he got a raw deal and were inclined to be supportive.

"You goin' to Merle's funeral?" was a question frequently asked at Club 250.

"Yeah. I didn't know her but this is going to be hard on Jimmy. He's bought me a beer anytime I was broke, figure I owe him." This was a common point of view. Normally people figured they'd paid for any beer Jimmy bought by putting up with his usually rude and shrewdly critical wit while they drank with him. Still, a funeral is different.

Then there were the down-time Anabaptists, who met in Club 250 on Sunday mornings until the cops started asking questions about them causing trouble. This was all the excuse Ken needed to throw them out. Complaints had been filed about a church they were starting just outside of Grantville's jurisdiction. Jimmy organized an armed escort to stand guard over the new church when the local Lutherans started getting nasty, in spite of the Anabaptists having the local count's permission. They thought well of him for it for it.

The biggest surprise was the number of people who showed up because James Richard Shaver had defended Grantville's honor on the fields of Philosophy in the face of a nasty stuffed-shirt German who still continued to bad mouth up-timers and up-time values. He asked Jimmy if war was mankind's greatest glory or greatest shame. "Neither," Jimmy replied, "our greatest glory is to love our wives and raise our children well, our greatest shame is an un-cherished child." The philosopher from Berlin didn't like the answer.

Bina Rae had a staff member from the home to say a few words and then there was a walk to the cemetery followed by a quiet, catered meal planned for the immediate family at Bina's house.

Jimmy found himself in the middle of the street between Club 250 and the Gardens with half of the people who walked back from the graveyard with him going one way and half going the other. Both halves were ready to buy him a drink. To everyone's shock, he went home to do his drinking alone.

Bina was dumbfounded at the turn out. Jimmy was a drunk. No one respects a drunk.

A life-sized angel with Merle's face carved in fine white marble stood at the head of the open grave. She had specified a simple grave stone to Alberto Ugolini down at the monument company. Jimmy had changed her order when he paid for it.

"Jimmy, that ain't what Bina ordered."

"I'm payin' for it. It's what I want. If you won't arrange it, I'll find someone who will."

"No, I'll get 'er done," Alberto answered.

* * *

Three days after the funeral, at about two-thirty in the afternoon, the door to Club 250 opened on a nearly empty bar. Bina came through the door, walked to the middle of the bar, hopped up onto a bar stool and said to her ex-husband, "Buy me a beer."

Without a word he waved two fingers at Ken, and two bottles and a glass arrived in short order. Bina poured her own when it was apparent Jimmy wouldn't play the gentleman and do it for her. She downed half of it in one long gulp and let out a sound halfway between a gasp and a sigh. "You loved her."

Jimmy didn't say a word.

"Jimmy, I didn't understand."

He sipped his beer out of the bottle. You can't talk while drinking. He took a breath and then he took another long sip.

"I was hurt, Jimmy."

He looked at the mirror behind the bar.

"I thought it was your fault."
He took another drink.
"I'm sorry, Jimmy."
He waved for two more beers.
"You're not the only one hurting you know?"
Silence still replied.
"Damn it, Jimmy. I'm sorry!"
He said nothing.
"Aren't you going to say anything?"
He gazed into the mirror, not seeing what was there.
Bina slid off the stool and left.

Before the door was closed behind her, Ken plopped a bottle of whiskey and a shot glass on the bar in front of Jimmy without saying a word. To Ken's surprise, Jimmy finished his beer and left without touching the whiskey.

※ ※ ※

As the sun went down, Old Joe Jenkins sat on the screened-in back porch watching the garden. An ancient, single-shot twenty-two leaned against the door jamb in case he saw a rabbit. Good things come to those with. There's no better bait for a rabbit than a vegetable patch. A raccoon or an opossum was almost as good though they took a little more fixin'.

There was movement off to the right where the trace led through the back of the neighbor's place and down to the hard road. "Company comin," Joe said. His old driveway was off to the left of the house and ran straight off the highest cliff left by the Ring of Fire. "Good thing I get on with the neighbors or I'd have no way into town."

"Hello the house," a familiar voice called out.
"That you, Jimmy Dick?" Joe called back.
"Yeah."
"Well, come on up."

Joe watched the man he knew to be in his fifties—and who looked ten years older than his age—make his way through the twilight. Tonight Jimmy looked even more haggard and worn than usual.

By Terry Howard

"Hey, Jimmy, come on in and sit a spell. I've got a jug my pa put down." Joe indicated an old brown jug of corn liquor. "Aged to perfection in a charred oak barrel and then put up in jugs. Let me get you a glass."

"Don't bother, I ain't thirsty."

"Thirty-year-old whiskey? Smooth as silk?"

Jimmy shook his head. "I'd take one of those if you got one to spare," Jimmy indicated a cigarette glowing in the ashtray next to Joe's rocking chair.

Joe pointed to a wooden box on the table next to the ash tray. "Help yourself."

Jimmy lit up and took a deep drag. "Damn, Joe have you been sittin' on a stash of up-time cigarettes all this time?"

"Nope. They'd be stale by now, even if you froze 'em. I rolled these. Years ago the wife got tired of me hand rolling the things. Said they looked nasty. So she bought me a roller and a crate of papers for Christmas."

"Yeah, but this is good, mellow up-time tobacco, not like that harsh cow shit stuff they sell in town."

"I got a plant growin' in the greenhouse out behind the barn."

"You're sittin' on a fortune."

"Can't grow it except in the greenhouse. Season's too short. The papers will see me out, but if I took to sellin' the things then when they're gone there ain't no more and I can't smoke the money."

"You could sell the seed and they could take it down to Spain and ship it back."

"Could. Then more people might take it up. Did you see the little book in German that was goin' 'round? Someone tryin' real hard to stop the trade before it starts." The truth was that lung cancer caused Joe's wife's death and the print run of the up-time study on tobacco and cancer was his doing.

"Joe, I know who paid for that book to be published," Jimmy said.

"Caught me, did ya'?"

Jimmy nodded.

"Well, I'm about done for and I figure a man oughta give somethin' back. Once it's out there then any damn fool who takes up with it deserves what they get.

THE LEGEND OF JIMMY DICK

"What brings you to my mountaintop this late in the day, Jimmy?"

"Needed to talk to you. I was wondering if you would teach me Latin?"

"Why in tarnation would you want to do that?"

"It's what you and Onofrio used with that Kraut. I've got the reputation of being a philosopher. It's embarrassing to have the name and not be able to talk the game. Did you know I'm getting mail from all over Europe? It's mostly all in Latin. If I'm going to be a serious philosopher these days, then I need to know Latin."

"Sorry to hear about Merle," Joe said.

"Thanks," Jimmy replied in what Joe thought of as an empty voice.

"Jimmy, if you want to learn Latin, talk to Onofrio. He's better at it than I am."

"I heard you with the Kraut that night in Grantville's Fine Foods. You're better at slingin' that yack than he is."

"He stops and thinks before he talks. No, Jimmy, his Latin is better than mine 'cause his English is. I think in ain'ts and oughtas and 'causes. He learned to think in book English. So he has book Latin. It's pure and mine is tainted. Besides, he's a teacher and I ain't. Then, too, he just retired again. So he has the time. I'm still workin' a farm up here."

"Yeah, I hear about Onofrio. Rev. Wiley's kid got the old man canned after he argued the kid into the ground over religion versus science." William Wiley's aggressive atheism ran up against Emanuel Onofrio, who pointed out to Will that ultimately he accepted science on faith. Having his world view challenged did not sit well with Will and he raised a stink, accusing Onofrio of teaching religion along with math. "Wiley should have taken a horse whip to that boy of his when it would have done some good."

"I hear tell he did, and I hear tell that's the problem. I also hear Onofrio could have stayed on if he'd wanted but he was ready to give it up anyway.

"Still, he's the one you want to get to teach you Latin. You're welcome to come up any time and give me a hand with the chores and practice your Latin when you've got some, but if you want book learnin', go see Onofrio.

"Shhh. Now sit easy and be quiet. There's a rabbit takin' a nibble of the head of lettuce I was going to make a salad out of tomorrow." Joe quietly stood up and eased the rifle out the screen door. The rifle popped and Joe smiled.

"Well, from the size of it, it's an old one. It looks like we'll be havin' rabbit stew for supper tonight. Why don't you go fetch it in and I'll start supper."

Jimmy left the next afternoon with a dozen 'real' cigarettes having, not had a drink of liquor all the while he was there.

* * *

Jimmy pushed up to his usual place at the bar. Club 250 was at its lunch crowd peak. Ken set a cold one in front of Jimmy without a word. Eye contact was made.

"Burger and fries," Jimmy said.

At the sound of Jimmy's voice, Julio looked up from his lunch, a cold beer in a glass with an absolutely fascinating bottom. "You're late."

"Didn't know I was on the clock." For years Jimmy was one of the first of the lunch crowd to show up. He was often still in the same spot at last call.

"Where ya' been?"

"The library."

"The library? What in hell are you doing in a library?"

"Working."

Julio snorted in disbelief. "Now that's funny.

"You never worked in your life until we landed here." This was not completely true, but it was close enough. Jimmy hadn't worked a day uptime since he came home to find his wife and daughter gone. Eventually he got by on a disability check. Now he got by on the rent from inherited real estate. "Then, as soon as we had a rail line from the coal mine to the power plant and we were over the hump, you quit workin' for the railroad. What's up, Jimmy? Where have you really been?"

"Told ya'. I've been down at the library working."

"Nobody works at the library. All you do there is read. What're ya' up to?"

"Julio, you know how the cops saw to it I've got the name for bein' a philosopher. Shit, you and Ken helped make it happen. Well, if I've got the name as a player, I figure I oughta at least be able to talk about the rules of the game. So I've been spending some time down at the library trying to find out just what the rules are."

Julio snorted. "It was a joke! Nobody but the visiting Kraut was serious. You ain't no more of a philosopher than I am."

"Tell me something, Julio. Have you got three letters from Italy and another one from Morocco sittin' at home asking questions or invitin' you to come visit?"

"Of course not," Julio said.

"Well, I do. That Kraut I had dinner with has been bad-mouthin' Grantville, up-timers in general, and me in particular all over the place. As far as the world is concerned, *I* am Grantville's foremost philosopher. Oddly enough, he is reporting what we told him accurately, and in spite of his ridicule it seems it's being well received. Under the circumstances I think I oughta have some idea what I am talkin' about. Don't you?"

An amazed Julio replied, "Three letters from Italy?"

"Yeah, I've got two invitations to visit Rome from two different cardinals. The other invite is from Venice."

Julio was impressed. "You goin' to go?"

"Hell, no. Least wise, not until I know what I am talkin' about. Joe and Emanuel got me through the dinner. If I went off without them, I'd embarrass myself and all of us. So I've been spendin'—spending—time down at the library reading philosophy and learning Latin.

"Emanuel is all over me about dropping letters and using contractions. He says if I'm sloppy with English I'll be sloppy with Latin, so he is after me to clean up my language. I tell you, Julio, being a philosopher is turnin'—turning—into a lot of work. But one of these days I am going to get cornered and Grantville's reputation will be at stake, so I need to know what I am talking about."

"Wow, Jimmy, I'm sorry. I didn't mean to land you in a situation like that. I mean, Ken and I just saw that Grantville was goin' ta be laughin' about the Kraut and we just figured we should help you laugh with 'em instead of bein' laughed at. I figured it would just blow over."

"I figured the same thing. It worked too, at least for a while. But I don't want to get caught short again. If you know what I mean."

Jimmy ate lunch, and left. He stopped in for a burger and fries for dinner and went home early. For the second, or at most the third, time in his adult life he had found something worth doing.

※ ※ ※

A bit over a month after Jimmy had spent the night, Joe opened the back door to his house shortly before sundown and was hit with the unexpected aroma of dinner on the stove.

Jimmy knew Joe's habit of eating a big breakfast, a solid lunch and a light dinner after the sun went down. When he stopped in town to pick up a bucket of Hungarian dumplings, he couldn't resist a pan of ready-to-bake biscuits. He also toted a six pack of a new root beer which had the teetotalers in town standing in line. At the sound of the door opening, without looking up from the book he was pouring over, Jimmy said, "Dinner in about half an hour. I figured it was my turn to cook."

"Thanks. A fella' can get tired of eatin' his own cookin'." It was a polite lie. Joe was a good cook and enjoyed cooking the dishes of his childhood. He glanced over at the book Jimmy was reading. Joe had left his German Bible on the table. When he'd read through it, he'd put it away and read the French. Now that he spoke Latin, he read it in turn, also. He was thinking of taking another stab at Greek and maybe Hebrew, just because he had the time to do it. "Your German is good enough to read it?" he asked Jimmy.

"I've been over John, Chapter Six in Latin so many times I've got it memorized. So if I don't know the words I still know the meaning."

"Emanuel is teaching you Latin out of the Bible then?"

"Yeah. He says philosophy is just secular theology and most philosophers are either arguing for or against scripture, so I need to know scripture to know what they're talking about. I think it's all bull. I think the Latin in the Bible is what he is most at ease with, so it's what he wants to teach."

Joe had a different opinion. He figured it was just a way for Emanuel to slip Bible study into a language-tutoring program. He also figured he might as well help it along. "Matthew Chapter Six? What do you think of what you're reading?"

"The Lord's Prayer is nothing new. But I think Judaism makes a whole lot more sense. You've got, what, six hundred and thirteen laws. Three hundred and sixty-five of them are things you can't do and the others are things you must do. So, you got a list. Do it and you're all right. Don't do it and God will get you. That I understand.

"But take the verse right after the Lord's Prayer. If you don't forgive others then God won't forgive you. Joe it ain't—it isn't—right. People do bad things in this world. I'm just supposed to forgive them and forget about it? I should just let them get off scot-free?"

"Who says they do? 'Vengeance is mine,' sayeth the Lord, 'I will repay. Be sure your sins will find you out. It is appointed unto man once to die and after this the judgment. Let no man deceive you with vain words: for because of these things cometh the wrath of God upon the children of disobedience.'

"The point of forgiveness is not for the benefit of the forgiven. It's for the benefit of the forgiver."

"What do you mean by that?" Jimmy asked.

"Someone does somethin' to you. So, you get even. How? By doing something bad back. You've just hurt yourself by taking on an evil deed. Then of course they're gonna get even and then you need to do something else. Vengeance does not go long un-revenged.

"Now let's say someone does somethin' and you don't get even. You just stay mad about it. So you carry the anger and bitterness around with you and it contaminates your whole life. You not only let them hurt you, you helped them to go on hurting you.

"If you've got a pack full of old hurts and grievance you're carrying around, then at the end of the day you're tired and worn out. If you dump 'em and let 'em go, your life goes easier. Chances are it doesn't make any difference to the other party if you forgave them or not. In most cases they don't even know it, unless you are actively tryin' to hurt 'em. Then instead of you havin' fun and enjoyin' life you're lettin' them dominate your life 'cause they're in your thoughts and you are just letting them drag you down. In most cases, even if they do know they don't care.

"Jimmy, the point of forgiveness is not for the benefit of the forgiven. It's to make life easier and more pleasant for the forgiver." Joe could tell from the look on Jimmy's face the idea was new to him. He figured he should let Jimmy think on it. "I've got a critter that's been eatin' up my garden. I'm gonna sit out on the porch and watch for him. You give me a holler when the vittles are ready."

Jimmy sat there staring at the text but not seeing it for the longest time. What the old man said made sense. For all these years what Bina did had dominated his life. She moved out and took his baby girl with her. Then she made life miserable and wouldn't let him have his visitation rights. What she took from him—his reason for living, his baby daughter and his loving wife, crushed him. It not only ended his life at the time, it rode him like an old hag, like a burden that was almost... no... *was* too much to bear. For all the years of Merle's life, his life was pain and emptiness, filled with hate for Bina and pity for himself.

It was time to just let it go. He wasn't a young man but he still had a life to live. Why in the world should what Bina did all those years ago ruin what life he had left?

"God, I don't know if I believe in you or not. But if you do exist, help me to forgive Bina and let go. And God... if you don't exist, I guess I'll just have to let go of it on my own."

Jimmy sniffed the air. Something was burning. "The biscuits!" he yelped. He stood up to get to the oven. What should have been just enough energy to lift his tired bones sent the chair flying and caused the table to move; he felt physically lighter, almost like he was floating.

"Everything all right in there? "Joe called.

"Yeah, Joe, I'm fine."

The biscuits weren't burned too badly. They could still be eaten. Jimmy smiled. Life was good.

THE BAPTIST BASEMENT BAR AND GRILL

Jimmy Dick moved down the bar to where Tom Ruffner was putting away the brews way too fast for a man who was going to walk home without taking a nap first. "Hey, Tommy? What's up? You don't hardly come in here anymore. You ain't had a fight with the wife, have you?"

"Jenny is going to kill me!" Tom said.

"Well, send her some flowers. That always helps."

"I did. I bought a big expensive vase from that Hungarian potter and I took it to the <u>flower</u> shop and had them fill it full of roses and take it to my wife this morning. But she didn't call the shop so I know she's still mad. She's going to kill me."

"So you decided on a self-fulfilling prophecy?"

"A what?"

"A self-fulfilling prophecy. Like what happened to Oedipus Rex."

"Ed who?"

"Oedipus Rex, the Greek who . . ."

"Oh, him? The one they named the Ed'ipus complex after. I know that one. The lady took her son to the shrink because the school told her she had to. The shrink told her, 'Mrs. Goldstein, your boy is suffering from an Ed'ipus complex.' And she said, 'Ed'ipus, shmed'ipus, as long as he loves his mother.'" Tommy tipped back his beer and signaled for another one. "What does that stupid joke have to do with anything?"

"Oh, there's a whole lot more to the story that that. First of all, when Oedipus was born it was foretold that he would kill his father and marry his mother. So Poppa told someone to get rid of the kid. Instead of killing the boy, that someone gave him away to some shepherds. When Oedipus hit twenty or so he got rowdy and the local law told him to get out of town. So he loaded up his chariot and took off.

"Along the way he ran into a mean old man coming down the road toward him who was suffering from road rage. The old man told him, 'Get out of the way or get run over.'

" 'Try it, you old fart,' Oedipus told him.

" 'Shut your mouth, boy, before I shut it for you. I'm king around here.'

"Oedipus laughed. 'You and what army?'

"So, the old man got out of his chariot and set out to teach the kid a lesson. He couldn't make good on the brag, and in the end, he died trying.

"Later, Oedipus met up with a mythical creature who told him he had to answer the most famous riddle of all time or get eaten."

"Which one?" Tommy asked. "What is your name, what is your favorite color, or what is the relative flying speed of a sparrow?"

"No, the other most famous riddle of all time." Jimmy said.

"Why did the chicken cross the road?"

Jimmy Dick gave up with a sigh, "Yeah, that one. When he answered it correctly the Sphinx was so upset it killed itself. Someone caught it on camera for the evening news, and since the city was short a king and he was a good-looking kid, they gave him the job. But to get it he had to marry the queen. She was a good-looking woman and a lot younger than her first husband, so Oedipus said yes.

"So, you see, if they had kept the boy and raised him up right the prophecy wouldn't have come true."

"What are you getting at, Jimmy?"

"If you get drunk, your wife will kill you."

"She's going to kill me anyway. So I might as well get drunk. Just one thing I want to know? What is the correct answer to why the chicken crossed the road?"

"That's simple. One ditch is birth, the other ditch is death, so the chicken has no choice. Just why is your wife going to kill you anyway?"

"Yesterday was our wedding anniversary and I completely forgot it."

Jimmy looked at him. "Ken, a bottle of whiskey and two glasses. We've got a wake down here."

Then Jimmy directed his words to Tom, "Shit, kid, you're right, Jenny is going kill you for sure, but not before she skins you alive. So you might as well go home dead drunk."

Jimmy poured a <u>healthy,</u> or unhealthy, double shot of whiskey in a shot glass and encouraged Tom to chug it. It wasn't very long before Tom was smiling from ear to ear and trying to sing.

"That should just about do," Jimmy told the younger man. "Ken, I need a bottle of <u>cheap wine</u>, if you please."

"For crying out loud, Jimmy, are you trying to give the man the worst possible hangover he can have?"

"Sure am."

Ken snorted. "I shouldn't let you do it, Jimmy. I need the customers, bad!" Ken put a half empty bottle on the bar. "Here, it's on the house. I won't be able to sell it anyway."

At that comment Jimmy raised an eyebrow and Ken walked off. Jimmy got a shoulder under Tom's arm, "Let's see about getting you home before you pass out." He grabbed the bottle, pulled the cork out with his teeth and handed it to Tom. "Here, have a hit of this."

At the Ruffner house, Jimmy got Tom settled into the porch swing. Tom started to lie down. Jimmy propped him up. "No, you don't, Tommy. Not until I get you to bed on the couch."

Jimmy knocked on the door. When Jenny answered it, Jimmy said, "Hi, Jenny. Help me get Tom on the couch before he falls asleep."

"Jimmy? He's drunk?"

"Yeah."

"What happened? It's still daylight. When he used to get drunk he didn't stagger home until sometime after midnight."

"That's because he stuck with beer. I got some whiskey and some wine into him on top of the beer and then I brought him home."

Jenny shook her head and frowned, "I ought to leave him on the porch for the night!"

"Haven't you already done enough? He's going to have what he'll be sure is the worst hangover of his life tomorrow morning."

"What do you mean haven't I done enough? I didn't get him drunk!"

"Really? The man didn't stop at the bar on the way home for a beer or two. He stopped to get drunk. He wasn't willing to face you sober. He was afraid to come home. Mostly what he said was, 'Jenny is going to kill me!' So, I don't see how you can claim it isn't your fault."

Jenny sucked her breath in between her teeth with a hissing sound and she blushed just a bit. "I guess maybe I was being a little hard on him. Let's get him to bed."

"No, put him on the couch. He needs to wake up with a sore back and a stiff neck along with the pounding head."

"Jimmy, you're mean!"

"Don't waste a good hangover by making it easy on him, and don't wait until he feels better to talk about it either, not if you want this to be his last one."

* * *

Jimmy was hardly back to the bar before Bubba came in.

"Hey, Jimmy." It was Thursday night. Bubba was broke, as usual, and thirsty, as usual. Jimmy Dick was perched on a stool at the middle of Club 250's bar, ready, willing and able to buy a beer for anyone who was desperate enough for a free beer to put up with his acid wit. There were few takers, as usual.

Jimmy waved two fingers at the bartender. Ken was already popping two cork-lined bottle tops off newly made bottles. Up-time beer bottles were now collectables and were turning up in curio cabinets all over Europe.

"What's up, Bubba?"

"You heard about the mess Al Green's kid got into?"

Oddly, all Jimmy said was, "Yeah?"

"Well, don't you think a preacher should have done a better job of raising his kids than that?"

"Bubba? Have I ever told you you're about as dumb as a box of rocks?"

"About once a week, Jimmy."

"Didn't you get in trouble when you were his age?"

"Yeah, but then my dad wasn't a preacher."

"And you expect a preacher to do something even God couldn't do."

Bubba picked up his beer bottle when the bartender plopped it down in front of him by sheer reflex unguided by any cognizant thought. His entire intellect was busy trying to get itself around what Jimmy had just said. In half a second he gave up. "Now how do you figure that?"

"Bubba, God raised Adam and Eve, didn't he?"

Jimmy was staring at a blonde. The waitress picked up the empties off of the table. When she got to "Big Dog" Carpenter she leaned over and said something quietly in his ear. Bobby looked up and replied but the waitress shook her head emphatically.

Jimmy caught the tail end of the conversation. Or at least he thought he did if he read Bob's lips right: "Let me finish my drink first."

When the waitress got back to the bar, Ken had two beers waiting. He told the waitress, "Go tell Bob, these are on the house, then tell him you're sorry, you misunderstood. He and his lady friend are welcome to stay as long as they like."

The waitress got mad and demanded, "What about the sign on the door?"

"I guess it's time for the sign to come down. I'll take it off in the morning."

"What happened, Jimmy?" Bubba asked. "It sure ain't like Ken to give out free drinks."

"Shit, Bubba, you really are as dumb as a box of rocks. The waitress told Bobby to get his down-timer girlfriend out of here."

"Shit, Jimmy. Yeah, the sign is still on the door, but Ken quit saying anything about that months ago. The Garbage Guys started bringing that Frenchman in here for a drink after work. Until he left town, he was here so often he was practically a regular. So how come she told the blonde to leave and never said boo to the Frenchman?"

"Ken will be taking to sign down in the morning."

"Yeah, but what's the difference? Why did she get on to Big Dog but not the Garbage Guys? I'd much rather look at the blonde than the Frenchman."

"Think about it, Bubba. Why do the girls work here? The money sure ain't all that good."

"Okay, Jimmy. Why?"

By Terry Howard

"To get looked at, Bubba. When the blonde came in every guy in the place was looking at her and no one was paying attention to the waitress any more. The waitress doesn't mind the Frenchman, she thinks he's cute. He sits at a table, drinks his wine, he's quiet, and he tips well. But she wasn't about to put up with having that kind of competition. There's only room for one queen bee in a hive, so one of them had to go. She was too much of a distraction."

"Yeah, that's a fact she surely was distracting, all right. A woman like that, well, it's kind of hard for a fella to think straight. Shit, it's hard for a fella to think at all when he's lookin' at somethin' like that."

"Said Adam when Eve handed him an apple. Like I said, Bubba, even God can't raise perfect kids. I don't see how you can expect preachers to do any better. Like I told Jenny when I took Tommy home, if you want to keep them, all you can do is love 'em, forgive 'em, and encourage them to do better next time."

❋ ❋ ❋

Late the next morning Ken was at the front door with a screwdriver when Jimmy walked up.

A sour faced Ken Beasley looked at him. "You're early, even by the old standards."

For years Jimmy Dick had often been Ken's first customer of the day, and he was usually there at closing. After Jimmy got labeled as Grantville's Greatest Philosopher, about the time his daughter died, Jimmy started changing and spent more time in the library than he did in the bar. That phase seemed to be tapering off, and the amount of time he spent in the bar was going back up.

"I wanted to see you take it down," Jimmy said.

Ken snarled. "Might as well. When the wife turns it into a beauty parlor I'll have to anyway. Most of her customers are Krauts."

Jimmy was taken aback. "Beauty parlor? What are you talking about?"

"Shit, Jimmy, her business is booming. Both chairs are booked solid and she could fill a third one, easy, and probably a fourth one if there was room."

"Where would she get another chair?" Jimmy said.

"She can get one made up. Except for the hydraulics it's just a reclining chair and the hydraulics are no big deal. Hell, a car jack will work, and there are plenty of those to be had. It don't even need to be hydraulic. A mechanical jack will do just fine. She's wantin' to expand but you of all people know what rents are like in town right now."

Jimmy nodded. He lost his veteran's disability check because of the Ring of Fire. Fortunately, the rents from the once empty buildings he had inherited on Main Street made up for it. Someone had bought them because they could be had on the cheap. After the Ring of Fire an empty building was not to be found in Grantville.

"So, she's nagging me to let her open up here. She wants to turn half of it into a salon and the other half into a coffee shop, a café for customers while they're waiting and people waiting for customers. If her numbers are anywhere near right, it's the way to go."

A pale Jimmy Dick quietly asked, "But where would we drink?"

"Jimmy, she don't care. I guess I shouldn't either. The place is never more than half full anymore. People off to the army and moving out of town don't account for all of it by a long shot. With so many new bars in town, people just don't come anymore. If they don't care, why should I? I can't afford to turn customers away. I guess I could still sell beer out of the coffee shop side of the business after hours."

"That would take care of the late-night regulars, I guess, but what about the lunch crowd? What about the faithful? You'd lose a lot of business anyway. Do you know what a beauty parlor smells like? Yeah, I guess you do. But you're used to it, so you don't even notice. I don't see how anyone could stand to hang out and drink there."

"Still, Jimmy, if I pay myself wages, I ain't making enough to break even. Even on New Year's Eve I'm only half full any more. The interest I'm paying on the loans that let me buy McAdam's whiskey and Old Joe's cigarette makings is eating me alive. The wife looks at the income and argues that a parlor is a much better use of the space. I've been arguing that it will turn around but I'm losing ground. It seems like there's fewer of us every month. More and more people are making down-time friends. They can't bring them here so they go across the street. If things don't turn around somehow, I'll have to give in and close up."

By Terry Howard

"Ken, I just raised the rent on the old shoe store. The tenant says he'll have to move if I don't come back down. That would be a whole lot better location for a beauty parlor than here anyway. And she'd have room to open a café if she wants."

Ken shook his head, "Can't afford it, Jimmy."

"Yes, you can. I'll see to it. We can start with a low rent and raise it as the business grows. If it doesn't grow, then she can move it back home."

Ken stopped unscrewing the sign and looked at Jimmy without saying a word for what seemed like forever. When he spoke it was one word: "Why?"

"Ken, this is . . . community, it's family, it's church for those of us who aren't churchmen, it's home." Jimmy's voice kept rising. "I can't let you do it to me or the other regulars. I just can't."

Ken bit his lower lip, something he was wont to do when he needed to think. "Let me run it by the wife. Thanks, Jimmy."

※ ※ ※

When Jimmy came in the next day, Ken popped the tops off of two beers and put one in front of him. Jimmy got quiet in his soul. In all the years of drinking in Club 250 he had rarely seen Ken drink and never with a customer.

Ken concentrated on drinking his beer until it was half gone. "Jimmy, thanks for the offer of the old shoe store. But I talked it over with the wife and she flat out said 'No.' I said, 'Why not?' and when she said why I couldn't argue the point."

"Ken, you can't do this. What was her argument? Surely we can come up with an answer that will get her to change her mind."

"I doubt it, Jimmy. She pointed out it was dumb to pay rent, even if it was a better location, when the Club was going out of business anyway. And it is, Jimmy. Even with the best whiskey in town . . ."

Jimmy spoke up, "Shit, it's the best whiskey in Germany."

". . . and even with the only supply of the next thing to up-time cigarettes . . ."

"I don't care if they are hand rolled. They're up-time cigarettes," Jimmy said.

". . . to exist these days, I ain't got enough customers to pay the toll. And it's only going to get worse. So why rent a space downtown? What am I going to do with this place when I close the doors? She's right. We might as well face reality and make the change now."

Jimmy's mouth opened and agony poured out, "Ken, you can't do it! Please? Think about it! Find another way!"

"Sorry, Jimmy. It's a done deal. She's moving the beauty shop here just as soon as we can do the remodeling. You're the last customer. I'm hanging the out of business sign on the door as soon as you leave."

"Then I'm not leaving. Please, Ken, find another answer."

"Well, if you're not leaving then I guess I'll just hang the sign and lock the front door before anyone else comes in while you're waiting." Ken picked up the hammer and the nails and the sign he had ready to hand behind the bar and headed for the door.

When he came back Jimmy had calmed down. "Ken, what are you going to do?"

"Like I said, Jimmy, we're turning the place into a beauty parlor."

"No, I mean what are you going to do when you're not running this place any more?"

"I guess I can find a job as a bartender, if I don't like being a house husband and gentleman of leisure. The wife says with what she'll make after she moves, I won't have to work if I don't want to. Shoot Jimmy, I almost hate to admit it, but as I get older the idea of farming is growing more attractive all the time, despite what I swore as a kid.

"When I sell off the stock and the furniture I might try to buy the old home place and raise some cane." Ken said with a smile. "I haven't been able to raise any cane in years. You really need to be on the other side of the bar for that."

"How much?"

"What?"

"For the stock and the furniture? How much?"

"I ain't tallied it yet."

"Give me first dibs. You owe me that much."

"What are you going to do with them? Open your own place in the old shoe store?"

"Maybe. And maybe, all I want is a lifetime supply. It's like the story about the man . . ."

"Jimmy, the bar is closed. I don't have to listen to any more of your dumb ass stories even if all I ever did was overhear them. I never did think any of them were funny. No, I take that back. There was one, the one about the Norse gods complaining to Buddha about Grantville. That one was funny."

✳ ✳ ✳

"Hey, what's going on?" a very puzzled Jim Allen demanded. All the tables and chairs were pushed to one side. Ken and Jimmy Dick were busy taking the bar apart.

"Didn't you read the sign?" Ken asked.

"What sign?" Eric Hudson asked.

"The one on the door," Ken clarified.

"The damned door was open! We didn't see any sign. What hell is going on?" Jim repeated.

"I'm out of business," Ken said.

"Out of business? You can't do that," Jim objected.

"Watch me," Ken replied.

"But, but, but why?" Jim asked almost stuttering in absolute amazement.

"Shit, Jim. I was losing money and it was getting worse seems like every week. I ain't seen you or Eric in over a month. Where were you when I was trying to make ends meet?"

"We've been in Halle," Eric said.

"Yeah, that's the problem. Half of my customers have moved out of town. Half of the ones who didn't got cozy with the Krauts and quit comin' in. I can't make a livin' no more and my wife needs more space for her beauty salon so I'm out of here and she's movin' in."

"A beauty salon? You're turning the best saloon in town into a salon? Ken? You have got to be kidding! You can't do this!" Jim said.

When Jimmy Dick heard the line 'saloon into salon' his sarcastic wit went to work. "So you lost your 'o', did you? Or maybe, if you take the salon out of saloon all you have is '0.' Or how about. . . ." But he set it aside for later and gave his attention to what was unfolding.

"I can, and I have. Fini, done, finished, complete, it's over. I can't keep a bar open without customers.

"I'm ready to take a break and I've got a few cold ones in back. Care to join me?"

Jimmy looked up. "It's like the story of the fellow who . . ."

Ken snarled, "Shut up, Jimmy. You guys want a cold one on the house or not?"

"Might as well," Eric said. "That's what we came in for. It's just not going to be the same in town without the club."

"I'm sure you'll find somewhere else to drink," Ken said. Looking at Jimmy, "Maybe someone else will open up a redneck bar."

Jimmy didn't say a word.

"Ken, it just won't be the same," Eric said.

"Hey, things change. They grow or they die. It's like a . . ."

"I said shut up, Jimmy, and I meant it."

"Well. Okay, but . . ."

Ken's look said it all. Jimmy shut up.

❋ ❋ ❋

"Hey, Tip. You heard the news?" Audrey Yost, the florist in town, asked as she stopped in for a beer and pretzel lunch.

"Yes, isn't it great. She had a litter of nine and all of them are pointed."

Audrey was purely puzzled, "What are you talking about."

"Hazel's latest litter, we were sure when there wasn't an unneutered male Siamese in town that we'd lost them. But she found a pure white to breed with. Only two of the first litter were fully pointed and they were both females. But she kept crossing back. It's taken years, but it looks like maybe she's bred the alley cat out of them. Now, when my cat dies, I can get another Siamese. Isn't it great?"

"That's news?"

"Sure, it's great news."

"I was talking about something important."

"Well, if you don't think keeping a breed alive is important, I do. What's your important news?" Tip asked.

"Club 250 has shut down and the beauty parlor is moving in. Never thought I'd see the day I'd be going there but it looks like I will now."

"Yeah, I've heard." Tip's voice held no excitement or approval. "I thought you said you knew something important."

Audrey was puzzled and disappointed. "Hey, with Ken shutting down, that leaves you with the only aged whiskey in town. Maybe you'll pick up some of his business."

Tip paled just a bit, "Gawd, I hope not. I don't want those rowdy rednecks in here making a lot of noise, scaring off my other customers, getting in fights, and busting up the place."

"Hm. Hadn't thought of that," Audrey said.

✼ ✼ ✼

Lorena Maggard's phone rang, "Hello?"

"Lorena, this is Carolyn, I've got the most wonderful news."

In her early seventies Lorena didn't get out much. On the other hand, you couldn't hardly catch Carolyn at home. A lot of her time was spent visiting down at the nursing homes and fetching groceries and such for various shut-ins . . . in other words, gossiping.

"You'll never believe it. And I wanted you to know right away so I didn't want to wait until I see you tomorrow. After all these years, our prayers have been answered. Ken has finally shut down that awful bar."

"No!"

"Yes."

"Halleluiah! It's about time! I didn't think I'd live to see it. What happened, Lorena? Did the cops finally close him down? The good Lord knows we called and complained about it often enough."

"No, his wife needs more space for the beauty shop so she made him let her take over the building."

"Lordamercy, I do declare. Well! God bless her. I guess I'll just have to go get my hair done. It's been ages."

"Lorena, it's been years and you know it."

"Well, then it's about time, ain't it? I've always wondered what the place looked like inside."

* * *

A bit later Phyllis Congden-Dobbs' phone rang. She picked it up and, of course, she said, "Hello?"

"Phyllis? This is Carolyn. Have you heard? Ken's closing down that terrible bar of his."

"Well, that's not surprising. I've been waiting for that to happen ever since he told Estil he couldn't be bartender any more because there wasn't enough business."

Carolyn was disappointed. Phyllis was neither excited nor surprised. After all, what's the point of "sharing the good news" if everybody already knows about it? Still, if you can't pass it along, then it's time to go fishing. Who knows, you might learn something you can share elsewhere.

"Say, I ain't seen Estil in a dog's age. What's he up to these days."

"Haven't you heard? He's got a job in Magdeburg."

"Well, I do declare. Will miracles never cease? Estil has a job?" Then her voice filled out with suspicion. "What kind of job? Is he tending bar?"

"No, he's a consultant."

"You don't say? What's he consulting on?"

"Up-time culture." Phyllis knew he was helping to set up a theme bar, but she wasn't going to tell Carolyn and have it spread all over town. Let her find out on her own. Estil was enough of an embarrassment as it was.

"You've got to be kidding? Estil? Well!" No one could do a *righteous, high and mighty* or an *offended martyr* any better than Carolyn Atkins. "I do declare."

* * *

Carolyn no more than hung up from speaking to Phyllis than she was dialing Lorena's number.

By Terry Howard

"Hello?" Lorena answered the phone's request for attention.

"Lorena, you won't believe what I just found out."

* * *

Melodie and Donnie Murray stopped into Marcantonio's Pizza. Everyone—except the Marcantonios—agreed it was the place to find the second best pizza in town. Carlina happened to be working the counter. When she put the order slip on the clip ring to the kitchen she called out in a stage whisper, "Leo?"

"Yes?"

"This one's for Donnie and Melodie." They hadn't been there in months, not since before they got married.

"Well, Saint Pepperoni be praised. For the Virgin's sake, woman, don't make any more wisecracks about Donny and Marie. They took offense, and I don't blame them. It wasn't funny anyway."

"Leo, if I've told you once, I've told you a thousand times, there isn't any St. Pepperoni."

"Sure there is. I asked Father who the patron saint of pizza was and he told me it was St. Pepperoni."

"Leo, he was pulling your leg, you old fool. There isn't any patron saint for pizza. And there never was a St. Pepperoni. I looked it up."

Leo knew it, of course, but there was no way he was ever going to admit it his wife.

"We have to share St. Carlos Borromeo with the cooks and the bakers, but I've told you that. I thought you would want to know they're back." What she was really saying was, "See, I told you it was no big deal."

"Well, you shouldn't have teased them about being Donnie and Marie. Still, with Club 250 closing, maybe they'll start being regulars again."

"That would be nice." She paused. "As long as they don't bring any of the riffraff with them."

"Damn. I never thought of that," Leo said. "I sure don't want Ape and Monkey hanging out here. It would be bad for business. This is a family-friendly restaurant."

THE LEGEND OF JIMMY DICK

❋ ❋ ❋

Casey was working the window at Casey's Take-Out. Dean Blackwood ordered a roast beef and Swiss on rye with mayo and a small bucket of beer. When he got his sandwich and his drink, he lifted the lid on the beer pail and took a heavy hit. "Hey, Casey, I said I wanted a small bucket of beer, not a bucket of small beer." Casey still had it in a keg. Small beer wasn't being bottled much. The people who drank it were used to it being out of a keg.

"Dean, that's the only beer I sell. If you want a stiffer beer go find a bar."

"Shit, Casey, ain't you heard, the only good bar in town just shut down."

"It was a good bar all right. Good for nothin'."

Dean let fly with the bucket of beer, "Keep your damned canoe beer!" Followed by the sandwich. "And your worthless sandwich too."

Casey ducked. Dean started to walk off, "Hey, you haven't paid for that."

"Paid for what?" Dean asked.

"The beer and the sandwich."

"What beer? That damned can wasn't beer, it was canoe."

"It was what?" Casey asked.

"It was damned close to water."

"If you don't pay up I'm calling the cops."

"Go ahead. See if I care!"

❋ ❋ ❋

Arch Pennock bumped into Mark Castalanni coming out of the Flying Pig. Arch was the one coming out, having just been cut off by the bartender. He wasn't at all happy about it. He was sure Ken wouldn't have cut him off for at least two more beers.

"Hey, Mark, have you heard? Ken's closed down."

"Yeah, I heard. That's a shame."

"As if you cared. You ain't been there in years. It's your fault you know. Ken didn't have enough business to stay open."

"Arch, I stopped going when I got married because I was getting harassed about it."

"Well, you didn't have any business marrying a Kraut."

"It's none of your damned business who I married. We're happy. She's a good woman."

"Not the way I hear it. I heard she could be had by anybody with a . . ."

Arch never got to finish his sentence. It's kind of hard to talk while someone is knocking your teeth in.

✳ ✳ ✳

The dispatcher put the phone down, "Lyndon, get over to The Flying Pig. There is a fight on the street. Mark Castalanni is mopping the gutter with Arch Pennock."

Lyndon let out a rattling sigh of disgust. "That's it; there's been one a night. Arch did his drinking at Club 250 and Ken kept a lid on things."

"Yeah," the dispatcher said. "I never thought I'd hear myself say it, but damn, I wish he hadn't closed the place down."

"I know what you mean. Even with the little old ladies calling in a noise complaint every Sunday after church it was a lot quieter in town with it open."

"Well at least we haven't heard from the Hole in the Wall yet tonight. Nor Tip's either."

"I don't think you'll hear from Tip's. The last fight happened when the bartender refused to serve them because they got into a fight the night before and the night before that. He told them to get out so they couldn't get into a fight with the patrons. So they got into a fight with the bartender instead. The chief made it official. If they go back there he'll see to it they end up doing ninety days on a work crew." The police had stopped holding any man in good health in the jail for any sentence of more than a week. Some crews did road work or logging or haying in season. Anyone who looked like they might run off ended up in a secure facility, tanning leather. The owner built a dorm, hired guards and contracted with the police for labor. Lyndon grabbed his hat and headed for the door. "I'm on my way."

THE LEGEND OF JIMMY DICK

✽ ✽ ✽

Jimmy Dick stopped into Tip's for lunch. The lass who took his order was cute, if a bit plump for Jimmy's taste. He was disappointed when Tip brought the order out instead of the waitress. He was a bit shocked when Tip pulled out a chair and sat down. "Jimmy, is it true you bought the tables and the bar out of Ken's place?"

"Yeah, want to buy some?"

"No. I hear you also bought up his stock and his kitchen."

"Yeah. I'll sell that, too."

"Please don't. I know a lot of people who figure you're going to open a bar."

"I thought about a philosopher's lounge but there isn't enough call for it. Couldn't make a living."

"No, what you need to open is a redneck bar and grill."

"Shit, Tip, if Ken couldn't make a living at it, how in the hell do you think I could? I don't have money to throw away any more than Ken does."

"But, Jimmy, they've got to have someplace to drink. When they mix with other people they mix it up. They need their own place."

"Look, Tip, I miss Ken's place as much as anybody. For years I spent more time there than I did at home. But the business just isn't there. Ken wouldn't have closed up if it was. I'm talking to the tobacco shop about buying the rest of the cigarette papers and the ongoing supply of mild tobacco. I sort of figured you'd buy the whiskey but if you don't want it I'm sure one of the other places will. If not, I'll find someone somewhere. It's damn fine liquor. I've got a line on a tavern in Magdeburg that is maybe interested in the furnishings. But I can probably make a whole lot more selling it off piecemeal as up-time artifacts. That leaves the grill and the refrigerator. But I don't think I'll have any trouble getting rid of them."

"I sure wish you'd reconsider."

"Tip, I can't make any money at it."

"But there are some things more important than making money."

"Oh? Like what?"

"Like peace and quiet. Those boys are going to drink somewhere, and when they do they're going to get loud and rowdy, and then they're going to get into a fight. They need to be quarantined."

"Yeah, I suppose you're right, but I don't see why I should pay for it."

"Surely we can find a way."

"Are you willing to pay for it?" Jimmy asked.

"Well . . ."

"See?"

Tip got quiet for a bit. "Jimmy, if I'm guessing right Ken was still turning a profit. He was at least coming close to breaking even if I know anything about it. Shit, if his wife hadn't wanted the building he could have gone right on breaking even for years. Now if I can come up a company to pay for it, and eat the loss if we have to, will you put up the furnishing and the stock? If there is actually a loss, it really shouldn't be that bad. I mean there are things Ken should have been doing that he wasn't."

"Look, Tip, if Ken had thought he could make that work I'd have rented him the old shoe store. I offered, and at a damned good rent too. But he was sure he couldn't pay the rent and his time and still make it pay for itself. Where are you going to get people interested in taking a loss?"

"Myself and other bars who want the damned rednecks to go someplace else. I can at least try."

"Do you really think you can make it work?"

Tip thought about it. "No. But I can try."

"This whole thing is like the story about the man who went hunting. He wandered off into the restricted game area where he found the bear, he took aim and the bear asked him, 'Hey, what are you doing? This is a closed area. You ain't supposed to be here.' Well, the hunter said to the bear, 'I'm cold. So, I need a bear skin coat to keep warm.' 'You don't say,' said the bear. 'So happens I'm hungry so I'm out here looking for a meal. Why don't the two of us talk about this?' So the man agreed to talk about it and in the end they both ended up getting what they wanted."

Tip snorted. "So the moral of the story is to be careful of what you ask for because it could end up eating you alive."

"Yeah, something like that." Jimmy said.

"Next time, Jimmy. I've got to get back to work."

THE LEGEND OF JIMMY DICK

✻ ✻ ✻

Two drunks, singing a song that was just plain disgusting, and, truth be told, their singing was worse, walked into the police station. The dispatcher looked at them, crinkled up her nose more in distain than at the smell, and asked, "What can I do for you?"

"We're lookin' for the retired president."

"Well, Mike Stearns sure isn't here."

"Naw, not him, the other one."

"The second drunk spoke up. "Yeah, we want to see Lyndon Johnson."

"He isn't here either."

"Well, get him here. We know he's on duty. We saw him earlier tonight."

"He's busy."

"Hey, do we have to start a fight to get him here? We can do that if we have to."

"Okay, have a seat and I'll call him."

The drunks set down and went back to singing.

She got on the radio and called the patrol car, "Lyndon, you won't believe it. Arch and Dean just walked in looking for you. They said they'd wait."

"I can hear 'em. What do they want?"

"All I know is they're here, they're plastered, and they insist on seeing you."

"Okay, I'll be there shortly."

Lyndon walked in and shook his head. The drunks spied him and one of them called out, "Lyndon, ol' buddy, good to see ya."

"Okay, guys, what do you want?"

"We're drunk."

"Yeah, I can see that."

"Well my friend here pointed out that if we got any drunker we'd end up in a fight and you'd have to come and get us and we figured that we'd save you the trouble of comin' and gettin' us— I said that already, didn't I? Anyway, we figured we'd save you the trouble of comin' and gettin' us and we figured we'd just come on down and meet you here."

Lyndon put a hand over his mouth to hide his face while he snorted from swallowing his laughter.

"You mean, you want me to charge you with being drunk in public?"

"Well, yeah, or you can let us go and then later tonight you can charge us with drunk and disorderly."

The dispatcher let out a deep sigh, "That bar is more trouble closed than it ever was when it was open."

"How about I just give you a ride home instead?"

"Yeah, that might work."

When the report came across the chief of police's desk, he read it twice and said out loud, even though he was the only one in the room, "We have got to do something. This can't go on."

* * *

Friday night rolled around and for a wonder the town was quiet.

"What's going on out there?" the dispatcher asked.

"Nothing," one of the new officers said.

"I know that much from just sitting here. The question is why? Where are the rednecks from Club 250? We scheduled a double patrol just to handle them."

"Did, you not hear? There is a big party?"

"Oh. Ken threw a party? Good."

"No. Mr. Beasley did not throw a party. He is not invited. It is a wake and they did not invite the man who murdered the deceased."

"You mean the man who killed the club."

"Yes, I said that, did I not?"

"No, you did not. You said murder, and you can't murder anything but a person."

"Oh, well, that is what is said. They are having a wake and the murderer is not invited."

* * *

THE LEGEND OF JIMMY DICK

The elders of the Grantville Anabaptist Church met in solemn assembly. All the elders of both congregations were present. Every one of them knew what Brother Treiber wished to propose. The kindest thing anyone had to say about the idea was, "Preposterous!"

Pastor Greiner, as the chairman for the evening, opened in prayer. It was his turn. When both pastors were present, they alternated as chairman. It worked because Pastor Fiedler and Pastor Greiner made it work. The two congregations agreed to alternate for the early church service and the later time slot year by year, that also worked for the same reason. There were many people who predicted the building would be for sale within months of being finished because it would not work with two congregations sharing a building, especially when they had such loud and public arguments. The Gardens finally told them to keep it down or to do their drinking elsewhere. One group was strictly pacifist; the other group wasn't. When they went in together to buy land and build a meeting house to be shared, a pool was opened, and bets were laid. So far, at least, the pool was still open, even though it was far past the time anyone of the first subscribers chose for the date the 'For Sale' sign would first appear.

When the amen was said on a rather short prayer–by the usual standards–Pastor Greiner said, "This is a called meeting of the joint elders as our by-laws require since we are discussing Brother Treiber's proposal, which involves a change in the use of the building.

"Brother Treiber, would you be so kind at this time to share your proposal?"

Treiber stood up. "As you know, Club 250 has closed down. I propose that we allow them to use the lower level of the church as a meeting place."

When they built the meeting house the only land they could afford was a steep hillside. They scraped off the dirt and quarried into the hill using the stone to raise the walls. When they were done there were two levels, each with a ground floor entrance. The upper level had stained glass windows. Some members of the congregations had taken an evening art class in stained glass at the high school, so they made the windows instead of buying them. That way they could be sure they did not offend. The lower level was darker and not suited to a joyous celebration of the glory of God.

"You mean as a drinking place," Brother Bollert, a rather recent addition to the membership, interrupted.

"Well, yes, that is the primary point of a club such as the one that closed," Treiber said.

"It is not a club! It is a tavern! We do not need a business selling in our meetinghouse. Christ cleansed the temple. What could you possibly be thinking?" Bollert asked, rising out of his chair in protest.

"Brother Bollert, sit down. It won't be in the sanctuary. It won't interfere with worship. So it won't be a problem."

"But it is just—"

"Brother Bollert, please. Brother Treiber has the floor; you will be heard in the due course of time."

"What I am thinking," Treiber said, "is that when we were thrown out of the Southern Baptist Church in the cold and snow and had nowhere else to go, Club 250 took us in, asking only a modest rent and that we be gone by noon. Now they need a place to meet and we can return the kindness."

Heydenbluth rose to his feet. The chairman looked to Treiber, who had the floor, and Treiber nodded.

"Brother Treiber," Heydenbluth objected, "that is not quite correct. We were not thrown out of the Southern Baptist Church. We were asked to leave, and we did not have nowhere to go. One of them offered us his garage to meet in."

"Whether we were thrown out or we were asked to leave, or we were thrown out by being asked to leave, is a rather finer hair than I am used to splitting. And yes, we were offered the use of a garage, but the owner asked at least every other week when we would be finding somewhere else so he could move his equipment back inside out of the weather. That is when Club 250 opened its door to us."

Heydenbluth nodded and sat down.

Bollert stood and was recognized. "But it is still a tavern selling beer. That should not be. It has nothing to do with us. Besides, we use the lower level in the evenings to teach catechism classes."

Treiber also nodded. "True, but we can move the classes upstairs. Otherwise the lower level is only used for communal meals and occasionally as shelter. We can open our homes as needed for that. It is not a good place to live, even briefly. Meals usually happen on Sundays, and we would reserve Sundays for our use. As for your objection to commerce, I agree with Pastor Fiedler. It won't be a problem. Is this a concern to anybody else?"

No one spoke up.

"Brother Bollert, you are outvoted."

"What about funerals?" Brother Senewald asked, without standing.

Treiber answered anyway. "Those are usually in the morning, and they do not open the club until lunch. We can work around it and ask them to let us reserve the space as needed, which should not be that often."

Pastor Greiner rose. "Brother Treiber, I know many of us would like to hear your reasoning. After all, these people you wish to befriend do not like us. There was a sign on the door that read, 'no dogs and no Germans.' These people are not friendly."

"Yes, Pastor. I was there, as were many of you. I saw the sign every Sunday morning as I went to help clean and set up before worship. We laughed about it often, saying 'on Sundays it did not count,' or 'do you suppose we are not Germans on Sundays?' and Brother Jenkins, who is now gone, once asked, 'does that mean that dogs are not dogs on Sunday?' But every Sunday we thanked the good Lord that we had found a landlord. That was before you came to Grantville. But some of us remember."

Several heads nodding in agreement, and some smiled at the memories.

"But the landlord threw us out," a voice called out. "Why should we do him a favor?"

"Yes, Ken Beasley did. But Brother Jenkins found us a very large tent for the summer, and he found us a loan to buy the land and the materials we could not harvest onsite or off of his land.

"Now Ken Beasley has thrown his patrons out to make room for his wife's business."

"There are plenty of bars in town. We do not need another one. Let them go there," the voice answered to a general murmur of approval.

"Just like us?" Treiber asked. "Was it not said, 'there are plenty of churches in town, let them go there'? But where did we fit? There is trouble in every bar in town. These people do not fit. Like us, no one wants them. Besides, we are not doing a favor for Ken Beasley. They call him a murderer, and will have nothing to do with him. We will surely deal with Jimmy Dick." Treiber looked to Brother Menges. "You remember him. When we opened a church just outside of the Ring of Fire, even though we had the count's permission and blessing, there was still trouble. Rocks were thrown and threats were made. Was it not Jimmy Dick who organized an armed guard for several months until the last of the troubles were over?

"We owe these people. We need to pay this debt."

Ritzman rose to his feet. "Brother Treiber, I know people who have worked in the mercury fulminate shop making primers. The owners of the shop are amongst these people. They have spitefully used and abused our people. Do we really owe them anything?"

Again there was a general murmur of consent.

"Brother Ritzman, that is a very interesting word, spitefully. Can you quote Matthew 5:44 and 45?"

Ritzman turned red and sat down without answering.

"Let me quote it for you.

"But I say unto you, love your enemies, bless them that curse you.

"Do good to them that hate you, pray for them which despitefully use you, and persecute you;

"That you may be children of your Father who is in heaven.

"These are the words of Christ. Are we followers of Christ or are we like the Catholics and the Lutheran and the Calvinists who have turned us out onto the road even in winter with nothing but the clothes on our backs, who have imprisoned us, and beaten us, and even executed us? Was there not a time when we could tell who ruled where by whether we were burned or hung or drowned?

"Have we also found peace here in Grantville and become so busy being a church and prospering that we have forgotten who we are and where we came from? Have we no compassion for others who are turned out and roaming the streets, just because they are not like us? Did not Peter write . . ."

Again a voice called out, "Surely you exaggerate. They can drink in any bar in town."

"Can they? I work for a real estate office." He did repairs, cleaned up, cleaned out, put up signs and took signs down. "If they can drink in any bar in town why did the chief of police ask the Lions, and the Moose,

THE LEGEND OF JIMMY DICK

and the Knights of Columbus and others—" The others included the Masons but Treiber did not want to mention them. They were not well thought of by some. "—to pay the rent on a place for a redneck bar? The office has been looking for someplace affordable and isn't having any luck. Nobody wants these people. Does this not sound familiar?"

The silence lingered.

* * *

"I was told that the chief wants to see me." Jimmy Dick told the dispatcher.

She picked up the phone, spoke quietly, looked up and said, "Go on in."

The chief said, "Have a seat, Jimmy. I don't have time to beat around the bush. I need you to open a redneck bar. I've got to get these boys off the streets. They're causing trouble."

"Chief, I'd like to help. Really I would. I miss having a place to drink. But it won't pay and even if it would, I'm not the man for the job. I had to buy to get anyone to drink with me."

"If I got you free rent?"

"I heard. What's up with that anyway?"

"The lodges in town are chipping in as a public service."

"Why?"

"Because I asked them to."

"Oh. But you can't find a spot? I know because they asked about the old shoe store, and I won't rent you the old shoe store for what you can pay. And I won't let you have the furniture. I had that out with Tip. I've got an out-of-town buyer, and he's paying me ten times what it's worth. You can buy the stock, but I'm not discounting it. Chief, it isn't going to work."

"We've got a spot. But they've specified that you have to run it. You don't have to work it. Hire the help. You just have to be the manager. If you don't, the deal is off."

"You've got a spot? Sure you do! Like huh. I ain't interested. Even if it could work, it's too much work."

"Free rent, and it's a good spot."

By Terry Howard

"Yeah? Where? I know this town. There isn't a good spot anywhere that you can get with the rent you're prepared to pay."

The chief smiled. It was nice being able to tell a know-it-all like Jimmy Dick Shaver that he is wrong. Unlike so many know-it-alls, Jimmy usually did know what he was talking about.

"Okay, Chief. I know that smile. Where? I just want to know, mind you. I still ain't interested."

"That's a shame, Jimmy, because if you aren't in, the deal is off."

"Where?"

"The lower level of the Anabaptist Church."

Jimmy's mouth fell open and then closed with a click. "Damn! Damn? That quarry hole in the ground. You're not kidding are you!?"

"Nope. It's on the level."

"Can I name it?"

"Jimmy, you can call it anything you want."

Jimmy got a twinkle in his eye, "I was thinking maybe we could call it 'The Baptist Basement Bar and Grill.' "

The chief blinked and then broke out in roaring laugh. Jimmy Dick just smiled.

LITTLE BIRD

Jimmy Dick looked through the plate glass window of the barber shop before entering for a haircut. He was getting it cut a lot more often than he did in years past. Before he became known as Grantville's foremost philosopher, it hadn't matter what he looked like. If his hair got long, so what? No one cared. That's what a drunk was supposed to look like. Now, though, what he said and what he looked like reflected on the town.

In the old days, what people thought of him was water off of a duck. Back then he just didn't care. But now, to some people, he represented Grantville, and what people thought of Grantville was another matter. So he retired his old Mr. Roger's cardigan sweater, got leather patches put on the elbows of his corduroy sports coat, gave up cigarettes and took up smoking a pipe, and started paying attention to what his hair looked like.

Besides, a man could spend only so many hours a day in a library. With Club 250 turned into a beauty salon he really didn't have any place to hang out. So if you timed it right to catch the barber shop full, you could end up waiting an hour or more for a trim and bullshit with the other customers.

As he pushed open the door, Walt the barber looked up with a smile on his face from the chair closest to the window as he hung a cape over his next customer. His son was cutting a head of hair on a patron in the second chair and did not look up. "Hey, Jimmy, have a seat." He glanced at the last empty chair in the waiting area along the wall. "It'll be a bit."

Renato Onofrio was sitting in the chair; Walt's son was standing behind it. "Well, I don't care what went on when he was a boy. He had no reason treating his wife like that. If she'd ever just shot him, she'd a got clean away with it."

"Well, you're probably right about that," Walt replied.

"Damn straight I'm right about that!" Renato looked at Jimmy Dick. Jimmy was willing to share the title of Grantville's greatest philosopher with Walt and Emmanuel Onofrio as part of a triumvirate, but that didn't mean Renato didn't still have hard feelings against Jimmy for raising his rent so that he had to move up to the attic. But living space was a premium in Grantville since the Ring of Fire, and a shoemaker's shop and living quarters now occupied the space Renato used to live in. Besides, with the government disability checks no longer coming in, Jimmy needed the rents off of the downtown buildings that a relative left to him as an inheritance in order to get by. "I bet you think it was all right, don't ya?"

"What's that?" Jimmy asked.

"The way Zeppi treated his wife all those years before she died. I don't care what kind of send off he paid for or how big a tombstone he bought. How he treated her all those years was just not right."

Jimmy nodded, "You're right. If she had ever shot him, she'd have gotten away with it. There weren't enough people in town to make up a jury who wouldn't have seen it that way."

"Is that all you've got to say?" Renato demanded, getting a little red under the collar. "Zeppi's a friend of yours. "He sneered. "You both used to hang out at Club 250. I'll admit he was a nice enough guy when he was sober, but what he did when he was drunk stunk." He waited awhile. When Jimmy didn't respond Renato wouldn't let it drop. "Well?" he demanded.

"You're right." Jimmy did his best to be agreeable and let it pass. "There are some people who shouldn't get drunk," Jimmy said.

"Is that all you've got to say? What I really want to know is why she put up with it."

Every eye in the shop that didn't belong to a barber turned towards Jimmy Dick. Both of the barbers knew enough to keep focused on the job at hand. Razors, scissors, and clippers can give a nasty cut if they end up someplace they shouldn't be. Jimmy Dick sighed inwardly. It looked like he was stuck. Sometimes have a reputation just plain sucks.

"Renato, I hear a story once about a robin in Edinburgh Scotland. She was on the small side and no matter how early she set out in the spring, by the time she got to Edinburgh all the best nesting places were claimed. So she settled for second best and being on the small size, and size counting towards beauty for a robin, she never could manage to attract the better mates. Some years she didn't manage to find one at all. One of those years she got to thinking: if she could find a warm place to nest and save up food, she could winter over and claim the very best nesting place. Then she might be able to attract that certain male she had the hots for.

"Things went along fine until the first true winter storm came along. Then our little bird realized she'd made a big mistake, and as soon as the weather broke she headed south. Somewhere over the North of England she got caught in a freezing rain, and with ice on her wings, she crashed into a barnyard where a cow almost stepped on her.

"Then to make bad matters worse, to make things absolutely humiliating, the cow dumped a fresh cow pie on her. But the thing about cow pies is that when they come out, they're body temperature. And as anyone who has ever been around a barnyard that had cows knows, in the winter the pies don't come out in those tight little balls. The come out in a thick stream. So it completely covered the little bird. But that turned out to not be all that bad. It melted the ice and kept her warm, and it kept the weather off of her through the night. When dawn broke so did the storm. Our little bird stuck her head out to see the blue sky and the bright sun. In the sheer joy of knowing she was going to live she began to sing.

"Now up on the porch of the farmhouse, an old yella' tomcat heard the bird singing its happy song. And he asked himself 'Whoever heard of a singing cow pie?' So he yawned and stretched and mosied over to take a look. When he got there, he carefully cleaned all the shit off of the little bird."

The other patrons nodded at the happy ending while wondering what the point was.

And when the timing was right—after all, timing is everything when it comes to humor—Jimmy Dick said, "Then he ate it."

There was a mixture of nervous laughter and frowns.

"Now any philosophical story needs a moral. The moral of this story is in three parts.

"Firstly, don't assume that someone who takes shit off of you is a friend." Some of the fellows who were waiting snickered. And one of them said, "You sure got that right."

"Secondly," Jimmy continued, "just because someone dumps on you doesn't mean they intend do you wrong. And then we get to the point that Carolyn lived by."

Jimmy Dick paused for effect and waited for a prompt.

Renato obliged. He was irritated that Jimmy was coming out looking good when he had hoped to box him into a corner, and it showed on his face for all the world to see. "Well? What's the point?"

"Oh, that's simple. If you're warm and happy livin' under a load of shit, then by all means keep your mouth shut and make the best of it."

Renato snorted. "And if you ain't?"

Jimmy waited for all of two seconds before he answered. After all, timing is everything. "Why then, shoot the bastard." Jimmy replied.

The room roared with laughter.

ONE NIGHT IN THE FLYING PIG

It was late in the morning when Chief Richards looked through the bars at James Richard, Jimmy Dick, Shaver. Jimmy had spent the night there. The skinny fellow was still dosing on the cot, fully dressed including his shoes. The police chief shook his head and then tapped with his ring on a crossbar of the cell until he had the occupant's attention. "It's been awhile, Jimmy. I'm not used to seeing you back here like in the old days. What happened."

"Does interrogating me at the crack of dawn count as a cruel and unusual punishment?" Jimmy muttered.

"It's nine o'clock, Jimmy. The sun has been up for four hours, and I've been up for three. And you've been sleeping for eight. I've read the report already. You got in a fight at the Flying Pig and put Renato Onofrio in the hospital. Are you going to tell me what happened or am I just going to let the judge throw the book at you?"

"Shit, Chief, it wasn't my fault. I was quietly drinking a beer, minding my own business, working at being an upstanding, respectable citizen when Renato decided he wanted to get into a fight."

"Uh-huh. And then what happened?"

"Well, you know how Renato always likes a shot of whiskey with each beer and has for the last fifty years. And he likes to think he can hold his liquor. And while he has the bulk to carry the load and keep it down, what he can't do is keep his head while he's about it. He's been banned from most bars in town."

By Terry Howard

Chief Richards nodded. He knew all about Renato's problems when he started drinking.

"Shoot," Jimmy said, "He was banned from Club 250 long before the Ring of Fire. Well, he sat in the middle of the Flying Pig, loudly espousing his views to anyone who wanted to hear them, and to anyone who didn't, for that matter.

"He was about ready to be cut off for the night. He was full of beer and even more full of himself. And then he said, "And another thing, while you krauts have proved yourselves to be decent, hardworking, good people, we do not need any more of these dumb Pollacks that have started turning up." He turned around a looked at me, where I was minding my own business at the bar that runs down the left-hand side of the tavern. And he asked, "Ain't that right, Jimmy?"

"You know I do most of my drinking in the Blind Pig since Ken let Kim turn Club 250 into a hair salon, and the Pig is a block and a half or so away from the house. And I don't spend the kind of time in the bars like I used to."

The Chief nodded again. It was true that Jimmy had cleaned up his act, mostly. "And what happened?"

"Well, I acted like I didn't hear him. So he said it again, but louder this time. "Ain't that right, Jimmy?"

"So I said, 'Oh, we've got plenty of dumb people in town, Renato.'"

The Chief nodded. He could see where this was going, even if Renato didn't realize Jimmy had just said he was dumb.

"But not all Poles are dumb," I told him."

"Oh, yeah? Well then, why ain't I ever heard of one then?"

"You ever hear of Madam Currie, Renato?"

"Ain't she the Frenchy who left a key between a photo plate and a block of uranium and discovered radiation? Yeah, that's right. She was. But she's French."

"Her husband was or would have been French. But Mary was Polish."

"And she had the good sense to marry a Frenchman and change her name. So she don't count."

"Does Copernicus count, Renato?"

"Ain't he the fellow what said the earth goes around the sun?"

"Yes, and he's Polish."

"Copernicus don't sound like a pollack name; it don't end in ski."

"Because he wrote in Latin like every other educated man in this century."

"Our school teachers don't know Latin!"

"Most of them are learning it, Renato."

"So that's two."

"Oh, there's a lot more," I told him."

"Never heard of 'em!"

"That's because you don't look for them. People see what they're looking for, not what's there."

"That's just stupid, Jimmy."

"Let me tell you a story Renato, so maybe you'll understand."

"Oh, shit. Here we go again. Another stupid Jimmy Dick story," Renato snickered.

"But I ignored the insult. After all, I'm the resident philosopher here in Grantville now, so I need to set a proper example. Right?"

The Chief nodded. "I appreciate that Jimmy; now, what happened?"

"I told him a story—"

"Sometime in the future, not long from now, in Poland of all places, a noble gave a land grant to a monastery that his father had sold to a village several years before. The monks started to plow it up, and the villagers objected.

"The monks answered, Well, we are the church, and we need this for a vegetable garden. You should give it to us."

"But we need it for a winter pasture for the sheep."

"Then we will have to stop you."

"How?"

"Any way we have to."

"You would fight us for it?"

"If we have to."

"But we are men of peace. How about we debate you for it?" The village did not like that idea, but the monks insisted. The monks sent for the bishop. When the villagers found out, they sent into the city for the great rabbi, Bal Shem Tov. But then they got to thinking, what would happen when the rabbi won, and the bishop looked stupid. Not wanting to risk losing the rabbi, the town agreed to send the one-eyed simpleton Shleml. But not wanting Shleml to look silly and embarrass them, the village insisted that the debate be held in silence. Well, even the bishop had heard of Bal Shem Tov. And when he heard that they wanted to hold the debate in silence, he agreed, thinking that he could not look as foolish in a silent debate.

On the appointed day, the bishop met Schleml in the middle of the field, and being a bishop, he stood on his dignity and went first. He held up one finger. Shleml clasped his hand over his breast and bowed his agreement, so the bishop continued and held up two fingers. Shleml bowed again. The bishop held up three fingers and then bunched them together. Schleml shook his fist. Then the bishop walked away.

"He is too wise," said the bishop to the waiting monks. "I can't defeat him."

"What happened?" asked the abbot. "We saw, but we do not understand."

"I held up one finger to represent the Father. He clasped his hand over his breast and bowed his agreement, so I continued. I held up two fingers for the Father and the Son. And he bowed again. I held up three fingers for the Father, Son, and Holy Ghost, and bunched them together to show three in one. And he held up and shook his fist, showing that all knowledge stems from the same single source but comes to mankind only with struggle and effort. I cannot defeat such a scholar."

The monks left, and the villagers asked Schleml what happened.

"He started out insulting me by saying I had but one eye. Well, he is a guest here, so I politely acknowledged his point. Then he bragged that he had two eyes. And I politely agreed. After all, I was chosen to represent the village. But then, he wouldn't let it go, and he rubbed in even further by saying there were only three eyes between us. And when I threatened to punch him in the nose the cowardly fellow ran away."

"So, you see, each man saw what he expected to see. Understand?"

"All I understand is that even the bishops are dumb in Poland."

"Well, Chief, I sighed. I mean what can you say to a fellow like that?"

"And what *did* you say, Jimmy?" the chief asked.

"I said, Renato, did you ever hear the story–and he interrupted me to say, 'Here we go again'–of the Italian from America who moved back to Italy and raised the average I.Q. of both countries? That is when he roared bloody murder and rushed the bar to try to spread my nose all over my face, so I broke a beer bottle over his head. And it was nearly full too, more's the pity."

"Do you realize you put him in the hospital?"

"Chief, what can I tell you? I shouldn't have hit him so hard. I've stayed out of fights for so long now that I forgot just how easy it is to break an empty head."

By Terry Howard

HAIR CLUB 250

Early Fall 1635

"Ken, when are you going to put up a new sign?" Kim Beasley asked her husband.

"I ain't," he said, reaching across the breakfast table for the butter. "That sign's been there all these years. It does a good job. We don't need a new sign."

"But all you did was add the word 'hair' to the old Club 250 sign."

"So? You didn't barely have a sign at all at the house, and it's hangin' on the door." The little sign read 'Kim's Hair Salon,' and it now hung where the sign reading "No Dogs and No Krauts" once hung. Which was good, because over half of her clients were down-timers.

"That was a residential neighborhood. I barely got away with running a salon out of the front room. I couldn't have but the one chair and one full-time employee or two part-time employees because of where it was. They wouldn't let me put up much of a sign. This is a commercial location, and I want a new sign. Or at least you need to repaint the old one. It needs to read 'Kim's Hair Salon' so people can find it."

"Nope. Ain't going to do it. They can find Hair Club 250 just fine."

"But it lacks class," Kim objected.

Ken tried to swallow a snicker and almost succeeded.

Kim started to throw her coffee cup at him and stopped since it was still half-full and coffee was expensive. Instead, she threw a biscuit at him.

By Terry Howard

It was an old discussion. Ken had long maintained that since this was Grantville and the salon was in the front room of the house, trying to be classy was just putting on airs.

Ken caught the biscuit, took a bite out of it, and threw it back. Kim laughed. Ken laughed. The two of them laughed a lot. They were a good fit.

"I want the sign repainted," she said.

"Then you do it."

"I don't have time. Since we moved, I'm swamped. Gals who haven't had their hair done in decades are making appointments. When can you get me that third chair? I can get the all the half-trained help I need. But I've got to have that third chair."

"Are you sure you're going to need it? It might be just the opening rush."

When they decided to move the salon out of the house and into the bar building they commissioned a new hydraulic lift chair (the works used to be a car jack that got reworked), and now she needed—or at least wanted—a third one.

"I got the clients to fill it. If I don't take care of them, I'll lose 'em. The opening rush will pay for it even if I don't need it. But if I have it, I think I can keep it busy."

Kim picked up the biscuit her husband had taken a bite out of. It had bounced off her chest and landed on her plate. She bit off and chewed the corner edge now covered in egg yolk and then put butter on the rest while she chewed what was in her mouth. "Get me another chair and have the tinker make up another copper rinse sink. And, yes, you can go ahead and tell me I told you so. That leather hose and the spray nozzle the tinker made up works just fine."

"Are you going to want another drying station?" Ken asked, leaning forward to grab another one of the still-warm, light, flaky biscuits off the plate in the middle of the table. Ken, who was a good cook, made good biscuits, which was a good thing, because as soon as the shop had opened up in the old bar building, business had boomed and Kim didn't have time to cook or clean house.

"Yes, please," Kim replied.

Ken nodded. "I'll see to it." When the electric heating element went out in '32 Ken had a gas heater and a blower made up. When they set up in the bar he had a tinker make a hood for it and he plumbed the divided heat run. Now it was running two dryer bonnets and looked like it could handle a third one.

"But I do want a new sign."

"Then hire it done. I ain't changing it."

Kim sighed. She knew the tone of voice. If she wanted the sign painted she would have to see to it.

Later that day

"Leota, do you know who they got to paint the sign for the hotel?" Kim asked. Leota's head was over the rinse sink. Kim had just finished touching up the dark roots of Leota's bleach-blonde hair. Leota was a night manager or something at the Willard. So she might know.

"Yeah, but why?"

"'Cause I want the sign repainted and my ornery husband says he won't do it."

"Kim, for the second time in his life he's right. Don't change it."

"The second time?" Kim asked.

"Hey, he married you, didn't he? Do you know how many women are coming in just to see what the inside of Club 250 looks like? Honey, after all those years, we won. Don't go taking that away by changing things."

"You really think it matters?" Kim asked.

Mary Katherine, who always came early for her appointment because she liked to hang out and gossip, was sitting at one of the tables left at the front of the building for an over-large waiting area, spoke up and intruded on the conversation.

"Of course it matters, Kim. If things ever slow down, you need to provide transportation to the old folks home. They got someone who comes in, but the ladies would like to get out and now you're barrier-free." At the house, you had to climb the front steps and some people couldn't. "They'd love to see the inside of Club 250. When I went for my regular visit, after word got out that you *were* moving, it's all they talked about. When I go back next week, they'll notice the new hair-do, and they're all going to ask me about what it's like in here."

"Well, if they want to see it, they'd better hurry before we start redecorating."

"Young lady, don't you dare. You'll destroy the charm of the place," Mary said.

"What? And spoil our victory? Every time I look in the mirror behind what used to be the bar, I snicker," Leota added. The salon chairs were set up so they could spin around and take a look in the old mirrors over the sinks where the back bar used to be.

Over the course of the day, whenever Kim mentioned the remodeling plans, she got variations on the same theme.

"You do and I ain't never comin' back."

"No. I like seeing what it looked like."

"That would be a shame."

✳ ✳ ✳

Kim's daughter Marisa, along with her high school chum Merrie Davidson, stopped in at closing time and sat down at a table to wait. The salon chairs were where the bar used to be. The dryer hoods were off to one end, away from the old kitchen pass-through and door. So that left more than half of the floor space open, and there were tables along the front wall for no other reasons than they kept the place from looking empty, and it was a cheap waiting area.

When everyone was gone, Kim sat down at the table and asked, "What's up?"

"Mom, Simone, is getting married, and Merrie and I want to throw her a shower—well, more of a bachelorette party, really. I don't have room at home. Can I use the salon on a Sunday when you're closed?"

Kim looked thoughtful for a full minute and then replied. "Marisa, I know you . . ." She glanced at Merrie ". . . and your friends. I ended up in the principal's office more than once because you two and Simone cut class or skipped school. But you're grownups now. So, yes, you can. But don't embarrass me. The business is doing well, so I don't need any bad publicity. So you make sure no one gets too drunk to walk home. And make sure you clean up after you're done. And you will pay for anything you get out of your father's stockroom. Is that clear?"

THE LEGEND OF JIMMY DICK

"Thanks, Mom."

❋ ❋ ❋

Out in the street Merrie said, "Okay, you got the place. I'll get Fred Astaire."

"You sure about that?"

"Hey, you saw him on the dance floor at the school dances. Shoot. You danced with him."

"Yeah. He can dance, but can he strip?"

Amanda smirked. "The way that boy moves? After I have him watch my Chippendale tape? Piece of cake."

"Okay, but will he?"

"Leave that to me." Merrie smiled a wicked, if merry, smile, "He'll do it."

"Hey, what's his real name, anyway?"

"I don't know. Hans something or other."

"Shoot, Merrie, every third or fourth Kraut is named Hans. If you don't know his last name how are you going to find him?"

"Everybody calls him Fred Astaire, I'll find him. Besides, he hangs out with that cartoon group that makes the flip books. So they will know where to find him."

❋ ❋ ❋

"Of course, it pays very well." Bobby McDougal told Fred as they leaned up to the bar tossing back the beer the Flying Pig was justifiably famous for.

"Hey, another round here," Bobby called out to the bartender. "That's a cold bottle for me and another one for Brent, and a room temperature draft for our buddy Fred here." He turned back to the down-timer, "Now like I was sayin', look at what they expect you to do."

"Hey, it's just a dance."

"Just a dance? Where did you get that idea?"

"Well, that's what Mistress Boyd said."

"And what else did she say? They aren't talking about a waltz here. Hey, don't take my word for it. Go look it up. It's called *droit du seigneur*. That's—"

"I saw *Braveheart*. I know what that is," Fred objected. "It might have happened in Scotland, but this is Germany."

"Yeah, well, think about it, why don't you? Do you know just how many of our families came from Scotland to the hills of West Virginia? We don't have nobility. That's why the King of Sweden is addressed as Captain General if he ever comes to Grantville. So since we don't have nobility, the local lord can't perform the rite of the first night. So Marisa Beasley is hiring a male stripper to exercise the rite. They hire a dancer to do the job and make a party out of it."

"You're putting me on. No one ever heard of that."

"Yeah, how many bachelorette parties have you heard about? If they have one, they usually keep it quiet for a reason. This is an old pagan thing. The priests and preachers don't approve, but it still happens."

"Look," Bobby continued, "you told me she said it was to give the girl a foretaste of things to come."

"Yes."

"Well, just what did you think that meant?"

"Yeah, but she gave me these special underpants she had made up called a G-string and—"

Bobby snickered. "The G stands for god. So since it's kept in a god string it's all right, it don't count since it's a god. Like it didn't count with the Virgin Mary having a baby 'cause it was of the Holy Spirit, so she was still a virgin, right? They expect you to dance to arouse the girl and then take her to the back room and acquaint her with what is going to happen. Haven't you heard any redneck jokes? I know you have. You were there when Brent here told the one about the boy who sent the girl home after the wedding because she was a virgin. You remember? The boy said, 'Shit, Pa, if she ain't good enough for her family she ain't good enough for ours!'

"Look up the Roman god Tutunus. I tell you they are hiring you to play the part of Tutunus in your god string. That's what Tutunus wore. Don't take my word for it. Go look it up. Get the anthropology texts and look up marriage customs. The books are full of lords and kings, elders and priests who, in the name of their gods, introduced girls into the ways of womanhood. West Virginia was a melting pot, right. We had people and ideas from all over. Ain't that right, Brent?" Bobby asked his sidekick.

"Sure is," Brent said with a straight face that took considerable effort to maintain.

Fred still looked skeptical.

"Hey, don't take my word for it go look it up. You need to know what you're getting into. Why do you think they didn't hire an up-timer?"

❉ ❉ ❉

The party was going strong when they brought in the dancer. He moved well to the music and then he started to strip. The problem was that the stripper did not stop stripping. Merrie thought it was understood when she provided the "G" string that he would keep it on. But the music continued, and so did he. The laughing gasps of dramatic affectations of shock ceased. The noise level dropped. Indeed, apart from the music and gasps of honest shock there was silence. This truly was going too far by anyone's standards.

Merrie muttered softly to Marisa, "You are in so much trouble when your mom finds out!"

"Momma is not going to talk to me for at least a whole year. There's no tellin' what Dad will say. And I don't even want to think about how my *husband* is going to react."

The rampant stud danced across the floor towards the guest of honor who stared in shocked dismay, not at all sure what she should do.

Fred extended his arms full out and placed his hands on her shoulder near her neck to slide her cardigan off her shoulders to encourage her to start undressing. He stepped back and did a slow turn to the music for all to see. When he was faced back, Simone pointed at his penis and laughed.

"Marisa? Where in the world did you ever find a little boy who could do that? And what I want to know is how many did you go through to find one that small and how much fun did you have looking?"

Marisa blushed.

Fred turned red in rage and started to slap the smirk off of Simone's face. But Simone was ready and as soon as his arm straightened to swing she kicked him in the balls. Not hard enough to do serious damage but it was hard enough to drop him to his knees. It definitely focused his attention. Slowly he got to his feet and with both hands comforting his distress, he hobbled to and out the front door as fast as he could.

The guests sat or stood by in shocked silence and couldn't decide whether to laugh or not. When one did, the rest joined in, and the room roared. When they finally calmed down, after more than one false start, Merrie said, "I suppose we should gather up his clothes and send someone after him." But when they did, they couldn't find him.

An obviously distressed, naked man staggering through the doorway of the Gardens generated a great deal of attention. "Get him out of sight and call the police." The manager said to his staff.

When the search party returned, before they were through the door, a police cruiser showed up.

"Marisa Beasley?" The chief demanded. "What in hell do you think you're doing?"

Marisa bit her lip. "We were just throwing a bachelorette party for Simone."

"And it got out of hand?" He asked.

"Hey, this is Club 250 isn't it?" Amanda Boyd asked with a chuckle.

※ ※ ※

Later, in the interrogation room at the police station, Hans Gruber, alias Fred Astaire, explained, "Honestly, I thought that was what I was hired to do. You mean they didn't intend for me to introduce the virgin to what was coming so she would not be shocked on her wedding night?"

"Where did you get an idea like that?"

"Well, Mistress Boyd said it was to give the bride a foretaste of what was to come. After I had a conversation with Bobby McDougal, I looked up bachelorette party in the library. I read the next article or two in a book about wedding customs of the world. . . ." Fred stopped. And in a quiet voice he asked, "You mean that wasn't what they wanted? But I thought—that bastard!"

The interrogator suffered from dry heaves of suppressed laughter.

Fred turned bright red while he played back the memory of his conversation he'd had with Bobby and Brent. "Oh, they are going to pay for this."

✳ ✳ ✳

When Kim opened the door to the shop on Monday morning, the phone was already ringing. "Marisa, you are so-o-o in trouble girl!" Kim said aloud though there was no one there to hear her. And the phone kept right on ringing all morning long.

At closing, a very subdued Marisa slipped into the shop and sat down at a table. When everyone else was gone, Kim joined her.

With tears running down her cheeks, Marisa said, "I am so-o-o sorry mom. It wasn't supposed to be like that and—"

Kim broke out laughing. Marisa's mouth fell open.

"Honey, the phone has been busy all day. For every cancellation, there were two or three people wanting an appointment. And get this: there were three inquiries about Sunday rentals and one booking, which you will have to handle, by the way. And they want the stripper. But they were adamant that this time he has to keep the G-string on."

"But—"

"So, I'm not mad. Everything is all right."

"No, it isn't, Mom," Marisa said. "I got a call early this morning from Simone. She said I don't have to worry about being a bridesmaid. Ethelbert heard about what happened and has called off the wedding."

"That's good."

"Good!? What!? How!?" the puzzled young woman demanded.

"Honey, what did I always tell you and your sister when you were growing up? Speak up, speak up—"

Marisa smiled and finished the saying, "—you have nothing to lose except your future ex-husband."

By Terry Howard

BIG DOG AND A BONE OF CONTENTION

August 31, 1635

Adam, still as trim as he had been when he was a football running back, leaned up against the bar in Tip's place and greeted his friend, "Hey Big Dog, did you see that old fool Jenkins go through town this mornin'?"

Big Dog had put on some weight since he had been a lineman in the front four before he moved to center. After he had, most of the team's gained yardage came from quarterback sneaks when Big Dog bulled ahead and the quarterback followed until they were piled on.

Big Dog, Harlan Carpenter, shook his head. "I heard about it, though. My boss down at the machine shop cussed up a storm for over half an hour. He says for Joe to do what he did he needed a lathe and a mill, not to mention an arc welder, which would be nice things to have here in town, back in the early days especially, instead of sittin' idle out there on a hillside. Not to mention the little steam engine he has pushing that old tractor that's going to end up rusting to pieces somewhere assuming the old cuss gets past Jena."

"Your boss don't think he'll make it?"

"Hell no. The boss says if we're lucky that old tractor with its cobbled-up steam engine will break down just outside of town, but there's no way he'll get past Jena," Harlan said in a big voice.

"I got a hundred bucks says he makes it all the way," Jimmy Dick piped in uninvited from down the bar.

"Bull shit! No way!" Big Dog said.

"Oh, he'll make it all right, or it'll kill him. But he's a tough old bird. Hundred bucks say I'm right and you're wrong." Jimmy Dick pulled his billfold out of his pocket.

Adam looked a Harlan, "Split it?"

"Hundred each," Jimmy called out.

"You're on!" Harlan said.

Adam got a sinking feeling, but pride wouldn't let him back down.

✳ ✳ ✳

Jena was in an uproar. They had seen so many cars and trucks, they were no longer notable. True enough, people would still stop and watch them, but their coming and going would not turn the whole town out to watch like it was a parade. This was somehow different. The Grantville trucks needed some special liquids, or rare atmospheres you might as well call magic potions, to run. This was one burned coal. Anyone could get coal, and if you couldn't get coal, then it would burn wood. So why couldn't anyone get an engine? Most trucks were self-contained, but this was like a railroad without the rails, one mighty engine pulling wagons. Everyone wanted to see it. It seemed like the whole town was turned out.

Albert stood, out of breath, at the back of the crowd, on the side of the road into town from the south. He had run all the way from the university, his scholar's robe flapping all the way since he had no time to take it off, to a spot where he could climb up on something to see what was coming. He was in time, but just barely. The sounds of cheering were cresting ever closer.

An hour earlier, the Professor, likewise dressed in a scholar's robe but with the addition of a hood showing his degrees by the color code in the lining, told him, "Albert, wait for the class to gather and dismiss it."

"Professor, no one will be here. Everybody has known it was coming since this morning." Updates came in at least every hour all morning. "If I stay I might miss it."

"And if I stay I might. One of us has to. I am a professor. You are an assistant. You are my assistant! Now, which one of us is staying?"

"But there is no need! There won't be anyone here!"

"There might be," the professor told Albert in a tone of voice leaving no room for further discussion. At least the professor got to walk at a dignified pace to the edge of town. The pilot or passengers aboard the coaches had announced that they were not entering the town but instead taking the by-pass.

Three students, properly dressed for class in student's robes, turned up at the top of the hour for the class. Two had been 'studying' together all morning, and the third slept late and had not stirred out of his quarters until it was time for the afternoon class. When Albert told them why the class was called off for the day they ran for the road and left him alone in the lecture hall. When the bell struck a quarter past the hour, Albert was at the door waiting.

Now he was at the road into town from Grantville to see what was being described as a coal burning engine pulling a train of wagons over the road without the need of rails. Albert had been to Grantville more than once. He had ridden in a 'school bus' and on a 'trolley.' He had seen an 'airplane' take off and land, he had also ridden on a railroad train. There were very few of the students who had not done the same. It was not far, and the point of being in the University was to receive an education, so going to Grantville was high on the 'must do' list. Still, the arrival of a self-powered machine run on common coal, or wood, of all things, caught the public's imagination.

The cheering crowd was not the only foreshadowing of the mighty engine's eminent approach. A plume of dark smoke and an occasional high piercing whistle also heralded the event. Albert waited. Any minute he would see the engine, bright yellow and the size of a school bus, pulling a train of wagons a furlong in length down the dusty road. The crowd thickened and spilled out onto the road. The whistle pierced the air, and there it was, the grand historical event, a little red . . . disappointment.

The engine was smaller than a team of big draft horse they used in the quarries back home, and the whole train wasn't much longer than a coach and six. The red paint on the engine was faded and dull, there were brown rust stains in places, and it looked like another color of paint, a light gray or green, poked through from underneath in places. He had seen the likes of it in Grantville: it was called a tractor, and this one was obviously not new by a long shot. The bright future, the wave of tomorrow, the new destiny of mankind was looking as old and tired as the white-haired coachman sitting behind the pilot's wheel of the sad little engine. If it had not been moving on its own, it wouldn't have been worth a second glance.

Herr Schroeder, the head provost's marshal's guard, came running past.

"What's got his tail up?" Someone in the crowd wanted to know.

Schroeder ran up to where the potentates from the town and the university were gathered. After a brief conversation, they all scattered like autumn leaves. A formal welcome was no longer on the agenda.

"Well, isn't that something. Wonder what we've got, a leper colony on wheels?"

The little engine pulling two wagons came on at a good walking pace. The news arrived much faster. Albert caught the first word, "Anabaptists!" then a snippet, "Up-timer bishop." Then he heard another snippet, "damn them all to hell, heretic anarchists." Then Albert heard a whole sentence: "The old man at the wheel is the up-time Anabaptist bishop who's stirring up trouble all over the place. They're heading to Magdeburg so he can install an altar and bless the Anabaptist church there. They wouldn't let him on the riverboat and up-timers don't know how to ride a horse, so he is taking a tractor if the authorities don't catch up with him and make him go back."

No wonder the official welcoming committee left," Albert said aloud to himself.

※ ※ ※

Halle was in an uproar.

Frau Schmitt went to the market for the day's vittles. The usual conversation, mostly complaining about the price of produce being higher because so much of it was going up the river to Grantville, had been displaced. One version had a demon from hell with red hair and white beard, passing himself off as an Anabaptist bishop, traveling in a coal-eating, fire-breathing machine on the way to Magdeburg to corrupt the government and damn the nation. He had been thrown out of Jena and stoned in Eulau. They would be wise to keep all the virginal girls and babies out of sight lest he despoil the first and eat the latter. The other version was a bit less colorful, if no more likely. Still, there was a stack of coal in baskets waiting down by the dock so there must be something to it. After a full day for the tale to grow, Frau Schmitt was not sure what to make of it. The demon should be arriving sometime early afternoon.

She stood with mixed apprehension in the quiet crowd, with a group of other grandmothers in scarves and shawls, lining the road into Halle. It was a hostile sort of quiet, a dry quiet, like tinder, just waiting for a spark to burst into an all-consuming riot. She watched as a fantastic machine, a coach and two wagons, all without horses, moved by themselves down the road, and she shuddered. If you had asked, she wouldn't have been able to say why. It was not really that different from the railroad. But the railroad politely stayed on the tracks. She knew about Grantville. Her son had gone there on a flimsy excuse and said it was all true. She thought she believed him. Still, seeing it for oneself is another matter. A young man sat on the coachman's seat. Another one stood on the open wagon between stacked baskets of coal and an oven.

Someone from the crowd called out, "Where is the old man?"

He's been shot!" the stoker replied. "We need a doctor."

Frau Schmitt's neighbor, who joined her for the walk to the edge of town said, "Well, if he can be shot then he can't be much of a demon." Frau Schmitt was not sure whether she was relieved or disappointed.

"Take him down by the dock. The doctor has a parlor there. What happened? Someone try to rob you?"

"No," the driver called back. "He was driving this morning, and a shot rang out. We never did see who did it."

Word preceded them, and the doctor was waiting. He pulled the bandage off of a chest wound and put it back. Shaking his head, he looked at the young men. "There is nothing I can do. He's already out of it with the pain." They didn't tell him they were giving the old man a pill every time he came to. "Get him to Magdeburg or back to Grantville. They might be able to do something, but I doubt it. Magdeburg will be better. The more he's bumped around, the worse it is, so a boat to the naval yard will be better than the railroad to Grantville."

By Terry Howard

Aaron turned to Johan. "You'd better be the one to go with him. One of us has to stay with the tractor and trailers. That should be me." Johan did not argue the point.

❋ ❋ ❋

"Hey Jimmy Dick, you hear the news?" Big Dog wanted to know. "You owe me a hundred bucks."

"I heard," Jimmy Dick said. "But you got it backward. You owe me."

"Bullshit. The tractor's in Halle."

"And Joe's in Magdeburg."

"If he ain't dead."

"The bet was he wouldn't make it to Magdeburg. It didn't say he had to be alive. Besides, there's nothin' wrong with the tractor. After they get him patched up, he can go back and get it."

"No way, Jimmy. You ain't weaseling out on me. Pay up."

Jimmy called out, "Tip, you got the bet slip?"

"Yeah." Tip brought the lock box he kept in the cabinet by the cash register. On top of the pile was an envelope with Jimmy's two hundred dollar bills and two IOUs along with a note initialed by all three parties. "Let's see," Tip said, "one hundred each, that Old Joe doesn't make it to Magdeburg."

"Yeah, but we meant he had to get there on the tractor," Big Dog complained.

"Sorry, Harlan. Ain't what it says. You initialed it. Next time make sure it says what you meant," Tip said.

Jimmy smirked. "Pay up."

"You old farts are in cahoots. No damned way I'm payin'. Ain't what we bet on."

"Kid," Jimmy said. "Your IOU. is in the box. If you don't redeem it, everybody who comes in here is going to know your note's no good. But I tell you what. Halle's half way. I'll go double or nothin' that the tractor finishes up in Magdeburg or comes back here under its own power."

"You're on," Big Dog said.

Jimmy instructed the barkeeper, "Write it up, Tip."

When Harlan came in, he had enough sense to cut his losses and pay up.

* * *

There was loud rapping on the door to the caravan, not at all a polite inquiry asking if anyone was inside, but a demanding pounding insisting on admittance. Aaron woke up and grabbed the shotgun. It was late morning, but he had been up all night. He figured no one was likely to do much in the daylight. The last thing he expected to see when he opened the door was a denim-clad up-timer with a pistol and hunting knife at his belt, another pistol in a shoulder holster still clearly visible when looking down the steps, and a pump shotgun on a sling over his shoulder. Aaron did not have the door open more than a crack when the man, in that hard-to-understand, ungrammatical German that was so popular in Grantville, demanded, "How is the old man?"

"Shot." A startled Aaron replied.

"Crap, I know that. How is he now?"

"Gone by boat to the Navy Yard in Magdeburg."

"But how is he?"

"I haven't heard. The doctor here said he is not likely to make it."

"Shit, let us fire this up and go find out." The up-timer stuck out his hand, "Name, James Richard Shaver. Old Joe is friend."

"I'm Aaron. Maybe we should wait."

"What the hell for? Take two, you, me." The force of nature pointed at Aaron and then tapped his own chest.

Aaron was rather bowled over.

Late afternoon they traded off, and James was driving. As it grew dark, Aaron waited for the driver to shut the tractor down for the night. Instead, James turned on the lights and kept driving.

"Aren't we stopping?"

"Hell no, why?"

"Do you know the way?"

James pointed off to his right, "river," he pointed ahead, "Magdeburg. How many coal?"

"What?"

"How many shitting coal we have?"

Aaron finally understood. "How much coal do we have?"

"Yes."

"Two baskets and a bit more."

"Save last one. Right?"

"Okay."

He drove until the coal ran out.

At dawn, Aaron awoke to a noise he had no reference for. James was down in the edge of the river with the noise in both hands turning a fallen tree into firewood apparently by sound alone. James looked up and yelled something in English which Aaron did not understand and could barely hear over the deafening onslaught. James set the noise cutter down, and the sound diminished. He picked a log up and tossed it up the bank. "You come, you get."

"But sir, the wood is not ours."

"You come, you get." James was insistent.

"The owner will object."

"We gone." James laughed. "Wood gone. Hell, let him object."

Again, in the face of a stronger will, Aaron's wishes were swept aside. As the last log was loaded on the fuel wagon, James put a black case holding the silenced noise cutter back in the caravan followed by a red, rounded-edged box. James shook it and said in English, "That's five gallons the army didn't get." Aaron had no idea what James was saying. James started the fire with coal and then went to the wet wood. Shortly he called for Aaron to stop and he cut up a second fallen tree in the river's edge. When a third one came in view, other people were visible on the road, and Aaron was relieved when James did not yell for him to stop.

Biere was in a small uproar, but then it was a small village. They stopped at the inn for a meal and Aaron was able to buy the bulk of the innkeeper's firewood. It would see them into the city. They would not have to steal any more trees.

They made their way into Magdeburg. The tractor wagon and caravan drew a lot of attention. The story of a coal burning engine on a land vehicle like the ones on the boats and how the old man was shot had lost nothing in the telling.

"See, son," one onlooker, who had worked at the naval yard and thought he understood how the steam shovel worked, directed his boy's attention to how things were. "Hanging behind the two big wheels on the red car in front is the steam engine. Now that thing that looks like an oven on the front of the first trailer is a boiler. You can see that they have a pile of wood on the back half of trailer to keep it burning and there are the water barrels to add more water for steam."

"It's not going very fast, father. Horses could go faster."

"True, Hans, but steam doesn't get tired."

The boy pointed to the third unit of the train. It looked like a Romany caravan. "Are they Gypsies, father?"

"No, son, it's worse than that, they're Anabaptist."

Some people were cheering, and a few were quietly hostile. James had his shotgun slung over his shoulder and was waving to the crowd. From time to time he would clasp both hands together and shake them over his head. Aaron ignored the people except as a driving hazard. The tractor was not very far into town before they were joined by mounted marines fore and aft. What cheering there was grew louder. When there was silence, it was deeper. There was very little of the 'fire breathing demon' talk going around Magdeburg, but the story of the Anabaptist bishop who was shot south of Halle was common. Some people openly said it was too bad he wasn't killed outright. Most folks just wished he would get well, get out of town, and take his fellow troublemakers with him. Still, the arrival of a coal or wood powered vehicle other than a boat was something worth seeing. The future was coming after all. The new streets were being laid out very wide to leave room for a trolley system like Grantville's.

Aaron took note of a wisp of a young strawberry blond with a grocery basket who was enthusiastically waving and calling his name.

He called to her from his seat on the tractor, "Would you like a ride, Sarah?"

She looked skeptical, but when Jimmy came to the edge of the tender and held out his hands, she ran forward, and with a jump was lifted up to the wagon. Her bright smile and "Thank you" as she gave a shake to check the fall of her skirt, warmed the old drunk's heart.

The mounted escort took them to the infirmary without asking. The Chief Corpsman was outside waiting for them. Before they had stopped,

Jimmy had nodded recognition to the corpsman, one down-timer to another.

"Hi, Jimmy." Came the response with the return nod.

"How's Joe doing?"

"If he weren't tough as wang leather he'd be dead. He might manage it yet. Getting shot can kill you. Fortunately, the bullet missed anything vital, so he'll probably make it. Still, he could die of old age at any time and who'd know the difference?"

Jimmy smiled in relief at the good news that his friend was still alive. The tractor and Joe, still alive, were in Magdeburg. Harlan would pay up or lose his standing as a member of the good old boys' club. Jimmy did not have to admit he cared about the old man.

"I've been wondering what to do with him since I couldn't send him home," the corpsman said. "Looks like you brought home to him."

Aaron and Sarah helped get the old man settled in the caravan. Then Aaron went to report into Brother Hess, the head of the family he stayed with, who was sponsoring him in the local Anabaptist fellowship, detouring a bit to see Sarah to her home.

✻ ✻ ✻

"Aaron, it is good to see you back safe and sound," George Hess said. "You've been to the naval yard? How is the elder?"

"They said he would be all right. They've moved him into the caravan. He's very weak and will be a long while recovering."

"Elder Ritter's family will be looking after him. Hansel said it was the least they could do since it was their idea for him to come, and it almost got him killed." George Hess half wondered if they didn't want him under their roof and obliged to them when the time came to, once again, discuss the question which brought the elder to Magdeburg. The same thought crossed Hansel's mind.

"Johan and John Ritter left on a boat for Halle yesterday. Perhaps they will be back today." George set the shoe on the last in front of him off of the stand. "Let us go see if the Ritters are ready for our guest and then get him moved in."

THE LEGEND OF JIMMY DICK

✴ ✴ ✴

While the Ritters were pleased and excited about hosting Joseph Jenkins, they had not anticipated Jimmy Dick. They did not know what to make of him or do with him. About the time they figured out he did not really speak German they developed a suspicion he was not a true Christian. Half of what German he did have was not suitable for a man of G-d to utter. So Hansel Ritter bluntly asked him, "Are you a devout man of G-d?"

"A damned what?" Jimmy asked.

"Are you a Lutheran, a Calvinist, or a Catholic?" Hansel asked when it was absolutely clear he was not truly a Christian. This question Jimmy understood.

"Hell, I not neither!"

"Well, then what are you?" Hansel asked.

Jimmy answered proudly, "I," he switched to English for the word, "hillbilly," while tapping himself on his chest, and then he switched back to German for the words, "red neck."

The words 'red neck' caught the attention of the Ritter family. The phrase had appeared in an article Joe had published, under the pen name of Leo Nidus, in a Magdeburg weekly paper put out by the committee of correspondence. The article told of how the men of Club 250 had stood guard over a startup church outside of the Ring of Fire until the locals got the message and left the congregation alone. Elder Ritter asked if he was one of them. With Jimmy's very poor German and the Ritter's complete lack of English it took a bit before Jimmy figured out what they were asking. "Hell yes. Was me!" Half of the family was puzzled when he sounded ashamed. The other half took it to mean he supported the non-violent ways of the true faith. This left them supremely puzzled over the vocabulary he peppered his German conversation with.

When he fired the tractor up to go back to the Naval Yard instead of staying with the elder, a sigh of relief found its way to heaven and caused the angels around the throne of G-d to chuckle in amusement. The fit Jimmy threw when the guard at the gate would not readmit the tractor caused Aaron to blush even if he did not understand three words in fifty. When Jimmy wound down, a young ruffian bystander said, "There's a vacant lot near the Golden Arches; you can set up camp there. You will be safe there." Aaron sacked out early. Jimmy went off to find a bar and returned late. This did nothing for his reputation with the Ritter family.

When Jimmy rolled out of the rack sometime between ten and eleven the next morning his first need could have been taken care of in a chamber pot in the wagon. Instead, Jimmy pissed on a wheel. As he tucked his shirt back in his pants, he turned away from the wheel and encountered a smiling face.

"You know," the face said in good English, "it is not strictly necessary to keep the hub of a metal wheel moist like it is for a wooden hub."

"I know," Jimmy growled. "But if it feels good, do it!"

"An interesting philosophy. Can I quote you? You are the infamous Dick Head, aren't you?"

"Shit, yes!"

"Shit yes, I can quote you? Or shit yes you are Dick Head?" The face asked with a big smile.

"Both!" Jimmy smiled. He found himself liking the young man.

"Stop over to the Arches, and I'll buy you breakfast."

Jimmy shuddered. "Not before I've had something to drink."

"There I am afraid I cannot help you. I am told Peter assured you that you could camp here without worry. "

"Yeah?" Jimmy said. His suspicion kicked into high gear, he was sure he was about to get hit up for rent.

"Well, he was right. But I was wondering if you might give some of us a ride sometime."

Jimmy smiled. "Tell you what, you stop back by in about an hour with a dozen husky friends and a cold beer, and you can show me the sights."

The face did not say a word. It only nodded.

Jimmy started a fire under the boiler, then dug a wrench out of the toolbox and pulled a bolt out of the floor in each corner of the caravan. Joe had, in his usual conservative way, built the caravan as a free-standing shed. When it got home, they could still use the hay wagon, and they'd have another storage building or a guest room. An hour later the young man's face was back. He had a bucket of beer and plenty of help. The beer was warm. Cold beer was not having any better luck getting a foothold in Magdeburg than it was anywhere else. The caravan was split into a shed and a wagon. Aaron was back from wherever he had been by then.

So Jimmy had him drive while he plopped himself down in the overstuffed easy chair Joe had bolted to the floor of the tender. When more fuel was needed, he told his new friend to add it to the fire. Everyone else hopped on the hay wagon, and they were off on the very first steam powered tour of Magdeburg.

Joe's recovery was slow, these things take longer as you get older. Meanwhile, Jimmy turned a very good profit on the excursion and tour business. Aaron stopped by the Ritter's daily when he got off work, to check on and then talk with the elder. Herr Ritter was impressed. The piety that this concern for the health of a near-stranger grew out of was surely laudable. If only the lad had not taken a turn as a soldier! That being the objection to his joining the fellowship.

If Jimmy stopped in for a chat, it was in the early afternoon, after he had his breakfast and before the tour rides started. Peter and friends set up a table in Hans Richter Square selling hand written tickets, then one of them would stoke while another would announce.

※ ※ ※

Big Dog slapped his hand down on the bar to Adam's left. Adam was looking right, and the sound caused him to jump.

"Got ya'," Harlan said.

"You're late," Adam said.

"The boss is busy with a pet project, so everybody else has to chip in and get his work for the day done too."

"Huh," Adam replied. "I hear Jimmy got the tractor to Magdeburg. Looks like you owe him."

"Hogwash, I bet him the tractor wouldn't get the old fool there, and it didn't. Jimmy Dick can't go cheating and expect me to pay up."

"Dog? Did you read the bet slip before you initialed it?"

". . . 'course I did."

Adam just shook his head.

By Terry Howard

* * *

After three weeks of chicken soup and pillow fluffing, Joe had enough. He needed to get some exercise to get his strength back, but he figured he could do that on the boat to Hamburg and the ship to England.

"Jimmy, you'll take the tractor back to Grantville for me?" Joe asked.

"You takin' the train?" Jimmy responded.

"No. When I got off the train coming back from my time in the army, I promised myself I'd never get on another one. I'm heading for London first and then maybe Ireland."

"You up to traveling?" Jimmy asked.

"At my age, if it kills me, what have I lost? Johan has agreed to go along. That leaves Aaron and that girl he's sweet on to go with you right after they're officially married. What to do about Aaron is the reason they sent for me. And since they sent for me, I started my farewell to life tour here instead of in Hamburg. Half of the local congregation wants to admit him to fellowship and half wants him thrown out. So I'm going to make them both unhappy. He's going to the farm in Grantville. But he's taking Sarah with him, and she's the daughter of the leader who wants the boy gone. They'll work the farm until Green gets the Bible college set up."

"Why London?" Jimmy asked.

"According to the histories, there are Baptist congregations in London. One of them claims to be in correspondence with three congregations in Ireland that they think has sound doctrine and that claim to go back to the days of St. Patrick. I want to find out if it's so. I can't settle the authenticity of the manuscripts, but maybe I can settle the lineage question."

"Good luck, Joe," Jimmy answered.

* * *

Jimmy parked the tractor and hay wagons in the street in front of Tip's Tavern. Fortunately, it was not in the part of town which was closed to vehicular traffic during daylight hours. "I'll buy lunch and then we can go on up to the farm," Jimmy told the newlyweds.

"Big dog, you owe me two hundred dollars," Jimmy called out when he saw who was at the bar.

"Bullshit. The bet was that the tractor wouldn't get the old man to Magdeburg and it didn't."

"The bet was double or nothing that the tractor wouldn't get to Magdeburg or back here on its own. Well, it did both seeing as how it's parked outside. Pay up!"

Big Dog snarled. But what could he say? That was the bet.

By Terry Howard

DUELING PHILOSOPHERS

September 11, 1635

Renato Onofrio slowly got up from the barber's chair like someone who had a bad back, which in fact he did. "Walt, something I've always wondered about. How's come you're letting that drunken scallywag Jimmy Dick steal your title as Grantville's greatest philosopher?"

"Well it's nice of you to ask," Walter Jenkins said. "And I don't mind you thinking I ought to have the title. But, you know the police gave it to him as a joke, don't you?"

Renato looked at the barber intently. When he didn't see any humor in the man's eyes, he asked, "Are you putting me on?"

"No, it's the gods' own truth."

"Well, it ain't funny. More philosophy gets talked about here in this shop than anywhere's else in town. People are taking Jimmy Dick seriously. You ought to speak up and take the title away from him. He don't deserve it. You've got to know more about philosophy than Jimmy Dick does. I've heard you quoting Augustine and I don't know who all else."

"Renato, it's kind of you to say so. But how would you go about proving something like that?"

"Challenge him to a duel."

"Pistols at dawn, or swords at high noon?" The waiting customers laughed at Walt's joke.

"No, you know what I mean, a verbal duel. What'a'ya call it?"

"A debate." Walt's son, Evan, answered from behind the second chair without looking up. When you've got scissors or a razor or even just clippers around someone's head, you really do need to pay attention and keep your eyes on the job.

"Yeah," Renato said. "That's the word. A debate. Walt, why don't you challenge that dickhead to a debate. Shoot, I bet you could even charge admission. I'd pay to see someone take the obnoxious little creep down a notch or two."

"Naw," Walt said.

"You think about it. You really should. I mean it. Seriously."

With these last words Renato went out the door. Joseph Daoud took his turn in the chair. "What's the burr under his saddle?"

"Renato?" Walt asked. "Two things. He used to rent a whole building downtown for little or nothing. They let him have it just to keep heat on in the winter as long as he did the maintenance. After the Ring of Fire, they raised the rent, and he had to move out of the store front on the ground floor. Then they raised the rent again, and he had to move out of the upstairs apartment. Now he's living in the attic, and since Jimmy Dick owns the building, Jimmy is who he's mad at.

"The other thing is, truth be told, he thinks the title should have gone to Emmanuel Onofrio. For that matter, he's probably right, but Emmanuel say he has his hands full as it is, so Jimmy Dick is welcome to the job."

"Still, though," Joseph said, "he's got a point. You've got as much right to the title as Jimmy Dick does. You really ought to debate him. Look, the Lions are wanting to do a fund raiser. The call for kids needing glasses is a lot higher here than back home, and it costs a lot more. Their budget is shot and there's still a waiting list. Why don't you let me see if they think it's a good idea?"

"Naw," Walt answered. His words said no; his tone of voice said maybe. You could tell he wanted to say yes.

Evan spoke up with a dry voice and with a straight face. "Why don't you, Dad? It's for charity. Besides, it would be good advertising. Walt the Barber challenges Jimmy Dick the Drunk to a verbal duel on philosophy for the title of Grantville's Greatest Philosopher. Marquis of Queensbury be damned. This will be a bare knuckles brawl. The last man standing will be declared the winner and will walk away with the title, 'Grantville's Greatest Philosopher.' "

Everyone laughed.

"I'm not joking," Joseph said. "Renato is right. A lot of people would come to something like this. I was eating at the restaurant when Jimmy dined with the German philosopher from Berlin. The place was packed. People were wanting to see the fireworks. Then it all happened in Latin and no one could follow it until the Berliner got up and stomped out. With the Lions selling the tickets, we could pack any place in town. It would be a great fund raiser and we could really use the money. The branch in Magdeburg is forever asking for help and we just don't have it to give."

"Let me think about it," Walt said.

Evan turned his head away so his father wouldn't see his smile.

"Stop smirking boy," Walt said.

"I wasn't smirking," Evan replied.

"Yeah, you were." Walt gave his son a mild reproof, passing it off as a joke. "I could've heard your face cracking if you'd been in the back room, much less at the next chair."

Evan left telling jokes and chatting up the customers to his father. The older man insisted it was as much a part of the job as cutting hair. Many were the times, he told his son, after a customer walked out and the shop was empty, "That fellow didn't need a hair cut, he just wanted to tell someone a joke, or share some gossip, or brag about something going on in his life, or complain about it, or whatever the reason other than a hair cut caused the man to be sitting in the barber's chair." On other occasions, when the shop was empty, he would tell his son, "We're as much psychiatrist as barbers. You need to get better at chatting up the customers. I'm not always going to be here to do it for you. It's the butter on our bread, after all."

✳ ✳ ✳

Over the next week, it seemed like every member of the Lions Club in town came in for a haircut, and every one of them asked pretty much the same question.

At the end of a week, Walter weakened and let them make him do exactly what he wanted to do.

✽ ✽ ✽

Everyone at the Lions Club meeting assumed Joseph would organize the debate; after all, he'd proposed the idea. Besides, most of the other members worked full-time. Luckily, Joseph had his personal retirement account in the bank in Grantville, so he didn't lose it like people with out of town assets did. After the Ring of Fire, his retirement hobby farm quit being a hobby. The garden doubled in size. Any other land they could plant went into grain, and the hog raised for slaughter became hogs for a cash crop.

Joseph, being stuck with the job for the crime of suggesting it, decided to make it as much fun as possible. Having sold the idea of a debate to the club, he now needed to sell the idea that it should be fun to the steering committee.

"Okay," Joseph said, "I've checked and they said it's all right to use the sanctuary." The Lions Club met in the basement of the Methodist church once a month unless something came up. "So we can sell three hundred advance tickets and still leave the hundred seats in the overflow area for tickets sold at the door."

Reyburn Berry spoke up. "Joe? Do you really think that many people will show up?"

Sondra Mae Prickett smiled. "Rey, it's all about promotion. I saw a time the store couldn't sell flip flops for two dollars a pair. When we advertised them as 'buy one pair for four dollars and get the second pair for free,' we couldn't keep them on the shelf."

Doris Debolt nodded. "Besides, it doesn't matter if they come or not, as long as they buy a ticket. This is a fund raiser. It's just an excuse to ask people for money."

"Not this time, Doris. This time it's a *fun* raiser. When you sell a ticket be sure to tell people to be there ten minutes before the opening bell because at five till, unclaimed seating will be considered open," Joseph said.

"The opening bell?" Rey looked puzzled, "You're making it sound like a prize fight."

"Yup. Sure am. It's what they discussed the day it first came up. A verbal duel, bare knuckles, no holds barred, the title goes to the last man standing. Everybody thought it was a hoot. Nobody would have given a damn about some stupid formal debate. Who cares about a debate? But a verbal brawl? We can sell every seat in the house for a verbal brawl. At ten dollars a seat, we're looking at four thousand dollars. The church is free, and we don't have to split the gate. Then we'll have a coffee and cookie mixer in the basement afterwards which will be worth another thousand dollars."

Rey looked almost cross-eyed. "Are you serious!? Do you expect to raise five thousand dollars out of this?"

"No," Joseph said in a flat voice.

"Good, I thought you were serious."

"I expect to raise at least ten thousand."

Rey yelped. "What! How?"

"We have a referee and a timekeeper with a bell. At the end of each round we pass the hat through the hall . . . two hats, actually. Then we tally the take and the round goes to whoever has the most votes at a dollar a vote."

Rey sputtered. "But—someone could buy the match."

"Good. Let them. I don't care who wins. I just want to raise some serious money because every penny we take in is one more penny to put glasses on some kid's face."

Doris, getting whiplash watching the tennis ball bounce back and forth, finally broke the cycle. "But what if someone complains about it being unfair?"

"Let them. We're raising money, not settling the fate of the nation. Actually, it would be good if they do. Then we can stage a rematch and do it all over again," Joe said.

"You're crazy," Rey sputtered.

Doris smiled. "He's crazy like a fox, Rey."

"How are you going to collect the money between rounds without taking up half the night?"

"Just like at a Billy Graham crusade. One man goes down one aisle handing out a bucket to each pew and someone collects them at the other end. It goes almost as fast as a man can walk. It will take longer to count it than it will to collect it. But we don't have to post the results before we start the next round. So, we're looking at ten rounds at a dollar a head for four hundred people—that could be another three or four thousand. But I'm only counting on one."

"I think you're counting un-hatched chickens."

"Sure am. But then, everything is donated so it won't cost us anything if it falls through. I cut a deal for ice cream sandwiches at cost, and we return any we don't sell as long as we keep them frozen. I'll hit the Abrabanels up to donate the coffee."

Sondra Mae smiled like a pig in a mud puddle. "Sounds good to me. When?"

Joseph shrugged. "Don't know yet; still got some details to work out."

Rey looked concerned. "Such as?"

"Walt's in. Haven't asked Jimmy Dick yet."

"What? You've booked the hall, arranged for snacks, and who knows what else—but you haven't asked one of the debaters if he'll come?"

"The 'what else' includes pricing the tickets and lining up a donation to pay for them, pricing the programs, and getting a donation to cover them too. We'll sell the programs for a dollar each. Best of all, I got a newspaper to agree this is news, not advertising. So the promotional space is free and front page."

"And you don't know if Jimmy will be there!"

"Oh, he'll be there all right. Walt will issue a challenge in the paper. Jimmy won't be able to show his face at any watering hole in town without being laughed at if he doesn't show up.

"The paper will run question requests up to a week before the debate at ten dollars a pop for processing, and we get half. If your question gets picked, you get to ask it live at the debate."

"Shoot, Joe, you gonna charge for air?" a bemused Rey asked.

"I would if I could figure out how to do it. We *will* charge more for front row seats, though."

"How much?"

"One hundred for the front row, fifty for the second and twenty for the third."

Rey gagged and sputtered, Doris smiled, and Sondra Mae laughed out loud.

Joseph also smiled. "So then, now we've got the finances out of the way, let's talk about making this thing fun."

❋ ❋ ❋

Renato Onofrio turned up out at the Daoud farm so early he must have gotten up at the crack of dawn.

"Renato. You're up early."

"Yeah, well, I wanted to make sure I caught you before you headed to town or something."

"What's up?"

Renato took out a check. "For starters, I want three front row seats. Then I wanted to ask if you needed any help, since you're organizing the debate."

"Sure. How would you like to be the timekeeper? You can do that from the front row and it will put you smack in the middle." Joseph paused, faintly embarrassed. "Listen, we don't have the tickets printed up yet."

"That's okay. Just write me a receipt and I'll pick the tickets up later, when you've got them."

❋ ❋ ❋

"Hey, Debbie, how's it going?" Joseph Daoud asked as he walked into her office.

Debbie Mora's face bloomed with a smile. The business and advertising manager of the *Grantville Times* said, "Great and getting better."

❋ ❋ ❋

Her boss, Lyle Kindred, was annoyed when he found out she had committed the paper to run what should be a series of ads as news. When he found out she had promised front page coverage, he blew a fuse.

Then she told him she agreed to split the income from selling ad space for prospective questions. He wanted to fire her on the spot. Instead, like the well-married man that he was, he stomped out of the office in high dudgeon. He went home so he could unload on his wife and cool off. He wanted to be calm when he came back and fired her.

When he got home and unloaded on his wife, to his utter shock, Mary Jo laughed so much she seemed almost ready to roll on the floor.

When he came back he called Debbie into his office. "My wife agrees with you. She says it is news, and she says we can afford to split the fee for running the proposed question. She says every question which comes in is five dollars we weren't getting before. She says the circulation will go up because people will want to see who asked what. She says it's going to be the best thing ever to happen to the paper." With each repetition of the words "she says," Lyle got a shade redder in the face.

"You had better hope she's right. Because if she isn't—well—let me put it this way, your job is riding on this one. If this proves to be something we've got to live down, you won't be here to see it. If we lose money on this, you're out of here one minute after I hear from the accountant."

✳ ✳ ✳

"My boss is eating crow and enjoying every minute of it. I don't mind telling you I'm enjoying it even more than he is. He's already apologized three times." Somehow, Debbie's broad smile got even bigger. "Circulation is up, and I mean way up. Advertising is up, and I don't mean the questions either. People want their ads in our paper because they're getting seen. Ad space on the pages with the questions is at a premium. It's the highest paying space we've ever sold.

"Joseph, you have got to figure out how to get a rematch. I'm telling you, this is a bonanza for both of us."

THE LEGEND OF JIMMY DICK

✳ ✳ ✳

On the way to the church to handle last-minute setup, Joseph's wife, Nina, said, "Joseph, I just noticed something. Almost everyone who volunteered who isn't a Lion is anti-Jimmy Dick. The rest are pro-Walt the barber.

"You noticed? Yeah, you're right. Everyone Jimmy Dick ever crossed, which is half of the serious drinkers in town, is coming out of the woodwork to buy a ticket. Seems like anyone Jimmy ever humiliated, which is half the people he crossed, is wanting to volunteer."

"Why?" Joseph's wife asked.

"Because they're hoping Jimmy will get knocked down a peg or two, and they're wanting to feel like they helped make it happen."

✳ ✳ ✳

There were no empty seats in the open seating section. Reserved seating did not lag far behind. The standing-room-only area overflowed, and people were being turned away at the door.

A modestly dressed young woman—they were in a church after all—walked across the stage holding up a large sign reading "10 Min. to Bell." Five minutes later, a second lass walked on stage. Her sign read "5 min. to bell." The first one followed with a sign reading, "Any empty seats are now open." There were only a few empty seats, so only a few standees were able to sit down.

Reyburn Berry sought out Joseph Daoud. The man grinned from ear to ear. "Joe, I've got the gate count. At six hundred sold tickets they started turning people away. I have never been so happy to be so wrong in my life. At ten dollars a head, plus the premium tickets, we've already broke ten thousand dollars, not to mention the programs are sold out, and early people who went downstairs to the bathrooms have already bought coffee and ice cream. Go ahead. Tell me 'I told you so.' I deserve to hear it."

"What did you say?" Joseph asked.

Reyburn repeated the admission, "I said, go ahead and tell me 'I told you so.'"

By Terry Howard

Joseph smiled. "Nope. It's been said twice already. I don't need to repeat it a third time. But there is one thing I would like to mention."

"What's that?" Reyburn asked.

With a completely straight face, Joseph said, "Well, this is a church, even if they are heretics. So I would like to say, 'Oh ye of little faith, did I not tell thee we would see at least te . . .' "

Reyburn tried to swallow a laugh and it came out as a snort.

✳ ✳ ✳

Promptly at seven o'clock the bell, borrowed from a gas station, rang a fast series of sharp peals. Benjamin Franklin Leek, having bought the privilege of doing so by paying to print the tickets and the programs, walked on stage before the ringing stopped. A young woman preceded him carrying a sign with his name on it. In the drawn-out voice expected of a ringside announcer, he spoke without a mike, the acoustics in the building being what they were. "Ladies and gentlemen, this verbal duel will be a ten-round match to determine possession of the title, 'Grantville's Greatest Philosopher.' "

"As published in the *Grantville Times*, who are graciously one of tonight's sponsors— for a complete listing of sponsors I refer you to the back cover of the program—this verbal duel will be decided round-by-round with the winner of the most rounds taking the title. If, perchance, it is an even tie, at the end of ten rounds there will be a sudden-death round to break the tie. Each round will be decided by popular vote. Two paper buckets, well, cones really, will be passed. Red for the challenger Walter 'Walt the Barber' Jenkins, and blue for the reigning champion James Richard 'Jimmy Dick' Shaver. You will cast your ballot for whomever you think the round should go to when the cones are passed. The ballot shall consist of paper money or personal checks only. Change will not be counted—and remember, be generous in your voting because all proceeds will go directly, and completely, to provide eyeglasses to needy children."

Benjamin stopped and waited. Nothing happened. Finally he said, "People, my script says I am to wait until the applause dies down."

THE LEGEND OF JIMMY DICK

A scattering of nervous laughter preceded a round of applause. This would have been completely inappropriate in a solemn Methodist church, but not out of place in a rowdy one. It set the tone for the evening by telling people that, for the balance of the night, the rules of conduct were somewhat relaxed.

When the clapping died down, Benjamin pointed stage left and, again in the ringside voice, said, "In this corner, wearing a three-piece suit from Huss & Zitzmann Fine Tailors and Haberdashery, weighing in with years of contemplation and study, Walter 'Walt the Barber' Jenkins." Then he faced the crowd squarely and with a hand signal encouraged them to clap, while at the same time one of the cute young lasses walked on stage with a sign reading "Applause."

Followed by his son, Walter walked out on stage wearing something rather like the dressing gown a boxer wears into the ring, hanging off his shoulders over a sharp three-piece double-breasted suit. The senior Jenkins lifted his hand over his head in a Rocky-style brag of triumph. Evan caught the robe as it fell off his father's shoulders, and then the younger barber exited stage left.

"And in this corner," Benjamin theatrically pointed stage right, "wearing pretty much what you will see him in any day of the week, weighing in with his famous sarcastic wit, is James Richard 'Jimmy Dick the Dickhead' Shaver." The young girl turned the sign over. It now read "Boo" and "Hiss." Again, nervous laughter chirped away, and a fair number of people did what the sign told them to do. Jimmy had not been prepped to expect the totally uneven treatment. If it flustered him in the least he didn't show it. Indeed, his reaction was a stifled yawn. This brought yet another set boos, along with some giggles from the floor.

"Gentlemen, yes, I mean you Jimmy . . ." Again, there was a twittering in the crowd. ". . . please remember, even though this is a no-holds-barred, bare-knuckles, last-man-standing event, we are in a church and certain proprieties will be observed. The first offending party will be thrown out." He stared pointedly at Jimmy Dick. The audience laughed. "Then his opponent will be declared the winner. Will the bouncers stand up please?" In the front row were two large, husky men with a reputation of being pugnacious and a history of not particularly liking Jimmy Dick.

Benjamin addressed the debaters, "Gentlemen, to your corners please."

At these words, each debater took a seat as they had been instructed. Walt's seat was a comfortable upholstered chair. Jimmy's was a wooden kitchen chair. The snickers from the audience made it clear that the uneven treatment of the contestants did not go unnoticed. A sense of resentment at the lack of fair play arose among the small minority of uncommitted people in the crowd. The supporters of Jimmy Dick were mad as hell and Walt's fans thought it to be funny as all get out, which is what it was supposed to be.

"It is my great pleasure," Benjamin said in the ringside voice, "to introduce tonight's interlocutor. He will introduce the winners of the questions contest. He will also ask the first question since it was asked much more frequently than anything else. It was also the only completely anonymous question to be asked. Ladies and gentlemen, I give you Artie Matewski. Let's give our interlocutor a big hand, shall we?" Enough applause to be polite answered the referee's request, but not a lot extra.

"Thank you, Benjamin. As our referee for this evening already said, the first question tonight was asked, with some variation, thirty-eight times. Over all, they boiled down to the same thing. And, for obvious reasons, it was always anonymous or pseudonymous or placed in someone else's name. There were several variations on the question, but in the aggregate all thirty-eight of them boiled down to the same thing. To wit: 'Why is Jimmy Dick such a jerk and an idiot and what is a jerk like Jimmy Dick doing with the title anyway?' "

"Thank you, Mister Interlocutor," the referee, turning to the participants said. "By previous agreement, according to the coin toss, the first response goes to the challenger." There was no prior agreement and there was no coin toss. The statement was completely bogus. "Mister Interlocutor, if you please?"

"Mister Jenkins, why is Jimmy Dick such a jerk?" Artie Matewiski asked.

"Mister Jenkins, you have five minutes," Benjamin said.

Walt rose from his seat, stepped to his podium and said, "Well Artie, those are not my words. I would never dream of calling Mister Shaver a jerk. I will concede he does have the reputation for being one. It comes from his sharp tongue, his acid wit, and his total lack of anything resembling tact." Having finished he set back down. There was a soft rumbling on the floor and a lot of heads nodded in agreement.

The referee rose from his seat in the middle of the stage and said, "Mister Interlocutor, if you please?"

Artie smiled a smile which could best be described as a shit-eating grin and said, "Jimmy, why are you such a jerk?"

James Richard Shaver rose from his chair, and without stepping to the podium said, "It is difficult to have a name of one who soars with the eagles when you dwell in the midst of anonymous turkeys." As he sat back down, the sanctuary roared with applause.

When he could be heard, the referee asked, "Mister Jenkins? Do you have a rebuttal? Jimmy, do you have a riposte? Mister Interlocutor, who is our first questioner?"

"Mister Referee, our first questioner is Mary Jean Slater."

Mary stepped up to the mike. "My question is something I have heard argued my whole long life. Is the eternal security of the believer conditional or unconditional?"

Benjamin said "Mister Jenkins? You have five minutes."

Walt rose to the podium. Seeking to avoid giving an answer, he said, "This is a theological question, not a philosophical one." And he sat down.

"Mister Shaver, you have five minutes."

"Philosophy is secular theology, man seeking to understand the meaning of the universe, which is co-extensive with God. So, likewise, theology is religious philosophy; the two cannot be separated. I would appreciate it if my esteemed opponent would answer the question."

Without waiting for the formal niceties, Walt rose and said, "As a Catholic I am instructed to leave the answering of religious questions to the church. The church teaches that anyone who is not baptized is doomed to hell. Of those who are baptized, sin must be repented and penitence must be completed in this life or in purgatory. So eternal security is conditional upon repentance and penitence. I have nothing else to say on the question."

Again, the crowed rumbled with approval. The Catholics in the audience, the majority of the down-timers, and a good slice of the up-timers present, understood and agreed completely.

The referee cut in before Jimmy could speak, "Mister Shaver, you have two and a half minutes for a rebuttal." While Benjamin spoke, a sign girl hung a large tile on a board behind the three men on stage. The first of eleven spots for cards in a Wheel of Fortune-like display announced to the world the outcome of the first round. Jimmy Dick drew first blood.

Between the applause and the cat calls, over a full minute passed before Jimmy could begin to speak. Still, the timekeeper let the clock run from when the referee said, "You have two and a half minutes."

"Mary, the answer must be both at the same time, because both are scriptural, so both must be true." Jimmy quoted several passages to support both sides. When he was saddled with the title, he undertook to study the field. This included reading the Bible again, after a long absence, and works on religious thought. "Now, how can this be? It is a matter of perspective. You see, it's like a brick thrown off a roof. To those on the roof, it is falling away; to those on the ground it is falling toward. Which is it doing? Is it falling away or—"

The ringing of the bell cut him off.

A call came from the floor in the midst of boos and cat calls, "You bastard, it is not fair, you are being," in the fluent, but accented, English of a Welshman.

Benjamin stood up and held up both hands for silence. "It is my job to referee this duel. I remind you of what I told the duelist about this still being a church. If we can identify who just said what I heard, the ushers will escort the party from the building." He sought eye contact with the head usher. "Did you see who said that?"

The man shook his head.

"Well, it came from somewhere over in that area," the referee pointed. "Watch it and if it happens again I want the impious fellow thrown out on his—" Benjamin paused. "—backside." A response of approval, disapproval, and laughter created a rumble in the audience.

This was the capstone over the relaxed atmosphere which pretty much finished establishing the tone of the evening festivities.

Benjamin spoke over the noise. "Mister Interlocutor? Who is our next questioner?"

"Mister Referee, our next questioner is Brian Early."

Brian, having won the right to ask his question, found his way to Grantville from Magdeburg for the weekend. "Aristotle and Descartes seem to be in agreement on many things. But . . ."

THE LEGEND OF JIMMY DICK

✳ ✳ ✳

The second and third rounds went to Walt.

At the end of the tenth round a pause ensued while the take—which is to say the votes—were counted. To fill the time Benjamin read a note he had been handed.

"Ladies and gentlemen, I have been informed that as of this time Walt the Barber is ahead on points by a significant margin. Still, this contest is not decided by popular vote, but rather by the number of rounds. If Walt wins this round the title is his by six rounds to four. If it does not fall to him, then there is a five-to-five tie and we will move on to the sudden-death tiebreaker."

The lass who hung the placards handed Benjamin a note which he read while she hung the card showing the round going to Jimmy Dick.

"Ladies and gentlemen, by a three vote lead, this round went to Jimmy the Dickhead Shaver. So now we move on to one last round. Let me remind you, you are voting on the merits of the debate and not solely on your personal prejudices."

There came a shout from the standing room only section, "Yeah, right! In your dreams, Benny boy! In your dreams!"

If ever there was a roar of angry laughter it was heard that night at that hour.

The evening went to Jimmy when he took the eleventh round by four votes.

✳ ✳ ✳

The arguments started long before people got as far as the coffee line in the basement.

"Who gives a damn about the point spread? Jimmy won fair and square!"

"Hey, man, all I said was—"

"I heard you, shithead. Walt won on the point spread. It don't matter a damn at all. Shit, do I have to point it out to you? In the Civil war the South won the point spread. Now you tell me who won the war. The point spread don't matter one bit. Jimmy keeps the title."

"Yeah, for now. But, what about the rematch."
"What rematch? It's settled."
"The one Walt has every right to demand."
"Yeah, if he's a bad loser! The South shall rise again."
"You want to go outside and repeat that?"

Fortunately, someone called the police station in the tenth round when they correctly gauged the mood of the crowd. In spite of a police presence that night, the troubles were not over, merely postponed.

✻ ✻ ✻

Someone approached Benjamin while he was drinking coffee. "Herr Leek, you are referee. Why are you allowing unfair to Jimmy Dick this way? A debate should be even."

"Sir, you are laboring under a misunderstanding."

"What?" asked the German. His English vocabulary was not as good as he thought it was.

"You got it wrong. This was not a debate. It was a verbal duel, a farce, a comedy, an entertainment. I was working from a script. You heard me admit it when the audience did not know its lines. This was a show, just a show. If you want a real debate, then we'll need to do it over."

✻ ✻ ✻

That night, over beer, another debate was going on.

"Where were the fireworks? Jimmy should have torn the man up," Brian complained.

"Hey, I've already told you. Jimmy's changed," Bubba answered.

"Yeah, sure. The leopard changed his spots."

"It's the truth. He's changed. Ever since they started calling him a philosopher, he's been spending most of his days in the library. Then his daughter died and he wasn't around for a while. When I saw him next—I don't know—he was different somehow."

"Well, he still should have torn the barber up."

THE LEGEND OF JIMMY DICK

✳ ✳ ✳

Three days later, the dispatcher looked up as Lyndon brought in a bloody nose with a split lip and what would be a beautiful shiner as soon as it ripened. The dispatcher winced.

"Hey," Lyndon said, "you should see the other guy."

"Yeah?" she asked, "Where is he?"

Lyndon, thinking about the serious damage the other man suffered, frowned. "He's on his way to the hospital."

"Really? Is this one pro-Jimmy or con?" the dispatcher asked.

"This one's con."

"When you've got him booked, put him in the far cell," the dispatcher instructed.

"It's getting crowded. Why not the middle one?" Lyndon asked.

"Because we don't need another fight through the bars."

"Did that happen?"

"Sure did. So the pros go in the first cell, the cons in the third one and anyone else in the middle cell." Shaking her head because the whole thing seemed like a waste and a mistake, a real tempest in a tea cup that was spilling over into the broader world, she asked, "Whose idea was this anyway?"

"Hey, they raised over ten thousand dollars for the Lions Club to buy eyeglasses for kids who won't get them otherwise," Lyndon said.

Shaking her head again, the dispatcher said, "Look at the trouble it's causing. Are you sure it's worth it? The debate happened three nights ago and it's still being argued about. Have you seen the front page of the *Times*?"

Lyndon shrugged. "Not today's."

The dispatcher held up the front page. The headline read, "Jimmy Dick agrees to a rematch."

"Shoot," Lyndon said. "This is never going to calm down now.

✳ ✳ ✳

"Hey, Debbie, how's it going?" Joseph Daoud asked as he walked into the office of the *Grantville Times*.

At the sound of his voice a grin blossomed on Debbie Mora's face. "Great, and getting better. Thank you for coming in on short notice."

"Hey, when you get a call from the chief of police telling you to meet him somewhere to see somebody ASAP, then you get yourself there as soon as possible. What's up?"

"Don't know for sure, though I think I've got a good idea. I'd rather not speculate. Let's wait for Chief Richards to get here. I guess he called me before he called you. I told him since I was brown-bagging it, I'd be in the office all day."

A police cruiser pulled up to the curb, cruisers and emergency vehicles being the only exceptions to ban on vehicular, daylight traffic in the downtown area.

"You saw yesterday's front page?" Deb asked Joseph.

"Sure. You got the rematch you wanted. I've got to admit you had more of an actual debate going on in the paper than we ever did on stage. I think they could have gone on forever trying to decide just how unfair it was and to whom it was more unfair."

"Yes, we do have quite a debate going, but I meant the headline. Besides, now the debate is pointless."

"I liked the day before yesterday's better. 'Civil Unrest and Uncivil Disagreements?'"

The chief came through the door. He nodded to Debbie. "Joseph, thank you for coming in early like this. We need something done, and since you created this mess, I figured you ought to be the one to clean it up."

Joseph gave an Italian half-shrug with two hands in the air about shoulder height. "If you're talking about yesterday's headline, what do you think I can do about it?"

The chief stared right through Joseph for a full three seconds before he said, "If it stopped there it wouldn't be a problem. Unfortunately, the front page isn't the only place that is dealing with the debate. It's affecting the emergency room, the jail, and business in half the bars in town. If it were just up-timers, it wouldn't be bad at all. The pro-Jimmy people know he's is a jerk. The problem is the down-timers who seem to think he's some sort of Saint Robin Hood."

"You have got to be kidding!" Joseph blurted.

THE LEGEND OF JIMMY DICK

The chief shook his head. "Nope. A lot of the down-timers have had that exact opinion of Jimmy, ever since he helped out the Anabaptists. When he organized the armed guard to watch over that start-up church just outside of the Ring until things calmed down, he made a lasting impression with a lot of down-timers.

"Mind you," the chief continued, "most down-timers don't have any use for the Anabaptists, but that's the really strange thing. While they don't like them, they see them as German when it comes to the anti-kraut attitude of Club 250. Somewhere they got the opinion that, while Jimmy drank at Club 250, he was pro-kraut."

The chief took off his hat and sighed. "It isn't true, of course. Jimmy never was pro-anything, unless it was pro-arguing."

Debbie spoke up. "Yeah, so I heard. Is it true one time he got in an argument one night and ended up in a fight and in jail, then the next night he got into it again arguing the other side and landed in jail a second time?"

The chief broke out in a laugh which sure looked like it hurt his belly. When he caught his breath and rubbed his eyes, he said, "No. Not one single time; more like a dozen times. More than once, Debbie, oh yeah, more than once. The point is, people who don't like Jimmy are mouthing off and down-timers are telling them to shut up. Then it turns into a brawl and the down-timers aren't interested in a social fight. People are getting hurt!"

"What do you expect me to do about it?" Joseph asked.

"When you sponsor the rematch, you need to do things a bit differently this time."

"I wasn't planning on sponsoring the rematch."

The chief stared through him again. Then he said, "You are now! And this time Jimmy Dick needs to lose, which he will if it is a fair and honest debate. It must appear to be absolutely fair and honest or we will never put this to rest."

Joseph looked perplexed. "What good would that do? You will still have strong opinions both ways when it's over."

"Look," the chief said, "the last debate was a farce. Yeah, you put on a good show and people got their money's worth. But the real problem was letting people try to buy the outcome. Plus some of your questions were just plain silly. Do it over, do it right, do it quick, and do it fair."

By Terry Howard

"Chief," Debbie said, "you aren't the only one who has a problem. The duel put us in the black. I told my boss I'd get him a rematch and we'd do it all over again. This ruckus and rematch will keep us in the black to Christmas. The third debate will carry us to spring. Then, with any luck, enough people will be in the habit of buying a paper. If we can milk this for enough exposure, we will be able to survive. I need thirty days to run three weeks of questions and sell the ad space which goes along with it."

"There isn't going to be a third debate. We've got to get this settled and over with. We need a clean, fair debate so Jimmy can lose and put this to rest." Chief Richards thought for a moment. "Okay. Set a date a month out. The prospects of a rematch should settle things down enough to get by until then. But you need to run the new format right away so people know it will be fair this time. Just one thing: if it doesn't settle down, the date will have to be moved up. Now, here is how you are going to run the next one. Drop most or all of the theatrics. It won't be as good of a show, but this is no longer about a good show. It's about the peace of the community."

* * *

The day's headline read "Police say Rematch Will be Completely Fair and Unbiased."

The lead article read, "This morning Chief Richards told the *Grantville Times* and a representative of the Lion's Club that he would personally see to it that the rematch would be completely fair. The two sides will choose a mutually-agreeable judge. The third-party judge will chose a second judge, and the popular vote will carry the weight of a judge. Each ticket sold will be printed in five sections allowing each person attending to cast five votes over the course of the event."

The second paragraph told about ticket information with the date, the time, and the new location for the event. The high school gym should accommodate everyone wishing to attend.

* * *

Seeing the chief in Club 250, brought some stares and muttered comments. But there he sat at a table with Jimmy, Walt, and Walt's son, Evan.

"Okay then," the chief said. "We've settled on a judge all three of us can agree will be fair-minded and even-handed. Now, if Pastor Green agrees, then he will find a second judge, but you two won't have anything to do with that and most likely you won't even know who it is until the night of the debate.

"Again, I want to stress this time it is a debate and not a verbal duel. We really do have to get this settled.

"I've twisted the arm of the CoC to provide the volunteers so we won't have those shenanigans this time. So, let's talk about the questions."

Jimmy lifted a beer and Walt lifted a hand, "Chief, I thought the questions were going to be chosen out of the paper like last time?"

"In theory," the chief nodded, "yes. But I am going to vet them. For instance, there will be no theological questions. As a devout Catholic, you can only answer with the official line of the church. Since Jimmy is a devout nothing, he can tear you up and there isn't any way you can come back because it's dogma."

At the words "a devout nothing," Jimmy looked over his horizontal beer bottle with a glare.

The chief ignored it. "So theology is out because it isn't fair. Then there will be no cheap questions like why is Jimmy a jerk. It's not fair to Walt."

Jimmy snorted and beer flew.

"Not fair to Dad? How do you figure?" Evan asked.

"First, your father has to be polite and Dickhead here doesn't. Second, Jimmy is used to cheap shots and has a whole slew of cute comebacks, like the anonymous turkeys line, ready and waiting in the bank, which are sure to be a big hit with the crowd."

Evan started to object. "Hey, my dad has a—"

"Thirdly," the chief said, "because I just said so. If you've got a problem with it, shut up." The chief was being high-handed and he knew it. He normally wasn't. But this was going to look completely fair. The best way for it to look fair was for it to be fair. And it would be, even if he had to be high-handed, hard-assed, and arbitrary about it. It was going to be fair, and Jimmy was going to lose. Jimmy couldn't possibly win a fair fight. It would be exactly fair, and it would have the outcome the chief wanted.

* * *

The seats on the gym floor cost more than the bleachers did. But this did not mean the people with the chairs got any more votes, just a better view. The chief watched as the CoC ushers moved the down-timers mostly to stage right and up-timers mostly to stage left. This being by instruction to keep the pro and cons separated as much as possible. Things had quieted down when the rematch was announced, but tensions were running high in the gym. Benjamin took the microphone needed to be heard—it was a gym after all, not a hall built with acoustics in mind. He addressed the crowd in a normal voice.

"Good evening, ladies and gentlemen."

In the absence of the ringside voice several cat calls rang out.

"People," Benjamin said, "this is not a verbal duel. This is a debate. As such there are stricter protocols than last time. Notably, inappropriate individual responses from the audience will be unacceptable. If this does not meet with your approval, see the cashier on the way out for a refund. Or not, since once again all proceeds will go to the purchase of eyeglasses for under-privileged children.

"Mister Interlocutor, who has the first question?"

The chief sighed.

Lyndon asked, "What was that about?"

"It's all downhill from here. Jimmy is toast, and the problems are over. The people who care will accept an honest defeat."

Lyndon was puzzled. "What makes you so sure he's toast?"

"Well, it isn't a secret, but it is a little-known fact. Walt studied for the priesthood when he was a very young man. He left when he decided he wanted to be a father in fact, instead of in name only. That was about the time he discovered philosophy and started asking question his superiors didn't want to deal with. They started asking if he really had a vocation. So you see? Walt has a clear advantage."

"Which is even more so because you slanted the questions."

The chief just smiled.
"Well, my money is still on Jimmy Dick."
"How much do you want to lose?"
"You're way too confident, Chief. Shall we say one dollar?"
"You're on."

When the first round went to Jimmy, Lyndon smirked. When the second round went to Jimmy, Lyndon chuckled. When the third and fourth rounds went to Jimmy, Lyndon kept his mouth shut and his eyes on the stage to avoid the chief's glare. Round five fell to Jimmy also. Then it seemed as if the barfly ran out of steam. The next four rounds were Walt's and Lyndon wondered if Jimmy could be grandstanding for the crowd.

"Mister Interlocutor, unless there is a tie, who has our tenth and final question for the night?"

"Mister Referee, the last question is from out of town. It is my privilege to read it. 'Is war mankind's greatest glory or greatest shame?' Mister Jenkins, the first response to this question is yours."

"War is mankind's greatest shame," Walt said. Then he gave a heartfelt, well-reasoned defense of his answer lasting four minutes and forty-five seconds. Walt had been supplied with an advance copy of the questions. Jimmy had not been, though Walt did not know this. The crowd, being full of people who had seen more of war than they wanted and were sick of it, responded with applause and a standing ovation.

"Well," the chief said, "we go to a tie-breaker. Care to go double or nothing?"

"No, Chief. I'll be taking enough of your money as it is."

"Mister Shaver," the interlocutor said, "is war mankind's greatest glory or greatest shame."

Jimmy stood and took the podium. "Neither," he said. "A man's greatest glory is to love his wife and raise his children well." Jimmy started to sit down.

The judge interrupted him. "Mister Shaver, you did not answer the question. The question is not what is a man's greatest glory. But rather, 'is war mankind's greatest glory or greatest shame.' " The judge emphasized the word mankind.

"War is only glorious when you win with an acceptable casualty rate. Any casualty rate is unacceptable to the casualties or their families. So, since there is always at least one loser in a war, it is glorious less than half the time. Still, mankind's greatest shame is not war. Mankind's greatest shame is an uncherished child." With this Jimmy did sit down.

No applause followed. At first there was only a dead silence and then a great deal of subdued conversation.

The hat was passed as it was at the end of each round. But the tabs were not counted. The two judges were in agreement. The referee announced the winner at six rounds to five.

Jimmy took the podium and said, "Ladies and Gentlemen—and yes, Benny, I mean you—" This, being a reference to when Benjamin said the same to Jimmy Dick in the first debate, got the laugh Jimmy wanted.

With the crowd laughing, he knew they were paying attention and that he could hold them. He had something serious he wanted to say. "A year ago, a man by the name of Wilhelm Krieger came to town. He is Germany's current greatest rising-star in the field of philosophy. No one here ever heard of him. He isn't even in the encyclopedias because he didn't live long enough to get published until we changed history. He asked me the same question about war, and I suspect this is the source, directly or indirectly, of tonight's last question.

"When I had dinner with Herr Krieger, I got lucky. Joe Jenkins and Emmanuel Onofrio went with me to dine with the stuffed shirt." Again, the way he said stuffed shirt, got the laugh he needed. "The two of them, being serious philosophers, conversed with Krieger in scholarly Latin so I didn't get a chance to embarrass myself." As he expected he got his laugh. "Or Grantville." Here he neither sought nor got any laughter.

"At the time, both were better philosophers than I will ever be. The title of Grantville's Greatest Philosopher should have gone to them, but it fell to me, and I have spent the last year trying to learn enough to at least talk the game since I will never be able to walk the walk in the footsteps of these two truly great men. And let me tell you, when a dumb hillbilly like me has to learn Latin just because he's been stuck with a title he doesn't deserve, well, it's a life changing experience. But Emmanuel Onofrio can parse Latin right fine-like—" Jimmy slipped in a traditional hillbillyism to let people know that he wasn't getting uppity, "—and Joe Jenkins can jabber away in it all day long, and that's without losing his hillbilly accent. So I set out to learn it. Among the other things I learned along the way was a great deal of humility.

"Joe has recently left Grantville and said he will not be coming back. Since he's a man of his word, we will never see him in town again."

Jimmy looked to where he knew Chief Richards stood watching as he had all night. They made eye contact and held it. "With his leaving, we have an empty slot at the top."

Jimmy watched the chief nod. Jimmy nodded back ever so slightly. They understood each other. Jimmy had gotten the message, loud and clear. In the opinion of the chief of police—the chief of police being one of those people whose opinions counted—Jimmy needed to be brought down at least two or three pegs. Jimmy's nod acknowledged the chief had won the day even if Jimmy had won the night.

"Walter's name is Jenkins, so we will not even have to change the letter head; and since he clearly deserves it, it is my privilege, on behalf of myself and Emmanuel Onofrio, at this time, to invite Walter to join the triumvirate as one of Grantville's Greatest Philosophers."

Emmanuel Onofrio turned to his co-judge Pastor Green. "He should have asked me first before sticking me with that title! Now, since he announced it before the world in the way he did, there is no way I can turn it down without being ungracious or looking like I do not approve of Walt getting the title."

Green looked at the old man he had co-opted to be a judge on the strength of his master's degree, his forty years in education, his irreproachable reputation, and the general respect of the community. The Baptist pastor laughed a light chuckle, and then used some inappropriate language. It being rather out of character for the pastor's public persona, but completely on the nail head for the occasion, he said, "Sucks to be you, don't it?"

"What will Jimmy do if someone else comes along that deserves the title, too?"

"Knowing Jimmy," Pastor Green said, "I suspect you will end up with a four person triumvirate."

At first silence filled the gym from one basketball hoop to the other, just like when Jimmy answered the last question. This time, the silence blossomed into a full blown roar of approval.

By Terry Howard

OVERFLOW: A SALON 250 STORY

Late fall 1635

The front door to 'Hair Club 250' opened. A howl of wind and a spray of sleet came through the door of the salon with a short dark-haired man. He shook himself like a dog, getting the just mopped floor wet again.

Kim Beasley, the owner and chief stylist of the salon, frowned. The floor would have to be mopped up or it would leave spots.

"Sheeit!" She mumbled. The man was someone who worked at the Thüringen Gardens across the street. She glanced at the clock. It was nearly 6:30 and the Salon closed up at 6:00 on Fridays. Kim had stayed behind to instruct the girl she'd just hired on the peculiarities of cleaning a hair salon.

"I should have locked the door," She muttered.

"Mrs. Beasley," the man strode toward her, "I am so glad you are still here. I don't believe we've met." He extended his hand for a handshake. "I'm Dieter Schliemann. I'm a shift manager across the street. I have a problem, and I believe you can help me out with it."

Kim took note that his English was fluent and polished. And he was polite. And while he was dark, he wasn't was tall nor handsome. She looked at the wet footprints on the clean floor and frowned again. "Yes, you do have a problem." She agreed. "That haircut is awful. But I don't normally do men's hair. And we *are* closed for the day. And I don't normally do walk-ins anymore, anyway."

"Okay, I have two problems." Dieter looked a little sheepish and ran his hand back through his wet hair. "The one you can help me with right now is that I have over-booked my private dining rooms. I've got two groups insisting on having a private meeting right now. And you have started renting out your waiting area on Sundays. I can pay a premium for the use of it this evening."

"Mr. Schliemann." If he couldn't read the tone of her voice, Kim's hands on her hips and her tapping foot clearly should have said she was annoyed. But he just did not seem to be noticing. She had just told him no, and still he kept asking for a favor. "My husband has dinner waiting for me at home. I hate to disappoint him. He's a good cook and puts a lot of effort into putting a meal together. And I am not going to leave the building unattended."

Heloise spoke up, trying to be helpful. "Mistress Beasley, I can stay."

Kim glanced at the stout young woman, wishing she hadn't offered.

"Mrs. Beasley, I can cover her wages on top of paying to use the space." While he was not reading her body language, she was reading his, and he was clearly desperate. "I have tried to get both groups to give me a break and take a table in the common room. But they will have none of it."

Kim continued to radiate hostility. She looked at him like he was something inconvenient that a storm had blown in. He shrugged and pushed onward. "Part of it is that the common area is too loud for a quiet conversation. And they each have their own musicians with them and they plan to sing their own songs."

He shuddered at the thought of what would happen if they tried doing it in the common room. "I've got a band onstage, and it's one the crowd really likes, so that isn't going to fly. But mostly it's that the two groups know each other." Dieter grimaced. "And they hate each other with a passion. And they sure aren't willing to back down. Not if it means that the other party gets the room. They'd rather die first."

Kim was not thawing. So Dieter tried explaining. "They both come from somewhere I never heard of. And they're both celebrating the same treaty or contract or something. I'm not quite clear, just that the date is important to them." He looked at Kim and tried some more. "Each side claims their grandfather skinned the other side. And the great victory absolutely has to be celebrated tonight." Kim, continuing to have her hands on her hips and her foot tapping, still did not give him anything to work with. So he plowed on. "And if I don't manage something, and quickly, they are likely to restart their grandfathers' war all over again, right now, in the middle of my bar. And that is not good for business. I've thought about throwing them both out." Dieter sighed. "But that's bad for business, too. And then they're just as likely to have a brawl in the street regardless of the weather."

Kim, thinking to end it, asked in a very dry voice, "How much are we talking about?"

A relieved Dieter named a price, which she knew was the full price he was getting for a room. She had checked on what that was when she started renting out the waiting area for private meetings when the salon was closed on Sundays. Kim countered by asking twice what he offered, assuming that would be the end of it.

Dieter shocked her when he said, "Done. But at that price you pay your help. And we use your linens and place settings."

"No," Kim said. "You still pay Heloise."

"Done."

Exasperated at letting herself get caught out, Kim said, "Heloise, get the sheets out of the closet in the kitchen and cover the styling chairs and the drying stations." She turned to Dieter. "How many place settings will we need?"

Dieter sighed in relief, "Fourteen or seventeen depending on who comes over."

Kim turned to Heloise and said, "When the stations are covered set out fourteen plates and flatware. Mr. Schliemann, we don't have tablecloths or cloth napkins. My husband didn't run that kind of business."

"Hold off on setting the places," He told Heloise.

Then he turned to Kim. "I'll send over linens. And Mrs. Beasley, I can't tell you enough how much I appreciate this. Thank you. I mean it. You really are a life saver."

"Well, pay your staff a premium because the tips go to Heloise," a miffed Kim said. She *really* didn't want to do this.

He nodded in agreement and left.

"Heloise, clean up again when they're done. You can leave the dishes in the drying rack after you wash them. Make sure the door is locked when you're finished, and come by tomorrow afternoon when you get off work at the diner and tell me how it went."

✱ ✱ ✱

Back in the Gardens, Dieter approached the head of the Maass family. The older fellow was a thin wisp of a man, even shorter than Dieter. He made up for his size in raw, pugnacious belligerence. With a quick sigh of relief at finding a way of avoiding an absolute, unmitigated disaster, Dieter said to the old man, "Your group will be moving to our overflow accommodations across the street."

"At the hair salon?!" the popinjay bellowed. "No way are we going to—"

His wife tugged on his sleeve. "Husband, that is where our neighbor, Niles Hanover, dances?"

The man calmed down. "Is Niles dancing tonight?"

"No," Dieter said. "That has to be arranged in advance."

"Oh. Well, *okay*. Maybe next time. Niles is a good boy."

Dieter had some trouble keeping a straight face but managed. He just could not come to grips with the idea that a male stripper was a good boy. "Have a beer on the house, and we'll get your dinner orders before you go over."

"Oh, we all have same thing. Is tradition. We must have soup. Then sauerkraut with sausage. And we told you when we reserved about the cake, yes?"

"Yes." Dieter nodded in agreement. "We have the cake ready."

With a sigh of relief, he went to tell the other group they could have the room.

"Okay, Herr Koehler," Dieter said. "The room is yours."

"They are getting free beer?" The leader asked, suspiciously glaring down at Dieter.

"And you are getting the room," Dieter replied sharply. He was already losing enough money on this deal. He wasn't giving out free beer to the party who was getting the room.

The leader looked smug. "And they are going home?"

"No, they're going across the street."

"To the salon?" A matronly woman asked. From the sound of her voice, you would have thought that the street in front of the salon surely must have been paved with gold.

"Yes," Dieter replied.

"We should have gotten the salon," she muttered. Her voice sounded bitter, hurt, and angry, and it was definitely tainted with jealousy.

"Well, you are getting the room you reserved."

"And they are getting free beer, and did I hear right, they are getting dancers?" The man was very unhappy.

"No. They didn't reserve the dancer in advance." It was clear to Dieter that he'd handled the whole thing poorly. He should never have had the conversation with one group where the other could hear it. Now this group was somehow sure that they were being slighted and that the ancient enemy was somehow getting an advantage.

It was clear to Dieter. When they left here tonight he was going to have unhappy customers leaving with bad memories. And, worse still, he was going to lose money doing it. When he found out who was responsible for double-booking the private dining room, someone was going to get an unpaid vacation. And if it was who he thought it was, then someone would be looking for another job if he had his way about it. Unfortunately, he didn't. She was a friend of his boss and she could probably get away with just about anything short of murder.

❈ ❈ ❈

When they got to the salon, the places were set with water glasses at each place setting, as Heloise was accustomed to doing from working breakfast and lunch in a café downtown. The Gardens' staff member who had brought the linens was gone. The server who had carried a covered wooden tub was staying. The tub held a metal bucket full of hot coals and a wooden bucket full of hot soup, along with baskets of bread. He had just put the warm bread basket on each table. As soon as people sat down, he started ladling soup out of the bucket into the tub where it sat on the floor. When he filled the first bowl, Heloise was there to collect the first two bowls and hurry back for two more. A second server arrived with three cases of bottled beer.

"That is not cold beer, is it?" the head of the family asked. It was a reasonable question. For the most part, draft beer from kegs was room temperature in Grantville like everywhere else. A cold beer like the up-timers wanted was normally in a bottle. If you wanted a cold pitcher at the Gardens, that was fine, but you had to ask, and the wait staff would tell you that the bottles were better and just as cheap. But if you insisted on cold beer in a pitcher, they would go to the kitchen and pour the bottles into a pitcher. Most places in town, if you asked for a bottled beer it was cold unless you specified otherwise.

"No sir." The Garden's employee assured the patron. "They're not chilled. But we can't be running back and forth across the street with beer mugs and pitchers in this weather, now can we?" He popped the caps and started pouring the beer into the glasses Heloise fetched for him. Drinking out of the bottle really was a redneck thing in this day and age.

The empty hot tub went back when the soup was served, and it returned shortly with the kraut and sausage. It was a good thing that there was a coal pot in the tub to keep the main course warm because the party was in no hurry about eating. During the soup course, they started toasting. And these people took their toasts seriously. Then they started singing.

* * *

While helping Ken wash the dishes after dinner, Kim said, "I wonder how the new girl is doing at the shop."

"I thought you stayed till she was done?"

"Well, I did mostly, but the manager from the Gardens came over and asked if he could rent the shop for an overflow party, and Heloise said she could stay."

"You mean to tell me that you've got a party of Krauts in the club and the only one watching them is another Kraut that we don't even really know?" Ken raised an eyebrow.

"Well, when it you put it that way?" Kim raised an eyebrow back at him. "Yes." They both laughed. "But the No Krauts and no Dogs sign ain't hanging on the door anymore." It had been on the front door when the building was a bar. The rowdy up-timers who had been Ken's regular patrons hadn't mixed well with the new locals. The new sign read Kim's Hair Salon.

He dropped the dish rag in the sink and headed for the coat closet. "I'd better go check before they burn the place down or they walk off with the cash register." It was a mechanical brass contraption, with mother of pearl inset keys. It had been a collectible antique when he got it to begin with. Now it was a priceless up-time relic.

✳ ✳ ✳

Heloise heard a noise in the kitchen and went to look. An unknown man promptly asked, "Are you Heloise?"

"Yes. Who are—"

Ken interrupted her question with an answer. "I'm Ken Beasley, Kim's husband. I'll be at the desk in the stock room if you need anything."

But he never got there. The Krauts were loud and rowdy. That was fine. He was used to loud and rowdy. But the tone of the toasting was belligerent. Ken's German was passable after four years of being around it. But he had no luck at all at following the dialect being spoken in the front room. He stood in the kitchen, out of sight, and listened with growing apprehension. One toast followed another, and each sounded more aggressive than the last. The party had that feeling which he knew all too well. He could feel it in his bones. They were spoiling for a fight and they weren't going to calm down or cool off or go home until they had one.

Ken picked up the old rotary phone and dialed the familiar number.

"Police station." The phone said.

"Yeah, this is Ken Beasley at Club 250. I've got a fight brewing. I need some help."

"Ken?" The dispatcher asked in shock. "What's up? Are you okay? Are you having a flashback?"

By Terry Howard

"Look! My wife rented the shop out for an overflow party from the Gardens. And they're getting ready to tear the place apart. Get me some help over here now! I don't have a shotgun under the bar anymore."

Ken heard the server from the Gardens loudly saying, "I just told you. You've gone through all three cases of beer. There's no more beer. And no I will not go get any more. I'm cutting you off. You've had enough."

"Shit," Ken said with a deep sense of dread.

"It's going to hit the fan," he told the police dispatcher. "Get your asses over here RIGHT NOW!"

Ken grabbed a case of beer and headed for the front hoping to delay things until the cops got there. He pushed through the kitchen door with the words, "Heloise, get in the kitchen, NOW!"

At about that time the front door opened. Ken was relieved. Then he realized it wasn't the cops.

"Oh shit!" A group of down-timers was standing in the door screaming bloody murder in the same dialect Ken had been listening to for the last half hour. A plate still half full of sauerkraut and sausages flew through the air, splattering all over the man in the lead. Some of the sauerkraut splattered everywhere. The plate bounced off the man and broke when it hit the floor. Three or four more plates followed, accompanied by a wordless bellow of rage. Screamed invectives mingled with threats of mayhem kept coming from outside with the sleet and the wind.

The older man of the party using the salon was up out of his chair bellowing like a bull. He charged the enemy, twice his size, who was standing in the doorway, in a headlong rush ending with his head butting into a stomach. This turned into a tackle filling the doorway, keeping the rest of the invading force out in the street. But it did not stop the three men who leaped up from the tables. They dashed over the two wrestling in the doorway as the wind blew sleet into the salon. The ladies were keeping three much younger boys from following. An old gray beard hobbled to the door and aimed a kick at a face. This resulted in blood on the floor.

"Heloise, I told you to get in the kitchen!" Ken looked at the server from the Gardens. "You too. In the kitchen. Now!"

"Aren't you going to do something?" she demanded, as she slid past him, since he was half blocking her way.

"I am doing something. I'm waiting for cops."

As the Gardens' employee passed him, he shoved the case of beer at him. Then he stood there and glared at the ladies who were standing around the tables, hanging onto the boys, as the sirens on the squad cars started growing louder.

In short order, the sirens stopped. Shortly after that, the noise outside changed and then stopped. And shortly after that Lyndon Johnson came in.

The solid, calm, and collected young man asked, "Ken, what in the world just happened?"

The frowning younger police officer glanced at the sauerkraut splattered walls and the floor and the sauerkraut mixed with blood. "Four men are headed to the hospital; one of them looks like he won't make it. Six men are on their way to jail." He glanced at the sheet-covered workstations of the salon. "I thought we were through with this sort of thing."

Ken shrugged. "I don't know a whole lot."

Dieter Schliemann showed up. Ken looked at him with a half-suppressed snarl. "These are his customers. Ask him?"

"I'm sorry about this," Dieter said.

"The breakage is extra," Ken replied.

"That's fair enough." Dieter agreed with a nod.

"Any idea what it was all about?" Lyndon asked.

"From what little I've gathered," the manager from the Gardens replied, "it sounds like what I was told about your Hatfields and McCoys."

A soft snort of a sound between a grunt and a growl, along with a nod, was Lyndon's only reply. He understood. Like a lot of people in West Virginia, he claimed some distant kinship. That is to say, he may have had some minor family connections, to one or both of the feuding parties. And anyone born and raised in the hills can tell you when it comes to feuds, what caused them is unimportant. When it came to a feud, the only thing which matters is the feud itself.

"Herr Schliemann," the server from the Gardens said to his boss, "We didn't need to bring the food over in hot tubs. They've still got a full kitchen over here. We could have kept the food warm in their oven or on the stove."

※ ※ ※

When Kim had heard the sirens, she came running. She took in the mess at a glance: the blood on the floor, the sauerkraut splattered on the walls and strewn across the floor, the broken plates. She shook her head. Heloise was clearing the tables so they could take their table cloths back across the street.

"When you finish," Kim told the girl, "mop up the blood first and then clean up the mess. I'll be doing the dishes."

She found Ken at the kitchen sink with his sleeves rolled up looking very solemn while washing soup bowls.

She gave him a peck on the cheek and said very softly, "I don't know whether to laugh or cry?"

"They think one of them is dead," Ken replied very quietly. "I never had anybody die in a bar fight before."

The chief of police turned up while Heloise was mopping up the last of the blood. He too took in the sauerkraut and sausage mess, although he identified the sausages as wieners. He found Ken in the kitchen washing dishes. Kim was drying and putting away. Ken looked at the chief. "Is he . . .?" the rest of the question hung in the air as if not asking might make it not so.

The chief answered the question with a slow shake of his head.

"Shit," Ken said. "I was always able to keep things under control."

"Yeah," The chief agreed. "It's rough. I thought when you closed the bar it was over. Instead, it's gotten worse than ever."

"Hey, it wasn't our fault!" Kim objected, on the verge of tears.

"That's true." The chief agreed. "But we both know who's going to get the blame. And the Gardens' reputation is not the one that is going to take it on the chin."

"That's just not fair," Kim said with silent tears running down her cheeks.

The chief took her into his arms and held her in a fatherly hug, patting her strawberry blond head as she cried on his shoulder. "You're right," He said. "It's not fair. But that's the way it is."

Ken grunted in agreement.

"It wasn't fair even back up-time." The chief sighed. "And the Good Lord knows, there ain't nothin' at all fair about our being here."

Ken watched as the police chief realized he was hugging another man's wife with the man standing there watching. The chief loosened his hold. Normally that would break the clutch. It didn't. She wasn't through using his shoulder. He couldn't just push her away. Ken kept on washing dishes, and he kept the smirk off of his face. Telling Kim no was not an easy thing to do. Eventually the chief tried, awkwardly, to engage Ken in conversation.

"With the blood and the sauerkraut, that's quite a mess you got out there."

"Yeah. Well," Ken sighed, "it's damned ironic. This wouldn't have happened when the sign on the door read 'no Krauts' allowed."

By Terry Howard

THE MCMANSION

Late May 1636

Brother Green stopped into the Baptist Basement Bar and Grill about the time the lunch rush was over. He was dressed in a short-sleeve shirt. He gave up wearing a suit coat and tie when he gave up the title reverend. Now he was Brother Green. He'd revert for weddings and funerals. But a farmer and a teacher didn't need to stand on dignity. He wandered down to where Jimmy was hanging out near the keg. The bar in the basement of the Anabaptist church opened when Club 250 closed to give the rednecks somewhere to go. But it didn't see many of the patrons from Club 250. It seems they were allergic to drinking in even the basement of a church

"Jimmy, how's business?"

"Not bad. We've got enough traffic through the bar to pay the bills. But I got to tell you, being behind the bar is nowhere as nice as being a customer. Now I've got to watch what I say. I keep coming up with the perfect insult, but I can't use it because I have to worry about offending people."

Green grinned. "That's too bad Jimmy. Listen, I stopped in to ask, how are things going with the Scottish Horde."

"I've got a dozen of them sleeping in my garage and no telling when more will turn up. They were there when I got back from Bremen with the two with the war pipes. After they marched in the Fourth of July parade, the powers that be decided they absolutely had to go on the trip. We had to borrow a drummer from the high school because the one they brought with them has a steady gig playing with little house pipes out at the Holiday Lodge. Some of them are slow about finding work. They came here to fight, and that's all they want to do. But I leave that up to them. They can go hungry if they want. It's not like you can't find eight jobs in eight hours in this town if you look. How are things going for you up on the Baptist Bible Mount Top Institute?"

"Not bad. But I've got a problem, and I think my problem can take care of your problem. This mess with the Scotts will blow over eventually. But you need to house them until they are ready to move on. So you've got a problem, and I've got a problem, or my wife does at work, which is the same thing. And I think we can use your problem to fix my problem."

"Oh," Jimmy asked. "And what is your problem?"

"The hospital has a fair number of indigent patients. They often come with families who can't afford a hotel room. So if we use your clansmen to build a lodge, when they move on the hospital can use the lodge to house charity families who are waiting while we are treating the patients."

"That is going to take a lot of money," Jimmy worried.

"Not all that much, as long as the labor is free. We can harvest the materials off of the Institute's land. We've got dried wood, so all your people have to do is cut and mill the trees and stack the lumber so it will dry to replace what is ready to use. The land took a little creativity, but the hospital will provide that. I can get some of the hardware donated, but a post and beam, wattle and daub construction doesn't have to use a lot of hardware. I've lined up a really big tent to house the crew while they're building the lodge. And the hospital will help out with feeding the workmen. And we know how to get around the problems of building in the winter."

"You say the hospital is coming up with the land? I can't picture where."

Green smiled. "You know the proposed bridge over the Deborah Creek? We turn the front porch of the McDonald house into the bridge."

At the image of a house with a stream running under it, Jimmy laughed.

FOR OLD TIMES' SAKE

James Richard, Jimmy Dick if you please, Shaver sang quietly to himself. Singing was not his long suit. As a child, he was told to sing tenor solo. That is to say, ten or twelve miles down the road and so low no one could hear him. It was one of the few bits of wisdom offered to him as a child that he actually paid any attention to.

"One rye whiskey
Two rye whiskey
Three rye whiskey
Floor
If you want a bigger headache
Then have one rye whiskey more.

"Anna, hit me." Anna the bartender smiled and poured another shot into Jimmy's glass. It was his second and would be his last for the night unless he went elsewhere to get it. Jimmy knew it from past experience. Anna's place, the Anabaptist Basement Bar and Grill, was not a place to get drunk. It was early on a Friday night, and someone was telling Bible stories to kids in one corner while the Anabaptist elders were passionately reviewing theological differences in another corner. Anna the waitress had just told them again to hold it down. Arguments in a bar are common. Theological ones are not unheard of, but where in the world, other than Grantville, would anyone be telling Bible stories to the children of the bar patrons in a bar on Friday night? Jimmy sighed. Getting drunk anywhere other than Club 250 was just not the same, and with the club now a beauty parlor, Jimmy's days of getting drunk were pretty much a thing of the past.

"Anna, put in an order for a brat and a beer." Jimmy saw Bubba come through the door. "Make that two beers and brats, please."

Bubba stopped and stood listening to the argument for a few minutes. One of the elders saw him standing there and pointed at the empty chair. Bubba respectfully shook his head no and headed for the bar.

"Hey, Jimmy, did you hear about the deaf child who was using swear words?"

"No."

"His mother threatened to wash his hand with soap."

"That was bad, Bubba."

"Yeah, but, it's not as bad as the last one you told me. Is there another word for synonym? You could have told me what it meant instead you told me to go home and look it up. I did just to figure out why it was funny. Is there another word for synonym? You could have explained it to me."

"Sure, but then you wouldn't have remembered it."

"In the old days you would have told me what it meant."

"In the old days I told you that you were dumb as a box of rocks"

"It wasn't true then and it isn't true now. Did you just pass up an invite to sit in on the argument?"

"Yeah."

"Why didn't you?"

" 'cause, I promised the wife I'd be home early and anytime I sit down at that table I'm here past midnight."

The brats and beers arrived, and Jimmy said, "Have a brat."

"I can buy my own, Jimmy."

"For old time's sake," Jimmy said.

Bubba nodded. Things change. Club 250 closed, and Jimmy opened a bar in the church basement. Bubba followed him since there was nowhere else he wanted to go, and he could still count on a free beer on Thursday nights. Then a French fanatic burned the bar and it reopened without Jimmy. The money was there, but it just wasn't fun. Bubba kept coming. He found himself listening to the Bible stories and then to the elders arguing. The next time his wife started nagging him about going to church, he told her he'd go if she would go with him to the church he wanted to go to. After all it, worked once so it should work all the time.

✱ ✱ ✱

"Mitchell Kovacs, if you want to go to mass on a regular basis, I told you when we got married I'd go with you to any church you wanted, but I am not going just once in a while."

Bubba nodded; he had given up telling her that the Baptist church doesn't call it mass. "I said okay then and I meant it. But if you want me to go to church with you tomorrow morning, then you need to be ready at 8:30."

"What gives?" Mary asked. "We always go to late mass so you can sleep in some."

Bubba answered, "I didn't say we were going to mass. I just said I'd go to church if we went where I wanted. And you know where that is."

"The Anabaptists in that new church they built?"

"I want to see if Rev. Greiner can preach as well as he argues."

"And you'll go on a regular basis?"

"If you want to get up that early," Bubba smiled, thinking he'd won.

By Terry Howard

FIRE AND BRIMSTONE

Grantville, summer of 1636

"What can I do for you, Mr. Underwood?" the young lawyer asked.

"I want an injunction compelling *that* bar to change its name. It's embarrassing," Deacon Albert Underwood said. "I asked the man politely to take that sign down, and he laughed at me."

Jimmy Dick found Albert's polite request rude and demanding, followed by an even ruder ultimatum. Jimmy laughed at him.

"They have no right to use the name. They aren't Baptist. That's why we threw them out. Drinking is a sin and calling *that place* The Baptist Basement Bar and Grill is insulting. Baptists do not drink!" The last words rang with passion, fire, and brimstone. "You know what I thought it said when I first saw it? What I thought it said was The Bargain Basement Bar and Grill; after all, it surely couldn't say what it does, could it? But I took a second look and, lo and behold, it did say what it does.

"I pointed out he could shorten the sign by two words and still use it. You know what he said? He said, 'If we take off *and grill* how will people know we serve food?' The man is a cretin and a fool; they should throw him in jail and throw away the key!"

The young lawyer found himself wondering if the old deacon ever said anything without filling it with passion. "Mr. Underwood, I understand, and I sympathize." He told a social lie, but then lawyers are . . . well, (I guess I'd better not say. I don't want to get sued.) "But I doubt if there is anything I can do for you. The word Baptist is in the public domain. It's not like you've got a trademark on it, and it is attached to a church after all."

"But they're not Baptist, neither the bar nor the church. They call themselves Anabaptist. They are against everything we stand for, like decency and order and right living. Ask any of the down-time pastors. The whole lot of them are anarchists. Can't you get them for false advertising or something?"

"Mister Underwood, it will not hold up. What defines a Baptist is adult-only baptism and baptism by full submersion which they have been doing since they opened here in Grantville, even if they didn't always do it before. So, I am sorry, there is nothing I can do for you.

"The chief of police is a reasonable man, and he has a lot of influence with Jimmy Dick. Why don't you talk to him?"

"I did! He told me to go see a lawyer."

"Then I guess you will just have to learn to live with it, sir."

"You mean the law will do nothing? Well, if *that* is the case, someone ought to just burn the place down."

"*That*, sir, would be illegal." Realizing someone as passionate about the subject as the old deacon clearly might actually go to such an extreme, the young lawyer thought to head off trouble before it started. "Since you've mentioned it, if anything happens I will have to tell the police about this conversation."

"Attorney-client privilege."

"First, you haven't paid a retaining fee, so you are not a client. Second, the privilege does not apply when a client announces ahead of time that they are going to do something illegal. Good day, sir. I cannot help you."

"Well, I wouldn't do it anyway. But someone should."

***

Not many nights later flames shot up from the roof high into the sky as if the spirit of the building sought heaven. The walls were quarried limestone, but the furnishings burned nicely as did the floor and the roof, except for the roof slates, which, along with the stained glass for the windows, were the only things the congregation purchased, except for songbooks, Bibles, and modern plumbing. Unfortunately, the fire burned the walls to lime. They were still standing, but the building inspector declared them unsafe. They would have to come down. Beyond question, it was arson. Someone used so much fuel oil or kerosene that some of it floated out on top of the water when the fire department got busy controlling the blaze.

***

At first light, while the coals were still glowing, Lyndon Johnson started investigating the fire. The fire chief estimated how much petroleum someone used.

"That much?" a shocked Lyndon asked.

"It takes a lot for some to float out like it did."

A radio call to the dispatcher and a few phone calls to the gas stations established for a fact; no one bought any diesel recently which did not go into a vehicle's tank.

"Well, that's a dead end. Looks like someone's been sitting on a stash all this while. We can look, but, if the sweep for fuel back in '31 didn't turn it up, it's not likely we will either," Lyndon told the fire chief.

"I didn't think it would be that easy," the fire chief replied.

***

Jimmy Dick stood there looking at the ash-filled hole in the ground. The sign over the door, by some fluke, somehow, survived. He shook his head. "We weren't even open a month. The worst of it is, I had insurance on my contents, but the congregation didn't have any insurance at all. At least it was all new stuff. I sold all the up-time furniture and furnishings to an Italian. I'm glad I kept the jukebox at my house, or it would be gone too."

"Why'd'ya do that for?" Bubba asked.

"Because, Bubba, it could be overheard upstairs. Some songs shouldn't be heard in church, even if it is through the floor."

"Oh," Bubba said sadly, looking at the ashes.

Lyndon asked, "Who wanted you out of business badly enough to do this, Jimmy?"

"I don't know, Lyndon. Not the other bars. They were happy to get rid of Ken's regulars. I can give you a list of the regulars who wouldn't come; some because they wouldn't drink in a church, others because I wouldn't keep the krauts out. But, damn it, Lyndon, it *is* kind of hard to tell your landlord he can't buy a beer in your bar. And if they were going to burn something down, they would have torched the beauty salon in the old building."

Lyndon's next question probed a bit deeper. "Who had it in for you personally?"

"Most of my family, half of the regulars, all of my ex-tenants and most of the current ones," Jimmy replied.

Lyndon pushed, "Why the tenants?"

"I raised the rent. My family, 'cause I ended up with the property, and they thought it should have been split up. The regulars because, over the years, when they were being stupid idiots I pointed it out to them, and I wasn't the least bit polite about it when I did it either."

Lyndon probed deeper still, "Sounds like you got half the world mad at you. Why, Jimmy?"

Jimmy actually looked a bit sheepish. "Because I enjoyed being a jerk? Freud told me I have a death wish."

"Like you talked to Sigmund Freud!"

"You mean you haven't?"

"Get me the list of the old regulars who don't come. I'll start there."

✳ ✳ ✳

Back at the station, Lyndon found a note in his inbox telling him to call a lawyer's office. Shortly he stood knocking on Deacon Underwood's door. "Mr. Underwood, have you heard the Anabaptist church burned last night?"

"Serves them right. They never should have opened a bar in the basement."

"Mind if I ask where you were last night?"

"Home, in bed."

"All night long?"

"I can't sleep like I used too. So I get up and read and then go back to bed."

"Anything you want to tell me?"

"You mean like, 'Yes, I kidnapped the Lindbergh baby.' Well, I didn't."

Lyndon did not trust the gleam in the old man's eye.

✳ ✳ ✳

"Hey, Jason, any ideas on who burned the bar?"

"Hey yourself, Lyndon, and what you really mean is did I do it, since I have a record as a suspected arsonist.

"They never proved it. I never said I did it, never said I didn't, either. In this case, I didn't. If I find out who did, I'll beat the crap out him before I tell you. He burned a church, Lyndon. I don't go to church, 'cept for weddings and funerals. It shouldn't have been there. But I would never burn a church.

"You ask me; it was one of the pious hypocrites. The churches are full of them. You know how you tell a Catholic from a Baptist in a liquor store? The Catholics will talk to each other; the Baptists won't."

"Well, you were in town, and you might have it in for Jimmy, you both being Shavers after all."

"I ain't got nothin' against Jimmy. But he shouldn't have opened a bar in the basement of a church. It just ain't right."

❈ ❈ ❈

A few days later the chief asked: "How is the arson case coming?"

"A lot of dead ends," Lyndon said. "The only thing I've turned up is Jason Shaver's being in town. He says everything is cool between him and Jimmy. I know better. So there's opportunity and motive. I'd question him again, but he's back in Magdeburg at the glassworks."

"How'd they move the fuel oil?" the chief asked. "It wasn't carried in by hand, not that much, not by one person anyway. Freight moves around town at night since the League of Women Voters got the daylight traffic ban voted in. Ask the haulers if they saw anything."

❈ ❈ ❈

"Herr John's Son?" Lyndon just stepped into the gas station to sign for the tank of gas for the cruiser. The attendant said, "I have a question."

"Yes?"

"The police called the day after the fire and asked if anyone had been buying diesel, and I said no except into trucks."

"Yes," Lyndon prompted.

"Is it important? One man buys ten gallons into cans once or twice a week."

"Do you know who he is?"

"No."

"The next time he comes in, call the station. Then stall him if you can and try to get a name."

"Yes, Herr John's Son."

❋ ❋ ❋

"Wesley, your electric truck was seen around town the night of the fire? Know anything about it?"

"Now that's the strangest thing. When I came in the morning after, I found the big door closed but not latched. Nothing missing or out of place, so I just figured we forgot."

"You're telling me someone could have used your truck without you knowing it?"

"Yeah."

"How'd they get in?"

"Through a window, maybe? I didn't check. Like I said, nothing was missing."

"Any idea who could have borrowed it?"

"Not offhand."

"You think of anything, let me know. I should talk to your partner too."

"Sure, she's home getting over having her appendix out. Been laid up all week."

"Just for the record, where were you that night?"

"Home in bed. Where else?"

❋ ❋ ❋

Three days later a message caught up with Lyndon to call Wesley at the conversion shop.

"Wesley?"

"Hey, Lyndon, after we talked I added a bar to the door. This morning the bar was upside down. There's some nicks you wouldn't notice if you weren't looking for them, and the chalk marks on the wheels were gone too."

"I'll be over in just a bit. Don't touch anything until I get there."

"Hey," Lyndon called out to the office, "I need a fingerprinter. Who's up?"

The chief came out of his office.

Lyndon addressed him. "Maybe we just got a break in the arson case."

A week later, on a rooftop in Grantville

"See anything?" the radio asked.

"What did I tell you an hour ago?" Rick asked, in nearly accent-free English.

"Nothing."

"What did I tell you the hour before that?"

"Nothing."

"What did I tell you once an hour yesterday and four yesterdays before that?"

"Nothing."

"Do you see a pattern here?"

"I see nothing."

"Have you been watching *Hogan's Heroes*?"

"Yes. Sergeant Schultz is a hoot. Talk to you in another hour."

"Hang on; I see a light. Someone is in the building." The soft noise of the carrier wave and the occasional mutter of voices in the background of the station were the only sounds for long enough to measure time in fractions of an hour instead of numbered minutes.

"Okay, they are opening the doors, and yes, the truck is rolling out. It's comin' down. Move."

"People are in place, Rick. Come on down."

"Let me guess, you've seen *The Price is Right*?"

"Sure, my landlady brought them home, and we watched them over and over. A panda is waiting for you in the alley."

"A panda?"

"Yes, a black and white patrol car."

"Where did you come up with that one? Never mind. I'm on my way."

Wesley's electric truck made its way to the fairgrounds, where things to be delivered downtown were left until the middle hours of the night, when traffic wouldn't endanger the swarms of kids and other pedestrians. The driver and passenger loaded up, made the three stops, and headed back to the conversion shop. When the two of them were exiting the side door of the shop, car lights came on at both ends of the alley.

A voice called out, "Freeze." Then, "Put your hands on your heads." Then, "Abe? Is that you?"

Abe, a known hillbilly-ophile answered, "Rick?"

"Yeah."

"What's going on?"

"You tell me."

"We were borrowing Wesley's truck. He said we could."

"No, he didn't."

"Yes, he did. We needed to help someone move, and we borrowed his truck. When we brought it back I said 'thanks,' and he said 'anytime.'"

"Abe, you know that is not what he meant."

"It is what he said."

"Come on. Let's go down to the station."

At the station, they called Wesley. "Sure, I loaned Abe the truck to move some old lady. But I didn't mean he could use it for free any time he wanted without asking."

Lyndon nodded. "Rick tells me it isn't a question of Abe misunderstanding either, even if he has the I-don't-know-English-too-good routine down pat. Shoot, his proper English is better than mine, and he can do hillbilly just fine."

"So," Wesley asked, "did they burn the church?"

"No. The dispatcher at the fairgrounds says Abe worked on the other side of town that night and he's got records to prove it. Only thing they've got to say is they saw a dark pickup truck go by on rubber tires and they sure wished your truck had rubber tires. So now I get to chase down every dark truck in town that still has tires, which is most of them."

"Are you going to press charges," Lyndon asked.

"No. They didn't hurt anything, but I am going to charge them rent."

✼ ✼ ✼

The next day Lyndon stopped for gas. Barely through the door to sign the chit, the attendant spoke to him.

"Herr John's Son, I have something to say."

"Yes?"

"I have a name. He is Abe Holt."

"Thanks. We picked him up last night."

"Then he burned the church?"

"No. He has a solid alibi."

"I have been thinking, Herr Underwood, he has been buying a lot of diesel into his truck. I have been wondering why so much driving. And now, after the fire, he has stopped."

"Oh, really?" Lyndon said. "Interesting. What color is Underwood's truck?"

"It is dark blue, Herr John's Son."

"Hm. Thanks, Johann."

"Anytime, Herr John's Son."

✼ ✼ ✼

"Hey, Lyndon," the chief called out when Lyndon got to the station. "What did you get last night?"

"A red herring. The fellows using Wesley's truck didn't do it. But they saw a dark pickup moving through town. So I follow that lead next."

"Well, over lunch someone from the CoC asked me about it."

✼ ✼ ✼

"Chief Richards, how is the investigation going in the religious discrimination case?"

"The what?"

"The religious discrimination case. Have you found out who burned the church down?"

The chief asked for an explanation, "It's religious discrimination?"

"Of course it is."

"Why?"

"Arson. The only church in town to be burned is a down-time church. Your up-timer churches are strange and crazy, but for the most part, they are staying put in Grantville . . . well, other than the Pentecostals. Those people are a long-standing despised minority. They are actively expanding under your protection."

"Maybe the bar was the target, and the church just happened to be over it?"

"Don't be crazy. Who would care about a bar? No. You need to be investigating the loud-mouthed Lutherans whose pastor, from the pulpit, called it an act of divine justice."

❋ ❋ ❋

"I got the distinct impression if we didn't look into it, the CoC would.

"I told him we weren't calling it a religious discrimination case at this time, and if the Lutheran pastor had an accident one dark night, I would come looking for him.

"So, if you don't have any other leads, check it out."

"I may actually have something. It turns out Underwood has a dark blue truck, which I know runs on diesel. He fills up way too often, but not since the fire."

"Oh, really," the chief said. "Let's go."

"Where?"

"To see Albert."

❋ ❋ ❋

The door opened, and Albert Underwood said, "Yes?"

"Brother Underwood," the chief said; they went to the same church. The archaic greeting matched the man being addressed. "I have a problem, and as a deacon of the church I thought you might be able to help me out."

"If I can I surely will. What's the problem?"

"I've got a suspect in an arson case who's got motive, opportunity, and ability, which is enough to bring him in and book him."

The old man paled. "I didn't do it."

"I didn't say you did. So far the evidence is purely circumstantial, so a judge would most likely throw it out. Without more evidence, I don't see any point in charging the suspect.

"But that's not the problem I want your help with."

"What is?"

"If someone in town got burned out, especially if they didn't have insurance, we, that is, the congregation, would take up an offering. Seems to me like we should help the Anabaptists out. Don't you think?"

Albert's mouth fell open. "You have got to be kidding! After they opened a bar in the basement? And called it what they did? No, absolutely not! It needed cleansing, and nothing cleans quite like fire."

"Albert? Is there something you want to tell me?"

"Yes. If you propose we take up an offering to help them rebuild, I will vote against it. And I'll make it stick, too."

"Albert, I got a situation. The CoC thinks this is religious discrimination. Those people tend to act on their beliefs. If they do, we've got serious problems. I need this settled. I need to make an arrest whether I can make it stick or not.

"Or come up with the money to rebuild the church. If an elder deacon says to take up an offering asks the other churches to do the same, and he seriously encourages people to give, we can raise enough to rebuild, and I can keep a lid on things."

"And you want me to do it?"

"That's the idea."

"What about the bar in the basement?"

"Nobody's business but theirs. You know they don't see drinking as a problem."

"I don't like it! Not one bit!"

"Needs to be done," the chief said.

"I didn't do it!"

"I didn't say you did."

"What about the name over the door?" Albert scrambled to salvage something since he understood he wasn't going to have any choice in the matter.

"Oh, I think, maybe, something can be done about that," the chief threw the old deacon a bone. "What do you say?"

"I don't like it!"

"Albert, I need someone to head up the funding drive to rebuild the Anabaptist church, and I need that someone to do it right."

Albert turned red. "This is blackmail."

"Really? Just what is it I am holding over your head? Why don't you stop down to the station tomorrow morning, bright and early, and let me know how I'm going handle this. See you tomorrow, Brother Underwood."

Back in the cruiser, Lyndon spoke for the first time since leaving the station. "Chief, that's just plain mean."

"Yeah. It is," the chief said with a chuckle. "Either he raises the money to rebuild, or he confesses. Either way, it doesn't really matter."

"So, Jimmy Dick is back in business," Lyndon said.

"He says no. There's not enough business. Too many of the regulars won't come. But things have quieted down with the old 250 crowd, so maybe we don't need it."

※ ※ ※

The next morning, Albert Underwood walked into the chief's office. "Brother Richards, I've got something to say."

The chief nodded.

"I've walked this earth for over eighty years. In my younger days, I did a few things I probably shouldn't have. Some called me a braggart and a bully, and looking back I'd have a hard time arguing about it. But I am not going to take the credit for doing something when I didn't do it. And come judgment day I do not want to explain to the Lord why I helped build a bar. I can't confess. I won't go to my grave with a lie on my lips. I won't do it."

"Albert, I need to know what you did with the diesel you were buying because right now it sure looks like you used it to burn a church down."

"I didn't do it. I'd be lying if I said I did. At my age, I'll be facing the Lord sooner rather than later."

"What did you do with the fuel?"

"I didn't use it to burn the church down."

"I didn't ask what you *didn't* do with it. I asked what you *did* do with it."

"I ain't telling."

"Albert you're the only lead we've got on where that much fuel oil came from."

"So be it," the old man said.

The chief got up from his desk and walked to the door. "Lyndon, I need you in my office."

When Lyndon entered, the chief pointed at the old man. "Book him."

***

In a bit over an hour, the chief's phone rang. The judge currently handling arraignments asked, "Chief, Albert Underwood's wife just came to my chambers. Is it true you've got him locked up?"

"Yes. He's our only suspect in the arson case."

"Do you consider him a flight risk?

"No."

"Do you think he did it?"

"I don't know. If he could tell me where the fuel he's been buying went, I'd say no. But he can't, or at least he won't."

"Just a minute."

After some faint mumbling, the judge said, "His wife says he's embarrassed to admit he's been selling out of town."

"If the fueling stations did that they'd be cut off. But there's no law against it."

"His wife says it bugs him because she's making all the money. His pension is gone, so he's been looking for some way to make money. This is all he's come up with."

"Shoot," the chief said. "I need something in the way of a break in this arson case."

"This isn't it," the judge said.

A minute later Lyndon's phone beeped.

"Yes?" Lyndon asked.

"We know what he did with the fuel. He's covered; let him go."

"Right, Chief."

A few minutes later Albert bypassed the receptionist and knocked on the chief's door.

"Come in."

"Brother, Richard, I've been thinkin'. Now don't get me wrong. I still think the place should have been burned down. But you're right. If it had been anyone else, I'd be happy to help in a fundraiser, but I won't help raise the funds to rebuild a bar. If you can assure me they won't open a bar back up, I'll raise the money for them to rebuild."

"Jimmy says he definitely is not going to open back up. Is that good enough?"

"I think so. But that's not what I wanted to tell you. Lyndon said you know what I've been doin'. I wouldn't want it to get around. An' I've been thinkin'. The CoC might be right. The fellows I've been selling fuel to picked up a load the night of the fire. If you don't have any other lead on where the fuel came from then, it might be the fuel I sold 'em. I talked religion with them some. If you think I'm angry with the Anabaptists, you ought to hear them. They hate 'em even more than they hate the Lutherans."

"So you think they stopped on the way out of town and torched the church?"

"Motive, opportunity, ability, what you said I had. Well, they had it too. They even had the supplies on the move that night."

"Brother Underwood, do you have any idea who they are or what they're doing with it?"

"I asked once. They said the French were paying top dollar for fuel at a research station. I wasn't selling enough to fuel anything much like a boat or a tank or something, and it's not aviation quality, so I didn't see any harm."

"How do they get in touch with you?"

"They stop by the house and ring the doorbell."

"Do you know when they'll be back?"

"Another three or four weeks."

"But you've not been buying any since the fire. How were you going to fill the order?"

"I'm ahead pretty close to a wagon load. After the bar burned down, the wife asked me what would happen to the house if what I had out behind the garage caught fire and if maybe I should keep it down. I decided she's right."

"Can you let me know the next time your buyers are in town? I think we need to talk to them."

"I'll give you a call," the old man said.

***

"At least this time it will be a short stakeout," Rick told his partner.

"Be quiet and watch," came the response.

A wagon full of barrels came down the road. But instead of turning left and heading out of town, it turned right.

"Shit." He clicked the handheld twice and waited.

"Go ahead," the dispatcher said.

"Call the army guys outside of town. Tell them they're not coming. They turned right instead of left."

"I'll tell them. Watch them as long as you can see them, then come on in. I'll get a tail on them."

Shortly Lyndon stopped by in a patrol car. "Hop in."

With the lights off, the cruiser crept along staying just close enough to see where the wagon went.

Lyndon grabbed the handset to the radio, "Holy smokes, they're stopping at the Baptist church. Get me some backup, pronto."

"Will do, Lyndon. Do what you can, but be safe about it," Chief Richards voice returned over the airways.

"Rick, you shoot one of the horses if that's what it takes to keep the wagon from leaving. Don't worry about anything else." Lyndon turned to the other man, "Come on."

One man waited on the wagon; the other walked out of the building.

Lyndon called out in German, "Hold it right there. Get your hands in the air." The man drew a gun and Lyndon dropped him. The driver kicked off the brake and slapped the reins over the horses' backs while at the same time yelling at them. It did no good because he now had a horse down in the traces.

Lyndon rushed the door. His companion took charge of the downed man. Lyndon rushed into the basement of the building to find a wooden barrel of diesel with the bung knocked out and fuel all over the place. A two-inch stub of a candle slowly burned its way down to the floor. The wooden stick match with a black head, made to a Grantville pattern, lay on the floor beside it. Lyndon carefully picked up the candle and carried it outside.

"How is he?" Lyndon asked at the door.

"He's dead."

Another car pulled up and slammed on the brakes. Four people piled out.

"There's a mess to clean up inside," Lyndon told the chief. "One down, and one in custody."

❊ ❊ ❊

Back at the station, the still-living half of the pair sang like a stool pigeon. "It was not my fault. I didn't know he was going to do it. It was my first time to come. His last partner quit him. I didn't know till we got here."

"We can check if you're new or not. If you are, then you're only facing one count of attempted arson. Did he say why he did it?" the chief asked.

"Yes, he said, he's part of the Society of the Sacred Heart. It's his God-given duty to stop the spread of heresy. He said this, too, is an Anabaptist church which re-baptizes people. It's an affront to God, the church, and the souls of men. It was his duty to burn it down. He wished he could burn it when the people were inside to send them off to hell all the quicker."

Chief Richards shook his head. "Book him."

❊ ❊ ❊

"Hey, Lyndon?"

"Yeah, Chief?"

"When you called in, was that supposed to be a pun?"

"What are you talking about?"

"When you called in, the first thing you said was, 'Holy smoke.' I want to know, were you making a pun?"

❈ ❈ ❈

Months later, Albert Underwood stormed into the chief's office. If anger was heat, he could boil water. "You promised me they wouldn't open another bar in the basement. I told a lot of people that when I went looking for money." The simple truth being, he bragged about it outrageously. "If you don't shut it down, I'm going to look like a fool. You promised. I expect you to shut it down."

"Now, Brother Underwood, just calm down. Think back to the day you got locked up and released. Now, just what did I tell you?"

"You said they wouldn't be opening a bar in the basement."

"Did I? Or did I say Jimmy Dick would not be reopening a bar in the basement? I remember. Those were pretty much my exact words. Well, Jimmy hasn't. The congregation has. They say it's an evangelical outreach. People stop for a beer and see they aren't a bunch of sticks in the mud like up-time churches. Part of the problem is the Gardens told them they can't come back until they promise to stop talking religion. Since there's nothing else they really want to talk about, they decided to open a place of their own.

"But Jimmy Dick has nothing to do with it, which is all I promised."

Albert stayed quiet for a moment. He didn't want the arrangement. Then he smiled. "Brother Richards, when you were standing on my doorstep the day before I got locked up, you told me you could get them to change the sign. Well, they're using the same sign, so they're still calling it the Baptist Basement Bar and Grill. I expect you to see to it they change it like you told me you would."

"Let me see what I can do."

❈ ❈ ❈

Preston Richards leaned over and rolled the passenger side window done. "Brother Granat, can I give you a lift?"

"Thank you," Rev. Granat said, opening the door and getting in.

"Don't mention it. There is something I need your help with."

Rev. Granat cautiously asked, "Which is?"

"The sign over your basement door at the church. Albert Underwood is offended by the use of the word Baptist. Do you think you could help me out? He says I promised. I didn't, but I did say something once, and I guess it could be construed as a promise. Whether it can or it can't, he sure is doing it anyway."

"After all of the money he raised, I think we can do something. The sign is okay as long as it doesn't have the word Baptist in it?"

"I guess so," Preston answered.

✻ ✻ ✻

The chief answered his phone the next day. "Brother Richards," Albert said, "thank you for taking care of the sign promptly."

"I haven't seen it. What did they change it to?"

"I have no idea. They haven't put a new one up. But the old one is down and you said the new one wouldn't have the word Baptist in it, so I really don't care."

Two days later Lyndon told something in the station, and everybody broke out laughing. The chief buzzed the receptionist and said, "Tell me about it? I could use a good laugh."

"Chief, the sign over the bar is back up. They cut the sign into two pieces and inserted a third piece large enough to carve three extra letters, "Ana," and put the sign back up. Lyndon hasn't seen it yet, but he says he heard about it while walking to work, and Anna and they couldn't have put it up more than an hour ago. The whole town will be laughing about it shortly. Well, at least those who aren't boiling mad or screaming bloody murder about it, anyway."

The next day about ten o'clock the chief answered his phone, "Hey, Preston, I'll buy you lunch if you'll pick me up."

"I can do that."

"Pick me up at eleven, so we can beat the rush."

Preston picked up the smiling judge.

"Where are we going?" the chief asked.

"Annas' place."

"Where?" a puzzled Preston asked.

"The Anabaptist Bar and Grill. Annas' place. I heard it called that three times on the trolley on my way to work this morning. Seems like everyone heard about Albert Underwood demanding they change the name, so they added Ana. Besides, the cook and the bartender and the waitresses are all named Anna. So it's Annas' place."

The judge continued, "I tell you, they couldn't have asked for better advertising. I want to see the sign. Besides, I hear the beer is good, and they say they've got a grilled brat that tastes just like the best brand name off a supermarket shelf."

Looking at the sign over the door, the judge said, "Those three letters on the unscorched wood sure do stand out."

When they were seated, a buxom matron came to their table, "I'm Anna Gisa. I will be your waitress. What can I get you gents?"

"Gisa . . ."

"No, Chief Richards, here I am Anna or Anna Gisa."

"Okay. Anna, where did you learn to take an order that way?"

"Is how Jimmy Dick's waitress did. Is not right?"

"Yeah, it's fine, just wondering. But why are you going by Anna?"

"Chief Richards, everyone is all the time calling Anna so is easier than to tell it is not our names."

When she left with their order for small beer and brats, the judge said, "See, I told you, Annas' place. If the food and the beer are half as good as people are claiming, they've got it made. But you know what is really funny?" The judge did not wait for the chief to answer. "Look over there in the corner. If you bring your kids with you in the evening, they've got someone telling Bible stories while you have a beer or two. A bar telling Bible stories, now don't that beat all?"

※ ※ ※

By Terry Howard

Months later, Chief Richardson stopped in around three o'clock for a brat. He'd missed lunch, and a brat sounded good. The lunch crowd gone; Preston sat at the bar.

He asked, "So, Anna, how's business?"

"Chief is very good. People like our beer, they like especially Henri's brats. The number of families bring children is good. They have a beer, maybe two, maybe dinner. The kids hear a story. Some children start coming on Sunday, a parent too, sometimes. Everything is good.

"The only problem . . ." Anna shook her head and tsked. "We have to tell our elders to argue more quiet. It disturbs other customers. Is getting tiresome. No wonder the Gardens told them not come back. Some nights I wish we could do the same."

BOUND FOR HAMBURG

"Herr Shaver?" The rising inflection clearly made it a question.

James Richard, Jimmy Dick, Shaver looked up from the first-rate meal on his plate. He had seen the kitchen. It absolutely could not hold two people. That someone could produce a gourmet meal in such cramp quarters was amazing. Across the table, in the almost equally cramped dining room of the new river boat, sat a prosperous merchant. Next to him was a less plump, younger copy. In their new clothes they looked ready for a Dutch master to immortalize then on canvas. The framed oil painting, hanging in the Met in New York, back in 1999, could have been titled Father and Son.

The stern-wheeled paddle boat was purpose-built for passengers and light cargo on the Magdeburg to Hamburg stretch of the Elbe river. The three staterooms were cramped with just enough room to get in and out of bed when the bunks were let down. You changed clothes with the bunks up. The dining room was tiny and seating was limited to first class passengers. Day passengers were fed in their seats, and their food was plainer. Deck passengers were fed on deck, and the meals did not come with the price of the ticket.

"Yes?" Jimmy Dick answered.

"Pardon me Herr Shaver? But my son insists that you are the famous Grantville philosopher, Herr Head?"

"I suppose I am." Jimmy Dick replied. When he figured out he was stuck with the title, out of embarrassment he'd spent time in the library reading philosophy and learning Latin. If you have the name you need to at least know how to play the game or you would look like an absolute idiot. That didn't bother Jimmy Dick. But he was the famous Grantville philosopher and if he couldn't walk the walk, Grantville looked bad, and that did bother him.

"I have read about you in the Berlin Philosophical Quarterly." His voice shifted slightly in pitch and rhythm as many are wont to do when they quote something. " 'A man's greatest glory is to love his wife and raise his children well.' You said this?"

"Yes."

"Is it true that you raised no children?"

It was not the first time he had been asked that. In fact, it was an almost inevitable question. "When I was a young man, I went to war in a country half way around the world, south of China; Persia is half way there. When I came home it was shortly clear that I was no longer fit company. Any woman who was worth having would have nothing to do with me, and any woman who would have anything to do with me was not worth having. You can die in a war. You can be crippled likewise. Sometimes the wounds are on the inside."

"But you are a famous philosopher?"

"That only happened after we ended up here in Germany, and it never would have happened if we hadn't."

"Still, you managed to heal."

"A man who would have been a monk who had been born in this century, along with a very holy hermit, helped me find my way through the darkness, and I was finally able to forgive myself."

"This is my son, James. Would you mind if he asked you a few questions?"

James smiled. "Children's questions are the hardest to answer." He looked at the boy. There was a light in the lad's eye that gave Jimmy pause, "If I say I do not know, will you accept that answer?"

The young lad looked at the up-timer in awe and nodded.

"Then, yes, I will answer your questions as long as we are at the table."

OLD GOATS ARE HARD OF UNDERSTANDING

"Jimmy," as his common first name, James Richard Shaver, looked up from the steaming plate of spaghetti and meatballs in marinara sauce. The smell of Thursday nights' special filled the room. An older, white-haired gent, one of Jimmy's neighbors, was standing across the table.

"Jim." Jimmy nodded and pointed at a chair. "Have a seat." Jimmy raised his hand and waived three fingers. "Have a beer. The spaghetti's good. Can I buy you dinner?"

"No thanks, Jimmy. What I need is some advice. What with the mob you've got comin' and goin' out of your place, I thought I'd get your opinion. You see, I'm having an argument with my wife. I want to close off the dining room and turn it into a bedroom and take on another boarder. The living room couch ought to be thrown out, and we could move the dining table into there. The dining room chairs spend most of the time in the living room anyway. Vellie admits we could use the money, but she says if we add another family the house will be too crowded. Which was the same thing she said years ago when it was just us and the kids instead of the fourteen people who live in the house now."

Jimmy Dick was sitting at his usual table next to the big window left over from years ago, when the Flying Pig used to be a small grocery store. The cinderblock building was empty for years, back up-time, and it became a tavern sometime after the Ring of Fire. The owners liked having someone they thought of as famous sitting in plain sight in the window, and they discouraged anyone else from sitting there until after Jimmy left for the evening. If he came at all, he'd generally be there by early afternoon, and usually he left in time to be home for dinner. Except, that is, for Thursday nights. On Thursdays, he had dinner at the pig and held court to closing time. He was often joined by old acquaintances looking to mooch off of him when they were broke at the end of the week. People learned to look for Grantville's Cracker Barrel Philosopher there on Thursday nights.

"Let me tell you a story," Jimmy told his neighbor. "There was an old couple with a small farm. Years ago, when they first started out, there was a little, old, one-bedroom house with a wood burning stove and no running water. The first summer, after he had the crops in, he sank a well and added a bathroom. When the wife got pregnant, he spent the next summer building her a big new home with five bedrooms and lots of space. But the dream of a large family didn't happen. They had one son, and that was it. They named him John III after his father and grandfather.

"When Little John grew up, he went off to the university, got married, had a baby girl, and graduated. But then he couldn't find a job, so he moved back home. While he was away, his parents rented out the big house and moved back into the little one. They needed the income since Big John, or now Old John since Little John was bigger than his father, couldn't manage the work, and they rented out the cropland. You see, little John swore a solemn oath never to be a farmer, and that's why he took a football scholarship and went to the state U. But since he was not good enough to go pro, and he was out of work, he had no choice but to move home and sleep on the hide-a-bed sofa in the living room.

"It wasn't long before Old John went to see a psychiatrist. 'Doc,' Old John told the shrink, 'That many people in that small of a house is driving me crazy. I have got to do something.' "

Bubba, one of Jimmy's old drinking buddies and the major reason Jimmy held court on Thursday nights, got a genuine shit-eating grin and interrupted. "I know that one. He told John to go home and move the goat and the chickens into the house and come back in a week. And a week later he said to move the goat out and come back in a week. And when he did the old man told him life without the goat was a paradise."

THE LEGEND OF JIMMY DICK

Jimmy took a long pull off of his beer bottle and thumped it down on the table. "That's the way it happened in Poland or Turkey sometime next year when the farmer complains to the priest. But John lived in America. When he came back to see the shrink, the shrink told him to move the goat out.

"John said, 'I don't think so, doc. You see, when I moved the goat in, our daughter-in-law said she couldn't live like that. And my wife gave her a ride into town to the women's shelter. Well, when the wife saw the free room and board, and someone else did the cooking and the cleaning, she decided that I had been mentally abusive all those years since I expected her to do the cooking and cleaning and canning and look after the animals and help with the harvest. So she stayed in town at the shelter too. My son declared that if his wife wasn't going to live with him, he might as well join the army, so he caught the bus into the city. Now if I throw the goat out I won't have anyone to talk too.'

" 'A month later the old man got sick and died, and the coroner said it was from living in a goat shed. He had insurance, and the old lady was the next thing to rich. So she and the daughter-in-law moved into the big house. Little John came home on leave. When he left, she was pregnant, again. And the kids just kept on coming every time he came home.' "

"I see," Jim said. "Thanks, Jimmy." And with the beer bottle in hand, Jim walked out.

"Well," Bubba demanded, "I get the point of the story the way I heard it before. It's all what you're used to. But what's the point the way you tell it?"

"Bubba, the point is that just because you think you have all the answers, like the shrink did, if you go meddling in other people's affairs and giving out advice, you never know how it will turn out. It might turn out badly, and then your friends are mad at you for giving lousy advice."

"Jimmy, that never stopped you before? Why is it going to stop you now?"

"Who said I had the good sense to follow my own advice?"

"But Old Jim figured it out?"

"Nope. Old Jim heard what he wanted to here. I'm sure he's headed home to tell his wife I agree with him. If you had ten dollars, I'd bet ya', three to one, I'll be in trouble over this before it's said and done."

315

By Terry Howard

SOBER IN THE MORNING

Becky, setting at the roll top desk in the office in her home in Magdeburg, looked over the slate of candidates and was pleased for the most part. There were solid people whom they needed in office on the ballot in places where the Fourth of July party was sure to win. There were good people in place where the seats were up for grabs. But there were still several districts that did not have a Fourth of July candidate. And one, in particular, was troubling. It was a crown loyalist stronghold. Still the Fourth of July party needed to put up a candidate for appearance sake. But they weren't going to waste someone who might actually have a chance of getting elected. So the problem was finding a Fourth of July man who they didn't really want, and who they surely did not need, who was willing to lose.

It wasn't easy. Anyone who stood for any office as a Fourth of July candidate, or for any party other than the crown loyalist for that matter, in the district was wasting their time. But the party organizers felt that someone had to stand for the honor of the party. And it couldn't be just anyone who was willing to lose. It had to be someone who would be a credit to the party. Preferably someone well-known who could be taken seriously. But they had to be willing to lose in a landslide. A willing loser is not easy to come by. A serious politician who will let a massive defeat be attached to his or her record and take the loss philosophically is as rare as hen's teeth. Any serious politician wouldn't stand for it. As the word 'philosophically,' an image popped into Becky's mind. As she thought about it, her smile broadened. She picked up her pen and turned to a clean sheet of paper.

Dear Mr. Shaver,
You once said if there was anything you could do for me. I only needed to let you know. Well, it would seem that–

Jimmy Dick agreed to stand as a Fourth of July party candidate for the House of Commons with the understanding that he would not have to serve since he had no chance of winning.

After a period of near sobriety, contemplation, and study into the art of being a philosopher, he had reverted somewhat to his old form of hanging out in bars and drinking heavily. There really wasn't a lot of call for a full-time professional philosopher, so he was willing to put in some time as a political candidate. As long as he knew he would not have to serve, he had only one other requirement. He expected his expenses to be met, and that included enough good liquor to keep him happy. He would do it as long as there was whiskey in the glass. There was no point of having campaign rallies, but someone had to take the stage in the debates. Jimmy Dick was willing. Give him a glass of whiskey before and another one after and there wasn't much he wouldn't do.

So there he was, behind the altar rail in the Lutheran church, being the largest indoor assembly in town. The original plans called for the band shell in the park. But there was a cold rain, so they moved inside. The house was packed without even any standing room left. Jimmy was three sheets to the wind. But from long practice, he was still steady on the feet in his shoes and the feet in his mind. He understood the issues, he understood the questions, he understood the answers, both his and the ones of his crown loyalist opponent. He understood that Mike Sterns was always right, and that when Becky Sterns walked on water, she only got wet as high as her ankles. But mostly he was a name on the ballot that would not look like the party was throwing away the district as unimportant. So if he was inebriated, nobody really cared. All the debate was, really, was a chance for the Loyalists candidate to bask in the light of local approval.

Still, stand he must and answer he must, and so he did. The local opinion could not be any worse for his attempt to defend the honor of his party and, considering just who Jimmy Dick was and the makeup of the district, it certainly was not going make things any worse. So his answers really didn't matter.

The topic was the discussion of an established church and its role in government. Jimmy had the floor after his opponent concluded his summation with the words, "–and in light of this, one can clearly see that a nation without an established church will not and cannot long survive and prosper."

When the overwhelming response of the audience had mostly subsided, Jimmy stood to lean against the podium while waiting for the last enthusiasm of the crowd to wind down.

"My noble opponent," which he wasn't since he was standing for the lower house, he was just the choice of the local nobles, "is speaking from the limited view of the history he has lived through. Grantville has provided us with three hundred years of a history that now will never be. In that alternate history, a great nation with providences as large and larger than all of the Germanys combined had, and perhaps somewhere still has, a very stable nation with complete separation of church and state. They had universal religious freedom. A man could be any religion he wished, including no religion at all. Therefore long term stability is possible without an established church. As to prosperity, all one has to do is to look to those areas which have and practice religious tolerance. Far from suffering from anarchy, as my esteemed opponent has put forth, the truth is they do not suffer at all. They prosper.

"And why is that? Could it be that the qualities, such as the strength of will and perseverance in the face of adversity, which allow an individual to be a non-conformist in the face of strong social opposition are qualities which promote individual prosperity? If the individual prospers does not the community as a whole also reap the benefits of that prosperity? Could it be that an individual who is ready, willing, and able to uproot himself and relocate, to abandon a lifetime of accumulated labor and commitment to start over, is also an individual who is ready to try new things? He is someone ready to take on a new profession, to start a new business, to strive and succeed, indeed to excel, when it would be easier to continue to go on as he always had, confident in the belief that as it was is the way it should be?

"Could we not use some prosperous non-conformists to bring up the standard of living, buying goods and services, selling surplus production? Would not the entire community profit from such a citizen?

"What my honorable opponent did not address was just which religion should be the state religion. Is he assuming that since he is Lutheran that the Lutheran religion is the right religion and therefore it would be the state religion? Do not Catholics feel the same? On top of that do they not claim a long and notable history?

"If one thinks stability and prosperity will be found in the way things are and have always been should one not chose to be Catholic because it has the longer history and is, therefore, the most stable and therefore the most prosperous? This is something we know not to be true. In becoming Lutheran have you not prospered? In rejecting Catholicism did you not reject staid and stifling traditions which were inhibiting progress? Perhaps it is time for us to find a new reformation and do it all over again.

"My esteemed opponent would force everyone into the same mold. And why is this? Is it because he is comfortable with the way things have always been done? Even if the way things have always been is not the way thing have always been. Does not Catholicism have a better claim to that than the Lutherans?

"If you are going to choose one religion, let us choose a small one, one no one has ever heard of, or better still, an obnoxious and objectionable one such as the Anabaptists, who would tear down all religion and rebuild it in their own image. Then the majority can band together to preserve their rights and liberties as my esteemed opponent has suggested that the minorities always do. Is sauce for the goose not also sauce for the gander? It is –"

A little old lady in a scarf and shawl stood up and called out in the middle of Jimmy Dick's speech. Her interruption caused Jimmy to use, without attribution, a quote which he stole from Winston Churchill. It was the only thing of note produced by a very predictable evening. And it would be remembered. She stood, and in the middle of his rambling interrupted him to say, "Mister Shaver, you are drunk and a disgrace, even for a member of the Fourth of July party."

"And you, Madam, are ugly." Which she wasn't. Well, not for an old woman, at least, even though she had never been a great beauty. Jimmy waited for just a few heart beats for the timing. Somewhere he had learned the trick of gauging just when the time was right. And then he finished his stolen quote, "but I will be sober in the morning."

The auditorium roared with laughter.

When the election returns came in, the party organizers were shocked to find Jimmy Dick only a few point behind the leader. Perhaps he deserved a second look? Was there more here that anyone had thought?

Printed by Amazon Italia Logistica S.r.l.
Torrazza Piemonte (TO), Italy